The final conflict
has begun

Outside the museum, in the grim murk of the sinking, clouded moon, a black shape—darker than the deepest shadow—moved silently through the deserted alleyway.

Into Well Lane the solitary figure stole, traversing the empty, gloom-filled street before he turned, causing the ample folds of his great black cloak to trail and drag across the pavement.

Swathed and hidden beneath the dank, midnight robe, his face lost under a heavy cowl, the stranger raised his unseen eyes to stare up at the blank windows of the spire-crowned building before him.

"The hour is at hand." A faint, mellifluous whisper drifted up. "The time of The Cessation is come, for I have returned."

WYRD MUSEUM

The Woven Path
The Raven's Knot
The Fatal Strand

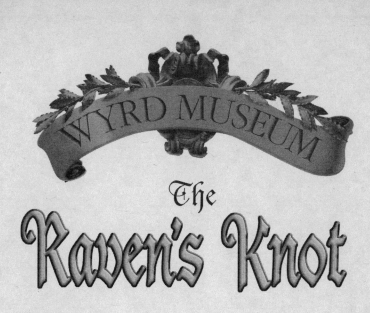

WYRD MUSEUM

The Raven's Knot

Robin Jarvis

Troll

CONTENTS

Five miles outside Glastonbury

2:58 A.M.

Brindled with bitter, biting frost, the plow-churned soil of the Somerset flatlands was bare and black. Hammered upon winter's icy forge, the earthen furrows were iron hard, unyielding as the great cold that flooded the moonless dark.

Deep and chill were the silent shadows that filled those expansive fields. As somber lakes of brooding gloom they appeared, pressing and pushing against the bordering hedgerows. Through those twisted, naked branches the unrelenting hoary darkness spilled, and the night was drowned in a black, freezing murk that no glimmer of star could penetrate.

Behind the invisible distant hills, shimmering bleakly on the rim of the choking night, the pale glare of mankind was weak and dim—the countless faint orange lights trembling in the frozen air.

In that lonely hour, in the remote realm of the wild, empty country, safely concealed by the untame dark, a sound—long banished from the world—disturbed the jet-vaulted heavens. Over unlit fields and solitary farm buildings the noise of great wings traveled across the sky, free at last of the tethers that had kept them bound for so many ages.

All creatures felt the presence of the awful force that coursed through the knifing cold. Upon the shadow-smothered ground, farm animals grew silent and afraid as the terror passed high above.

Horror and dread spread across the dim landscape that separated Wells and Glastonbury. Owls refused to leave their barns, and a fox, cantering leisurely homeward, suddenly flattened itself against the freezing ground when rumor of the unseen nightmare reached its sharp ears.

Dragging its stomach over frost-covered furrows, its brush quivering in fright, the fox darted for cover, tearing in blind panic toward a thicket of hawthorn. It lay there, panting feverishly, straining to catch the slightest sound upon the winter air.

But the unnatural clamor that had so alarmed the fox had already faded, and a new, more familiar noise was growing.

Through the night a vehicle came, the faint rumble of its engine a welcome distraction from the fear that had so gripped the fox's heart, and yet the animal remained crouching beneath the hawthorn until daybreak.

Over the icy road the car swept, the broad beams of its headlights scything through the dark veils in front, snatching brief, stark visions of hedge and ditch as they flashed by.

Inside the vehicle the heater was finally blowing hot air through the vents, and the toes of the driver and his passenger were thawing at last. Mellow music issued from the radio, coloring the dark journey home with a languid harmony, reflecting the relaxed and sleepy mood of the car's occupants.

Resting her head upon her husband's shoulder, a pretty young woman murmured the few lyrics she remembered of the romantic song and sank a little lower in her seat.

Her voice stopped as she felt him tense, and she lifted her head in surprise.

"Tom," she began. "What is it?"

A frown had creased the man's forehead, and he hastily lowered the volume of the radio.

"Ssshh!" he said. "Hazel, did you hear that?"

Disconcerted, the woman listened for a moment.

"Sounds all right to me," she answered. "Probably something rattling around in the trunk."

"I'm not talking about the car," he said sharply.

"What then?"

"*Outside.*"

Hazel brushed the hair from her eyes and stared at him in astonishment. Her husband was doubled over the steering wheel, gazing up through the windshield at the pitch black sky, scanning it fearfully.

"Tom," she ventured. "There isn't anything."

"There is!" he said emphatically. "Hazel, it was weird—sort of screaming."

She shifted on the seat and folded her arms as she began to look out of her window at the dark countryside passing by.

"What? . . ." she began nervously. "Like a person? That kind of screaming?"

"There was more than one," came his muddling answer. "But it wasn't quite human. It . . . it was weird."

"Oh, well," she breathed with relief, "if it wasn't human . . ."

The golden glow of Glastonbury's streetlights was now clear in the distance, with the majestic outline of the Tor rearing behind them. Another ten minutes and she could be in bed.

The car had been steadily picking up speed, and now the woman noticed for the first time the beads of perspiration glistening on her partner's face.

"Tom," she said. "Slow down. There's black ice all over these roads."

"We've got to get home, Hazel!" he told her, and the urgency in his voice was startling. "We've got to get home, and fast! It's too open here. I don't like it."

Before she could respond, something tapped lightly on the windshield. It was only a twig, but Tom's reaction to it was surprising.

"Where did that come from?" he demanded, his voice rising with mounting panic.

The woman gaped at him in disbelief. "Where d'you think it came from?" she asked. "It's a twig! Please, Tom, slow down."

"There are no trees on this stretch of road," he replied gravely.

Bewildered, Hazel threw her head back. "The wind blew it, a bird dropped it—I don't know! I don't care—but you're driving too fast. Listen to me!"

But Tom hardly heard her. All his senses were focused on the road ahead, yet not one of them prepared him for what happened next.

From the night it tumbled, out of the blind heavens it dropped, hurtling down with ferocious force. By the time he saw it, it was too late.

Into the bright light of the headlights it fell—a monstrous, massive bough. Raining insanely out of the sky, the mighty limb of ancient oak came plummeting toward them.

With a tremendous, violent crunch of metal, the huge

branch slammed into the hood of the car, and the windshield shattered into a million tiny cubes.

Screaming, Hazel threw her arms before her face as the vehicle buckled and shuddered beneath the vicious impact, and she braced herself as the tires skidded on the icy road.

His face scored by the twigs that had come whipping and flailing in through the splintered window, Tom gripped the wheel tightly and struggled for control as the vehicle shot into a wild, careering spin. But the windshield was utterly blocked, and all he could do was shout to Hazel to hold on.

"NO!" the woman yelled, clinging to him frantically as the car flew across the road and burst through the hedgerow. Into a field it thundered, with the branch still wedged on the hood, and over the frozen furrows it charged.

Then, with a lurch, the spin ended, and after one final jolt, the terrifying madness was over.

Gingerly, Hazel unfastened her seat belt and reached across to Tom. His hands were still clenched about the wheel, and when she held him, she discovered that he was shaking as much as she was.

Neither one of them spoke. Both pairs of eyes were fixed on the enormous oak branch that had dropped so unexpectedly and so illogically from above.

"It might have killed us," she whispered, reaching out apprehensively to touch the rough, glass-strewn wood. "But where? . . . Where did it come from?"

Tom made no reply. His heart was pounding in his chest, and his eyes widened as he stared upward.

"There's that noise again," he whimpered.

This time Hazel heard it, too, and her hands clasped tightly on his.

High above them the sky was filled with a terrible yammering, a foul, screeching cacophony that grew louder with every awful instant.

"The engine!" Hazel cried. "Tom, start the engine—quickly!"

Her partner fumbled with the ignition, but the car merely coughed pathetically, while overhead the dreadful shrieks mounted steadily.

Down the ancient nightmares swooped, bawling and squawking at the tops of their voices, down to where the puny chariot struggled in the frozen mire. They crowed their hideous delight at the prospect that awaited them.

"Lock the doors!" Tom cried. "Don't let it inside."

"But what is it?"

"I don't know!"

Screwing up his face, he tried the key again, and the engine turned over.

But it was too late. With a great downdraft and a clamor of high, screeching voices, they were caught. There came the beating of gigantic wings, and the car roof buckled as large dents were punched in the metal beneath the weight of many descending objects.

Then the enormous branch was flicked from the hood as easily as if it were a piece of straw. The yammering was deafening now, and Hazel's own voice joined it as she let loose a desperate scream.

Into the car, curving under the roof, there came a great and savage claw that gripped the contorted metal, and the vehicle was shaken violently.

A piercing clamor ensued as the automobile was

punctured and talons stronger than steel began to rend and rip. Like a can of peaches, the car was opened, until the two stricken occupants were staring straight up through the torn, jagged rents and they knew their deaths had come.

For a moment, as they were seized and dragged into the upper airs, Tom's and Hazel's screams equaled the vile, raucous laughter of the foulness that had captured them.

Then the two human voices were silenced, and once the feast was over, the night was disturbed only by a slow, contented flapping as dark, sinister shapes took to the air.

Across the Somerset flatlands all was peaceful again, except for one remote field just outside Glastonbury, where the engine of an empty, wrecked car chugged erratically and the radio softly played romantic melodies.

A force dormant for centuries was loose once more— the first of the Twelve were abroad, and in the days that were to follow their numbers would increase.

CHAPTER 1

OUT OF THE BLACKOUT

Over the East End of London a bright moon gleamed down on the many spires of the strange, ugly building known as the Wyrd Museum. But below the somber structure's many roofs, its cramped concrete-covered yard was illuminated by a harsher, more livid light.

Bathed in glorious bursts of intense purple flame, the enclosed area flared and flickered. With every spark and pulse, the high brick walls leaped in and out of the shadows, and everything within danced with vibrant color.

Lovingly arranged around a broken drinking fountain, a tribute of withered flowers appeared to take on new life once more as the unnatural, shimmering barrage painted them with vivid hues of violet and amethyst.

Yet behind the second-story windows, the source of the lustrous display was already waning as the last traces of a fiery portal guttered and crackled until, finally, the room beyond was left in darkness. Then a child's voice began to wail, and a light was snapped on.

The Separate Collection and everything it had housed were almost completely destroyed. Vicious smoldering scars scored the oak paneling of the walls, blasted and ripped by blistering bolts of energy that had shot from the center of the whirling gateway.

Yet from those sizzling wounds, living branches had sprouted, and now the room resembled a clearing in a forest, for a canopy of new green leaves sheltered those below from the harsh electric glare of the lights and dappled them in a pleasant verdant shade.

Neil Chapman was drained and weary. His mind was still crowded with images of the past and the frightening events he had witnessed there.

Together with a teddy bear in whose furry form resided the soul of an American air force lieutenant, he had been sent back to the time of World War II to recapture Belial, a demon that had escaped from the museum. They had eventually achieved this harrowing task, but the bear known as Ted had not returned to the present, and the boy didn't know what had happened to him.

Now all he wanted to do was leave this peculiar, forbidding room and surround himself with ordinary and familiar objects. To be back in his small bedroom whose walls were covered in football posters and to sleep in a comfortable bed was what he craved above anything—and to forget forever the drone of enemy aircraft and the boom of exploding bombs.

His thoughts stirred briefly from the dark time of World War II to the present again, as his young brother's cries pushed out all other considerations. Neil and his father, Brian Chapman, tried to comfort the little boy.

"Blood and sand!" Neil's father spluttered, unable to wrench his eyes from the bizarre scene around him. "What's going on? Blood and sand . . . blood and sand."

Standing apart from the Chapman family, Miss Ursula Webster, eldest of the three sisters who owned the Wyrd Museum, viewed the destruction with her glittering eyes, the nostrils of her long, thin nose twitching as she contained her anger.

Arching her elegant eyebrows, the woman examined the wreckage that surrounded her. All the precious exhibits were strewn over the floor, jettisoned from their splintered display cabinets, and she sucked the air in sharply between her mottled teeth.

"So many valuable artifacts," her clipped, crisp voice declared. "It is an outrage to see them unhoused and vandalized in such a fashion."

Turning, with glass crunching beneath her slippered heel, she clapped her hands for attention and pointed an imperious finger at Neil's father.

"Mr. Chapman," she began. "You must begin the restoration of this collection as soon as possible. Such treasures as these must not be left lying around in this disgraceful manner. I charge you to save all you can of them, for you cannot guess their worth. My sisters and I are their custodians for a limited period only. They enjoy such shelter and guardianship as this building can offer and what slight protection our wisdom can afford."

With a quick, birdlike movement, she turned her head to observe her two wizened sisters, who were stooping and fussing over a young girl, then returned her glance to Neil's father.

"Mine is a grave responsibility," she informed him.

"See to it that you obey me in this. When you have cleared away the rubble and removed this ridiculous foliage from the walls, throw nothing away. I must inspect everything prior to that, do you understand? We cannot afford to make another mistake."

Brian Chapman nodded, and the elderly woman gave him a curt, dismissive nod before turning to her sisters.

Miss Celandine Webster, with her straw-colored hair hanging in two great braids on either side of her overripe apple face, was grinning her toothiest smile. At her side, Miss Veronica was trilling happily, her normally white-powdered countenance a startling waxy sight, covered as it was by a thick layer of beauty cream.

Edie Dorkins, the small girl brought from the time of the Blitz in World War II London to the present by the power of the Websters, took little notice of them or the Chapmans. She was staring at a large piece of broken glass propped against the wall and gazing at her reflection. On her head the green woolen pixie hat, a gift from the sisters, sparkled as the light caught the strands of silver tinsel woven into the stitches, and she preened herself with haughty vanity.

"Doesn't she look heavenly?" Miss Celandine cooed in delight. "And there was I worrying about the size— why, it's perfect! It is, it is!"

Leaning on her walking cane, Miss Veronica bent forward to touch the woolen hat and sighed dreamily. "Now there are four of us. It's been so long, so very, very long."

"Edith!"

Miss Ursula's commanding voice rapped so sharply that the girl stopped admiring herself and fixed her almond-shaped eyes on the eldest of the Websters.

Picking her way through the debris, Miss Ursula took the youngster's grubby hand in her own.

"I have said that you are to be our daughter, Edith, dear, the offspring that was denied to us, and you have accepted. But do you comprehend the nature of the burden you have yoked upon your shoulders?"

An impudent grin curved over the child's face as she stared up at Miss Ursula. "Reckon I do," she stated flatly.

The fragment of a smile flitted across the woman's pinched features, but her bony fingers gripped Edie's hand a little tighter, and when she next spoke her voice was edged with scorn.

"Wild infant of the rambling wastes!" she cried. "Akin to us you may be, and many drafts of the sacred water have you drunk, but do not think you know us yet, nor the tale of all our histories."

But Edie was not cowed by the vehemence of the old woman's words, and baring her teeth, she snapped back, "So teach me 'em! Tell me about the sun, the moon, an' the name of everything that grows. What has been—an' all of whatever will be."

Miss Ursula loosened her grip, and her eyelids fluttered closed as she breathed deeply. "Well answered, Edith, my dear. Tomorrow we shall begin your instruction."

"No," the girl insisted. "Start now!"

Miss Ursula studied her, then gave a grim laugh. "Come with me!" she cried. "As this is the hour of your joining with us, it is only fitting that you are shown our greatest treasure at once."

With her gown billowing around her, Miss Ursula strode swiftly from The Separate Collection, and Edie Dorkins, her eyes dancing with an excited light, ran after her.

"Where is Ursula taking our new sister?" Miss Veronica asked in bewilderment. "There's jam and pancakes upstairs. I prepared them myself. You don't think they'll eat them all, do you, Celandine? Do you suppose they'll leave some for me? I love them so dearly!"

Miss Celandine's nut-brown face crinkled with impatience as she stared after the figures of Miss Ursula and the girl disappearing into the darkness of the rooms beyond.

"You and your pancakes!" she snorted petulantly. "I'm certain little Edith can eat as many as she likes of them—and most welcome she is, too. . . ." Her chirruping voice faded as her rambling mind suddenly realized where the others were going, and she threw her hands in the air in an exclamation of joy and wonder.

"Of course!" she sang, hopping up and down, her braids swinging wildly about her head. "Ursula will take her *there!* She will! She will, I know it—I do, I do! Oh, you must hurry, Veronica, or we may be too late."

And so, bouncing in front of her infirm sister like an absurd rabbit, Miss Celandine scampered from the room, and Miss Veronica hobbled after.

Alone with his sons, the dumbfounded Mr. Chapman pinched the bridge of his nose and gazed around forlornly.

"I . . . I don't understand," he murmured, staring up at the spreading branches overhead. "I want to, but I don't. Neil, what happened here?"

The boy pulled away from him, but he was too exhausted to explain. "It's over now, Dad," he mumbled wearily. "Josh and I are safe. That's all that matters."

"What's over? Who was that scruffy kid? She looked like some kind of refugee."

But if Brian Chapman was expecting any answers to his questions, he quickly realized that none were forthcoming. Neil's face was haggard and his eyelids were drooping. Remembering that it was past three in the morning, the caretaker of the Wyrd Museum grunted in resignation and lifted Josh into his arms.

"I'd best get the pair of you to bed," he said. "You can tell me in the morning."

Neil shambled to the doorway but paused before leaving. Casting his drowsy eyes over the scattered debris of The Separate Collection, he whispered faintly, "Good-bye, Ted. I'll miss you."

* * *

Down the stairs Miss Ursula led Edie, down past a great square window through which a shaft of silver moonlight came slanting into the building, illuminating the two rushing figures.

"Are you ready, Edith, my dear?" the elderly woman asked, her voice trembling with anticipation when they reached the claustrophobic hallway at the foot of the stairs. "Are you prepared for what you are about to see?"

The girl nodded briskly and whisked her head from left to right as she looked around in the dim gloom.

The paneling in the hall was crowded with dingy watercolors. A spindly weeping fig dominated one corner, while in another an incomplete suit of armor leaned precariously on a rusted spear.

"Here . . . here we are," Miss Ursula murmured, a

little out of breath. "At the beginning of your new life. The way lies before you. Let us unlock the barrier and step down into the distant ages, to a time beyond memory or record."

Solemnly she stepped over to one of the panels and rapped her knuckles upon it three times.

"I used to have to recite a string of ludicrous words in the old days," she explained. "But eventually a trio of knocks seemed to suffice. This place and I know one another too well to tolerate that nursery rhyme nonsense."

Striding back to Edie, she turned her to face the far wall then placed her hands on the young girl's shoulders and whispered somberly in her ear. "Watch."

Edie stared at the moonlit panels and waited expectantly as, gradually, she became aware of a faint clicking noise that steadily grew louder behind the wainscoting. Out into the hallway the staccato sound reverberated until it abruptly changed into a grinding whirr, and with an awkward juddering motion, a section of the wall began to shift and slide into a hidden recess.

"The mechanism is worn and ancient," Miss Ursula confessed, eyeing the painfully slow, jarring movements. "In the past hundred years I have used it only seldom. Come, you must see what it has revealed."

Edie darted forward and gazed into the shadowy space that had been concealed behind the panel.

The dusty tatters of old cobwebs were strung across it, but in a moment the young girl had cleared them away. With filaments of grimy gossamer still clinging to her fingers, she found herself looking at a low archway set into an ancient wall. Tilting her head to one side and half closing her eyes, Edie thought it resembled the entrance to an enchanted castle, and she tenderly ran her hands over the surface of the roughly hewn stone.

"Here is the oldest part of the museum," Miss Ursula's hushed voice informed her. "About this doorway, while my sisters and I withered with age, enduring the creeping passage of time, the rest of the building burgeoned and grew. This was the earliest shrine to house the wondrous treasure of the three Fates. We are very near now, very near indeed. What can you sense, Edith? Tell me, does it call to you?"

The girl stood back and studied the wooden door that was framed by the arch. Its stout timbers were black with age, and although they were pitted and scarred by generations of long-dead woodworm, they were as solid as the stone that surrounded them. Into the now steel-hard grain iron studs had once been embedded, but most of them had flaked away with the centuries, leaving only sunken craters behind. The hinges, however, were still in place, and Edie's exploring fingertips began to trace the curling fronds of their intricate design, until her hands finally came to rest on a large, round bronze handle.

At the bottom of the door there was a wide crack where the timbers had shrunk away from the floor, and a draft of cold, musty air blew about the child's stockinged legs, stirring the shreds of web still attached to her.

Edie wrinkled her nose when the stale air wafted up to her nostrils, but the sour expression gradually faded from her puckish face, and she took a step backward as the faint, moldering scent entwined around her.

The smell was not entirely unpleasant. There was a compelling sweetness and poignancy to it, and she was reminded of the roses that had been left to grow tall and wild in the gardens of bombed-out houses, their blooms rotting on the stems.

She had adored the wilderness of the bomb sites. In the time of the Blitz, the shattered wasteland had been her realm, and of all the fragrances that threaded their way over the rubble, the spectral perfume of spoiling roses had been her favorite.

The tinsel threads woven into her pixie hat glittered for a moment as the haunting odor captivated her, and watching her reactions, Miss Ursula smiled with approval.

"Yes," she murmured. "I see that you do sense it. Nirinel is aware of you, Edith, and is calling. If I needed any further proof that you were indeed one of us, then it has been provided."

Crossing to the corner where the armor leaned against the panels, she lit an oil lamp that stood on a small table and returned with it to Edie. Within the fluted glass of the lamp's shade the wick burned merrily, and its soft radiance shone out over the elderly woman's gaunt features, divulging the fact that she was just as excited as the child.

Then, with her free hand, Miss Ursula took from a fine chain around her neck a delicate silver key, but before turning it in the lock, she hesitated.

"Now," she uttered gravely, "you will learn the secret that my sisters and I have kept and guarded these countless years, the same burdensome years that robbed us of our youth and harvested their wits.

"No one except we three has ever set foot beyond this entrance. Prepare yourself, Edith. Once you have beheld this wonder there can be no returning. No mortal may gaze upon the secret of the Fates. Your destiny will be bound unto it forever."

Without taking her silvery blue eyes from the door, the girl said simply, "Open it." Then she held her breath as Miss Ursula grasped the handle and pushed.

There came a rasping crunch of rusted iron as slowly, inch by inch, the ancient door swung inward.

At once the stale air grew more pungent, yet Edie reveled in it. Holding the lamp aloft, Miss Ursula ducked beneath the low archway.

The darkness beyond dispersed before the gentle flame, revealing a narrow stone passageway that was just tall enough to allow the elderly woman to stand.

"Be careful, Edith," Miss Ursula warned. She lowered her hand so that the light illuminated the ground and showed it to be the topmost step of a steep flight that plunged down into a consummate blackness.

"This stairway is treacherous," she continued, her voice echoing faintly as she began to descend. "The unnumbered footfalls of my sisters and I have rendered each step murderously smooth. In places they are worn completely and have become a slippery, polished slope."

Down the plummeting tunnel Miss Ursula went, the cheering flame of the lamp bobbing before her, and keeping her cautious eyes trained on the floor, Edie Dorkins followed closely behind.

Deep into the earth the stairway delved, twisting a spiraling path beneath the foundations of the Wyrd Museum. Occasionally the stonework was punctuated by large slabs of granite.

At one point a length of copper pipe, encrusted with a thick layer of verdigris, projected across the tunnel, and Miss Ursula was compelled to stoop beneath it.

"So do the roots of the modern world reach down to the past," she remarked. "Yet, since the well was drained, no water flows from the drinking fountain above."

Pressing ever downward, she did not utter another sound until she paused unexpectedly, causing Edie to bump into her.

"At this place the outside presses its very closest to that which we keep hidden," she said, bringing the lamp up to the wall so the young girl could see that large cracks had appeared in the stones.

"A few feet beyond this spot lies one of their tunnels. A brash and noisome worm-boring, a filthy conduit to ferry the people from one place to another like so many cattle. Perilously near did their excavations come to finding us. Now, when the carriages hurtle through that blind, squalid hole, this stairway shakes as though Woden himself had returned with his armies to do battle one last time."

Miss Ursula's voice choked a little when she said this. Edie looked up at her in surprise, but the elderly woman recovered quickly.

"It is most inconvenient," her normal clipped tones added. "Thus far they have not discovered us, yet a day may come perhaps when these steps are finally unearthed by their overzealous probing. What hope then for the unhappy world? If man were to know of the many terrors that wait to seize control of his domain, he would undoubtedly destroy it himself in his madness. That is what we must save them from, Edith. They must never know of us and our guardianship."

Her doom-laden words hung on the cold, musty air

as she turned to proceed down the well-worn stairs.

"Still," she commented dryly, "at least at this hour of the night there are no engines to rumble by and impede our progress."

Farther down they traveled, until Edie lost all sense of time and could not begin to measure the distance they had come. Eventually the motion of her descent, joined with the dancing flame from the oil lamp, caused her to imagine she was following a glowing ember down the throat of a gigantic, slumbering dragon. Down toward its belly she was marching, to bake and broil in the scarlet heat of its rib-encased furnace. A delighted grin split the fey girl's face.

"Pay extra heed here, Edith," Miss Ursula cautioned abruptly, her stern voice cutting through the child's imaginings. "The steps are about to end."

As she spoke, the echo altered dramatically, soaring high into a much greater space, and Edie found herself standing at the foot of the immense stairway by the mouth of a large vaulted chamber carved out of solid rock.

Miss Ursula strode inside, and Edie saw that the curved walls of the cave were decorated with primitive paintings of figures and animals.

"Stay by my side, child," Miss Ursula told her. "This is but the first in a series of chambers and catacombs. Do not let your inquisitiveness permit you to stray. It might take days before you were found."

Edie toyed with the exciting notion of wandering around in the complete subterranean darkness, but she was too anxious to see where she was being led to contemplate the idea for long.

Into a second cavern they went, and again the echoes

altered, for here great drapes of black cloth hung from the ceiling, soaking up the sound of their footsteps.

"Gold and silver were those tapestries once," Miss Ursula commented, not bothering to glance at them. "Very grand we were back then. Several of the chambers were completely gilded from top to bottom. There were shimmering pathways of precious stones, and crystal fountains used to fill the air with a sweet tinkling music. There was even a garden down here, lit with diamond lanterns and replete with fragrant flowers and fruit trees, in which tame birds sang for our delight."

The elderly woman pursed her lips contemptuously as she proceeded to guide Edie through the maze of tunnels and caves.

"However," she resumed, "the passage of time stripped the pleasure of those decorous diversions from our eyes. Weary of them at last, we allowed the hangings to rot with mold, the jewels we gave back to the earth, and the garden was neglected until the birdsong ceased. For us there was only one treasure, and we ministered to it daily. Now, Edith, we are here at last."

They had come to a large gateway that was wrought and hammered from some tarnished yellow metal. Raised in relief across its surface was the stylized image of a great tree nourished by three long roots. Miss Ursula bowed her head respectfully as she reached out her hand to touch the image with her fingertips.

"Behind this barrier is a most hallowed thing," she murmured with reverence. "Throughout the lonely ages my sisters and I have served it with consummate devotion, and now you too shall share the burden. Behold, Edith—the Chamber of Nirinel."

Chapter 2

The Chamber of Nirinel

Swiftly and in silence the gate opened, and suddenly the darkness was banished. A golden, crackling light blazed before them, and Edie screwed up her face to shield her eyes from the unexpected, dazzling glare.

Through the entrance Miss Ursula strode, her figure dissolving into the blinding glow until finally the child's sight adjusted. She stared at the spectacle before her in disbelief and wonder.

The Chamber of Nirinel was far greater than any of the caves they had passed through. Immense and cavernous was its size, and Edie stumbled forward to be a part of this awesome vision, in case it was abruptly snatched away from her goggling eyes. Into the light she went, absorbing every detail of the scene before her.

Fixed to the vast, encircling walls a hundred torches burned, casting their splendor over the richly carved rock where, between the graven pillars and sculpted leaf patterns, countless stone faces flickered and glowed. All manner of creatures were depicted there, and the untutored Edie Dorkins could only recognize a fraction of them.

Edie gurgled in amusement and hugged herself as the dancing flames made this chiseled bestiary appear to peep down at her with curious stares. Even the monstrous serpents seemed to be astonished at her arrival.

"And why shouldn't they be?" Miss Ursula's voice broke in, reading Edie's thoughts. "The poor brutes have had an eternity of looking at me."

Edie laughed, then curtsied to the silent stone audience, craning her head back to see just how high the carvings reached up the walls.

It was then she saw the titanic presence that dominated that cathedral-like place. Her mouth fell open at the sight, and the giggles died in her throat.

From the moment she entered the chamber, Edie had been aware of a great shadow that towered over the cavern, but not till now did she realize its nature, and she froze with shock.

Rising from the bare earthen floor and rearing in a massive arc into the dark heights above, where not even the radiance of so many bright torches could reach, was what appeared to be the trunk of a gigantic tree.

Up into the impenetrable gloom its colossal girth soared, vanishing into the utter blackness of the chamber's immeasurable height, where it straddled the entire length of the cavern before plunging downward once more to drive through the farthest wall.

So monumental were its proportions that Edie could only shake her head, yet she noticed that no branches grew from that mighty tree. Only gnarled, knotted bulges protruded from the blighted, blackened bark, like clusters of ulcerous decay, and in places the wood had split to form festering and diseased wounds.

Slowly, Edie rose from her crouching curtsy. That withered giant was the source of the deliciously sickly scent, and she took a great lungful before tossing her head and considering the forlorn marvel more closely.

"What killed it?" she asked bluntly.

Miss Ursula put her arm around the girl's shoulders.

"You are mistaken, Edith," she said softly. "Nirinel is not dead—not yet. A trickle of sap still oozes deep within the core of its being, and while it does so, there is hope."

Leaping forward, Edie ran over the mossy soil until the gargantuan arch of putrefying bark loomed far above her. Shouting gleefully, she began to twirl and dance with joy.

"The tree's alive!" Her high voice rang within the cavern. "It lives, it lives!"

"Again, I must correct you," Miss Ursula told her. "This is no tree. It is but the last remaining root of the mother of all forests. We are in the presence of the last vestige of the legendary World Tree: Yggdrasill, which flourished in the dawn of time and from which all things of worth and merit sprang."

The child ceased her dancing and stared up at the immense, rearing shadow.

"This is a sacred site," Miss Ursula breathed. "But come, Edith, I will explain."

Where the massive root thrust up out of the ground, a circular dais of stone jutted up from the floor. Upon this wide ring, which was covered in a growth of dry moss and rotting lichen, the elderly woman sat and patted the space at her side for the girl to join her.

"I shall not begin at the beginning of things," she said, "for that time was filled with darkness. My tale commences when Yggdrasill first bloomed and the early rays of the new sun smiled upon its leaves.

"In that glorious dawn, the World Tree flourished, and it was the fairest and most wondrous sight that ever was, or shall ever be. In appearance it was like a tremendous and majestic ash, but many miles was the circumference of its trunk; its three main roots stretched about the globe, and its branches seemed to hold heaven aloft. Like a living mountain it rose above the landscape, but its great magnitude cast no despairing shade upon the ground below, for Yggdrasill's foliage shone with an emerald light, and in its cradling boughs the first ancestors of mankind were nurtured."

Edie gazed up at the vast root, vainly trying to imagine the unbounded size of Yggdrasill.

"The first civilization was founded at the eastern side of the World Tree," Miss Ursula continued, "and Askar was it named. In that early time there was no sickness and its people knew no death. All were content, and Askar flourished and thrived."

Miss Webster's voice trailed off as she stared into the flames of the torches.

"Was you there then?" Edie asked. "Is that where you're from?"

The elderly woman smiled gravely. "Yes," she murmured. "My sisters and I were born in that sylvan shade.

"Yet there were other beings who roamed the globe,"

she continued, shivering slightly. "Before the first blossom opened upon Yggdrasill, unclean voices bellowed and resounded in the barren wastes of the ice-locked north."

Edie grinned and leaned forward, eager to learn more. "Was they monsters?" she demanded. "Is that where Belial came crawling out?"

"No," was her patient reply. "Compared with them, Belial's evil deeds are like those of a mischievous schoolboy. Although he will one day pour fire upon the world, they shall come after. They were here before and they will be here at the utmost end."

Relishing every word, Edie squirmed and rested her dirty chin on her hands. "Who are they then?" she urged.

"Spirits of cold and darkness," Miss Ursula breathed, "drawn from the freezing waters when the world was formed, who clad themselves in chill flesh as giants terrible to behold. In a desolate, forsaken country, where none of the World Tree's roots had delved, they dwelt. A great gulf and chasm that stretched down to the very marrow of the earth separated their unhallowed realm from the main continent, and over the never-ending darkness they reigned absolutely."

Miss Ursula paused to gaze up at the huge, decaying root and clicked her tongue with irritation.

"You and I can only suspect the extent of their fury when the first light burst forth to herald Yggdrasill's unfurling," she said. "They had considered themselves to be lords of an echoing darkness, and now their dominion was threatened by this unlooked-for challenge."

"What did they do?"

"Sought for ways to destroy it," Miss Ursula told her. "For it was prophesied that as long as there was sap within the smallest leaf of the World Tree, their previous lordship and tyranny would be denied them. So began the building of the ice bridge to span the great chasm. Malice and loathing seethed in their frozen hearts, but the people of Askar were unaware of the peril that awaited them . . ."

"*Oh, Ursula!*" cried another voice suddenly, and with a jolt, Edie turned to see Miss Celandine and Miss Veronica standing by the gate.

Their gaze fixed on the withered root, the two sisters shambled inside. Then, leaving Miss Veronica to lean on her stick, Miss Celandine skipped forward, clapping her hands in delight and cooing dreamily.

"It's been so long since you let us come down here!" she declared reproachfully. "You are a meanie, Ursula. You know how I adored Nirinel so. Why, look how shriveled it has become. We must anoint it with the water like we used to and make it hale again."

Anxiously she trotted over to where Edie and her sister were sitting, then checked herself sharply and gazed at the circular dais in consternation.

"But, the well!" she gabbled in a flustered whine. "Such neglect. Ursula, what has happened? Why is nothing the same? First the loom was broken and now this!"

Clambering up beside them, she feverishly dragged the dead moss away, and Edie saw that the stone platform was embellished with a sumptuously molded frieze overlaid in tarnished silver and small blue gems. But even as Edie admired the decoration, Miss

Celandine's knobbly hands pulled away a great swath of moldering growth, and there in the center of the dais she uncovered a wide and precipitously deep hole.

Over the brink Miss Celandine popped her head, casting handfuls of the dead lichen down into the darkness, waiting and listening for the resulting splashes. But no sound rose into the cavern, and a look of comprehension slowly settled over the woman's wrinkled face.

"I . . . I had forgotten," she whispered in a small, crestfallen voice. "The waters are gone, aren't they, Ursula? The well is dry. It is, isn't it?"

Her sister nodded. "The sacred spring dried up many, many years ago," she said wearily, as if repeating this information was an hourly ritual. "And every last drop of the blessed water was drained over fifty years ago in order to vanquish Belial."

"Oh, yes," Miss Celandine sighed in regret. "So we can never heal Nirinel's wounds. It makes me woefully sad to see it shrunken and spoiled. Oh, how lovely it was when we first arrived, how very, very lovely. Veronica, do you recall? Veronica?"

She whirled about to look at the sister she had left by the gate, then gave a little yelp when she saw the expression on Miss Veronica's face.

Resting heavily upon her cane, Miss Veronica was staring up at the tremendous root with a ferocious intensity that was alarming to witness. It had been an age since she had last been permitted to venture down here and now the sight of it was stirring up the muddied corners of her vague, rambling mind.

"I see four white stags ahead of us," she uttered

huskily, wiping a trembling hand over her brow and smearing the beauty cream that covered it.

"I don't want to follow them," she wept, edging backward. "Let me return, I must . . . I . . . there is something I have to do!"

Lurching against the carved wall, Miss Veronica lifted her cane and waved wildly about her head as if trying to ward off something.

"Urdr!" she shrieked, staring at Miss Ursula with mounting panic. "Do not force me to go with you. I must go back—I am needed!"

"Veronica!" Miss Celandine called, hurrying back to her stricken sister. "You have nothing to fear. That time has ended. We are safe—you are safe."

Her sister's eyes grew round with terror and she threw her arms before her face. "Safe!" she wailed hysterically. "We are old, ancient and haggard, accursed and afflicted from that very hour. Won't someone save me? The mist is rising. I beseech you, before it is too late. Please, I beg you, my sister. Release me! Release me . . ."

Her cries melted into sobs as she buried her anguished face in Miss Celandine's outstretched arms.

"Hush," her sister comforted. "Come back, Veronica, it's over now. It is, it is." But as she soothed the crumpled, whimpering figure, she shot a scornful glance at Miss Ursula.

Still seated on the edge of the well, Edie Dorkins watched the elderly woman at her side and was astonished to see the extent to which her sister's outburst had distressed her.

Sitting stiff and as still as one of the stone images that swarmed over the walls, Miss Ursula blinked back the tears that glistened in her small, piercing eyes, and Edie could sense her inner struggle as she battled to control her emotions.

Then, mastering herself at last, Miss Ursula rose, and clenching her fists until they turned a horrible, bleached white, she said, "Celandine, take Veronica back to the museum. This is no place for her. The . . . the musty atmosphere is injurious to her. You know that neither of you is allowed down here. I shall lock the doorway behind me next time."

It appeared to Edie that Miss Celandine was on the verge of retaliating with some choice words of her own, but she must have thought better of it, for she turned and helped the weeping Miss Veronica hobble out through the gateway.

"It was her," Miss Veronica's blubbering voice sniffled and warbled. "She made me do it. I didn't want to come. . . . I didn't want any of this."

Rigid and wintry, Miss Ursula watched them depart the sacred chamber.

"An unhappy family have you joined, Edith," she said, keeping her voice level, hoping she betrayed nothing of the turmoil that boiled beneath her stern exterior. "My two poor sisters are wasting away in mind and in body. Their lives and mine are bound closely to that of Nirinel. As it fades, so, too, do we."

Edie eyed her shrewdly. "And mine?" she demanded.

"The young will not perish as swiftly as the aged," came the unhelpful reply. "I do not foresee what is to come, for the loom is damaged and the web was never completed, but I believe you shall be our salvation—in one way or another."

The child looked down at her feet. Then she asked, "What happened to the ice giants? Did they kill the World Tree?"

"The lords of the ice and dark?" Miss Ursula paused. "The rest of that tale must wait. You have learned much this night, but now I am obliged to go and make certain that Veronica is settled. Let us return to the museum. I, too, find this environment disturbing. I have recounted all I care to for the time being, and you must be patient."

Edie jumped from the dais and took hold of Miss Ursula's proffered hand, but the woman's palm was cold and clammy. The girl knew that Miss Veronica's words had shaken the older woman more than she dared to admit, and Edie could not help but wonder why.

CHAPTER 3

THOUGHT AND MEMORY

Far above the subterranean caverns within the Wyrd Museum, all was at peace. Only fine, floating dust moved through the collections, the same invisible clouds of powdery neglect that had flowed from room to room since the day the smaller, original building was founded.

Night crawled by, and the museum settled contentedly into the heavy shadows that its own irregular, forbidding bulk created.

In the small bedroom he shared with Josh, Neil Chapman cast his fears aside with the old clothes he had brought from the past, and the eleven-year-old boy was steeped in a mercifully dreamless slumber. Beside him, his brother snored softly, while in the room beyond, their father was stretched on the couch, a half-drunk cup of tea teetering on the padded arm.

Outside the museum, in the grim murk of the sinking, clouded moon, a black shape—darker than the deepest shadow—moved silently through the deserted alleyway, disturbing the nocturnal calm.

Into Well Lane the solitary figure stole, traversing the empty, gloom-filled street before he turned, causing the ample folds of his great black cloak to trail and drag across the pavement.

Swathed and hidden beneath the dank, midnight robe, his face lost under a heavy cowl, the stranger raised his unseen eyes to stare up at the blank windows of the spire-crowned building before him.

From the hood's profound shade there came a weary and labored breath as a cloud of gray vapor rose into the winter night.

"The hour is at hand." A faint, mellifluous whisper drifted up with the curling steam. "The time of The Cessation is come, for I have returned."

The voice fell silent as the figure raised its arms and the long sleeves fell back, revealing two pale and wizened hands. In the freezing air the arthritic fingers drew a curious sign, and from the hood there began a low, restrained chanting.

"Harken to me!" droned the murmuring voice. "My faithful, devoted ones, know who speaks. Your Master has arisen from His cold, cursed sleep. Awaken and be restored to Him. This is my command—I charge you by your ancient names—Thought and Memory. Listen . . . listen . . . listen . . . and yield."

Steadily the whisper grew louder, increasing with every word and imbuing each one with a relentless yet compelling power.

"Let dead flesh pulse," the figure hissed, the voice snarling beneath the strain of the charm it uttered. "Let eye be bright and cunning rekindle to obey my bidding once more."

Up into the shivering ether the strident spell soared, propelled ever higher by the indomitable will of the robed figure below, until the governing words penetrated the windows of the Wyrd Museum and were heard in the desolation of The Separate Collection.

Among the jumble of splintered display cabinets and fallen plinths, over the shards of shattered glass and buckled frames, the mighty sonorous chant flowed, summoning and rousing, invoking and commanding, until there, in the broken darkness—something stirred.

Responding to the supreme authority of that forceful enchantment, a muffled noise began to rustle amid the debris. At first it was a weak, labored sound—a halting, twitching scrape, like the fitful tearing of old parchment. But as the minutes crept by the movements became stronger, nourished by those mysterious, intoning words.

Suddenly a repulsive, rasping croak disturbed the chill atmosphere, and a horrible cawing voice grunted into existence.

In the shadows that lay deep beneath a toppled display case, half buried in a gruesome heap of shrunken heads, a black, wasted shape writhed and wriggled with new life.

Brittle, fractured bones fused together, while mummified, papery sinew renewed itself and hot blood began pumping through branching veins. Within the sunken depths of two rotted sockets a dim light glimmered as the gray, wafer-thin flesh around them blinked suddenly, and a pair of black, beadlike eyes bulged into place.

In the street outside, the cloaked figure was trembling, struggling beneath the almighty strain of maintaining the powerful conjuration. From the unseen lips those commanding words grew ever more forceful and desperate, spitting and barking out the summons to call his loyal servants back from death.

Answering the anguished, grappling voice, the movements in The Separate Collection became increasingly frantic and wild as the room was filled with shrill, skirling cries accompanied by a feverish, scrabbling clamor.

In the shadows the shrunken heads were flung aside and sent spinning over the rubble as a winged shape dragged and heaved its way from the darkness.

Emitting a parched croak, the creature yanked and tore itself free, staggering out from under the fallen display case to perch unsteadily upon the splintered wreckage.

In silence it crouched there, enwreathed by the sustaining forces of the incantation as, within its small skull, the crumbled mind was rebuilt and the eyes began to shine with cruelty and cunning.

Bitter was the gleam that danced there—a cold, rancorous hatred and loathing for all of the objects in the room, and its talons dug deep into the length of wood it balanced upon. Soon the rebirth would be complete.

Suddenly, outside the museum, there came a strangled wail, and the cloaked figure collapsed on the pavement. He had not been ready. The effort of invoking and sustaining those mighty forces had drained him, and he lay there for some minutes, gasping with exhaustion, the breath rattling from his spent lungs.

Immediately the link with the creature in The Separate Collection was broken, and giving a startled squawk, it tumbled backward.

But its lord's skill and strength had been just enough. The infernal charm was complete, and the shape floundered on its back only for an instant before righting itself. Then, with a flurry of old discarded feathers, it hopped back onto its perch and spread its replenished wings.

Yet no beauteous phoenix was this. The bird that cast its malevolent gaze about the shadows was a stark portrait of misshapen ugliness. Coal black was the vicious beak that speared out from a sleek, flat head, and powerful were its tensed, hunched shoulders. As a feathered gargoyle it appeared, and from the restored gullet there came a chillingly hostile call.

Stretching and shaking its pinions, the raven moved from side to side, basking in the vigor of its rejuvenated body, scratching the splintered furniture with its claws, and cackling wickedly to itself. The Master had returned to claim it back into His service, and the bird was eager to demonstrate its unswerving obedience and fealty.

Fanning out the ebony primary feathers of its wings, the bird flapped them experimentally and rose into the air, cawing with an almost playful joy. It was as if the uncounted years of death and moldering corruption had only been a dark, deceiving dream, for the bird was as agile and as supple as it had ever been.

Yet the euphoric cries were swiftly curtailed, and the creature dropped like a stone as a new, terrible thought flooded that reconstructed brain and its heart became filled with an all-consuming despair.

Leaping across the wreckage, the raven darted from shadow to shadow, hunting and searching, its cracked voice calling morosely. Through the litter of exhibits the bird searched, tearing aside the obstacles in its path as its alarm and dread mounted, until finally it found what it had been seeking.

There, with its head twisted to one side, its shriveled face covered in shattered pieces of glass, was the moth-eaten body of a second raven.

The reanimated bird stared sorrowfully down at the crumpled corpse, and the sharp, guileful gleam faded in its eyes as it tenderly nuzzled its beak against the poorly preserved body.

Mournfully its yearning, grief-stricken voice called, trying to rouse the stiff, lifeless form—but it was no use. The second raven remained dead as stone, and no amount of plaintive cawing could awaken it.

Engulfed by an overwhelming sense of loss, the bird drew back, shuffling woefully away from the inert dried cadaver, its ugly face dejected and downcast.

Abruptly the raven checked its staggering steps—it was no longer alone. Another presence was nearby. The atmosphere within the room had changed, and curious eyes were regarding it intently.

Jerking its head upward, the bird glowered at the doorway, and its beak opened to give vent to an outraged, venomous hiss when it saw a human child.

Her face was a picture of fascination, and she was not at all astonished or afraid at the emergence of the revivified creature.

Immediately the raven's sorrow changed to resentment, and it swaggered forward threateningly, pulling its head into its shoulders and spitting with fury.

The girl, however, merely stared back and made a condescending truckling sound as she patted her hands together, beckoning and urging the bird to come closer.

Incensed, the raven gave a loud, piercing cry and leaped into the air, screeching with rage.

Up it flew until the tips of its wings brushed against the ceiling, and with a defiant, shrieking scream it plunged back down.

Edie Dorkins watched in mild amusement as the bird dived straight for her like an arrow from a bow. But the pleasure quickly vanished from her upturned face when she saw the outstretched talons that were ready to pluck out her eyes and slash through her skin.

At the last moment, just as the winged shadow fell across her cheek, the girl spun around and fled from the room.

Yet the raven was not so easily evaded. A murderous lust burned within its invigorated heart, consumed by the need to avenge the death of its beloved companion and break the fast of death by slaking its thirst with her sweet blood.

Into The Egyptian Suite it pursued her, dive-bombing the hapless child, harrying her fleeing form, instilling terror into those tender young limbs.

Through one room after another Edie ran. But wherever she scurried, the raven was always there, beating its wings in her face, pecking her fingers, or clawing at the long blonde hair that had slipped from the pixie hat.

Breathlessly, Edie burst onto the landing and began tearing up the stairs, calling for the Websters, but the evil bird had tired of the game and lunged for her.

Into the soft flesh of her stockinged legs it drove the sharp talons. The girl yowled in pain, smacking the creature from her with the back of her hand.

Down the steps the raven cartwheeled, only to rise once more, shrieking with malice as it plummeted down, the powerful beak poised to rip and tear.

Edie squealed and threw out her arms as she leaped up the stairs, but the bird crashed between them and viciously seized hold of her exposed neck.

The girl yelled, and at that same moment the raven let out a deafening screech. It thrashed its wings, demented with agony. One of its claws was caught in the stitches of the pixie hat, and the flecks of silver tinsel began to shine, becoming a mesh of harsh, blinding light that blazed and flared in the darkness of the stairway.

Furiously the creature wrenched and tugged at its foot, for the wool burned and blistered, and a vile, stench-filled smoke crackled up where it scorched the scaly, ensnarled claw.

Edie whirled around, trying to grab the raven and pull it loose, but the bird bit her palm and its lashing feathers whipped the sides of her face. The pain was searing, but however much it battled, the creature could not break free of those stitches, for the Fates themselves had woven them.

In a last, despairing attempt, the raven screamed at the top of its shrill voice, closed the beak about its own flesh, and snapped it shut.

There was a rending and crunching of bone as the bird twisted and wrenched itself clear, then warm blood spurted onto Edie's neck.

With crimson drops dribbling from its wound and staining its beak, the bird recoiled, fluttering shakily in the air as it regarded the girl with suspicion and fear. Yet even though it despised her, the creature did not attack again but circled overhead, seething with impotent wrath, before flying back into the exhibitions, crowing with rage.

*   *   *

Standing alone on the stairs as the glare from her pixie hat dwindled and perished, Edie pulled the severed talon from the stitches and pouted glumly. Her fey, shifting mind suddenly decided she had enjoyed the raven's deadly company and wanted to play some more.

An impish grin melted over her grubby face as she decided to follow the bird and chase it from room to room, just as it had done to her. But even as she began to jump down the steps, there came the faint sound of shattering glass, and she knew that the bird had escaped.

From one of the windows in The Separate Collection the raven exploded, rocketing out into the cold dregs of night, where it pounded its wings and shot upward.

Up past the eaves it ascended, soaring over the spires and turrets, letting the chill air currents stream through its quills as the fragments of broken glass went tinkling down to the ground far below.

"Thought," a frail, fatigued voice invaded its mind. "To me . . . to me."

The raven cawed in answer and immediately began to spiral back down. Above the small, bleak yard it flew, fluttering over the empty street, its gleaming eyes fixed on the hooded figure now standing once more.

"Come, my old friend," the stranger uttered, wearily leaning against the wall as he raised a trembling hand in salutation. "Too many ages have passed since you flew before me in battle. It gladdens my heart, my most faithful attendant and counselor."

Wincing from the pain of its mutilated and bleeding claw, the raven alighted upon a cloaked shoulder and bobbed its head to greet its ancient Master.

"Now do I begin to feel whole again," the figure sighed. "How am I to wreak my revenge without the company and valued assistance of my noble, trusted beloveds?"

The bird croaked softly and brushed its feathery body against the shrouded head.

"I ought to remonstrate with you for not fleeing that accursed place sooner," the voice chided gently. "You were rash to assail that child of lesser men, for she has the protection of the royal house. The Spinners of the Wood have favored her."

The raven guiltily hung its head, but its Lord was chuckling softly.

"That lesson you have already learned, I see. Look at your foot. Is this how you repay the gift of life? To risk it at the first instant, to let spite and hate overcome your wisdom? Such an impulsive deed I might expect from your brother but not of you, Thought. In the past you always considered the consequences of your actions. . . . But where is your brother? Why has he not joined us?"

The unseen eyes within the hood stared up at the broken window of The Separate Collection. "I cannot sense him, not now nor before. Tell me, where is he?"

The raven called Thought rocked miserably to and fro, avoiding its Master's questioning glance.

"Answer me!" the cloaked figure commanded sternly. "The trivial art of speech was my first gift to you both. Have the wasting, dust-dry years robbed you of that, or do you merely wish to displease me?"

Blinking its beady eyes, the creature slowly shook its head before opening its black beak. Then, in a hideous, croaking parody of a human voice it spoke.

"Allfather," the raven uttered in a cracked, dirgelike tone. "Alas for mine brother, I doth fear the words of Memory shalt forever be stilled. The days of his service unto thee art ended indeed. His dead bones lie yonder still, unable to hear thy summons. The weight of years did ravage him sorely, more than their corroding action did unto mine own putrid flesh."

Its Master lifted a wizened hand and caressed the bird tenderly. "It is to be expected," he murmured sorrowfully. "The ages have plundered my strength and my greatness wanes."

"Never!" the raven squawked. "Thy cunning and craft endure beyond aught else!"

"Lift your eyes, my slave, and look about you. This is not the land you knew. You have been embraced by death many thousands of years. Since you and Memory penetrated the encircling mists at the vanguard of our forces, the world has changed beyond recall."

"In truth," the bird muttered. "Is it indeed so long? Then the battle was lost and the Three were victorious."

"Can you remember nothing of those final moments?"

Thought closed its eyes. "The span of darkness is wide since that time," it began haltingly. "But hold, I can see the field of combat that lay betwixt us and the woods wherein our enemy did lurk. The day is bright with swordplay and the air rings with the music of steel as I ride the wind and view the glorious contest raging below."

"What else do you see?"

"Mine eyes are filled with the glad sight of our conquering forces. The Twelve are with us, and no one can withstand their fury. But wait—Memory, my brother, he hath hastened toward the wood before the appointed time. I call yet he cannot hear. I fear for him and charge after, yet already he hath gained the trees. To the very edge of that forest I storm, 'til the mist rises and it is too late. I see but briefly the daughters of the royal house of Askar standing beneath the great root, and then there is darkness."

The raven became silent and ruffled its feathers to warm itself.

"Locked in their custody you have been for all this time," the cloaked figure concluded. "Yes, the battle was lost, and even the Twelve were routed. I, too, was defeated, but the war was not over and still it continues, for I have arisen. Though I am weak and ailing, so, too, are they. The enchanted wood is no more. The stags are departed and the well is dry."

Thought cocked its head to one side as its Master continued.

"There is a chance, but we must be careful. Although the mists no longer shroud the attendants of Nirinel, they have amassed a great store of artifacts within that shrine of theirs. It is the combined power of those treasures that now protects them. If we are to succeed, we must draw the loom maidens out, shake the web, and when the spiders fall, smite them."

Upon his robed shoulder, Thought began to hop from side to side. "Verily!" it cried shrilly. "Strike the treacherous scourges down and show unto them no mercy. Dearly will they pay for the doom of mine brother. I shalt feast on their eyes and make a nest of their hair. Tell to me how this delicious prospect may be achieved, my Lord. I ache for their downfall."

"Many treasures they have acquired over the sprawling centuries," the hooded one answered gravely, "yet the greatest prize lies without their walls. A marvel so rare and possessed of such surpassing power that it could bring about their ultimate ruin."

Crowing delightedly, the raven jumped into the air. "How is it the witches of the well have been so blind and blundered so?"

"Oh, they are aware of its existence," came the assured reply. "Urdr knows. She recognizes this thing for what it is and fears it, as do I."

"Thou art afraid of this treasure?" Thought cawed in astonishment. "How so, my Master?"

"Much has transpired since you passed into oblivion," the figure said darkly. "The prize I seek is hidden and cannot be won, save by one who has drunk of the sacred water. I must endeavor to compel one of the three sisters to deliver it to me, and in this you are to play an important role. Many leagues from here, where this mighty thing is bestowed, the trap is already set, and into it I have poured my failing enchantments."

The raven landed back upon the shoulder and stared into the darkness beneath the hood.

"Yes," the unseen lips answered. "I have labored long to call them back, my most terrifying and deadliest of servants. Daily their numbers increase, and soon they will be Twelve again."

Cawing softly to itself, Thought shook its wings and glared up at the sky.

"Once more the old armies shalt ride, inspiring dread and despair into the stoutest of hearts."

"And you will lead them," the figure instructed. "The Twelve are wild creatures of instinct and destruction. They have need of commanding, but I must remain here to gather what little strength I can for the final days. I had hoped to despatch both you and your brother to order their movements, yet you shall not go alone. Someone shall go with you."

"Who, Master?"

The figure took a last, despising look at the museum before turning to shamble back along Well Lane.

"Come," he said. "There is a great deal to be done and the time is short. There is one nearby who will aid us. Although he does not yet know it and will have to be deceived into our service, I believe he will suit the purpose very well. His good must be subverted. We must erode his will and entice him to do our bidding. When the treasure is found, it is he who must wield it. Soon the webs of destiny will be destroyed forever, and the shrine of Nirinel will be a smoking ruin."

With the raven cackling wickedly upon his shoulder, the cloaked stranger shuffled across the street and melted silently into the dim gray shadows of the nearby, derelict houses.

CHAPTER 4

THE LORD OF THE DANCE

A leaden sky and a drenching drizzle heralded the dawn, and the thick, slate-colored clouds that reached across London ensured the dismal weather was there for the rest of the morning.

It was an uninspiring start to the first day of school after the Christmas break, and by the time they splashed into the building, the students at the local middle school were a damp and straggly rabble.

Built just after the war, the school was a dreary collection of concrete boxes that, by nine o'clock, were awash with dirty footprints and dripping coats.

For Neil Chapman it was as if he had awakened from a long sleep. That morning was the first time he felt truly free of Miss Ursula Webster's influence since he and his father and brother had moved into the Wyrd Museum over a week before. It was a peculiar sensation. That forbidding building and the manipulating controllers of destiny it contained had fueled his thoughts from the very first day. Now the real, normal world seemed pale and unimportant by comparison.

The boy shook his head, startled at his own thoughts. Now that everything was as it should be he was finding life a bit dull. At breakfast that morning, Josh had been his usual annoying self. He made no mention of what had happened, almost as if he had forgotten the entire episode—either that or he had been made to forget. Then, when Neil tried to explain it to his father, he could see that Brian didn't believe a word.

Regretfully, Neil realized that it was no use pining for excitement. For him the adventures were over. He had completed his task for the Websters and would now have to get used to living a mundane life again.

Looking around him, he tried to take an interest in his new surroundings, but he wasn't impressed. His old school in Ealing had been much more modern and better equipped, with its own swimming pool and three playing fields. This one had to make do with an all-purpose field and very little else as far as he could tell.

As for the pupils, they appeared to be a rough-looking, slovenly crowd, and the uniform that his father had been assured was essential hardly seemed to be adhered to by the majority of them.

Laughing and calling out names, they boisterously jostled their way around the building, scuffling outside classrooms and jeering at each other as they boasted about what they had been given for Christmas.

Waiting at the office, Neil watched them barge by. Hardly anyone bothered to look at the new boy, and if they did it was only to snigger and nudge their friends.

"Chapel, did you say?" droned a nasal, unenthusiastic voice. "Can't seem to find you anywhere."

The boy turned and looked across the desk at the school secretary. She was a large, middle-aged woman with bleached hair, and she wore a turquoise blouse that was one size too small for her ample figure.

"It's Chapman," he said with mild annoyance, exaggerating his lip movements in case the chunky earrings she wore had made her hard of hearing.

The woman dabbed at the computer with her pudgy fingers and without looking up at him said, "You're in Mr. Battersby's class. Room 11a, down the hall on the right."

"Thank you," Neil muttered, slinging his bag over one shoulder.

"They won't be there now though," the secretary added. "There's an assembly this morning. They'll have gone to the drama center, across the courtyard and to the left. You'd best get a move on—you're late."

Neil didn't bother to answer that one. He hurried from the main doors and into the rain again. Over a bleak blacktopped square he ran, to where a low building stood, and he hastened inside.

Fortunately, the assembly had not yet begun, and Neil slipped in among the students still finding their seats.

The drama center was a modestly sized theater where school plays, concerts, and assemblies were held. It consisted of a stage, complete with curtains and lighting equipment, and tiered rows of seats to accommodate the audience.

Today the atmosphere was rowdy and irreverent. The stale smell of damp clothes and wet hair hung heavily in the air as the congregated pupils settled noisily into their places. The watchful teachers patrolled up and down, keeping their expert eyes on the troublesome ones. Several of these had pushed their way to the back of the highest row but were already being summoned down again to be divided and placed elsewhere under easy scrutiny.

Neil's eyes roved around the large room. At the back of the stage there was a backdrop left over from the last school production, depicting the interior of an old country house complete with French windows, and he guessed that it had been a murder mystery.

In front of the scenery was a row of chairs that faced the pupils, and some of the teachers had already taken their places at them. There were two female teachers and three male, but against that painted setting they looked less like members of staff and more like a collection of suspects.

Mentally performing his own detective work, Neil wondered which of them was Mr. Battersby. Of the three men sitting there, one was fat and balding, another tall and slightly hunched, but the last one Neil dismissed right away for he was obviously some kind of vicar, dressed in long black vestments.

Suddenly the level of chatter died down as a small, stern-looking woman with short dark hair strode into the room. One of the male teachers who had not yet joined his colleagues raised his hand as though he was directing traffic, and at once the children in the theater stood.

Neil did the same. This was the principal, Mrs. Stride.

"Good morning," she said, briskly rubbing her hands together.

The children mumbled their replies.

"I said, 'Good morning,'" she repeated, a little more forcefully.

This time the response was louder, and Mrs. Stride appeared satisfied. Nodding her head, she told them to be seated, and the room echoed with the shuffling of over three hundred pairs of feet and the usual chorus of pretended coughs before she could begin.

Only half listening, Neil watched the principal pace up and down the stage, but his attention was quickly drawn away from her and directed at the person sitting beside him.

Here was a slight, nervous-looking boy with untidy hair and large round glasses, whose threadbare blazer was covered in patches. With one watchful eye on the teachers, the boy lifted his bag with his foot, unzipped it, and drew out a science fiction magazine that he laid on his lap and proceeded to read, ignoring everything else around him.

Lowering his eyes, Neil peered at the colorful pages and read the bold type announcing "real life" abductions by strange visitors from outer space.

"Now"—Mrs. Stride's voice cut into his musings, and Neil returned his gaze to the front of the stage—"you all know Reverend Galloway. He came to see you quite a few times last semester to talk about the youth club before it burned down. Well, I haven't a clue what he's going to tell us this morning, but I'm sure it will be most interesting. He's even gone all out and put his cassock on for us. Reverend Galloway."

The principal stood aside as the man in the vestments rose from his seat, and a distinct groan issued throughout the theater.

"Not the 'God Squad' again," complained a dejected voice close by, and Neil looked at the boy at his side, who had glanced up from his magazine to contribute this mournful and damning plea.

Neil studied the vicar more closely. Apparently he was a familiar and unpopular guest at these assemblies.

The Reverend Peter Galloway was a boisterous young man with a haystack of floppy auburn hair and a sparse, wispy beard to match. Suddenly he broke into an enormous, welcoming grin, and his large green eyes bulged forward as if they were about to pop clean out of his head. Then he held open his arms in a great sweeping gesture that embraced the whole audience.

"I hope you all enjoyed Christmas," he said benignly.

The students eyed him warily, as though he was trying to sell them something, and an agitated murmur rippled throughout the tiered seats.

Peter Galloway looked at the sea of blank faces. The pupils' expressions were those of bored disinterest, but that did not deter him; in fact it spurred him on. For the past seven months, ever since he had left college, he had ministered to the spiritual needs of this difficult neighborhood and never once suffered any loss of confidence, whatever the reaction to his exuberant ministries. His soul brimmed with the joy of his unshakable beliefs, and he never missed an opportunity to try and share this with others.

In this short time, however, the Reverend had become increasingly aware that the church was failing to capture the hearts and minds of the younger members of the community, and he was grieved to learn of the trouble they got themselves into. If they could only channel all that youthful, restless energy into celebrating life as he did, they could enjoy a faith as strong as his own.

This mission to welcome the youngsters into the fold had become a crusade with him. He was passionate about it and tried many different ways to show them that the church could be fun. There had been concerts of Christian pop music, youth groups, debating societies, sporting events, and even sponsored fasts in aid of the Third World. Yet none had been a resounding success, in spite of his finest efforts. The teenagers he saw hanging around in gangs and loitering at street corners never came along to any of the events, but that only served to make him even more determined.

Today he had resolved to take a more direct approach with the children, and he returned their apathetic stares with a knowing glare of his own.

"Let us not forget," he addressed them, "that Christmas is not merely a time for exchanging gifts. We must remember its tremendous significance. At that season the Savior of Mankind was born."

At the back of the audience a girl began to giggle into her hand. Neil looked across at the teachers and found that they, too, appeared bored.

"Can you imagine the wonder that the people felt at the time of the Nativity?" the Reverend Galloway continued, jabbing his finger in the air. "It must have been absolutely incredible for them. Think of the shepherds who fell on their faces in terror when the white-robed angel appeared, revealed in glory."

At Neil's side the bespectacled boy muttered in a loud whisper that everyone heard, "I'd be scared if the Reverend appeared before us in a white dress."

The children burst into fits of laughter, and although the teachers looked stern and accusing, several of them could not completely disguise the smirks that had crept onto their faces.

Peter Galloway waited for the mirth to die down, but he gazed in the direction that the mocking voice had come from and nodded in energetic agreement.

"But that's precisely my point!" he exclaimed to everyone's surprise. "If we are to get anywhere, you have to dismiss the silly, archetypal image of an angel. That's utter, utter rubbish and belongs only on the top of a Christmas tree. A messenger of God isn't a person dressed up with wings and a halo, holding a harp. That's an invention by medieval artists, who had no idea how to illustrate or express such an amazing, celestial being."

Lowering his voice slightly, the vicar leaned forward to speak to them in a hushed, conspiratorial voice.

"Imagine," he began, drawing his hand from left to right as if pulling back an obscuring curtain. "Picture it in your mind, the stony landscape outside Bethlehem. Upon those barren, exposed hillsides it is dark and cold. To live there takes a certain type of stamina and courage. The people won't tolerate any sort of nonsense. These shepherds are used to the brutalities and hardships of Roman rule. Only something truly terrifying could possibly frighten them.

"There they are, encamped around a small fire perhaps, when suddenly their hearts are stricken with a mortal and petrifying dread. The angel of the Lord! Now, we here today haven't a clue what that really means, but it was a sight so awful that it put fear into those brave men. What can it have looked like, this monstrous vision? Was it merely a fierce, bright light, or did the angel have a more tangible, unhuman form? What is the real shape of a heavenly messenger? Whatever it is, it scares ordinary people like you and me."

At Neil's side, the boy with the magazine listened intently before glancing down at the glossy pages, where a painting of a grotesque, nightmarish alien roared up at him, and he nodded appreciatively. "Yeah," he murmured.

"All you have to do is think about it," the vicar went on, sensing with mounting excitement that his audience was paying attention.

"These events really happened. They're not legends or myths—they are historical facts. This man with the strange, radical ideas actually lived, and when he was only thirty-three, he was executed because he had dared to think them."

Taking a breath for dramatic effect, the vicar drew himself up and swept the wild mop of auburn hair from his eyes.

"Do any of you know what it means to be crucified?" he asked.

The pupils nodded, but the Reverend Galloway shook his head. "No, you don't," he told them. "Oh, yes, you've seen all the pictures and statues of Him, with His arms outstretched upon the cross, with nails in the palms of His hands and embedded in His feet. But the truth was far, far worse and bloodier than that."

"Cool," said Neil's neighbor, letting the magazine fall to the floor while the teachers shifted uncomfortably on their chairs and Mrs. Stride uttered nervous little coughs.

"No, the nails didn't go through the hands. The

bones aren't strong enough there—they'd shatter and wouldn't support the weight of the arms. Through the wrists the nails were hammered, and if you were lucky, they'd sever the arteries and you'd bleed to death. But if you weren't, then the feet would be skewered to the cross, only they'd be pinned to it either side, with the nails driven through the heels."

For the first time in over a dozen visits, the vicar knew that the children were listening to him. Some of the more squeamish ones might have been appalled at the gruesome details, while others were morbidly fascinated, but all of them were enthralled.

"When the hammering was over," Peter Galloway resumed, "the cross was hoisted upright, and there you'd stay until you died. Most people probably perished from shock, but others suffocated. Hanging there, with your head slumped on your chest, the only way to draw a proper breath would be to push yourself up by the nails impaling your heels. But to stop the prisoners from doing this, the Roman guards went around to each one and savagely broke their legs.

"That is what happened to the man born in Bethlehem—His legs were smashed and splintered, but still He lived. Although the agony and the suffering was excruciating, somehow He managed to cling to life. However, the following day was the Sabbath, and no one was permitted to be on the cross during that time. Having survived all this torment and pain, our Lord was finally killed by a Roman spear thrust viciously into His side."

The principal had never known the theater to be so full and yet so silent. Looking worriedly at the children, she had already decided to have a word with the Reverend Galloway afterward. If she ever allowed him to speak to the pupils again, she would make certain she knew what he was going to say beforehand.

Taking a step toward him, she hoped to lead the outrageous man from the stage and let the children return to their classes. But the Reverend was not done yet.

"Yes," he cried, reveling in the unfamiliar but immensely gratifying experience of holding the students' undivided attention. "That man hung on the cross. He was tortured for the sins of the world, but He rose from the tomb, and because of His ultimate sacrifice, we can all find forgiveness and know true happiness."

Trembling with excitement, the Reverend ran to the edge of the stage, where he had placed a tape recorder on a table, but he hesitated before pressing the play button.

"This is what it's like to feel the joy of forgiveness," he enthused. "To know that incredible elation of the soul. The Lord lives in me and in all of you if you'll let Him. He is knocking on the door of your heart right now—don't turn Him away. He is the light of the world, the Son of Man—'the Lord of the Dance.'"

With that, he punched the button down, and the tune to the hymn with that name began to blare from the speakers.

In one practiced movement, Peter ripped open his cassock to reveal a full-length black leotard, and at once he began to leap around the stage in time to the music.

Waving his long arms in the air, he capered around in a wide circle, waggling his head from side to side and tapping his feet as the hymn played on.

For a whole minute both the children and the

members of staff could only gape at the zealous young man as he endeavored to illustrate the overwhelming joy that so consumed his spirit.

No one could quite believe what they were witnessing. The sight of the Reverend Galloway cavorting about the stage, twisting and gyrating to the music, was the strangest spectacle most of them had ever seen, and they were frozen with astonishment.

To and fro he gamboled, and the expression on his face was one of perfect serenity. In his mind's eye he was as graceful as a swan, exquisitely conveying in the poetry of his movements all that he could not form into words. In reality, however, in that black leotard and with his wild haystack of hair, he looked more like a member of some bizarre circus launching into a peculiar and ungainly mime. Blissfully unaware of the effect this unexpected performance was having, he danced on—but it did not last for long.

As the tape recorder continued to thump out the tune, gradually the general amazement thawed, and the pupils began to stir and look at one another. Quickly the shock subsided, and in one great united voice, the entire theater erupted with a terrific peal of laughter.

Totally unprepared for this explosive reaction, when the shrieks and hoots of ridicule came, Peter faltered in his steps, and he stared around him, bewildered and dismayed.

"No," he protested. "You don't understand. All I'm trying to do . . . it's the beauty of God's love . . . please. I just wanted to show how wonderful it makes me feel . . . can't you see that? Listen to me. Children, listen."

But it was no use. The respect he had commanded

only a few minutes before when he appealed to their bloodthirsty natures was gone. There was no way he could reclaim it, and to his horror, he saw that the teachers too were sniggering behind their hands. Staring at them, with the children's derisive laughter trumpeting in his ears, he felt the color rise in his face as a bitter coldness gripped the pit of his stomach, and he realized the full extent of his humiliation.

Just as the audience had begun to harken to his words and think about what he was trying to communicate to them, he had thrown it all away by his own misjudgment. How could he have been so blind not to consider the preposterous exhibition he was going to make of himself?

His hopes and spirits crushed, the Reverend Galloway walked over to the tape recorder and turned it off. Then, retrieving his cassock, he left the theater with the laughter still resounding in his ears and branded upon his heart.

"All right, all right," Mrs. Stride called. "That's enough, the fun's over. Back to your classrooms."

So Neil's first day at his new school commenced. But when he trailed off to his first class, he found himself longing once more for the excitement of the Wyrd Museum. Already he missed the dark, shadowy corners of its lonely galleries and the display cabinets with their unusual exhibits. Yet as he sat at his desk, the time when the Webster sisters would need his help again was already drawing near.

CHAPTER 5

JAM AND PANCAKES

Ever since her outburst in the Chamber of Nirinel, Miss Veronica had been sullen and silent. Now, sitting in a worn leather armchair with her cane resting on her lap, she stared vacantly at the small square window, watching the rain streak down the diamond-latticed panes.

Over her white-powdered face the faint drizzling shadows fell, but whether she was aware of the soft, rippling light or was lost in a corner of her jumbled mind it was impossible to determine.

A plate of her favorite delicacy, jam and pancakes, lay untouched on the table at her side, and this fact alone worried her sister.

Miss Celandine Webster had tried everything she could think of to coax and cajole Miss Veronica out of her tedious sulk, but the wizened woman in the armchair was oblivious to all her urging.

"You're no fun today, Veronica," whined Celandine. "It's not fair—it isn't!"

"Let her be, Celandine," a curt, impatient voice interrupted. "If Veronica wishes to be childish, do not spoil it for her."

Miss Celandine turned her nut-brown face to the fireplace, where Miss Ursula, resplendent in a black beaded evening gown, stood cold and detached.

"But it isn't like her, Ursula!" she protested. "Veronica never mopes, not ever!"

"Then she's obviously making up for lost time," came the cold reply. "Leave her alone."

The Websters' quarters were a poky little apartment situated at the top of the Wyrd Museum. Cluttered with bric-a-brac collected over the endless years, it was almost a monument to the building's history.

Images of the place in various stages of its enduring existence covered the shabby wallpaper: from a small stone shrine to a twelfth-century manor house. A later watercolor showed the building to be a graceful Queen Anne residence surrounded by well-tended gardens. But the final portrait of the ever-expanding abode of the three Fates was a faded sepia photograph of the stark and severe-looking Well Lane Workhouse, and this grim print brought the record to a bleak and melancholy close.

Unaffected by the tense, oppressive atmosphere, Edie Dorkins paid little attention to the Websters' squabbles. She was too busy examining the dust-covered ornaments and fingering the collection of delicate antique fans to care what the others were doing. For her, the place was a treasury of enchantment. She felt so blissfully at ease and welcome that sometimes the rapturous sense of belonging swelled inside her until she wanted to run outside and hug every corner of the ugly building.

Lifting her gaze to the mantelpiece, Edie looked only briefly at the oval Victorian painting of the three sisters before staring with fascination at the vases that stood upon either side. Never had she seen anything like the peacock feathers that those vessels contained, and she quickly pulled a chair over to the fireplace to scramble up and snatch a handful.

"Lor'!" she exclaimed, shaking off the dust and holding the plumes up to the dim light. "They're lovely. Can I keep 'em?"

"They are yours already, Edith, dear," Miss Ursula replied. "Everything here is yours, you know that."

Edie chuckled and gloated over the shimmering blues and greens, like a miser with his gold.

"I never seen a bird with fevvers like this," she muttered. "Much nicer'n that big black 'un last night."

Miss Ursula smiled indulgently. "I really must get that fool of a caretaker to board up the broken windows," she said. "I cannot have the museum overrun with pigeons."

"Weren't no pigeon!" Edie cried. "Were the biggest crow I ever saw. Bold he were, too. Chased me clean through the rooms downstairs and tried to bite, he did."

Hoisting the hem of her skirt, she pulled and twisted her hole-riddled stockings to show the others the raven's claw marks.

"Make a real good scab, that will." She grinned. "I was gonna teach him a lesson, but the mean old bird took off before I could catch him."

Miss Ursula's long face had become stern, and her elegant eyebrows twitched with irritation.

"A large crow," she repeated in a wavering voice. "Are

you quite certain you are not mistaken, Edith?"

The girl fished in the pocket of her coat, pulled out the talon that the creature had left behind, and flourished it proudly.

"There!" she declared. "That don't come from no mangy pigeon—see!"

Miss Ursula stepped forward, the taffeta of her dress rustling like dry grass as she moved, and took the severed claw between her fingers.

"No . . ." she whispered uneasily.

Gingerly she held the raven's claw as if it was the deadly sting of some venomous insect. Then Miss Ursula's expression changed from disbelief to horror and dismay.

In silence, Miss Celandine padded up beside her, and she too appeared frightened as she sucked the air through her prominent teeth and bit her bottom lip.

Edie glanced from one to the other, their unspoken fear alarming her.

"Did I do wrong?" she asked. "You won't send me back, will you? I doesn't want to go back to that time, even with its pretty bombs. I don't know what the bird was."

For a whole minute no one answered her. Miss Ursula's face had grown even more pale than usual, and Miss Celandine seemed to be on the verge of panic. Then a sorrowful, whimpering voice said, "I know."

Edie and the others turned sharply. There, still seated in the armchair but now with her head turned to face them, Miss Veronica was peering at the thing in her sister's hand, and a thoughtful scowl creased her powdered face.

"A raven!" she announced, her vermilion-circled mouth widening into a jubilant smile. "The talon belongs to a raven."

Closing her eyes, she struggled to remember more, but the pathways of her muddled mind were too tangled and meandering, and she tapped her walking cane with impatience.

Her sisters regarded her cautiously.

"Veronica!" Miss Celandine trilled, dashing over to the armchair. "Do have a pancake, or would you like me to read you a story?"

Miss Veronica ignored her. "But weren't there two of them?" she muttered under her breath, trying to wade through the neglected memories. "I'm sure there were."

Still clutching the claw in her hand, Miss Ursula glared at Edie. "Have you told me the truth, child?" she demanded fretfully. "Did you really see this creature in the museum last night?"

The girl backed away. Miss Ursula was usually so composed and controlled. To see her afraid was startling and distressing.

"Answer me, Edith!" the woman snapped, seizing her by the arm.

Edie nodded resolutely, and Miss Ursula drew a horrified breath.

"Then I can only hope you are mistaken," she hissed. "It is too soon. Nothing is prepared, we are not ready! Can the hour I have long dreaded be here already? Have I been caught out at the last?"

Casting a final, fearful glance at the confused figure in the armchair, the eldest of the Websters whirled about and hurried quickly from the room.

Miss Celandine scowled at Edie. "You mustn't upset us so," she chided. "Fancy mentioning the ravens, and in front of Veronica, too. See how agitated you've made her? Veronica, speak to me, Veronica."

Edie wanted to run after Miss Ursula, but even as she hastened to the entrance her quick, capricious mind had already decided against it.

If she was caught spying, there was no telling what might happen. Of the three sisters, Miss Ursula was the most formidable, and Edie knew she had to be wary in her presence. The other two were much easier to handle. Perhaps she could learn what she needed from them.

Sitting beside the armchair, the girl looked at Miss Celandine's ripe, wrinkly, walnut-like features, framed by her straw-colored braids, and Miss Veronica's haggard, overly made-up face.

"Why is Ursula so scared?" she asked.

Neither of the Websters replied. Miss Veronica seemed to have drifted off into her own world again, and Miss Celandine was nibbling her lip as if wondering what to do.

"There are some things even you can't be told," Miss Celandine eventually blurted. "I thought you were here to look after us, but that hasn't happened at all—quite the opposite. It is, it is! Well, I shan't say anything to you unless Ursula tells me to—and Veronica won't, either."

But her words did not deter Edie. Apparently unconcerned, she lifted the plate of pancakes and sniffed them experimentally.

"Put them down!" Miss Celandine squealed. "They're not yours, they're not, they're not!"

Impudently Edie arched her eyebrows and proceeded

to stuff two of the pancakes into her mouth, much to Miss Celandine's outrage.

"Wicked!" she clucked, beating her fists upon her knees. "You stop that! At once, at once—ooh, you naughty child. You are, you are!"

Edie ignored her and looked instead at Veronica, who was also staring at her in shocked disbelief as yet another pancake disappeared inside the young girl's mouth.

Suddenly the woman in the armchair could bear it no longer. Yowling like a singed cat, she grabbed the plate from Edie and rammed its scrumptious jam-daubed dainties into her own crabbed lips.

Several minutes passed as Miss Veronica chewed and devoured her most favorite food. Then, when the last morsel was swallowed, she frowned at Edie and poked her with a bony finger.

"There were two ravens," she said, her eyes glazing over as she struggled to recall the fleeting memories. "Two of them, and they belonged to someone . . . someone very special. What were their names? Why don't I know? I'm sure it's important."

Leaning back in the chair, the elderly woman sighed heavily and shook her head.

"You are shameless," Miss Celandine berated Edie. "Veronica mustn't remember, you mustn't make her."

The girl eyed her mutinously. Perhaps if she asked about something else she could catch her off guard. "Tell me what happened to the land of Askar," she piped up unexpectedly.

At the mention of that name Miss Celandine brightened, but she glanced suspiciously at the doorway in case Miss Ursula was lurking there. "Come," she whispered, "over here—we'll sit by the fireplace."

Together they rose, and Miss Celandine settled herself in one of the chairs by the hearth. She raked a poker through the cold, dead ashes as if stoking a heap of flaming cinders.

Edie waited until she had finished before she said, "Ursula started tellin' me yesterday about the ice giants. Did they build the bridge and kill the World Tree?"

Miss Celandine brushed the ash and coal dust from her fingers and gazed mournfully at the charred, scattered cinders.

"Oh, yes," she murmured. "The chasm that separated the green lands from the icy wastes was spanned. Oh, but it was so heavenly in those days. Askar was at its most beautiful and Yggdrasill at the height of its power and majesty. It really was glorious—oh, it was, it was.

"Everyone looked so handsome and attractive then, the gentlemen were tall and dashing. Oh, what dances we had, what a delicious time."

Miss Celandine's voice trailed off as she slipped into a delightful reverie, and Edie had to nudge her to continue.

"What about the giants?" she urged.

Miss Celandine's goofy grin disappeared. "I don't want to talk about them," she snapped. "Mayn't I only remember the nice bits?"

"No."

"You're as beastly as Ursula," the elderly woman bleated. "Very well.

"When those terrible ice lords first stepped upon the shores of the fertile lands, they saw in the distance the wondrous light of the World Tree and knew in their black hearts that they could never hope to attack it. Spanning the chasm had weakened them dreadfully. So, at the edge of the green realm, they quarreled about what to do, until their leader—the tallest and proudest of them, who wore a crown of icicles upon his big head—was so disgusted at their cowardice that he stormed off on his own.

"Over the pretty hillsides he rampaged, drawing ever closer to the emerald shadows of Yggdrasill. When at last he reached the lowest and most outlying of boughs, he leaped up and swung his great axe."

Miss Celandine drew her breath and covered her mouth as she let the tragedy of those words imprint themselves upon the intrigued child.

"Hacked it clear through, that monster did!" she uttered sadly. "The world shuddered, as did we all, and after that the sun never seemed to shine quite as brightly again. A horrendous shiver traveled through the great ash, from its topmost leaves to the bottommost root, and suddenly we were all afraid."

"Is that when the tree died?" Edie asked breathlessly.

Miss Celandine ran her fingers through the stained and ragged lace that fringed her velvet gown before answering. "No," she said simply. "Only the bough was hewn. The ogre could do no more damage, for the massive branch toppled right down on top of him and broke his frozen head to bits. Served him right, it did, but that was no comfort to us. The World Tree was injured, and we did not know how to heal it.

"Oh, the poor thing. Three days it took for the people of the city to ride about the trunk to where the sap seeped from that hideous gash. I couldn't look; it was Ursula and our mother who went with a company of guards. Veronica was away at the time, but she returned as soon as she could. She was often away in those days, exploring the outlying regions, blessing the wild forests, and standing on distant hills. I wanted to go with her sometimes, but she always said no. Sometimes she could be so mean and tiresome—I do hope she isn't lapsing back into old habits."

"Then how did Yggdrasill die?" Edie pressed, before the elderly woman had a chance to be distracted.

"It was the others!" she cried, astonished at the girl's ignorance. "I thought everyone knew that! It was the other giants. They saw what happened to their leader and knew that weapons more cunning than axes would have to be used to be rid of it. They drew silly, weak people and unwary creatures into their service, until eventually they discovered the whereabouts of two of the World Tree's roots.

"Oh, it was terrible. Into them they fed the bitterest poisons, fouling the waters of the wells and springs that nourished them with their dirt and filthy charms. How we cried when a second shudder quaked the earth and Yggdrasill sickened. We thought that the end had come, but a ray of hope still glimmered, for no one—not even the enemy's watchful spies—knew where the third and final root could be found, and so the tree survived."

Resting her chin in her hands, Edie closed her eyes and recalled the impressive sight of the withered Nirinel in the subterranean chamber far below the museum.

"But they did in the end," she muttered glumly.

Miss Celandine stroked her head. "Don't be silly," she said. "The end hasn't happened yet, at least I don't think it has. Ursula would have told me, I'm certain. The ice lords haven't returned, have they? The sun still shines, doesn't it?"

Turning to the window, she stared at the dismal day outside and sharply drew her breath. "Has the last day closed? Are they stirring in the frozen wastes? We must get Ursula. The darkness is coming—the cold and dark are here!"

"No, Celandine," Edie assured her. "It's only raining. Tell me what happened next, after the two roots were poisoned."

The elderly woman squinted once more at the window and shifted in the chair.

"Great expanses of the World Tree started to rot," she murmured sadly. "In those decaying wounds, all the sicknesses and plagues were spawned. There was no death in Askar in the early days, but soon the bleak northern winds began to carry disease and the spores of pestilence. Many fell ill and perished, and so the glory of Askar began to dwindle and wane."

"That's sad," Edie mumbled as Miss Celandine sniffled into the lace of her collar.

"It was, and is," the old woman agreed, blowing her nose on the sleeve of her dress.

"But the Frost Giants were not wholly successful," she added. "They had not killed Yggdrasill completely, for the third root was still sustaining it, and while they continued to hunt and search for its whereabouts, something wonderful happened."

Running her fingers over the child's pixie hat, she beamed to herself and tilted her head to one side.

"When the first bough was hacked from the ash," she said, "no one knew what to do with it. Obviously we couldn't just leave it there for the ogres to make their nasty weapons out of. The wood was that of the World

Tree, and no one could imagine what powers it might possess. Then our mother had a vision in which she saw what had to be done."

"Did the people of Askar listen to her?" Edie asked doubtfully.

Miss Celandine stared at the child in surprise. "Of course they did!" she declared. "She was their queen! Hasn't Ursula told you?"

Edie grinned and gazed at the old woman as if viewing her for the first time. "Then you're a princess!" She laughed.

"I was," Miss Celandine answered mournfully, "a long, long time ago when my name was different. I don't know what I am now. I forget so much of the in-between years, after the great early days. Sometimes I wonder how we came here, and all I want to do is get away from Ursula and go dancing down through the galleries. Veronica feels the same, but her legs are bad. If it weren't for her pancakes, I don't know how she'd . . ."

"Celandine!" Edie said firmly, assuming a tone not unlike that of Ursula at her most severe. "What did they do with the fallen branch? What did the vision tell your mother to make out of it?"

"Why, the loom of course!" the elderly woman grandly declared. "The loom of destiny, where we weaved the fortunes of mankind and the webs of doom. Veronica would measure the threads, I would spin them, and Ursula would cut them. For many, many years we ordered the affairs of everyone and everything—the whole world was caught in our tapestry, no one escaped us. No one at all, even we were trapped."

Thrilled to the marrow, Edie marveled at Miss

Celandine's words, and her skin prickled with excitement. "Doooom," she echoed. "Loooom of Doooom."

"Of course," Miss Celandine added, "at first nobody dared to string it, and so the very first day it was completed the loom was left in the courtyard until the night came."

"What happened then?"

Miss Celandine turned and pointed to a small painting half hidden in the shadow of a bookshelf.

Edie peered at it. Within the dusty frame there was a woodland scene enshrouded by dense curling mist, and from the swirling vapors reared the dim outlines of four great stags.

"In the dead of night," Miss Celandine said, "Ursula looked out of her window and saw those milk-white creatures come boldly into the court and carry the loom away on their silver antlers. Of course, she raised the alarm at once, but it was as if they had vanished. No one could find any trace of them."

"But you did, didn't you?"

Miss Celandine, however, was growing restive, and she looked across the room to Miss Veronica, who was peeping over the back of the armchair with a curious, intense look graven upon her face.

"I won't say any more!" Miss Celandine announced, putting one of her braids into her mouth and chewing it stubbornly. "I've said too, too much!"

"Please!" Edie cried. "What happened next?"

Miss Celandine clenched her teeth and refused to utter another word, then she folded her arms over her chest and dug her heels into the frayed carpet.

"It was Ursula's fault," Miss Veronica's voice piped up. "It was she who walked under the leaves, she who learned too much, more than was good for her—or any of us."

Miss Celandine spat the hair from her mouth and tutted disagreeably. "Veronica, stop it! Oh, Edith, you are a wicked child—look, you've made our sister go and remember. It's better if she doesn't, Ursula always says so. How could you be so hateful?"

But Edie wasn't listening to her any longer. Drawing near to the armchair, she brought her face close to the heavily painted eyes that peered over the back and smiled persuasively.

"It was years later," Miss Veronica continued, "on a night of calm. Ursula was roaming under that part of the tree that was still untouched by poison when, in the rustling of the leaves, she heard a whispering voice."

"Stop her, someone!" Miss Celandine squeaked, hopping from her place by the hearth and clapping her hands over her ears. "I had nothing to do with it, I swear. I didn't make her remember, I didn't, I didn't. It was that disobedient girl. Why, I wasn't even here— I was downstairs. I'm not here now. I'm down there, that's what. I'll tell her that, too, if she asks."

Miss Veronica watched her spring about the cramped room, and she gazed dumbly at the folds of faded velvet that thrashed madly around her sister's wizened form, making a sound like great flapping wings. With a start, the old woman gripped her walking cane.

"The ravens!" she cried out abruptly. "Thought— Thought and Memory! That's what they were called!"

Miss Celandine stumbled to a standstill and shuddered before she let out a shrill squeal and pointed at Edie in fear.

"You've done it now!" she scolded. "Oh, you've done it now!"

CHAPTER 6

THE CROW DOLL

Along the curiously named Coursing Batch, the stretch of main road that cuts across the lower slopes of Glastonbury Tor, a plump figure with a mass of curling, carrot-colored hair strained at the pedals of her bicycle.

Lauren Humphries scrunched up her face as yet another heavy truck thundered by, and she wobbled unsteadily in the buffeting draft of its passing.

"Thank you!" she growled through gritted teeth, her cheeks spattered with dirty water thrown up from the wet road. The truck roared away, and the girl gently squeezed her brakes, stopping beside the narrow sidewalk to wipe herself clean.

Although she was now seventeen, she had lost none of the chubbiness that had made her childhood so miserable. There were so many unkind names for idiots to choose from when shouting abuse; it was like a sport that anybody could play. Lauren had grown used to it. From an early age she had taught herself to ignore the cruel taunting, but that did not make it hurt any less. No matter how hard she tried, sometimes the insults hit their mark and stung her.

Mopping a handkerchief over her freckle-covered features, she glowered at the receding, rumbling truck, her hazel eyes lost amid the fleshy expanse of her round pink face.

Pulling away from the curb, she set off once more, past the gates of the large boarding houses whose rooftops screened off the view of the Tor, to where Coursing Batch seamlessly became Edgerly Road.

Here, only the hedgerow separated her from the great green bulk of the strangely shaped hill that rose high up on her left.

Glastonbury Tor, with a solitary tower dedicated to Saint Michael spiking up from its summit, was a singular, stately sight.

A holy place, venerated through the ages by countless pilgrims seeking truth and enlightenment, it rose from the Somerset flatlands like an enchanted, enduring symbol of faith. Deep were the foundations of Glastonbury's appeal, and like a magnet it attracted things esoteric and occult from all over the globe. Obscure sects of enigmatic religions founded temples there, people sought healing from its everflowing springs, and legends both Christian and pagan abounded.

Nowhere else was quite like this small town. It was a special, haunting place, and the powerful vision of the Tor presided over all.

Lauren hated it.

She had lived there for only four months, but already she loathed the district, and as she cycled homeward, she did not take her eyes from the road to even glance at the Tor's majestic, imposing outline.

Hoping that her father would be back before she arrived home, she sailed by the high banks of the reservoir and saw in the distance ahead a group of five boys hanging out by the roadside.

Still carrying their backpacks, they had obviously just left school, and Lauren pitied them. There was little for young people to do in small towns such as this. It was fine for the tourists who came to see the ruined abbey, investigate the legends, climb the Tor, and explore the beautiful countryside, but to grow up in such a place had to be difficult. Vacationers and seekers of wisdom could leave when they wanted to, but that was impossible for a child born into the bleak rural landscape.

Yet as Lauren cycled closer to the group, a furrow creased her brow, and any sympathy she had felt vanished as her small eyes stared at them suspiciously.

Their voices were jeering with laughter, and that was a sound the girl knew only too well.

"Crazy Tommy!" they cried. "Crazy Tommy!"

Only then did Lauren see that in the center of the gang was a pitiful-looking old man, and with anger bubbling up inside her, she began to pedal furiously.

Surrounded by the group of twelve-year-olds, the man known locally as Tommy laughed good-naturedly, nodding like a donkey at everything the boys shouted in his ears.

"Show us yer teapot, Tommy! What do dogs do, Tommy?"

The white-haired old man crooked one arm in compliance and waggled from side to side, pouring imaginary tea from the pretend spout of his hand as he yapped like a terrier.

"That's right, Tommy!" the boys goaded, pushing him roughly. "What else do dogs do? Cock your leg—go on!"

Like a performing monkey he obeyed them, acting out stupid and humiliating tricks for their callous delight.

"Give us yer hat, Tommy," one of them called, reaching across and grabbing the battered cloth cap from his head.

"Pyeeuuurrgh!" the boy cried, mangling it in his hands. "It stinks! When was the last time you had a bath?"

The old man grinned, revealing an almost toothless set of gums. "Was a Tuesday," he declared.

"What year?" the gang shouted back.

"Tommy doesn't know," came his mild reply. "Can he have his hat back now?"

"You'll have to catch it first!" they taunted, throwing the cap from one to another.

"Please," Tommy asked politely. "It's getting dark. You lads should get yourselves home. Give Tommy his hat, he's got to get going."

In front of his ruddy face they dangled it, only to snatch the cap away as soon as his large, red-knuckled hands rose to claim it.

The old man staggered to and fro as they threw the cap over his head and back again, yet not once did he lose his temper or cry out in despair.

"Hey!" Lauren's angry voice interrupted the cruel game. "Stop it! Leave him alone."

Propping her bicycle against the hedge, she pushed

her way into the middle of the group and pulled the thoughtless boys away.

"Let go!" they yelled as she yanked them aside until only one was left, the cap still in his hands.

Graham Carter, the oldest of the bullies, glared at the girl, and a horrible leer twisted his face, which was already pocked with the first flush of acne.

"What do you want, fatty?" he asked with a snigger.

Incensed, Lauren dashed forward and knocked him into the hedge, but as he fell, Graham threw back his arm and let the cap go sailing into the road.

"Get off, you fat cow!" he bawled when she pushed him even farther into the thorns. "Get your sweaty, lardy hands off me!"

"Least I haven't got a face with craters in it like the moon!" she retorted.

"Better than being as big as the moon!"

Lauren stared at him as he squirmed in the hedge, then stepped back, ashamed that she had allowed herself to trade insults with this boy. "Just go home," she said gruffly.

Graham tried to pull himself from the thorns, but two of his accomplices had to help him to his feet.

"You wait, blubber mountain!" he warned, inspecting his sweater for holes. "We'll be looking for you next time."

Lauren shook her head. "Oh, drop dead," she told them.

Grudgingly the boys walked off, singing out a string of insults.

"Tubby or not tubby—fat is the question."

The girl ignored them and looked around to see if the

old man was all right. At once all thoughts of the stupid boys were flung from her mind as she saw Tommy go wandering into the middle of the road to retrieve his cap—walking right into the path of a speeding vehicle.

"Watch out!" she screamed.

Stooping, the old man glanced up as the driver of the truck gave three warning blasts on the horn. There was no way he could stop in time, and all Tommy could do was blink in timid surprise.

With a hideous squeal, the tires skidded over the road as the brakes were stomped on, but still the vehicle came. Then, at the last moment, Tommy snatched up the cap and leaped nimbly aside. The truck plowed past, finally lurching to a halt yards beyond where the old man had been standing.

"You stupid old codger!" the driver bellowed, sticking his head out of the window. "You nearly got yourself killed!"

Tommy placed the hat on his head. He chuckled as if the man had said something funny and then proceeded to do a little dance upon the grassy shoulder of the road.

The driver drew a hand over his forehead and directed his anger at Lauren instead.

"Why don't you keep a closer eye on your granddad?"

The girl opened her mouth to object, but the driver was already revving his engine.

"Useless fat lump," she heard him mutter just before the truck roared off.

Leaving a cloud of choking blue exhaust fumes in its wake, the truck lumbered away. Lauren pulled a face after it, hoping the driver was looking in his mirror.

"That's not very ladylike," a gentle voice said.

The girl gazed at Tommy and shrugged. "It wasn't meant to be," she answered. "But how are you? Are you all right? Did those boys frighten you?"

The old man stared at her, bewildered. "Frighten?" he murmured. "Why should Tommy's pals frighten him? We was only playing a game. They wouldn't want to scare old Tommy."

Lauren groaned and walked back to her bicycle.

"You were a bit rough with them," he added. "That's no way for a pretty young girl to behave now, is it? You'll never get a boyfriend acting like that, you know."

Exasperated, she turned to stare at him. Tommy was a peculiar-looking character. His face was a florid map of broken veins. Fine silver stubble bristled along his chin, and although he had never been seen without a smile, there was an element of sadness about his wrinkle-webbed eyes.

He was a sorry, tramplike sight. Under his shabby secondhand overcoat, over a collarless shirt, he wore a handknitted purple sweater that had been mended umpteen times. A long piece of grubby string served as a belt to hold up his baggy, colorless trousers.

Lauren had seen him around the town on numerous occasions, but she had never before spoken to him. At first she had assumed him to be one of the forlorn crowd who gathered outside the church on the benches to drink themselves silly during the day and to shout at passersby. Yet during the short time she had lived there, the girl had never seen so much as a can of lemonade in Tommy's large, clumsy-looking hands.

"That's a good bike," he observed. "Got two wheels to go around and around. Tommy likes bikes."

Lauren smiled indulgently.

"I should learn to drive really," she said.

The old man tutted and sucked his few remaining teeth. "You doesn't want to do that," he commented. "Tommy sees folk chargin' here and there all the time in their big hurries. 'Tain't natural. A bike's good enough for you, I'd say."

"Really?" she mumbled, tiring of his chatter. "What would you know about it?"

"Takes you to your college and back, don't it?" he replied.

Lauren eyed him uncertainly. "How do you know where I go to?" she asked. "You been watching me or something?"

Tommy laughed and nodded.

"Yep," he admitted proudly. "He knows a lot, does old Tommy. He knows when the rain'll fall by the smell of the soil. He knows how much fruit the apple trees'll have come autumn by the shape and color of the leaves. He knows how far down the rabbit warrens go and where hares lie in the field during the day. He knows what's goin' on in this place, he knows what's happening—oh, yes, he knows."

Clicking his tongue, he looked thoughtful and afraid for a moment, then he tugged at one of his ears, and the mood passed as he added, "He knows where you live, too. Your mom and dad had many guests yet?"

Wanting to ride off but not wishing to appear rude, Lauren started to push the bicycle along the sidewalk and walk beside him.

"Not a lot," she said, "and she isn't my real mother— not even a real stepmother yet."

"Tommy knowed that, too. Your'n died nigh on three year ago, didn't she? Arr, Tommy done seen a lot of folk come down here from the city to try what yours are a-doing. Not many manage. 'Tis hard work that, and mighty sore when the people don't show. Still, when they do, it ain't all rosy."

Trotting a little way in front of her, the old man raised his cap and in a high, affected voice proclaimed, "Do you got any softer pillows? This frying egg hain't yellow enough. Another bit of toasta here, more marmylady there. Mine tea is gone a coldy and the cup is a chippta. What, no hotty water for the scrubbing of my daft holiday makey face? I not be a-staying at this kennel again, you betcha!"

Lauren smiled. "Some of them are a bit like that," she confessed. "I try and keep out of their way."

Tommy displayed his gums again. "Good place, yours, though," he put in. "Tommy likes it there—builded strong and safe."

"The roof needs to be fixed," she told him.

"Ah, but there's shutters on them windows," he murmured in a low whisper as he looked warily over his shoulder. "Nice solid shutters to keep out the wind—arr, the wind and all else what wants to get in."

"We've got a burglar alarm," Lauren said, slightly perturbed at the hunted look that had settled upon his craggy face.

Tommy peered at her. "Have you now?" he breathed. "Well, that just might not be enough. Depends on what them burglars want to steal, don't it? Not all after silver forks and bangles, you know, no, not all of them. There's worse 'uns out there."

"I'll be sure to tell Dad," she said, humoring him.

"You do that," he warned, his gaze wandering up past her head to squint and scrutinize the sky.

"Dusk's coming," Tommy uttered apprehensively. "Time to be indoors. The dark's no place to be outside no more, not around here it ain't."

Unnerved by this unexpected, earnest sincerity, Lauren found herself asking why.

"'Tain't safe," the old man answered. "You not heard 'bout the womenfolk falling sick and lyin' tired an' drained in their beds during the day? Strange things is ridin' under the stars—Tommy knows, Tommy heard 'em. He knows what they're about and it scares him, it does, and rightly so."

The girl tossed her head and climbed onto the bicycle. "Well, if it's only vampires," she said with a laugh, "then I'll be all right. I love garlic."

Tommy took off his cap and crumpled it in his fists. "Don't be a dafthead!" he cried. "Tommy never said nothin' about vampires. These are older'n that, older and meaner. They'll freeze your flesh as soon as look at you! But you're right about one thing, they'll have your blood all right. Arr, and your bones 'n' gizzards an' all."

With that he rammed the cap back onto his white hair, spun around, and pushed through a gap in the hedge to trundle away over the plowed earth of the field beyond.

Lauren was still wondering where he was going and where he lived when she saw his faintly ridiculous, tottering figure pause in the distance and she heard his woeful voice cry out, "Get on home, girlie, and you watch out! Watch out!"

* * *

Painted a pleasant chalky blue, the Humphrieses' recently acquired bed and breakfast was a large house just off the main road, situated on an acre of land and surrounded on three sides by a sprawling field.

The tires of Lauren's bicycle crunched on the gravel as she entered the front gate, and remembering what Tommy had said, she looked up at the large windows with their white-painted, sturdy-looking shutters.

"Poor old nut case," she said to herself, dismounting and propping her bicycle beside the back door.

As she feared, her father was not yet home, which meant she would have to spend some time alone with her "stepmother." Still, there was a chance that she could creep upstairs without being heard, and she opened the door as quietly as she could.

"Hello, Lauren," a woman's voice said immediately, and the girl's heart sank. "How was your day?"

Lauren managed a polite grin and hung her coat on the rack while a pair of keen, observant eyes regarded her from the kitchen table.

"Look at that baggy old coat of yours," the voice said critically. "It makes you look like a sack of potatoes. We really ought to buy you a new one."

"It's fine," the girl replied firmly. "I don't want a new one."

The woman put up her hands in surrender. "Only a suggestion—don't bite my head off. Come sit with me for a minute. We hardly ever get a chance to talk."

Inwardly groaning, Lauren poured herself a glass of orange juice and sat down.

Sheila was a pleasant-looking woman in her late thirties. Although not blessed with any natural beauty, she knew how to make the best of her appearance so that she seemed more attractive than she actually was. Her bobbed auburn hair was highlighted with tints of red, and about her soft gray eyes her lashes were lightly brushed with blue mascara.

Lauren had never been able to figure out why she disliked this woman so much. Sheila hadn't tried to take the place of her real mother, and Lauren understood that Guy, her father, needed to have someone other than herself in his life. Yet the very first time Lauren met Sheila, she knew she could never warm to this meticulous, slightly bossy person.

She was certain that moving away from London had been entirely Sheila's idea, and this was another strike against her. Sometimes Lauren wondered what her stepmother was trying to run away from.

Sheila lowered her eyes. "You're not happy here, are you, dear?" she murmured regretfully. "You haven't made a single friend in all this time."

Taken aback by the directness of the question, Lauren gulped her orange juice.

"Not really," she found herself saying.

"Not even at college?"

The girl gave a vague shrug. "S'pose not. Everyone there knows each other from high school. They're all right, but I'm just not into making friends here."

"Perhaps if you were to make more of an effort? Do something about yourself? You haven't touched the makeup I bought you for Christmas."

Lauren gritted her teeth and changed the subject.

"Sheila," she began, "what do you know about Tommy?"

The woman sniffed. "Tommy who, dear?"

"Dunno his last name. I think the locals just call him Tommy."

"Lauren, we're locals, too, now, don't forget. Oh, do you mean that funny old tramp? He's not all there, apparently. I always walk on the opposite side of the road if I see him. Last week he followed me, grinning like a baboon and talking to himself. I had to go inside a shop to get rid of him."

"Where does he live?"

Sheila coughed in astonishment. "How should I know? Honestly, Lorrie, you do ask the strangest questions. In a shelter, I suppose. Or with the rest of the winos."

"Tommy's not a wino," Lauren said defensively. "He's just a sad old man. He ought to be properly taken care of. Hasn't he got any family?"

But Sheila's attention was now directed at a package lying on the table and wrapped in dark blue paper printed with silver stars and circles. She proceeded to open the parcel with a curious look of pride on her face.

"I'm sure I don't know or care," she mumbled distractedly. "I've had my fill of losers. Now, what do you think of this, Lorrie? I bought it in one of those new-age shops in town."

From the blue outer wrappings she brought out a mass of violet tissue paper that she carefully unfolded, sheet by sheet.

"You'll never guess how little I paid," she blithely continued. "I wasn't sure at first, but that woman with the dangly earrings in there persuaded me in the end. Now, what do you think?"

Having arrived at the center of the tissue, Sheila gazed at her purchase for a moment then held it up for Lauren to see.

The girl stared at the object in her stepmother's hands and wrinkled her nose.

There, with a shred of violet paper still clinging to one of its legs, was the most outlandish doll that Lauren had ever seen.

Made entirely from scraps of patterned cloth, it was a crude representation of a creature that was half crow, half woman. A tiny straw hat sat on its black birdlike head, and in the shadow of the brim there sparkled two shiny beads that had been sewn on either side of a long yellow beak.

Around the neck, the bizarre effigy wore a checked red-and-orange scarf, and poking from the sleeves and the hem of a padded gingham dress to form spiky hands and feet was an assortment of painted twigs. Around the doll's stomach there was a plain calico apron, the pockets of which were stuffed with dried leaves. Onto this creamy fabric, above a row of mismatched buttons, the word "HLÖKK" was embroidered in thick black thread.

"What is it?" Lauren asked.

"The woman in the shop called it a crow doll," Sheila replied, not minding the girl's obvious aversion to it. "Only had a few left—I was very lucky to get this one."

"You were robbed. It looks homemade, and it's hideous and creepy."

Sheila turned the cloth figure over in her hands and inspected the workmanship. "Actually she hardly wanted anything for it," she declared. "I was rather embarrassed, in case she thought we didn't have much money."

"What does 'Hlökk' mean?"

"I didn't ask. Maybe it's a foreign word for doll or crow."

Lauren gave a slight shudder. "Well, I hope you're not going to put that thing anyplace where a guest might see it," she said. "Probably give them bad dreams."

"How funny," Sheila murmured.

"What is?"

"That you should mention sleep. You see, it's stuffed full of herbs. That woman said it would help my insomnia. She told me to hang it above the bed."

Lauren grimaced again. The doll was truly horrible, and those tiny shining beads seemed to be staring at her. "Better you than me," she muttered, turning away to look out the window.

"Quite frankly, I'd do anything to help me get a decent night's sleep," Sheila said, giving the beak a playful pinch. "Besides, it doesn't look too bad. I think it's rather cute—pretty even, in a macabre kind of way."

In the fields beyond the Humphrieses' bed and breakfast a number of genuine crows were circling in the darkening sky, and Lauren watched them with a growing sense of unease.

"I've never liked crows," she whispered, staring at the ugly black birds wheeling above, their harsh, croaking voices faint through the window glass. "They're vile birds, like vultures."

Sheila arched her plucked eyebrows. Guy's daughter could be odd at times. Lifting the doll to her nose, she gave a tentative sniff then rose and walked to the door.

"I'll just go hang this upstairs then," she said, stifling a yawn.

But Lauren wasn't listening. "What do you call a group of crows?" she asked herself. "I ought to know this. It's not a flock. It's something weird like a mob or a gang. No, wait a minute, it's a . . . oh, I can't remember."

Sheila opened the door to the hall, but before climbing the stairs, she turned and, with the doll swinging in her grasp, said, "It's a *murder* of crows, Lorrie, dear."

CHAPTER 7

IN THE SHADOW OF THE ENEMY

"Blood and sand!" Brian Chapman grunted as he thrust the saw blade through the soft rind of a slender branch.

Perched on a high stepladder, the caretaker of the Wyrd Museum could not believe what he was doing. The floor of The Separate Collection was already covered in fallen twigs and leaves. There were still two more walls to be pruned, but he was having serious difficulty in coming to terms with it all.

On the ground, playing amid the fallen foliage, Neil's brother, Josh, crawled into a den of dry, crackling leaves and made noises like fierce animals in the jungle.

He loved his new home and didn't miss the old house in Ealing at all. Of course, he still yearned for his mother and asked about her, but today there had been so much to do that he hadn't thought of her once.

Before he had attempted to tackle the panels, Brian Chapman had boarded up the shattered windows, cleared away the broken cabinets, and carefully sorted the scattered exhibits into various boxes. Josh had enjoyed that part of the morning, for he had played with shrunken heads and frog skeletons and had gleefully kicked an enormous leathery globe about the room like a football until his father caught him and put the object out of his reach.

Now the four-year-old crouched in his leafy cave, listening to the rhythmic bite of the saw.

Suddenly the sound of urgent footsteps entered the room, and the boy cautiously peeked through the roof of his den to see who it was.

Into The Separate Collection came Miss Ursula Webster, and Josh regarded her with displeasure. That camel-faced old woman had been unkind to him when he first arrived at the museum, and he didn't want her to find him now.

Returning below the leaves, he lay on the floorboards and waited for her to go away again.

Overhead the sawing ceased as Brian looked down, but the elderly woman didn't even glance up at him. She hastened to the far end of the room where he had stowed the exhibits and began to hunt through every box.

"Miss Webster?" Brian began hesitantly. "Are you looking for something?"

Ignoring him, she continued to rummage and search.

"Where are they?" she hissed under her breath. "They must be here! They must!"

Into a chest crammed with fragments of broken sculpture the old woman probed, her tapering fingers trawling through chipped marble limbs and noseless plaster busts.

"He cannot have returned so soon," she attempted to

reassure herself. "We are not ready, the child is not prepared! Have I endured these endless years only to be confounded at the last? Why did I not act sooner?"

Pouncing upon another box, she feverishly spilled its contents over the floor and rooted through them like a wild, scavenging animal.

From his high vantage point, Brian stared down at her foraging form and decided that it might be best if he kept out of the way. Miss Ursula was obviously upset, and her tongue was sharper than the teeth of his saw. He scratched his head uncertainly.

"Where are you?" her growling voice shouted into the boxes, until suddenly she stiffened and threw back her head to give a great, glad shout as she pulled a black, scraggy bundle from a large chest.

Overcome with relief, Miss Ursula triumphantly brandished the object above her head for an instant, then inspected it closely.

Here were the stuffed remains of the second raven, and her shrewd, sparkling eyes examined every aspect of the poorly preserved bird.

It was a sorry-looking specimen, so badly damaged it was almost comical. Many feathers had fallen from the dried, flaking skin, and on the top of its head the creature was completely bald. Both eyes were shriveled, sunken sockets, and the lower part of the beak was hanging loosely on a shred of papery flesh, so that when Miss Ursula turned the dilapidated creature over in her hands it wagged up and down, making the bird appear to laugh silently.

Lifting the tattered effigy to her ear, the old woman shook it gently until, within the fragile skull, she could hear something rattling. A thankful smile spread across Miss Ursula's thin face.

"There now, Memory," she whispered, giving the black beak a scornful tap. "You certainly won't be going anywhere. How gratifying to find you still dead and inert. In life you were a vicious, spiteful imp, a vindictive little spy enslaved to a deceitful master."

Holding the raven away from her, she squinted at it through half-closed lashes. "I find you much more pleasing embalmed and shriveled like this," she remarked with a definite nod.

"Since the blood ceased to pulse in your veins, you and your brother have become useful to me. Now you are a pair of pickled gauges, my two fine barometers sitting out the ages, waiting to tell me when . . ."

The old woman's voice failed, and she glanced uncertainly into the chest once more.

"And yet," she muttered, "where is your brother? Where is Thought?"

Clasping the stuffed bird to her breast, she whirled about and stared up at Brian Chapman. "Where is it?" she demanded forcefully. "What happened to the other raven?"

Neil's father gave a nervous cough. "I'm sorry, Miss Webster," he began. "That's the only one I found. There wasn't another."

"You lie!" she stormed accusingly. "What have you done? Did you give it to the infant to play with? I know he skulks within the fallen boughs. Did he in his savagery destroy the bird, or has the brat lost it? Don't stand there dithering, you incompetent oaf, answer me! I command you!"

Brian pinched the bridge of his nose. "There was only one stuffed raven," he replied emphatically. "It was on the floor with everything else. If there had been another one I would have seen it. I'm sorry, but there you are."

Miss Ursula cast him a withering glance, but she had known all along that he was telling the truth, and a hideous chill crept down her spine. Closing her bluish, translucent eyelids, she cradled the raven in her hands, and her expression became set and grim.

"Then Edith was right," she breathed in a mortified whisper. "Thought has indeed escaped. His master has returned to assail us once more!"

She let the stuffed raven fall from her grasp and gazed dejectedly at the jumbled remains of The Separate Collection.

"None of this will avail me now," she murmured. "Against *Him* these defenses are trifling. A barrier of broken threads and frayed strands, nothing more. We are helpless, our protection lacking. What are we . . . what am I to do?"

Clasping her hands together, she paced toward the boarded windows, her elegant brows twitching and knotting as the situation bore down upon her.

"The time is now come," she eventually said aloud, as if announcing it for the rest of the museum to hear. "One of the ravens has awakened, a sure signal that the enemy of old walks this land once more."

Her cryptic words echoed about the paneled room, and it seemed to Brian that the electric lights became dim. He was not an imaginative person, but even to his drudging, doubtful mind it was as if the building had responded and was now troubled and brooding.

"We must forget our fears," Miss Ursula continued in a tone similar to a parent speaking to a fretful child. "One of the most trusted of the Captain's messengers has been called back from death. Why he has failed to rekindle Memory I do not know. I can only hazard that his powers are not as strong as he believed them to be. Either that, or . . ."

Miss Ursula's face fell, and when she next spoke her voice was filled with dread. "Either that, or he has spent them elsewhere," she uttered slowly. "Has he exhausted himself to bring his other, more deadly servants back into the world? If that is so, then our peril is even greater. We cannot indulge ourselves any longer. For the first time, Urdr will break her vow. The device that I refused to shelter long ago must be brought here straightaway. Without it we are lost."

The difficult decision made, she assumed a frozen dignity and strode purposefully toward the doorway, too absorbed in her turbulent thoughts to even glance at Brian Chapman.

From within his den of leaves, Josh watched her depart and pulled a rude face. High above him, on the stepladder, his father resumed his pruning.

"A madhouse," Brian Chapman muttered to himself. "That's what this place is—a blinkin' madhouse!"

*   *   *

"Thought and Memory!" Miss Veronica declared when Miss Ursula returned to the Websters' apartment.

Miss Ursula stared at her in wonder.

"Thought and Memory," Miss Veronica repeated.

Her sister regarded her warily. "Is that all you remember of them, Veronica?" she asked softly.

The white-faced figure in the armchair gave a wistful sigh before turning back to stare out of the rain-streaked window. "Both gone now," she murmured. "Both dead and gone, no more sweet messages. No more."

Curled up in a gloomy corner, her walnut features buried in a shapeless cushion, Miss Celandine suddenly sat bolt upright.

"It wasn't me, Ursula!" she denied vehemently. "It was the girl! It's all her fault! She made Veronica remember. She did, she did!"

Miss Ursula gazed at her coldly before turning to look at Edie.

The child had been drawing squiggles with her fingers in the thick ash that lay heaped on the hearth, and Miss Ursula placed her hands lightly upon her shoulders.

"The hour has come when perhaps we must remember," she said flatly. "Edith was quite correct. Last night, Thought's mortal remains were indeed renewed. He has flown from the collection, and the end I have long feared has arrived sooner than I had guessed or planned. We have been idle and complacent while our old adversary has not."

"The ice giants?" Edie cried excitedly. "Is it them?"

At this, Miss Celandine rocked back and hooted with laughter.

"Celandine!" Miss Ursula scolded. "Behave yourself, or else I shall send you out of the room!"

The old woman in the faded red velvet clapped her mouth shut and sullenly folded her arms. "Ice giants!" she said in a grumbling whisper. "The silly girl doesn't know anything. What would the ravens have to do with them?"

"Enough, Celandine!" Miss Ursula snapped. "I will not tolerate you in this ridiculous humor. Do you not understand? We are in the shadow of the enemy. The power we resisted long ago has arisen once more, but now we are defenseless."

Miss Celandine pressed her lips together tightly in case they said something else to offend her sister, but she glowered at Edie all the same.

"Come, Edith," Miss Ursula began, taking the child's hand and sitting her down. "Only you can aid us in this. Your first labor has arrived sooner than expected. If you fail in this then we are all doomed. All our hope and fortune reside now in you alone."

Squirming in her seat, jealous of all the attention Miss Ursula was paying to the child, Miss Celandine could bottle her voice up no longer.

"But what can she do?" she blurted. "It isn't fair, Ursula—it isn't, it isn't! I want to be important, too. I do, I do!"

"Silence!" Miss Ursula demanded sternly. "This is a task beyond even us, Celandine. You, Veronica, myself—we are bound wholly to the museum. Away from its cloistering walls we are even weaker than we are now. It is from Nirinel we draw our strength, you know that."

Miss Celandine huffed with dejection and hugged the cushion sulkily.

"If you hadn't broken the loom and if the well wasn't dry, we'd be as strong as ever we were," she mumbled.

"Those things are gone forever," Miss Ursula said crossly. "We must seek to protect ourselves as best we may. Only one path is open to us now. Edith must retrieve the one dread item that can save us. That one thing alone can stave off the approaching attack."

The child grinned. "What do you want me to do?" she asked.

Fingering the strings of jet beads about her throat, Miss Ursula stared keenly at her. "Many years ago," she explained, "a most perilous device was interred far from here for safety's sake. It was a mighty, magical thing, far too dangerous to keep within the confines of my museum.

"The Separate Collection was originally intended to be a sanctuary, a refuge where the forces too treacherous to remain in the outside world could be safely deposited and forgotten. Yet this one, singular device was different. Even I fear this object, and when it arrived in this land from far over the seas, I refused to accept it here."

Bowing her head so that the piled white curls flopped forward, shaking loose a fine drizzle of dust that floated onto her lap, the old woman passed a hand over her eyes and clicked her tongue in self-condemnation.

"I perceive now that I was mistaken," she confided. "If this device had been stowed here from the first, there would be no need of haste now and we would be secure. Yet need there is, and you, Edith, must venture out to fetch this terrible thing. But do not worry, child, you shall not go alone. Should this modern age bewilder your young head, I have decided that a guide will accompany you upon the journey."

"Who?" Edie asked.

"One in whom I have complete trust. There are still in this world some of the old race, those learned in the history of the former time. Fragmented remnants descended from the spoils of Askar are they. Distant heirs of those who once dwelt in our mother's realm. They know their proud lineage, and at the commencement of every year they congregate in the yard below to pay a tribute of flowers, decorating the fountain in memory of what was.

"Over the years I have seen the numbers dwindle. Ever they seek a sign from us, and always they depart unanswered. But now it is time for me to speak. Among those folk there is one man in whom the blood of Askar runs almost pure. It is he who will go with you, Edith, and now, sisters, we must summon him."

Miss Celandine cooed in delight and dragged her chair across the room to join them.

"Goody, goody!" she trilled. "I always enjoy it so, I really do."

Miss Ursula turned to the figure sitting by the window. Miss Veronica was staring fixedly ahead, and her sister called to her in a surprisingly warm and tender voice.

"Veronica, we need your assistance."

The painted face blinked impassively then moodily looked away.

"You know we cannot do this without your help, Veronica."

"Oh, don't be a meanie!" Miss Celandine moaned. "You're so stingy all of a sudden, Veronica. Please join in. I want to see, I want to go."

The wizened Miss Veronica pursed her vermilion lips then gave a begrudging nod, and Miss Celandine bounded over to help her from the chair.

"I can manage," Miss Veronica said defiantly, doggedly gripping the handle of her walking cane and taking a few hobbling steps forward. Her face frowning beneath the flour, she eased herself down again and laid the cane across her knees.

"Draw the curtains, Edith, dear," Miss Ursula prompted, rising to turn the armchair around to face the center of the room and pushing it closer to the others.

Intrigued, Edie ran across to the window.

"We are ready," Miss Ursula announced, waiting for Edie to sit beside her once more. "You may begin, Veronica."

Edie watched in fascination as Miss Veronica lifted the cane and held it out toward her sisters.

"Reach out, Edith," Miss Ursula told her gravely. "Touch it lightly with your fingertips."

The girl complied, her dirty hands looking tiny next to Miss Celandine's twisted fingers and as black as coal compared with Miss Ursula's pale, violet-veined skin.

Miss Veronica drew a deep breath and lifted her face to the ceiling.

"Let the measure find the one we seek and take us to him," she whispered.

For several protracted minutes no one moved, and Edie began to wonder if the sisters had fallen asleep. But gradually she became aware that the shadows were increasing and the sound of the rain pattering on the window was fading.

Absolute silence swamped the room, and from beneath the curtain, meager chinks of drab light no longer crept over the threadbare carpet.

Edie held her breath, for the only noise she could hear was that of her own breathing, and still the darkness deepened.

Then, very softly, Miss Ursula began to chant. "Aidan," she said. "Aidan, Aidan, Aidan."

Edie gasped, for the tips of her fingers were tingling, and when she stared down at the walking cane, the girl almost cried out in amazement. The black rod was glimmering. Within the polished wood, from the tip of the handle down to the silver-banded stub, a faint green radiance was coursing through the grain.

Swiftly the light welled up, shining into the four intent faces, and Edie marveled.

Directly opposite her, Miss Veronica's blanched skin looked even more ghastly than usual, and her grubby white robe reflected the glare so brightly that it was painful to look at.

Miss Celandine was so excited that she bit her lower lip with her goofy teeth to keep herself from squealing in delight. Her bright eyes bulged beneath her wrinkled brows, while the magical light continued to shimmer and spill outward, spreading its vivid splendor like an ever-widening iridescent pool.

Over the furniture the powerful, pulsing brilliance flooded, pushing the hollow shadows farther and farther back.

"Aidan . . ." Miss Ursula repeated, her gaunt features solemn and creased with concentration. "Aidan . . . Aidan."

At the quivering brink of the dazzling circle the deep darkness swirled, pressing close to the apartment's confining walls as the light steadily increased in might.

Steeped in the flaring heart of the lustrous, glistening beams, Edie shifted her gaze from the Websters and finally let out a desperate yet incredulous breath.

The glare had moved right up to the walls, passing straight through them and beyond. They were no longer within the room, and she almost pulled her hands from the walking cane in astonishment.

Above her the ceiling had melted away, and the obscuring shadows churned wildly as they parted to reveal an open sky that was already growing dark with the approaching evening.

The first of the early stars pricked out of the stretching heavens, and Edie shook her head with disbelief as she lowered her eyes and saw a hilly landscape unfurl all around them.

To her complete delight, she realized that she and the Websters were no longer in the Wyrd Museum.

CHAPTER 8

AIDAN

At the edge of a Somerset wood, three miles from Glastonbury, two vehicles were parked on the grassy shoulder of the road.

The largest, a rusted, barely roadworthy bus, was over twenty years old. Most of its seats had been removed and replaced with mattresses, blankets, clothes, pots, pans, large water containers, and those trinkets its owners could not bear to be parted from.

In its former life, taking day-trippers on excursions to the beach, the bus had worn a sober cream-and-purple design, but now its paintwork was a riotous, clashing multitude of garish flowers, rainbows, and sunbursts.

Directly behind this emblazoned vision sat a pale blue van. But in the waning half light, as the wintry sun dipped behind the rim of the trees, even the bus's brash, declaiming colors appeared dim and gray.

Around a small campfire a group of travelers discussed the day's events, as they did every evening. To them, the area around Glastonbury was their spiritual home, and they never journeyed far from its mystical influence. Unlike many of the other wayfarers and modern-day pilgrims who haunted the small town, those who traveled in *Eden's Bus* never marred the countryside with litter or provoked trouble with the locals.

On their scattered rugs the five nomads laughed and chatted in light, happy voices, while, nuzzling into their laps and lazing before the welcome flames, their two dogs—a honey-colored Labrador and a Jack Russell—lolled and panted.

Usually three men and two women sat around the fire, but that night a fourth man had joined them, and his unexpected arrival was the cause of glad celebration. In the company of their honored guest there could be no sorrow or care.

Their friend and mentor was a mysterious figure who never stopped in one place for any length of time, flitting about the country like a jackdaw, and he was known to them simply as Aidan. If he had ever possessed a surname no one had heard it, and his origins were equally enigmatic. He never mentioned his family, and he was careful never to put down any permanent roots that might bind him to any particular place or person.

Dressed in a baggy frock coat of chocolate-colored velvet, much patched about the pockets and elbows, he was a small, swarthy man who looked more like the traditional image of a gypsy than did any of those around him.

A ragged scarlet bandanna was tied loosely about his throat, while a battered top hat sat tilted far back on his head. Beneath its silken brim his long, dark hair trailed down past his shoulders. A dignified, finely sculpted nose jutted from his face, overshadowing his wide smiling mouth. Under his dark, bushy brows two grass-green eyes gleamed with both cunning and wisdom.

To the oppressed and despairing, this strange little man with the persuasive voice and kindly face was a champion of their cause, and everyone who spent any amount of time in his society respected and admired him.

"So where have you been since we saw you last?" queried one of the women, filling six mugs with home-made elderflower wine. "The grapevine's been very quiet concerning you since midsummer."

At her side Luke, her husband, passed the brimming vessels around and nodded in agreement. "But then it always is," he conceded.

Aidan considered them both while he gratefully received the wine then, nursing the mug in both hands, wafted it under his nostrils to savor the bouquet.

"What I always say," he uttered at last, with a great, dramatic exhale, "is that no one brews a better elderflower than you, Rhonda."

The woman bowed in playful acknowledgment, but she would not let him wriggle out of it that easily.

"And there's no one like you for avoiding a question with flattery and playing the fool," she added.

Aidan and the others laughed, and the dogs pricked up their ears.

The gypsy-looking man doffed his top hat at Rhonda. "I stand, or rather sit, corrected and chastised. Caught in the act of evasion, I must try and be cleverer about it from now on. I do hope I haven't lost the art altogether.

I must practice my bamboozling an hour a day at least. Tell me, about the wine, do you think the secret is in gathering the flowers at precisely the right moment? Or is the answer in the fermentation?"

Luke raised his cup and took a sip. "Give it up, Rhon," he advised. "Aidan's business is just that. You can't squeeze him for news. No one ever can."

"I'm sorry," she sighed. "It's only because we miss him when he's away, don't we, Dot?"

Her face partly hidden by a mug, the other girl gurgled a definite affirmation, and Rhonda grinned.

Aidan placed his own drink in the space between his crossed legs and curled the whiskers of his sideburns around his fingers. "To answer you, Rhonda, my little alewife," he began lightly, "I have been hither and yon as usual, and tomorrow I shall be elsewhere, but for tonight I am here, and that is good fortune enough for me."

"That doesn't stop us worrying about you," she remarked.

"Worry about Aidan!" cried a large, curly-haired man upon whose lap the Labrador rested its head. "You might as well fret about the sun not rising or wonder when the rain will fall."

"My, my," Aidan spluttered in embarrassment. "What a testimonial, Patrick—and quite unmerited, I might add. Any more of that and I shall have to find a bigger hat."

"What about a story then?" asked the one who had not yet spoken. "Go on, Aidan, how about a tale—no, a tune! That's it, give us a tune. We could all do with a pick-me-up."

"If you wish it, Owen," Aidan assented, nodding

graciously as he reached into one of his bulging, capacious pockets. "Only an ill-bred, discourteous fellow with an adamantine heart could decline such a plea."

From the frock coat he brought out a beautiful silver flute that, in the firelight, appeared to be made of molten gold. Holding it delicately in his small, nimble hands he raised the instrument to his lips.

"Play something lively-like," Owen said. "One of your own melodies. They're always the best. Cheer me up, they do."

With the flute still poised at his mouth, Aidan regarded the man and saw the strain revealed on his face, then slowly he gazed around at each of the other travelers. Resting the flute across his knees he said, "I think the music can wait a mite longer."

His friends glanced nervously at him, but no one could meet Aidan's penetrating glance.

"Which of you will tell me what is going on?" he demanded in a gentle, yet impatient, voice.

Rhonda fidgeted and shrugged, feeling foolish. "It's nothing really," she began. "You'll think we're being so silly. Oh, Owen, did you have to go and give it away like that? Cheer you up, indeed!"

"But it isn't nothing, Rhonda!" Owen answered forcefully. "You know it isn't."

The woman put her wine down and groaned softly. "Isn't it? I just don't know anymore. Oh, Aidan, I'm sorry. We didn't want to bother you with our problems. It . . . it just seems so ridiculous. It's paranoia on our part, that's all."

"Paranoia?" Aidan's bright eyes narrowed and his swarthy face lost all trace of merriment. "But then," he deliberated, "I'd be pretty paranoid, too, if I'd spent the past few weeks around here."

The others looked up sharply.

"Then you know already?" Owen cried. "You see, Rhonda, it is serious."

Aidan removed his top hat and set it on the ground. "Only fragments and snatches of gossip," he replied, "that's all. But it was enough to set me worrying. Now, tell me all you can."

"Difficult to know where to start," Luke put in.

"A little while before that car wreck," Owen said, "that's when it was."

The girl called Dot shuddered and held on to Patrick. "Utterly horrible that was," she murmured. "They never did find that young couple. Utterly, utterly weird."

Aidan leaned forward. "I heard about that. The car was ripped open, was it not? What else do you know?"

"Just bits and pieces really," Rhonda admitted. "Nothing concrete, nothing we can explain. It's just— well, it isn't the same around here anymore."

"We've even been thinking of leaving," Luke confessed shamefully. "Moving on completely, after all this time. Dunno what we'll do or where we'll go. Never thought I could live anywhere else."

"The whole atmosphere around here is different now," Dot insisted. "Totally changed. I've never known the locals to be so rude and antagonistic. It's really, really unbearable."

Luke shook his head. "People always lash out when they're scared, and outsiders are usually the first to feel it. Plus there's this weird sickness going around. I don't want Rhon to catch it."

"Nor Dot," agreed Patrick.

Meditatively tapping his fingertips together, Aidan listened to their fears, and his forehead furrowed so markedly that it seemed as if he had only a single eyebrow.

"This curious malady," he began. "Are you saying it affects only the womenfolk?"

Rhonda nodded, hugging herself in spite of the crackling fire and the thick woolen sweater she was wearing. "About ten of them, last I heard," she said. "Too exhausted to do anything but stay in bed all day. Don't think the doctors know what it is. Dulcie Pettigrew came down with it first. When she does manage to haul herself out of bed she looks awful. What if it's in the drinking water?"

"Then it's a very selective and discriminating little microbe," Aidan drawled skeptically. "But there's something else, isn't there? I can see by Owen's face that there is."

Owen scratched the Jack Russell's ear before he answered. "The others think I'm crazy," he said. "But for the past few nights I've been aware of, well, I don't know how you'd describe it . . . evil, I suppose, though that sounds plain crazy."

"Evil is many things," Aidan commented softly and with an earnestness that was both startling and uncomfortable. "But it is never 'crazy.' It always knows precisely what it is doing. Go on."

"Well, the dogs've noticed it, too. Cower under the bus, they do. I've heard 'em whinin', I have—poor little things. There's somethin' right nasty out there in the dark. Somethin' I'd like to get a good distance away from."

Rhonda and the others looked at their guest in silence while the outlandish little man contemplated all they had said. Eventually he cleared his throat and, to their surprise, smacked his lips as he lifted the flute once more.

"Well?" Owen said, just as the man was about to play. "What do you think of it all? Are we plain bonkers or what? I thought you understood."

With the flute resting upon his bottom lip, Aidan gave him a solemn smile. "Oh, but I do, Owen, I do."

"Then what do you suggest?"

"Oh," came the matter-of-fact reply, "I should get out of here as fast as you possibly can. The environs of Glastonbury have become a most dangerous and deadly place. Take my advice, pack up and go first thing in the morning—earlier if possible."

With that, he took a practiced breath, and from the flute there came a most beautiful, uplifting music that soared above the campfire and drifted high into the now star-crowded night.

The travelers looked at each other in consternation, disturbed by their old friend's words. But as the delicious, meandering refrain played over them, the melody entered their hearts and minds, instilling peace and banishing their anxiety.

Closing his gleaming eyes, his face a comforting picture of serenity, Aidan played on, quelling the qualms of these five frightened people. Enchanted, they gazed into the flickering flames, their thoughts conjuring up visions of a verdant land dappled by the emerald shade of a great and stately tree.

Abruptly both the Jack Russell and the Labrador jerked their heads away, and whimpering in fright, with their tails fixed firmly between their legs, they bolted for the shelter of the bus.

Completely absorbed in the music, Aidan continued for a few moments more, until Owen let out a fearful shout.

Aidan opened his eyes and stared at the man questioningly, but Owen was not looking at him. He was staring in disbelief at his friends, his mouth gaping wide.

Curious, Aidan turned to them, and the flute fell from his hands.

Sitting before him, taking the places of Rhonda, Luke, Dot, and Patrick, yet still arrayed in the travelers' clothes, were three old women and a young girl.

Immediately the small man leaped to his feet and bowed low, the tails of his frock coat flapping wildly behind him. He knew at once the identities of these three elderly ladies, and although he had yearned for this moment throughout his entire life, he had never dared to hope it would come to pass.

With the greatest of reverence he eyed them, but he was too overcome to utter a sound except for a feeble, choking splutter.

"Aidan!" Owen cried, shattering the wondrous, worshipful moment. "What's happening? Who are they? Where are the others?"

"Calm yourself," Aidan managed to say, mastering his tongue at last.

"But they've . . . they've snatched their bodies! For pity's sake!"

"Keep quiet, man! Show some respect."

Incongruously dressed in Rhonda's chunky sweater and jeans, Miss Ursula Webster paid Owen no heed but stared long and hard at the strange little man still bowing beyond the flames.

"Oh, Ursula!" Miss Celandine grumbled at her side as she flapped her hands within the long sleeves of Patrick's overcoat. "Why do Veronica and I always end up with the horrible clothes? Look at Edith. That charming dress is far too big for her, but those pretty necklaces are so darling!"

Aidan's sparkling eyes roved from sister to sister. Miss Veronica wore Luke's denim shirt and patterned vest but in her gnarled hands she still carried the walking cane.

She did not return his interested glance. Instead she looked around, trembling as somewhere deep down she thought she recognized the pleasing contours of this buttery land.

Sitting alongside her, retaining her green pixie hat but swamped by Dot's orange caftan, Edie Dorkins chuckled at the sight of Aidan's awestruck face.

"You . . . you are most welcome here," Aidan stuttered, returning his gaze to Miss Ursula. "This is the highest possible honor. I cannot . . ."

"Enough!" the old woman interrupted tersely. "It is gratifying that you know who we are. Yes, there is much of Askar in you."

"How . . . how could I not recognize you?" he gasped. "All my life I've waited . . ."

Miss Ursula waved him into silence.

"Listen closely to me, Aidan," she rapped sternly. "There is a task I wish you to perform."

"Name it."

"First, you must come to the museum without delay. There you will learn all you shall need to know concerning the high office that dire necessity compels me to command you to undertake."

"I . . . I will leave at once."

"You had better. Now we must be gone and return your friend's companions to him before he catches any more flies in his gawking mouth."

Hearing this, Miss Celandine began to protest. "Oh, but we've only just arrived!" she mewled.

Her sister ignored her. "When you are ready, Veronica," she said.

But the old woman wearing Luke's clothes was too wrapped up in her reverie to hear her, and Miss Ursula had to prod her sister to bring her out of it.

"Remember, Aidan," Miss Ursula said as the cane was raised once more, "do not delay for anything. You must come to us at once . . . at once."

Then, as suddenly as they had arrived, with Miss Ursula's instructions still hanging on the ether, the Websters and Edie disappeared, but not before Miss Celandine had spied the wine and taken a great, gurgling gulp.

Aidan looked up from his reverential bow. The four apparitions were nowhere to be seen, their unlikely figures replaced by those of his friends, but on the still evening air a distant child's voice called out, "I liked your music, Mister!"

"What happened to my wine?" Patrick asked, peering into the empty mug, not able to recall finishing it off.

"Owen!" Rhonda laughed. "What's the matter? You look as if you've seen a ghost. Aidan, why have you stopped playing? That was lovely."

Aidan stared at her, then gave Owen a reassuring yet desperate look.

"I've got to go," he announced with tremendous urgency. "There's something I have to . . . attend to."

"Aidan?" Luke protested. "But you can't go yet, Rhon's going to make one of her famous stews."

Owen grabbed his friend's arm. "Let him go," he said in a quavering voice. "Believe me, he's got more important things to do."

* * *

In the Websters' apartment, Edie pulled back the curtain and was mildly shocked to find that, in the East End of London, it was still raining.

"I liked that," she told Miss Ursula.

The old woman rose from the chair and smoothed out the creases in her evening gown.

"As soon as Aidan arrives tonight," she instructed, "you are to go with him. Do you understand, Edith?"

"I wish we could flit about like that every day," Miss Celandine lamented, wrapping her crimson velvet about her as she twirled in a circle. "It's so much fun being other people."

Hunched in the armchair, Miss Veronica stroked the stem of her cane. "I knew that land," she muttered under her breath, frowning slightly. "I was there, long, long ago, before the mists took me."

Nobody heard her, for Miss Ursula was explaining to Edie what she must do.

"If you do not succeed in bringing the device here to me," she warned, "then we shall fail."

"Will the enemy kill the big root?" Edie breathed.

Miss Ursula shook her head. "No," she replied with a

cold ring in her voice. "The one whom the raven serves would never dare to injure the last remaining root of Yggdrasill. He does not wish for the ogres of the deep cold to reclaim the world any more than we. No, Edith, it is *us* he is bent on destroying. He will never rest until our dominion over the destiny of mankind is ended."

Edie grimaced. "He sounds real 'orrible," she said.

Miss Ursula held out her hand for the child to take. "Come," she insisted, heading for the curtained doorway, "let us descend to the Chamber of Nirinel, and there I shall tell you all you must know."

"Ursula!"

Everyone jerked their heads around to see Miss Veronica struggling from the chair. Slowly she unbent her buckled back and raised her shriveled arm to point the cane at her sister in grievous accusation.

Edie stared at the painted face and was stunned to behold the bitter acrimony that contorted her white, wizened features.

With a little yelp, Miss Celandine hid behind a cushion. She had not seen her sister so upset and furious since the beginning of their confinement, and the spectacle dismayed her greatly.

Pressing her lips together and drawing herself up to her full, imperious height, Miss Ursula looked quizzically at Miss Veronica.

"There's no need to shout," she said archly. "I can hear you well enough."

Miss Veronica's half-blind eyes grew large and staring. Her bright mouth twisted into a condemning snarl as, at long last, the confusion that had clouded her mind for so long cleared and anger boiled within her ancient breast.

"I remember now!" she stormed. "It was your fault, Ursula—yours alone! Who told my Captain how to attain godhead? Who else but the one who had listened to the voice in the leaves! You were always jealous of what we had together, that I knew. But I never suspected the depths to which you would stoop to steal him from me."

"Veronica!" Miss Ursula commanded, but her sister would not be silenced.

"Your words!" she snapped. "It was your words that pinned him to the tree as surely as the nails that were driven through his flesh. Nine nights he hung there, nine terrible nights in which I searched for him and nearly perished in the wild. Yet all the time you knew where he was and still you refused to tell. Oh, yes, I found him in the end, but too late. When the sun dawned upon that tenth day he was no longer mortal!

"You denied me all that I ever wanted. Beyond the reach of my heart you set him. You are a vile, despicable creature, Ursula—I loathe you! With every breath I curse your base, spiteful soul!"

Aghast at the ferocity of Miss Veronica's hostile attack, Edie looked up at Miss Ursula. It was plain that the old woman was horribly shaken and distressed.

Reaching out her pale hands in supplication, only to have them resentfully struck away with the end of the cane, Miss Ursula struggled to make herself heard.

"You are wrong, Veronica!" she cried. "It was the only way. He was the only one suitable. Do you honestly believe it was my decision? You forget the dire peril our people were facing. His valor bought our escape."

"Escape?" Miss Veronica raged, striking the armchair

so fiercely with the stick that a cloud of dust exploded into the musty air. "Better to have met death than go running to this wretched jail where we've rotted ever since!"

Her sister recoiled as though another, more powerful blow from the cane had smote her, and staggering to the doorway she hurriedly drew her hands across her eyes.

"Come, Edith," she said huskily. "There is much you must learn."

Glancing back at Miss Veronica, who was still quaking with fury, the girl followed, but the old woman hesitated before leading her from the apartment.

"All that I have done," she declared, turning to face Miss Veronica, "was for the greater good. Vilify me if you will, but I know that my path was the only possible way."

Miss Veronica shifted around so that she might not have to look at her sister any longer.

Glancing briefly at Miss Celandine, who was still cowering behind a cushion, Miss Ursula departed, and Edie trailed after.

"Go," Miss Veronica breathed, leaning heavily on the cane as she listened to their footsteps descend the staircase. "Nothing you do can prevent it, Ursula. Bring the magical device to this accursed, benighted place—it won't avail you. The Captain was always tenacious. You, Celandine, and I, we shan't escape him. Even now the servants he created to depose us may be racketing across the sky. This time the Gallows God will be victorious."

CHAPTER 9

SPECTERS AND ALIENS

Neil Chapman strolled home from his first day at his new school, hands in pockets, tie askew, his bag slung over one shoulder. At his side Paul Roberts, the boy he had sat next to at assembly, enthused about his science fiction obsession, and Neil listened politely.

"Course, some people think they've only been visiting this planet for the past thirty years or so, but I reckon they've been here for ages. Take that guy this morning."

"Who?"

"The trendy vicar!"

"You don't think he's an alien, do you?"

"Don't be silly! Although, the way he was prancin' around, you'd think he might have come from another planet."

Neil sighed sadly. "I felt sorry for him."

The boys ceased walking, for they had come to the cheerless block of apartment buildings where Paul lived, and Neil could see in the near distance the spires of the

Wyrd Museum spiking up into the darkening horizon.

Half closing his eyes, he remembered that same view as he had seen it fifty years earlier during the war, and with a shiver, he recalled the trumpeting voice of Belial blaring in pursuit.

Paul goggled at Neil, then honked with laughter. "You felt sorry for him! You're a scream, Chapman!" he guffawed. "I love it! Hey, I gotta go. See you tomorrow, okay?"

"Sure." Neil nodded as the boy headed toward his building. "I certainly won't be going anywhere. My part's done now, and I'm stuck here for good. The adventure's all over."

Kicking an empty can along the street, he continued down a narrow cobbled alley that ran between a series of derelict warehouses and an empty industrial site. When he entered the cramped lane that led to the museum, he gazed up at the blank Victorian row houses that led up to the museum's rearing bulk and stared at their dark, almost menacing, façades.

Some of the houses were undoubtedly empty, their windows and doors covered with boards. But others were still inhabited, and he wondered who would want to live in such a desolate spot, with only a high blank wall on the opposite side of the road to stare at and the peculiar Wyrd Museum at the far end.

Squinting at the grim dwellings, Neil imagined their owners might be strange goblin creatures who shunned the light, only creeping out in the darkness to dance around the museum and with high squeaking voices praise the three sisters who resided there.

"Four now—there's Edie, too," he corrected himself,

raising his eyes to study the magnificently bizarre building ahead.

With the failing light behind it, the squat shape of the museum seemed even more like a gigantic, crouching animal than ever before, and although he disliked the Websters, Neil found he was actually glad that his father had come to work there.

"Not pretty, is it?" said a voice unexpectedly.

Neil started and looked around. Hidden by the blanketing shadows that converged at the junction of the row houses and Well Lane was the dim figure of a man. Although Neil could not see him properly, he could tell that the man was staring straight at him.

"Funny old pile, isn't it?" the stranger said, stepping from the gloom. The first glimpse Neil had of his face was of two blank, leaden discs as the evening sky reflected off a pair of eyeglasses.

The boy instinctively shrank away when the man approached.

He was an old, grizzle-haired character with a craggy, lined face, and he wore a light brown raincoat. He looked like any other senior citizen on his way to the social club, but there was something about this one that Neil thought he recognized.

"Surprised to see anyone hereabouts," the man said, turning on an ingratiating grin. "Funny, quiet district, this. Not surprising really, with that monster sitting there like a slumbering dragon."

Neil peered at the stranger, wondering why he seemed so familiar.

"The museum?" he muttered. "It's all right. You get used to it."

The man's high forehead creased, and the grin vanished as swiftly as it had appeared. "You know it's a museum?" he stated in wonder. "Well done, boy, well done. Not many know it's even here at all, much less what it is. Well, well, well."

"I'd be pretty stupid if I didn't," Neil replied, not liking the stranger one little bit. "I live there."

The craggy face changed abruptly, and the old man appeared shocked and stunned.

"You . . . you live in there?" he stammered. "Get away, lad."

Neil wanted to do just that, but he had provoked the man's curiosity, and it was apparent that he wouldn't budge until he had learned what he wanted.

"My dad's the new caretaker," Neil said bluntly.

At this the stranger became excited. "Tell me," he said, casting an eye at the museum's square Georgian windows. "What about the sisters who live there. Have you ever seen them?"

"Of course I have," Neil answered, but he wondered who this person was and why he was so interested in the building.

The man saw the boy's puzzlement and drew a small business card from the inside pocket of his raincoat.

"Here . . . the name's Pickering—Austen Pickering. Have you ever noticed anything . . ." he paused to find the appropriate word, ". . . peculiar about that place? Odd noises, unnaturally cold areas? Have items disappeared only to emerge somewhere different a few days later?"

Neil smirked unconsciously, thinking how mundane those occurrences would be compared with the things that really happened within those forbidding walls.

"Have I noticed anything peculiar?" the boy murmured, more amused than anything else.

"It's a very ancient site," Mr. Pickering interjected. "Ancient and watchful. I've been studying it for quite some time now. I've seen it in most of its moods, from brooding to antagonistic, self-pitying to jealous. Old structures are like that, lad, they absorb the atmosphere of the times in which they stand, and if the buildings are particularly archaic, that's when they can prove most tricky—and dangerous, too. Some places grow to just plain bad, from chimney to cellar."

"Studying it?" Neil whispered as the realization struck him. "Now I know where I've seen you before. When we first moved here—when those people brought the flowers—you were standing outside the yard."

"Ah!" the man cried. "Then you witnessed the procession, did you? Worth a couple of chapters on its own, that will be. Amazing, wasn't it—very nearly medieval in its structure and performance."

"Chapters?" the boy repeated. "Listen, what is all this?"

Mr. Pickering cleared his throat and pushed his spectacles farther up his bulbous nose, the thick lenses shielding his eyes so that Neil could no longer see them.

Then, in a clear, proud voice he said, "I'm a ghost hunter."

There was an embarrassing silence in which Neil wanted to laugh, but the man was deadly serious.

"I'm not joking, lad," he barked bluffly. "That building is, I believe, one of the most haunted locations in this country."

Neil looked away, and all trace of amusement left him. "You might be right," he said softly.

"No doubt about it, lad, no doubt at all. I've done my research, and I'm always very thorough. It's been many things, you know. Between the wars it was an insane asylum, before that an infirmary, then an orphanage, then a workhouse . . . all good meat for a ghost hunter to get his teeth into. I should dearly like to investigate it more fully, execute some scientific tests, conduct a few controlled experiments—collect data."

"So you can write a . . . book, was it?"

Mr. Pickering tutted and pulled a disgusted face. "A paper to the Psychical Society, that's all I'd write. No sensationalism, only more facts to add to the already overwhelming body of evidence."

"Then why don't you?"

"I've tried. I've written countless letters to the Webster family but nothing, not even a courteous refusal."

Neil rolled his eyes, acknowledging the stubbornness of the Websters. "Then it looks as if your paper's going to go unwritten," he said.

"Hang the paper!" the man snapped. "That's the least important aspect of my investigations. Don't you realize? There are hundreds of tormented souls locked up in that museum. My one ambition is to set them free and help them attain peace. Heaven knows they deserve it after all this time trapped in there!"

The impassioned speech was more than Neil could bear. This so-called ghost hunter was too intense, and the boy decided it was time to leave.

"Well, I really ought to get back," he said, edging past

him and wishing he was already within the small caretaker's quarters. "I've go a lot of, er . . . homework to do."

Mr. Pickering made no attempt to follow him, but his words had had more of an effect on Neil than the boy had expected. As he made his way around to the back of the building to let himself in the rear door, he could not help but think that it was all true. The Wyrd Museum did guard a wealth of dark secrets.

Wavering before he turned the key in the lock, Neil hesitated as, from over the high walls, the ghost hunter's chill voice came echoing.

"Beware that place, lad. Be careful of the lonely, unquiet spirits that tread upon its boards and roam under cover of night. Don't approach them. Not all are gentle with good intent. That site is like a great psychic sponge—it sucks up souls and covets them jealously. If you can't protect yourself, you'll never escape it, and you'll be doomed with all the rest!"

CHAPTER 10

VALEDICTION

Night crept over the Wyrd Museum.

While Neil slept fitfully in the bed he shared with his younger brother, far below in the Chamber of Nirinel Miss Ursula Webster stared up at the withered root and waited.

On the third floor, in the sisters' cramped apartment, Miss Celandine sat before a tarnished mirror, a lighted candle in her hand as she gazed morosely at her reflection, her meandering thoughts recalling happier times.

Nearby, the armchair closest to the window was empty, and upon a silver tray, another heaped plate of jam and pancakes brought to placate Miss Veronica remained untouched.

Downstairs, within the labyrinthine galleries illuminated only by the slanting moonlight, a bowed, crippled shape limped its way through the building. Like a phantom of some ancient pagan priestess driven out of her sacred grove, the hunched figure moved through the endless rooms, the grubby material of her flimsy white gown shifting around her shriveled form as the different drafts billowed about her.

Into The Separate Collection Miss Veronica hobbled, her eyes blinking in the gloom as she surveyed the swept devastation.

Haltingly she crossed to the far side where the crates and boxes stood and found at once what she sought.

With the powder on her face crumbling, her expression became one of intense sorrow, and leaning her cane against the wall, she tenderly lifted out the remains of the stuffed raven.

She held the long-dead creature to her bosom, and a great, uncontrollable sob surged up into her throat as the cold, bleak knowledge of who she was returned to torment her.

"Verdandi," she whispered desolately, the tears welling up into her eyes. "Oh, Memory. What did she do to you? Why did I allow it? Forgive me, my sweet little messenger, forgive me."

Down her face the tears streamed, plowing long, dribbling channels through the plastered white makeup as they coursed to her chin, dangling for a moment before splashing on the moldy feathers of the bird in her gnarled hands.

"Verdandi," she sobbed. "Verdandi of the royal house, why did you harken to the words of your sister? Why did you let her take him from you? Look what you have become—a dried, old, haggard corpse, no better than his beloved raven. At least, Memory, you were permitted the indulgence of death. Not for me any sweet closure of this burdened life, not for Verdandi. As Veronica she must endure to shamble through the coming seasons of the world. Pity poor Verdandi."

The old woman fell silent as she surrendered to the consuming grief, and the bird in her grasp was awash with her sorrow, its broken beak flapping uselessly and filling with salty tears.

Yet Miss Veronica was not allowed to mourn the wasted years and miseries of her life for long. Even as she wept, a black shape flew across the one unboarded window and alighted upon the sill outside.

A pair of sharp black eyes that burned with a fierce, calculating intelligence switched to and fro as the creature peered into the room. When it was satisfied that the woman was alone, it pecked fiercely on the glass.

Engulfed in her woe, Miss Veronica did not notice the sound at first, but as the noise became increasingly more frantic and compelling, she raised her head and gasped in bemused confusion.

Silhouetted against the window, its sleek, inky feathers edged by the cold moonlight, was perched another raven—only this one was very much alive.

Miss Veronica let out a small shriek while the bird executed a mannered bow in greeting.

"Thought!" the old woman exclaimed in wonderment. "Can it really be you?"

Letting the tear-drenched, mortal remains of Memory fall back into the box, she seized her cane and waddled excitedly to the window, where she pressed her face against the pane.

"How can this be?" she cried, her fervent breath steaming up the glass.

The raven hopped up and down in agitation, scratching at the window with its talons.

"I can't open it," Miss Veronica wailed.

Unfurling his shadowing wings, Thought took to the air and beat upon the glass with them before whirling suddenly to one side, where its claws raked on one of the wooden boards covering a broken pane.

Miss Veronica understood, and using the handle of her cane as a lever, she started to pull the board free.

With a loud clatter, the wood fell to the floor, and into The Separate Collection the raven flew.

"Dear, dear friend!" Miss Veronica called, raising her hands in welcome as the bird settled upon a table, shaking his feathers and eyeing her keenly.

"What marvel is this?" she cried. "I heard Ursula and the child talk of you, but I did not understand. You live, you are back among us. Oh, do not let this be a deceitful vision wrought by my decayed mind. Yet even if you prove to be born of my fancy, or a poisoned overindulgence of jam, it does my aged heart good to see you again."

The creature nodded its head three times in reverence. "Hail to thee, daughter of Askar," his dry voice cawed. "Verdandi, youngest of the three princesses. No dream standeth before you. Thought hath indeed returned. Long years have passed since the fair green day when thou didst entrust unto my Master the two orphaned chicks thou hadst found upon the borders of thy mother's realm."

"I remember!" She laughed, smearing her streaked

makeup as she wiped the tears from her face. "You poor things were nearly dead, but he nursed you with his own hands and loved you both so dearly. Like his own children you were to him."

"And more than parent was He unto mine brother and me," the raven croaked. "Willingly did we serve Him, and no gladder than when He bade us convey His messages unto thee, fairest of those who dwelt in that blessed age."

The old woman sniffed. "But that was so long ago. See how I have aged. I am as old as the stones and more frail than a moth's wing. The countenance that once drew the Captain of the Guard has caved and putrefied."

"Yet the inferno of thy spirit blazes still."

"If there is any spark left to burn," she sighed, "then it is all but extinguished. This is a rare moment for me; at present my thoughts are clear. Likely this clarity will soon fade and I shall be Veronica once more—a sleepy hag who recalls nothing."

"Not thou, O keeper of my Master's heart."

Miss Veronica gave a meek laugh. "You are wrong, Thought," she said. "I lost any claim to him when he listened to my sister's words and nailed himself upon the World Tree. When he became a god, there was no room in the chambers of his heart for anyone, least of all Verdandi."

"Blame not my Master," the raven squawked. "'Twas thy sister who beguiled Him. If any blame can be placed upon my Lord, then scold the folly of His callow youth and His rash though valiant desire to save the realm. If thou accuseth Him then condemn

His trusting nature, but never doubt the unbounded love He had for thee."

Leaning upon the cane, the old woman gave a sad smile. "What does it matter now?" she murmured. "What was done is past. From Yggdrasill he attained godhead, and that was an end to my dreams ever after. It is good to speak with you, Thought, even if you are imagined, but I feel Veronica's rusted wits creeping up and clouding my senses. It is late. Upstairs there awaits a plate of pancakes, which she shall surely devour."

Turning, Miss Veronica began to shuffle away, but the raven beat its wings furiously and flew before her.

"Hold!" he crowed. "Mine errand hath yet to be accomplished."

"Errand?" she said, faintly amused. "Can a phantasm have any purpose other than to tease and stir the stagnant waters of remembrance?"

"If thou doth not believe in my substance then trust in my words," Thought told her. "One last message hath my Master instructed me to deliver unto you."

Miss Veronica gripped the handle of the cane and uttered a dismal cry. "Why do you torment me?" she whimpered. "Begone! Verdandi is no more. She ended when the mists claimed her."

"A final message," the bird insisted, circling about her head until the old woman began to feel giddy. "Wilt thou not listen? Wouldst thou turn thy back on Him?"

Having reached the entrance to The Egyptian Suite, Miss Veronica leaned against the doorway and in an almost fearful voice said, "Tell me then. Impart your last message and begone."

Thought alighted upon one of the sarcophagi, and clearing his rasping throat, he recited what he had been commanded to relay.

"Princess, all quarrels must finally end. If it were of any avail I would crave your forgiveness, but your sweet pardon is more than I may hope to expect. Permit me then to look upon you one last time."

The raven concluded his rehearsed speech and stared up at the old woman's face expectantly.

Miss Veronica looked as if she might faint. "The Captain wishes to see me?" she murmured eventually.

"Verily," Thought answered. "If thou canst recall any warmth for my Lord, then grant Him this one boon."

"Is he outside?" she asked, preparing to limp back to the window. "He must be made welcome."

The raven outstretched his wings. "By thee, perhaps," he cawed. "Yet not by thy sister. No, Verdandi, thy beloved will never enter here. He is far from this place, and even now He awaits thee."

"Where?" she gasped, breathless with excitement.

"Canst thou not presume to guess? Hast thou forgotten the trysting place of thy youth? Whence didst thou ride in the days of the World Tree's glory? To which isle didst thou journey?"

A withered hand covered the pale, powdered face as Miss Veronica suddenly remembered the marshy landscape of her secret rendezvous, with its majestic Tor dominating the sapphire blue sky.

"Ynnis Witrin!" she cried. "Is it there he has gone? Does it still mean so much to him?"

Thought strutted across the golden face of the

sarcophagus and assured her it was so. "No place doth my Master hold so dear," he told her.

"Yes," Miss Veronica agreed, "we were both very much in love—or so I imagined."

The raven hopped up and down, his black eyes sparkling as he sensed that his mission was nearly achieved. "At sunset tomorrow," he squawked encouragingly, "my Lord will be waiting for thee. Come alone, for there is much He doth desire to explain. Do not disappoint or dismay His high hopes. Let not the final message of the last raven go unanswered."

"Have no fear," Miss Veronica whispered. "I swear I shall go to him. How could I refuse?"

A sly gleam flashed in the bird's eyes, and Thought spread his wings to take to the air.

"Then until the morrow's ending," he cried, flying back into The Separate Collection, where he wheeled around in a wide circle before bursting through the shattered window again.

"Wait!" Miss Veronica wailed, holding up her hands in consternation. "Ynnis Witrin—how do I find it? The land has changed much since I last scaled that noble hill. Thought! Thought! I am old and spent. How am I to reach it?"

But the raven was gone, and Miss Veronica cast the walking cane upon the floor in despair. How could she make such a journey when she could not even walk unaided? Bitterly she knew that away from the influence of Nirinel her strength would diminish even further. Her garishly painted mouth formed a silent shriek as the knowledge of her impotence came crushing down upon her.

Slumped against the doorway she wept forlornly, until gradually an unfamiliar resolve began to harden within her breast. For unnumbered generations she had suffered under the domination of her sister. It was Miss Ursula who forced her to ride into the mists and assume the mantle of Fate. She had never wanted to measure the span of people's lives, and resentment of her sister now tempered her uncertainty into conviction.

Slowly the tears stopped flowing, and Miss Veronica crouched down to retrieve the cane. Then, with a grim determination mastering her fears and casting aside her doubts, she knew what had to be done.

* * *

The main hallway of the Wyrd Museum was swamped in darkness. Down the stairs Miss Veronica came, clutching the banister and nervously glancing at the floor below in case Miss Ursula was standing in wait. To her relief she saw that the shadows that flooded that space were empty, yet from somewhere close by a chill, damp draft was blowing.

Halting on the steps, Miss Veronica strained her imperfect vision to glare into the murk. The hidden entrance that led to the subterranean caverns was yawning open. Catching her breath, Miss Veronica hoped her eldest sister was still in the Chamber of Nirinel and not returning up the winding stairway. If Miss Ursula found her sneaking off in the middle of the night, there was no telling what she might do.

Summoning up her courage and reminding herself who awaited her, Miss Veronica continued her descent.

Over her white, diaphanous robe the old woman had pulled on a large, heavy overcoat. Stuffed into one of its pockets was a crumpled envelope, and the tip of it could plainly be seen. It was addressed to Brian Chapman, and inside were the caretaker's wages. Miss Veronica had discovered the money on the mantelpiece of the Websters' apartment, and being lucid enough to realize she would need money, she promptly stole it.

At last her slippered feet gained the parquet floor, and she moved stealthily toward the main entrance, putting an arthritic, deformed finger to her lips as she passed by the suit of armor.

No one would know where she had gone, and without the power of the cane to assist them, her sisters would be unable to determine her whereabouts. It would serve Ursula right. Let her worry and wring her bony hands together—it would never atone for the tremendous wrong she had done to Veronica—to Verdandi.

Concentrating on being as silent as possible, the old woman stole by the blank panel and paused a moment to listen for any sound of footfalls upon the worn stairs. But there was nothing; she was safe. Miss Ursula was too far below the ground to hear her depart, and even if she did she would have no time to stop her.

Unable to prevent a proud smile forming upon her face at the thought of outwitting her sister at last, Miss Veronica waddled to the entrance and placed her hands upon the stout oak door.

"Hey!" cried a voice suddenly.

Miss Veronica twisted around, and there, sticking

her face through the museum's ticket window, was Edie Dorkins. The pixie hat was still fixed firmly on her head, its silver strands glittering in the dark.

"Where d'you think you're off to?" the child demanded. "You're not s'posed to go outside, are you?"

Miss Veronica tapped the cane irritably on the floor. It was too cruel to be caught at this, the final obstacle, and she whined in dismay.

Edie scowled and clambered through the hatch to drop onto the floor before her.

"Don't tell Ursula!" the old woman begged. "Please, Edith, she must not stop me, not this time. Let Verdandi live again, just for a short while. Let her be free before Veronica returns."

The girl scrutinized her then, with a slow, deliberate movement, turned her head toward the open paneling.

"No," Miss Veronica pleaded. "Ursula would be furious. You have never seen her angry, child. Nemesis some name her, and in that dreadful temper she suits it well. Would you see me locked away against my wishes for the rest of my unending days?"

Edie clasped her hands behind her back and rocked on her heels as she considered the situation, while the old woman stared beseechingly at her.

"Ursula can be a mis'rable old hag," the child eventually said. "I've found that out already. Expects me to do everything she says. Well, I done decided. If you're goin' to leave, there's only one way to keep me from telling on you."

Miss Veronica eyed her uncertainly. Could she trust the young girl, or was she merely playing some cruel trick? Edie Dorkins was a law unto herself, and no one could ever guess what she might do next.

"I'll let you go and not say a word . . ." she continued belligerently, enjoying the power she held over the old woman, "only if . . ."

"If what?" Miss Veronica cried. "Don't torment me. What do I have that you could possibly want?"

Edie grinned and haughtily tossed her head. "Only if . . ." she teased, "you take me with you!"

Miss Veronica stared at her in surprise. "I cannot," she murmured apologetically. "I must meet my Captain. He asked for no one to accompany me."

"Then I'll just go shout down to Ursula," Edie threatened.

"Why do you wish to leave so soon? What of Celandine and Ursula?"

Edie shrugged dismissively. "P'raps I don't want to do what droopy-drawers Ursula wants me to," she said. "P'raps I reckon that I've seen all I want to see in here and wanna know what lies out there now."

"Then she was wrong about you," Miss Veronica uttered sadly. "You were never the One."

The girl giggled and took a furtive step toward the gap in the paneling. "Let's go and tell her you're leaving then . . ." she taunted.

"No! No!" the old woman cried. "I agree. You may join me, you terrible, willful child. But we must go at once."

Edie let out a high, gleeful laugh, and Miss Veronica glanced apprehensively at the large black opening nearby.

"Get a move on then," urged the girl. "Open the door."

Miss Veronica placed her crippled hands on the door handle and, with her heart in her mouth, gave it a twist.

The great arched door swung inward, and for the first time in many ages Miss Veronica crossed the threshold of the Wyrd Museum.

For a moment she stood on the topmost step, framed by the bronze statues that adorned the imposing Victorian entrance. Taking a cautious breath of the cold, bracing air outside, the old woman let her eyes roam around the litter-strewn alleyway. She could not quite believe that this moment had arrived.

A droplet of water splashed on her head, and she craned her neck to glance upward. There, surmounting the sign that bore the building's name, the severe-looking sculpted figure above the arch was weeping.

"Ursula!" Miss Veronica cried, cowering in alarm.

Behind her, Edie followed her gaze and nudged her crossly. "'S only a bit of old rain dripping off the statue," she said.

A wan smile spread over the elderly woman's face. "Of course it is," she uttered in breathless triumph. "After all these years, I've finally managed to escape her. No more commands, no more squabbling. I'm free—at last."

Taking care in the gloom, she descended to the second step and gazed at the sculpted form on her right.

"Farewell, dear Celandine," she whispered. "The hardest part of leaving is knowing that I am abandoning you. Don't let Ursula bully you too much. Perhaps you might leave yourself one day, when your time comes."

With that she lowered herself to the third and final step and shifted around to examine the left-hand statue.

The image was that of a beautiful young woman dressed in royal fincry, and Miss Veronica reached out to caress the cold, molded metal.

"So the incarceration of Veronica is over," she muttered, "and away from the surviving root, who knows, perhaps a final ending will be granted to her."

Slowly she turned and moved away from the steps, allowing Edie to follow her. Not bothering to glance at the sumptuous Victorian artistry that embellished the entrance, the girl capered to Miss Veronica's side.

"Where are we going?"

Miss Veronica took one last, lingering look at the brooding shape of the Wyrd Museum and let out a long, contented breath before giving her answer.

"Even in my time it was known by many names, Edith," she said. "The isle of apples, Ynnis Witrin, Mewtryne, Avilion—but I believe it became known in the later years as Glassenbury."

"Never heard of it."

Miss Veronica smiled simply. "No reason you should," she stated. "It is far from here, and we must make haste if we are to reach it by sunset tomorrow. I think I once heard Ursula complain of great iron carriages that travel at thunderous speeds upon rails of steel. Come, let us avail ourselves of this marvel."

And so, leaving the monumental bulk of the Wyrd Museum behind, Miss Veronica Webster and Edie Dorkins wandered into the darkness. Yet from the dangers that lay ahead, only one of them ever returned alive.

CHAPTER 11

DECEIT AND LARCENY

Transforming the wet roads into rivers of reflected amber jewels, the street lamps of Bethnal Green buzzed in the cold night, but the Reverend Peter Galloway neither saw nor heard them.

He walked through the East End, his long, unkempt hair clinging to his skull, his wispy beard dripping with rain, his head full of questions, and his soul heavy with disappointment.

For over an hour he had been walking aimlessly and tussling with the issue that had tormented him the entire day. Ever since that morning, when he had been laughed off the stage at the school's assembly, his mind had been forced to challenge and reconsider his beliefs.

All he had wanted to do was demonstrate how wonderful faith could be, yet he had succeeded only in making a complete spectacle of himself.

Peter winced when he remembered and clenched

his fists so tightly that he drove his fingernails into his palms. For the first time since he had been entrusted with this difficult parish, he was downhearted and at a loss as to how to proceed. He had failed the younger members of his flock and had no idea how to go about repairing the damage he had done.

With these desperate concerns churning within him, he had roamed without an umbrella or a raincoat. Finally, when the deluge stopped, his jacket was drenched and he was soaked to the skin.

Down the back of his collar the rain had trickled, and he had trod in so many puddles that his socks squelched when he walked.

Yet to him, such corporeal discomforts did not matter. His one anxiety was the problem at hand, and his lanky frame continued to range through the quiet streets until finally he began to shiver. Then Peter realized that it was time to return home.

It was past two o'clock when he neared his street. He hurriedly crossed the main road and decided to cut through the small park nearby.

Away from the sodium glare of the streetlights, beyond the iron railings and screened by the trees, the park was layered with shadow, and the empty rectangles of the rose beds quilted the ground with darkness.

With his feet making ripe, sucking sounds inside his waterlogged shoes, the vicar strode onward until he drew close to the old library, where a wide pool had flooded the path, stretching back as far as the small cenotaph.

Bringing himself to a sudden standstill, he gazed

down at the perfect stillness of the water, unwilling to mar its flawless, glasslike surface with his careless passing.

As a liquid mirror the rain lake appeared, and leaning over its smooth edge, Peter regarded his reflected face, which in turn stared back at him.

The image was such a disheveled, weary sight that he hardly recognized himself, and he jumped back, startled.

"Stay," called a quiet voice.

Peter whirled around and saw, standing by the white stone cross of the cenotaph, a robed figure whose features were hidden beneath the folds of a great hood.

"Who's that?" the vicar demanded.

The black recesses of the cowl turned to face him, but Peter still couldn't see any clue to the stranger's identity.

"I don't have any money, if that's what you want," he shouted, casting around to see if the nearby shrubbery concealed any more bizarrely dressed muggers.

A low chuckle sounded within the shadows. "You have no reason to fear me, Cephus," the voice soothed. "A moment ago, you were alarmed by your own reflection. Is all mankind now so abashed and afraid?"

Peter continued to watch the figure suspiciously. "It's been a tough day, that's all," he mumbled. "Wait—what did you call me?"

"The waters show but the outward aspect," the mellifluous voice resumed, letting the question go unanswered. "Only the heart can tell what lies within. I have looked and I have seen. You are the one I have chosen."

The Reverend Galloway swept his hands through his bedraggled hair. "Look," he announced with mounting impatience. "I don't know who you are, but go play your crazy games with someone else. I'm tired and have had more than my fill for one day."

"I have returned, yet all I see is despondency and faithlessness. The dance is faltering. Will you not help me restore the hopes of mankind?"

Peter grew angry. It stung him to think that this might be one of the older children he had performed before that morning.

"That's enough!" he bawled. "How can you be so twisted? Clear off!"

Unperturbed, the figure raised one of its hands. "Peace," he said. "I know the pain that drives you. It is a sadness we both share. You look around and grieve for those who have spurned their Maker. You have tried to lead them but they will not be led. Your attempts fail at every turn, yet still you pursue your goal. The determination of your faith is like grains of gold shining in the muddy riverbed. You are hope itself, Cephus."

Peter narrowed his eyes, his curiosity overpowering his indignation as the robes about the figure stirred and the stranger moved a step closer, into the center of the pond.

"Do you still not know me?" the voice asked.

The vicar made no reply, for he was staring at the water in sheer disbelief. Although he had just witnessed the mysterious stranger walk through it, not a ripple disturbed the perfect surface, and he rubbed his eyes incredulously.

"Again you see only the outward aspect," the voice told him. "Look deeper. What do you behold, there, in the dark inner depths?"

Peter stared down at the shallow water, catching his breath when the pool shimmered and the image of the robed figure dissolved, to be replaced by an expanse of thickly swirling mist. But the dense, writhing clouds quickly dispersed, ripped savagely apart by a blinding spike of lightning, and gusted swiftly away to reflect an entirely different scene from that of the park.

Filling the surface of the water, the vision of a vast and mighty tree creaked and groaned as a storm boomed and raged about its squall-lashed branches, enmeshing them in a brilliant net of bolting fire.

"What . . . What is this? . . ." Peter breathed in awe, his stunned face flaring in the intense flashes erupting from below.

"The tree is the world," the figure replied cryptically. "Is there anything else you see?"

Peter stared harder at the wondrous mirage unfurling within the pool, and then, his eyes widening in dumbfounded amazement, he beheld a man impaled upon the gargantuan trunk, with large iron nails hammered through his wrists.

From his wounds, rivers of blood streamed down the bark, and the tempest beat into the man's upturned face as he called out in his searing agonies. But his cries were snatched by the ferocious gale, and the lightning licked about his tortured body, splintering the boughs overhead and setting flame to the wind-torn leaves.

"Long I hung there," the robed stranger said, his voice wavering as he recalled the pain. "Never have I known such torment, but the sacrifice had to be made."

The scene within the water faded with his words, and the mist flooded across the image until it was hidden from view. With a shiver, the pool grew black and once more reflected the cloaked figure and the park around him.

Battling to comprehend what he had witnessed, Peter jerkingly raised his face and gazed at the stranger in stupefaction.

"I have said that I am returned," uttered the velvety voice. "Now do you know me?"

The Reverend's legs were shaking visibly, and as they buckled beneath him, he finally, mistakenly mouthed, "Dear Lord!"

Into the water he fell, landing with a great splash upon his knees, and in that prostrate state he clasped his hands together in worship, humbly hanging his head and weeping like a child.

"Tears?" the figure intoned.

"They . . . they are sobs of joy," Peter declared. "I . . . I don't know what else to do . . ."

"Then let them fall, and I shall tell you of my purpose here. The faith of the world has diminished and must be forged anew. It is up to you, Cephus, to deliver unto the doubters and skeptics the proof they require."

"Proof?" the vicar murmured. "What further proof can there be? Let them come. Speak to them, let them know."

The cowl moved gently from side to side. "Not yet," he said. "That time has not arrived. All doubts and suspicions must be brushed aside. This is your blessed crusade, my friend. In the sacred heart of this favored land, where once my own feet did tread and where now grows the Holy Thorn, lies buried a testimonial to the passion. Go seek out this thing, then display it to the world that they will know what is written is indeed the hallowed truth."

"Me?" Peter gasped. "You want me to do this? What is this thing? Where will I find it?"

Slowly the figure stepped back to the memorial. "A companion shall I send with you," he said, "for guidance and counsel upon the road. Farewell, my Peter."

The stranger stepped into the deep shadows, and suddenly he was gone.

Still kneeling in the pool, Peter took a deep, thunderstruck breath and shook his head.

"I didn't imagine it," he told himself strictly. "I didn't—I didn't!"

Gingerly he rose and peered at the memorial, half expecting to glimpse the hood peeking up over the stone. But no, the figure had vanished into thin air.

"Then . . . what do I do now?" he whispered.

With water running down his trousers and leaking into his socks, he paddled back to the path, not knowing whether to sing out loud or weep uncontrollably.

As he stood there like a saturated scarecrow, his attention was abruptly seized by the sound of beating wings, and he looked up into the night to see a large bird circling the park.

Suddenly the creature swooped from the sky and zoomed over the grass at tremendous speed. Still reeling from his encounter, Peter watched the raven in bemusement until he realized that the bird was heading straight for him.

Like a bullet the creature hurtled, and the vicar threw up his hands to ward it off. Then, at the last possible moment, before its glinting beak rammed into his chest, the raven soared upward in a perfect, graceful arc.

Crowing with amusement, Thought wheeled about and touched down upon the path only inches from Peter's sodden feet.

The man stared down at the curiously tame bird, and the raven cocked its head upward, its eyes twinkling at him.

"No time, no time," Thought cried, and Peter's jaw dropped open.

"Thou must leave this night. Make haste, make haste."

A delighted chortle sounded from Peter's lips.

"What other marvels am I to see?" He laughed. "A talking crow!"

The raven glowered and prowled around him, his flat head pulled into his hunched shoulders, until, with a shake of his primary feathers, he rose from the ground and alighted upon Peter's shoulder.

"Cease thy prattling," Thought demanded gruffly,

snapping his beak dangerously close to the vicar's earlobe. "Thou must prepare to obey His bidding."

"Then, you—you're to be my guide?"

His beady eyes glaring at him, the bird gave an indignant squawk.

"What of it?" he cried. "Dost thou doubt the wisdom of thy Lord?"

"No, no, of course not!" the vicar rapidly apologized. "It's just that . . . well, wouldn't a dove be more appropriate?"

His feathers bristling, the raven cackled quietly, bobbing his ugly head from side to side. "No more questions," the rasping voice said. "We must leave without delay."

"I'm not sure where we're supposed to be going," Peter began nervously, "and . . . if it's a long way . . . well, I don't possess a car, only a bicycle."

Thought clicked his beak in agitation then shuffled nearer to the man's ear and, in a low, persuasive whisper, said, "Falter not at this, thy first trial. Much trust hath been placed in thee. This is the hour to prove thy devotion. Many leagues lie twixt us and our destination. We must be fleet."

"I understand." Peter nodded uncertainly. "In the morning I can ask my sister if we can borrow her car."

"Nyarrk!" Thought shrieked, digging his sharp claws deep into the vicar's shoulder. "Didst thou not hear?" he snapped. "Upon this very instant our journey must begin. If thou hast not one of these wagons, then we must contrive a way to take one."

"What, you mean steal?"

"Consider the glorious outcome of this most sacred

quest," the raven goaded. "What matter a borrowed trifle against the wealth of rejoicing that is to come?"

His judgment impaired by the momentous experience and inspired beyond all reason, Peter readily agreed.

"Then let us forsake this dreary place," Thought told him, "and cast thine eyes to where the highway drains into yonder road."

Peter began walking and looked across the park to Roman Road, where he saw the headlights of a car pulling into a residential street.

"The driver must live in one of those apartments," he muttered. "But it's no use, we'll need the car keys. I can't just smash the window, climb in, and fiddle with the wires!"

The raven gave an impatient hiss and took to the air. "Thought shalt do this," he cawed. "Be sure thou art ready when I command. Get thee to that wagon as fast as thy spindle-shanks allow!"

With a final, petulant grunt he flapped his great dark wings and rushed headlong toward the street.

* * *

In Victoria Park Square a maroon hatchback eased into the only remaining parking place, and its driver, a small, chubby man, squeezed himself out of the car then pulled the seat forward to retrieve his briefcase and a sheaf of papers.

Slamming the door with his foot as he set off along the sidewalk, he waved the remote control over one shoulder. The lights blinked as the alarm was activated.

Suddenly, from out of nowhere, a black-feathered mass crashed into the man's face, shrieking and screeching, battering him with its wings.

Panicking, the driver dropped his case and papers as the nightmare clawed at his face then pecked at his pudgy fingers until the keys fell from his grasp.

At once the raven plunged after them, snatched the tumbling prize in his beak, then rocketed upward, the keys jangling discordantly.

"Hey!" the man cried when the initial shock had abated and he saw what the lunatic bird had done. "Give me those, you demented parrot!"

Thought landed on a railing just out of his reach and shook his head teasingly, making the keys jingle even more.

The driver rushed forward to grab him, but the raven was too quick and leaped away, drawing the man farther down the road and cackling with mischief.

"Miserable bird!" the man fumed. "Stay just where you are."

With one eye fixed on the figure creeping self-consciously from the park gates toward the maroon hatchback and the other trained on the approaching driver, Thought waited. If he could only lure the annoyed human away a little more then all would be well.

"That's right," the driver said, trying not to startle the wretched bird, "you just drop them keys, and Uncle Donald might not wring your thieving little neck."

The raven lingered a moment longer then hopped backward, enticing him even farther from his car.

"Stay put, you cat's breakfast!"

Thought scowled and almost dropped the keys in anger, wanting to squawk at the man. Then flitting from the railing to the top of a mailbox, he executed a neat, taunting jig, mocking him unashamedly.

Enraged, the driver lunged for the mailbox, and emitting a shrill cry of scornful, victorious glee from the side of his beak, the raven tore back to the car, where the Reverend Galloway was waiting.

In disbelief, the driver whirled around to see the bird drop the keys in the vicar's hands, and shouting at the top of his lungs, he raced back to stop them.

"Make haste! Make haste!" the raven shrieked, perched on the car's sideview mirror and watching Peter fumble with the remote.

Flustered, the Reverend glanced down the road at the angry man charging toward them, and in his consternation, the keys fell to the ground.

"Idiot!" Thought yelled. "Simpleton! Oaf!"

Peter hastily retrieved the key ring, and the headlights flashed as he pressed the button to release the locks.

"Hey!" the driver bawled. "Stop! Police! Police!"

His heart pounding, the vicar yanked open the door and threw himself inside.

"No, you don't!" bellowed the owner as he ran up to the car, seized hold of the door frame, and lunged inside to haul the petrified vicar out.

At once Thought flew at the man, raking his talons through his flesh and pecking fiercely at his hands. The driver let go of Peter and thrashed his arms to fend off the attacking bird as the violence of

Thought's onslaught propelled him back across the road.

With a final, savage nip to the man's cheek, the raven abandoned him and flew into the car, screeching wildly.

"Go! Now! Now!"

Peter thrust the key in the ignition and turned it sharply.

The vehicle spluttered to life.

"The door!" Thought squawked. "Close it! Close it!"

The vicar looked to his left and saw the owner of the hatchback come lumbering back, his face now streaked with blood. Frightened, Peter reached out, and the car rocked with the force of the door as he heaved it shut and locked it.

Immediately the driver began thumping on the windshield and banging his fists on the hood.

"What must I do?" Peter cried.

"We must away!" Thought commanded, hopping up and down on the headrest of the passenger seat. "Before the glass is broken."

With an apologetic wave to the true owner, Peter put his foot down and the car roared forward, crunching the bumper of the vehicle in front. There was a screech of tires and a scraping of metal against metal until, lurching, the hatchback shot from the parking space. The owner leaped back as his car went tearing around the corner and disappeared behind the trees of the park.

His hands locked tightly on the steering wheel, Peter Galloway stared out of the windshield at the main road ahead, sweat pouring off his face.

"Well done," the raven congratulated him. "Art thou certain thou wert never a footpad or cutpurse before now? The mantle suits thee well."

"I've never done anything like this before," the vicar proclaimed, wrenching his eyes from the road. "Joy riding! What would they have said at the youth center?"

Thought chuckled dryly. "Peace," he said. "Dost thou not know a jest when it is uttered? Nay, be not aggrieved by this act, for it is the first step toward the great gladness that is to come."

Peter swallowed and reminded himself of that fact. "Yes," he murmured. "So, where exactly are we going?"

"Didst thou not listen to our Lord?" the raven asked mildly. "To a place most sacred in this verdant land—to Ynnis Witrin, the blessed isle of Avalon."

The car kangarooed as the Reverend Galloway lost his concentration and sighed with unparalleled joy.

"Now I understand," he uttered. "I know the legend. So it really is buried there. Oh, yes, what better testament to The Passion can there be? I can't believe it—it's fabulous!"

Thought said nothing and let the vicar avow his happiness. They were far from their destination, and there was still much to be done.

Yet even as the maroon hatchback scooted off into the night, in the small town of Glastonbury the terrors that the raven's Master had rekindled there were to find their numbers increased by a new recruit.

CHAPTER 12

RIDING THE NIGHT

At the Humphrieses' bed and breakfast, Lauren's stepmother twisted in sweat-soaked bedsheets, groaning and complaining in her sleep. As the woman turned fitfully upon the pillow, her face was waxy and pricked with perspiration, and the breaths that wheezed over her swollen tongue were shallow and labored.

Gulping at the cool air, she rolled onto her back, and her eyes suddenly snapped open.

Like large spots of ink, her pupils stared up at the ceiling, and massaging her painful throat, she pulled the coverlet further up the bed. In spite of the sweat that poured down her face, Sheila was shivering, and she leaned across to the slumbering figure at her side.

"Guy," she uttered with a choking cough. "Wake up, Guy!"

Lauren's father made no movement, so she nudged him anxiously.

"Guy!" she spluttered. "I'm . . . I . . . I think you'd better call . . . call the doctor!"

Still no answer. The man remained fast asleep, and Sheila shook him with what little strength she could muster.

"Guy!" she pleaded.

It was no use. Nothing she did could rouse him, and weakened by her exertions, she collapsed back on the pillow, panting and spent.

Dim was the moonlight that seeped into the room, but it was bright enough to spread across the floor and shine its pallid glow over the wall against which the bed stood.

Gasping and straining for breath, Sheila let her swimming eyes rove blearily around, until gradually they focused on the patterned cloth of the object that hung upon the bed's headboard.

She glared at the crow doll she had placed there earlier that evening in the hope of attaining a good night's rest. As she heaved her aching ribs up and down, she found the contradiction infuriating.

The eyes that were sewn on either side of the yellow beak appeared to gleam in the chill moonlight, and Sheila sobbed as her fever caused her to imagine that the effigy was moving.

The checked material of the doll's dress stirred as if blown by a draft, and jutting from the neatly sewn sleeves, the twiggy fingers flexed slowly.

Sheila moaned, shakily reaching out for the bedside lamp to dispel these delirious illusions, but before her finger found the switch, she froze and stared in horror.

It was not her imagination. It *was* moving—the doll was alive.

On the plain calico apron, the stitches that formed the word "HLÖKK" glimmered, and a ruby light shone through the thread until the letters burned fiercely.

Hanging on its cord, the doll twitched and jerked to life. Beneath the small straw hat, the bird's fabric head turned until the bead eyes were staring down at Sheila, and the twigs clattered together as it squirmed to unhook itself from the bedpost.

"No!" the woman cried, throwing the blankets from her and leaping out of bed. "Guy! Help me! Help! Lauren!"

Too late she fled for the door. The doll had worked itself free, and with supernatural force, it launched itself toward her.

Her hands scrabbling at the door handle, Sheila screamed when the nightmare creature leaped onto the back of her head. Her anguished voice grew shrill and wild with terror as the twigs tangled in her hair and the fiery letters scorched into her scalp.

"No!" she yelled, writhing and twisting like a rabbit caught in a snare. "Lauren! Get it off! Get it off!"

Through her hair the doll's fingers stretched, snaking and growing about the woman's head and neck as it clung with vicious strength, and though she tried to tear it from her, there was no escape.

Shrieking, Sheila collapsed against the door. The sprouting, flourishing twigs wrapped about her, and she was lost in a well of deep, crackling shadow.

* * *

In the adjoining room, Lauren was startled awake by her stepmother's cries. She snapped on the light as she dragged herself out of bed.

"Dad? Sheila?" she called, hurrying from her room, a hundred drastic possibilities flashing into her mind. "What's going on? What's happened?"

Onto the landing she ran. She pushed at the door but it refused to budge, as if something heavy was lying against it. The girl pounded on it with her fists.

"Let me in!" she demanded. "Dad! Dad!"

The frightened wails were subsiding now, but within the main bedroom there came a series of frantic bumps and crashes, and the door shivered in its frame as something smashed against it.

Fearfully, Lauren stepped back, and to her consternation, she heard a low, hideous, dry voice begin to croak and scream.

"What's in there?" she breathed in despair. "Dad! Sheila! What is it? Answer me!"

Standing there on the landing as the ghastly, bestial voice continued to snap and squawk on the other side of the door, Lauren felt horribly alone and helpless.

She desperately wanted to race downstairs and phone the police, but that would mean abandoning her father and stepmother to whatever was in the room. All she knew was that it certainly wasn't human, and feeling wretched and afraid, she waited as the seconds dragged by until the voice finally grew more faint.

Then there was silence.

Her plump face buried in her fists, Lauren gingerly moved closer to the door, pressing her ear to the wood.

The only sound she could hear was the dull, rapid beat of her own blood in her eardrums. Whatever had uttered that repugnant voice was either deliberately being quiet, or its mouth was otherwise preoccupied.

Filled with this horrific, sickening thought and dreading the grisly sight she might encounter, Lauren gave the door a ferocious kick.

"Dad!" she cried when the barrier shuddered open and she tore inside, heedless of her own safety.

Lauren stumbled to a halt as she viewed the scene before her. On the bed lay her father. She could see quite plainly that he was only sleeping, and relief at this discovery coursed through her tense limbs. Yet she could find no sign of Sheila.

A bitterly cold draft filled the bedroom. Lauren shivered in the large T-shirt she used as pajamas as she crossed to where her father lay and shook him gently.

"Dad?" she murmured. "Wake up, please, Dad!"

Yet the man merely snored in reply, and she pulled away, her face creasing with concern.

"Sheila?" she called miserably. "Sheila?"

Lauren caught her breath and rubbed the goose-bumps that had prickled over her arms. The window had been thrust open, and the net curtains were rippling with the breeze.

Nervously she walked over and peered outside, fearing she would see a broken body sprawled on the gravel below. But no—the driveway was empty.

Casting her eyes back to her unconscious father,

Lauren wondered what she ought to do. What had happened here? Where was Sheila? She couldn't have jumped down from the window without hurting herself. And what—or who—had made that hideous caterwauling?

It was then that she discovered four deep claw marks gouged into the wooden sill. As she stepped nearer to examine them, something soft brushed against her toes.

Lauren cried out and jumped back in case the unseen creature bit her. Then, staring down, she shook her head.

Lying on the carpet was an immense jet black feather.

Crouching to the floor, the girl flicked it warily then picked it up and held it in the moonlight.

The feather was nearly as long as her arm, and there was a quality about it that made Lauren screw up her face in a distasteful grimace. Whatever creature this quill belonged to was like nothing she had ever seen, and her skin crawled even to touch it.

Throwing it out of the window, she wiped her fingers and frowned. What was she to do? Had Sheila been snatched by some demonic nocturnal bird of prey? The whole notion was preposterous, yet there was the feather, and it would account for the terrible shrieks that had awoken her.

Only the prone, slumbering figure of her father prevented her from running to fetch help. There was more to this than she could ever explain. If she waited until daylight, the situation might appear less unnatural, and a more down-to-earth answer could possibly be found.

Reaching for the window, Lauren prepared to close it, then checked herself and returned instead to her own room.

There, with her knees tucked underneath her chin, she sat on her bed and waited for the dawn.

* * *

At the edge of the Somerset wood, where *Eden's Bus* remained parked on the shoulder, the two dogs, who slept in a large box beneath the dilapidated bus, pricked up their ears and started to whimper.

Within the old, rusted vehicle, the five travelers were sleeping peacefully. A small nightlight had burned low, and its waning flame cast a trembling glow over the shadowy interior.

Snug inside his sleeping bag, Owen grunted and turned groggily onto his side as the Labrador's whine became a frightened yowl underneath the floor and the Jack Russell yapped in terror.

Rubbing his eyes, the man sat up, and a rush of icy fear washed over him as he listened to the petrified dogs outside.

"Not again," he muttered, clambering out of the bag.

Behind a draped curtain a woman's voice asked in a drowsy whisper, "What's the matter with them now? Get them to keep quiet, will you?"

Owen pulled on his jeans. "They won't listen to me," he said. "Can't you feel it, Rhon? There's something awful out there. The poor brutes are scared witless."

Rhonda's sleepy face appeared beneath the curtain. "Well, bring them inside then," she told him. "But keep them down at your end of the bus. I don't want to be slobbered on all night."

"What's going on?" Luke's voice complained.

"Go back to sleep," Rhonda said testily. "You'll wake the others."

Hopping over the sleeping bag, Owen moved toward the door and pulled it open.

"Come on!" he called. "Get in here."

Yet the dogs refused to budge from their shelter beneath the bus and howled all the more.

Owen jumped to the grass and knelt on all fours to shine a flashlight under the vehicle.

The eyes of the two dogs flared bright green and yellow as the light beam blazed on them. Owen was dismayed to see that their mouths were speckled with white froth and that they were shivering uncontrollably.

"Hey," he said warmly. "It's all right, boys. Old Owen's here now. Come on, lads, it's nice and warm in the bus."

Neither animal moved. Their pitiful eyes stared woefully up at him, but they were too paralyzed with fear to leave the sanctuary of their box.

Owen frowned and rose. "Suit yourselves," he murmured, returning to the door and climbing back inside to find Rhonda waiting for him.

"Where are they?" she asked.

"Wouldn't come in." The man shrugged. "Should see their faces though, Rhon. Awful, they are."

Rhonda hugged herself. "We should've listened to Aidan and left," she said.

"I know," Owen answered.

At that moment the dogs ceased their yammering, and Rhonda swallowed nervously. "What can that mean?" she breathed.

Owen didn't know what to say, but then they heard a different, more disturbing sound, and they stared at each other in dread.

High above, echoing across the sky, there came a horrible, frantic clamoring.

"What on earth? . . ." Rhonda whispered. "Birds? . . ."

"Doesn't sound like any flock I ever heard."

Lit by the wavering flame of the nightlight, Rhonda's face turned pale, and she listened in mounting horror as the foul noise grew gradually louder.

"Mad geese perhaps?" she suggested, trying to sound lighthearted but not succeeding.

"No," Owen said softly, "more like a demented mob, rioting through the darkness."

"Those are not animal voices, Owen."

"Nor are they human," came his ominous reply.

"It's getting closer."

"What is that racket?" called Luke's voice abruptly.

Rhonda turned to see her husband come blundering from behind the curtain, scratching his head and yawning stupidly.

"Quiet!" she hissed, afraid that his loud voice might attract the attention of whatever was flying overhead.

Above the surrounding wood, the shrill screeching continued to draw nearer, and the last vestige of Luke's sleepiness vanished completely.

"I don't like it," he said, lunging for the driver's seat. "We've got to get out of here right now."

"No!" Owen cried, dragging him back. "You'll only draw attention to us. Let them fly past!"

Rhonda ran to the window and pressed her cheek flat against the glass as she peered up into the star-flecked night. "I can't see anything," she said. "But they're definitely getting closer. Just listen to it now."

"They must be directly overhead," Owen whispered. "Stay quiet."

Rhonda and Luke nodded. The raucous sound was unbearably loud, and they held each other's hands desperately as the wild, blaring shrieks reverberated above the trees.

In fearful silence, Patrick and Dot came blundering from their bunks and gazed at their friends with ashen faces.

Owen stared back, then his expression changed to one of panic.

"The light!" he blurted. "Put it out!"

Rhonda whirled around and ran to the shelf where the dwindling nightlight was still burning and hastily extinguished the flame.

In the darkness that engulfed them, they heard the dogs yelp in terror, and through the windows they saw them bolt from beneath the bus and flee into the nearby wood.

"Why did they do that?" Dot whispered. "Patrick, what's out there?"

Before anyone could answer, the shrieking suddenly erupted all around them, and they clapped their hands to their ears as the very air shook from the clangorous din of the unearthly, piercing screams.

"Stop it!" Dot bawled, dropping to the floor and crawling into a corner.

Then, abruptly, the bus quivered, and the roof buckled as a great weight came crashing on top of it— followed by another and another.

Violently the vehicle shuddered as more of the unseen creatures landed on it, their terrible croaking voices crowing and screeching.

"Save us!" Rhonda prayed, glancing fearfully up at the battered and dented ceiling.

Seized by powerful, malevolent forces, the bus suddenly lurched beneath the impact of a tremendous blow. The travelers within were hurled against the sides, floundering into the windows and tearing down the partitioning curtains in their desperate battle for balance.

From the shelves and out of the cabinets whose doors were flung open all the ornaments, mugs, and plates went careering, shattering and smashing on the floor. Suspended from hooks, the pans clanged and crashed together like tuneless cymbals as they swung madly, striking Luke across the temple when he stumbled by.

"Make it stop!" Dot yelled hysterically. "Make it stop! Make it stop!"

With an almighty crunching of metal, a third pounding shudder rocked the bus and for Dot it was too much. Before Patrick could stop her, she leaped up and pelted for the door, screaming at the top of her voice.

"Let me out!" she hollered. "We'll all die in here! We'll die!"

Even as she tore the door open, strong hands gripped her, and Owen twisted her around to push her back with the others.

"Listen to me!" he shouted. "God knows what's up there, but you won't last five seconds if you . . ."

His voice was suddenly lost, and the others could only watch in mortified despair as, through the open door and reaching down from above, a great, repulsive talon came stretching.

Before Owen could turn to face it, the black scale-covered claw flashed out and drove deep into his shoulder, puncturing the flesh and hooking deep inside his ribs.

Howling in pain, yet struggling for all he was worth, the man was dragged outside, and when his wide, tormented eyes glared upward to view the creatures on the roof, he let out a final, soul-tearing scream.

Inside the bus, Dot shrank against Patrick, screwing up her face. The others, stricken into silence and inaction, could only watch as their friend was hauled skyward, his legs kicking and flailing past the windows until they disappeared above, and the glass was spattered with a crimson rain.

"Owen . . ." Rhonda mouthed. "Dear God, no . . . Owen!"

Yet her grief was shortlived, for in that terrible instant, the roof splintered, and through the perforated metal a dozen vicious, iron-hard talons came stabbing, curving in to grip and grasp.

Luke snatched up a stick, ramming it toward the nearest claw, savagely beating it with all his fear-fueled strength.

Immediately Rhonda and Patrick joined him, using anything they could find as weapons—pans, brooms, bottles.

"They won't get in!" Luke raged.

But the talons of the unseen enemy were strong, and the creatures above ignored the travelers' fervent attempts as they spoke to each other in harsh, repellent squawks.

Trembling all over, Rhonda threw down the broom handle she had taken for a weapon and slowly shook her head.

"You're wasting your time," she murmured flatly.

Luke turned on her. "What are you doing?" he demanded. "Help us—we have to keep them out!"

The woman held up her hand for them to stop.

"They don't want to get in," she stated in a parched whisper. "If they did, they'd have done it by now."

"What then?" Dot asked, cringing against the bunk. "You saw what happened to Owen."

Suddenly the bus buckled, and a creaking groan rifled along its rusting bodywork.

Rhonda rushed to the window and stared outside as the vehicle rattled and strained. "No, please," she uttered.

"What now?" Patrick asked.

She did not need to answer, for as soon as the words were out of his mouth he knew.

With a dreadful teetering roll and a sickening pitch to the front that sent them reeling once more, the bus was lifted off the ground, and the stunned travelers saw the trees beyond the windows fall away.

Above them, mingled with the strident clamor of the ghastly voices, they could hear the steady beat of great wings, while below them the ground dropped sharply.

Up from the grassy shoulder of the road *Eden's Bus* was plucked, up into the cold wintry air, rising steeply with each downward sweep of powerful primeval feathers. To the tops of the trees the unwieldy vehicle was lifted, until it soared above the roof of the bare, leafless wood and beyond.

Higher the dark winged shapes hoisted it, their grotesque forms obliterating the stars, while the heavens rang with their awful screeching.

"This isn't happening, right?" Dot mewled, staring down at the shrinking landscape beneath them. "It's just utterly impossible."

The wood appeared tiny now, like a clump of withered flowers in a garden border, and the meandering network of roads seemed like the shimmering trails left by slugs.

Rhonda glanced across the night to where a curiously shaped hill reared in the far distance, and the woman smiled in spite of her fear to think it would be one of the last sights she would ever see.

Then it happened.

Above them the shrill cacophony of shrieks and squawks changed into a vile, skirling laughter that was filled with scorn and hatred.

The flight had come to an end.

The curved talons were withdrawn from the roof,

and the bus toppled downward, turning over in the rushing air as it plunged and plummeted through the night.

* * *

For a moment, the Somerset wood knew peace. High above, the stridulous laughter had grown silent, and the black winged shapes veered across the sky, not bothering to view the evil they had done.

Then, with a thunderous crash, the bus came ripping through the treetops, and with a deafening roar it pounded into the ground.

A dull boom rent the night as the gas tank exploded, and before long, most of the wood was ablaze.

CHAPTER 13

MEMORY FORGOTTEN

Before either his brother or his father was awake, Neil Chapman stole out of the caretaker's apartment and crept through the various galleries and collections toward the main entrance hall and the staircase.

The Wyrd Museum was silent as a tomb, and the sound of his footsteps chimed off the polished floors as he roamed through the ancient building. The doom-laden words of the self-proclaimed ghost hunter he had met the previous evening had troubled him all night.

Climbing the first step, the boy noticed that a section of the paneled wall was missing, and in the dank space beyond he could see a flight of stone stairs descending into darkness.

Neil wavered, wondering whether to go exploring, but he guessed that Miss Ursula Webster was bound to be down there and she would not appreciate his inquisitiveness.

Tapping the banister with his fingers, he resolved to complete what he had set out to do that morning and hurried to the second floor.

Into the room that had once housed The Separate Collection he went, and began looking inside the chests and boxes.

Presently he found what he searched for—the contents of the cabinet that had held Ted for over fifty years. A sad smile passed over Neil's face as he removed each item and studied it carefully.

There was a stirrup pump and bucket, a handbell, a shovel, yellowing leaflets and ration books, a gas mask, and a pile of old comics and film magazines.

"Wherever you are Ted . . . or Angelo," the boy murmured, "I hope you found peace."

Taking a deep breath, he shoved his hands into his pockets then kicked a broken piece of wood across the floor and decided to return downstairs. Another day of school beckoned, and he was already dressed in his uniform.

Yet as he ambled back toward The Egyptian Suite a movement caught his eye, and he spun on his heel excitedly.

"Ted?" he cried. "Is that you? How did you get back?"

Running over to a large tea chest he looked inside, then straightened his back in astonishment.

Quivering and jerking, as though tugged by an invisible thread, the damaged stuffed raven that Miss Veronica had wept over was struggling on its back, feebly waving one wing and kicking its legs in the air.

Neil stared at the thing in wonderment. The bird

had regenerated itself, yet the creature was still impaired. Only one eye had reformed, while the other remained a sunken knot of withered skin. Upon its flat head the feathers had not yet grown, and so it continued to look moth-eaten and bald, and the right wing hung limp and broken at its side.

Opening its black, feather-fringed beak, the raven let out a plaintive cheep then shook its head. The lower part of its jaw gave a faint click and locked open so that it was stuck in a painful-looking yet silent howl.

Writhing uncomfortably, the raven squirmed and clawed at its mouth, bashing its head against the side of the tea chest until the beak snapped shut once more and the one eye fluttered closed in blissful relief.

Finally the bird became aware of the boy peering in at it and vainly attempted to right itself, like an upturned beetle.

"Don't worry," Neil said gently. "I won't hurt you. But if I help you stand, you'd better not bite me."

Slowly he slid his hand beneath the feathers and lifted the raven so that the scaly feet were standing on the edge of the chest.

The creature shook itself and, with its single eye, leered gratefully up at him.

Unfortunately its balance was still rather shaky, and emitting a squawk of surprise, it promptly tipped over and fell headlong onto the floor at Neil's feet.

Clucking and quacking in alarm, it wriggled helplessly on its back, once more gazing up at the boy in despair.

Neil came to its rescue a second time.

Swaying unsteadily, the raven eyed its surroundings

quizzically, but when the bird tried to take a step forward, it tottered and staggered while flapping its one good wing in perplexed agitation, unable to coordinate its movements.

"You look drunk," Neil chuckled.

The raven stumbled back, squashing its tail feathers against the chest and tripping over a fragment of timber. Then, fixing Neil with its ogling eye and looking so comical and impish that the boy laughed out loud, the creature opened its beak and spoke.

"Fie!" it cried in a gurgly, piping voice. "As merrie as a malted mouse this knave doth be . . . nay, as a boiled owl!"

Neil stared at the bird in delight. He was already too familiar with the strange goings on within the Wyrd Museum to be surprised by a talking raven.

"He that eateth the king's goose doth void fethers a hundred years after," the creature rambled, lurching and teetering precariously. "I doth thank heaven thy father wert borne afore ye, most generous of esquires. How goeth the day?"

The boy crouched down and brought his face close to the ranting, incoherent bird. "I'm fine," he said. "But are you all right? My name's Neil. Can you remember yours? You don't seem very sure of anything."

"A malmsey dowsing of the noddle-tree, oh courteous gallant," the raven replied, shaking its head and hitting it with its wing. "The even that brimmeth over doth make for a cloudy morn. No recollection have I of whom or whence, nor know aught save the briny tang in mine gullet and the hammers in mine pate."

Bobbing its head up and down, the bird cast its

monocular glance about the room and gave several chirps of interest.

"Skewer me for a mallemuck! 'Tis a most uncommon dungeon—no danksome cave nor maggoty oubliette. Behold there is light, the chariot of the day is risen and peepeth through yonder window! Its glory is never worse for all it shineth on a dunghill. Day and night, sun and moon, air and light—all must have, yet none may buy."

"What are you talking about?" Neil said. "This isn't a prison, it's a museum."

The confused raven doddered forward, trying to comprehend the boy's words. "How sayest thou?" it burbled.

"Museum," Neil repeated. "A place full of old things—collections of this and that."

"A treasure house?" the bird declared. "A prince's hoard? What hoddy-doddy raving is it thou speaketh? To place a rogue in such a midst—he that stealeth an egg may steal the oxen. The thief is surely sorry he is to be hanged yet not that he is a thief."

Neil raised his eyebrows. "Are you saying that's what you are?" he asked.

"Dost the wolf perceive itself as such?" the creature answered, sorrowfully hanging its bald head and dropping its shoulders. "Dost the new day remember the old? In mine brains there is naught to glean, neither repute nor miscreance. The gems of this wretch's mind are robbed and squandered, the casket of the skull is bereft and full of lack. No ember can tutor me in name or descent, yet I am sensible of a darkness behind me, though I know it not, nor from whence it stems. Alack and alas for I."

The boy smiled reassuringly. "Well, you don't seem like a villain to me," he said. "But I'll have to call you something."

"Wilt thou not appoint unto me a name of thine own choosing?" the raven begged, waddling up to Neil's face, dragging its broken wing across the floor behind it. "Squire Neil, fill this hollow pan with a surfeit of tidings and reason, let me gorge upon new wonders and truths. Yea, though 'tis said 'gluttony killeth more than the sword,' let me perish with more learning than I do now possess and with wit enough to answer unto a fair-sounding title."

Feeling sorry for the poor creature, Neil considered his plea for a little while then grinned. "I know," he said. "I'll call you . . . Quoth."

The raven cocked its head to one side and muttered the word under its breath before ruffling its scant, frayed feathers and bowing low until its beak tapped upon the floorboards.

"Verily and amen to that," he cried gladly. "Henceforth the tale of Quoth shalt begin, aught that he wast can molder and remain forgot evermore."

Suddenly a distant scream echoed through the galleries, and Quoth ducked under Neil's arm in fright.

"Zounds!" he squeaked, his quills standing on their ends. "Beat the alarum! Wind the battle horn! 'Tis murder! Fiends! Ogres! Foes!"

Neil scrambled to his feet. "That was one of the Websters!" he exclaimed. "What's happened?"

"Hold!" Quoth pleaded as the boy hurried to the doorway. "Forsake not this callow wretch. If the banshee is abroad, I doth not wish to yield up mine green soul for its harvest."

"Well, keep up," the boy instructed, hastening into The Egyptian Suite and the rooms beyond.

With his claws clattering over the polished wooden floor, the raven trotted after him, marveling at each new group of exhibits and clicking his beak admiringly.

* * *

Down the stairs Miss Ursula Webster came, her gaunt face a portrait of anguish and despair. Gone was the imperious, aristocratic air. Transcending her immortal flesh, she looked at that moment like a frail, frightened old woman who felt the long ages of her life pressing down upon her.

Clutching at the banister she descended, taking each step as though every slight movement was a torment to her brittle, aged bones.

Floating down from above, the sound of Miss Celandine's weeping filled the upper story, but Miss Ursula was too stricken to mourn and mechanically continued on her way.

Only when she reached the second-floor landing did she notice her surroundings, for a figure moved by the doorway, and she turned woodenly. There was the oldest Chapman boy, but her stony face displayed no recognition, and he came forward uncertainly.

"Miss Ursula?" Neil ventured, taken aback by her frozen appearance. "Is everything all right?"

The usually bright, shrewd eyes stared hollowly at him, and the jet beads in Miss Ursula's white hair trembled as she slowly shook her head.

"They are gone," came her whispered, leaden reply.

"Who?"

"Veronica and Edith. While I kept the vigil below, they left the sanctuary of the museum. Celandine and I have searched everywhere, but to no avail. Can you imagine how long it has been since Veronica left the safety of this building? In this modern age she is utterly defenseless."

Neil didn't know what to say, but even as he tried to think of something, the sound of the raven's swaggering gait pattered up behind him, and Miss Ursula lowered her grim gaze to see him approach.

"So!" she snapped, her expression abruptly changing as her fury exploded. "You, too, have returned!"

Quoth blinked at her in fearful astonishment. "Avaunt!" he wailed. "Squire Neil, the turnkey hath caught us. Take flight while ye may, she doth have the look of the basilisk! Devil take the hindmost!"

Before the frightened bird could scuttle backward, Miss Ursula seized him by his good wing and snatched him from the ground.

As he dangled from her hand, his feet waggled forlornly and Quoth jabbered and trilled in panic. "Death when it cometh shalt have no denial! Farewell, mine good days, they shalt soon be gone!"

"Stop!" Neil fumed as Miss Ursula shook the poor raven and glared at him fiercely. "You're hurting him!"

The old woman gripped the bird even tighter, hauling him up to stare into his woeful face.

"The disappearance of Edith and Veronica is your Master's work!" she spat. "The power of the Fates cannot be contested. You know that, and so does He."

"Mercy!" Quoth yammered, twirling helplessly in her unforgiving grasp. "This tender lamb knows naught!"

"Do not lie to me, Memory!" she raged, closing the fingers of her other hand about the bird's neck. "I know your deceits all too well! Shall I wring your falsehoods from you?"

"Leave him alone!" Neil cried, rushing forward to drag her hands away. "Can't you see he's telling the truth? He doesn't know anything about it."

Miss Ursula snarled at the boy, then hesitated and examined the raven more closely. Catching her breath, she looked at the damaged wing, the bare patches of skin where the feathers had molted, and at the shriveled eye socket.

"Can it be so?" she muttered. "Are you indeed blameless in this?"

"Course he is," Neil told her. "I've only just found him in one of those boxes back there."

The old woman handled the raven more gently, and her piercing gaze penetrated deep into his good eye.

"Yes," she eventually murmured, "the damage was too great for Him to repair. No, it was the tears of Fate that recalled you, Memory. This is a most curious chance. It had better not prove ill."

Turning to Neil, she handed the bird over to him, and Quoth pressed his beak into the jacket of the boy's uniform, hiding his face from that formidable old harridan.

"I see that a bond has already grown between the two of you," Miss Ursula observed. "Are you certain he recalls nothing of his former life?"

"As far as I know," Neil answered, soothingly stroking the raven's limp wing. "He doesn't even know his name. What did you call him . . . Memory?"

Miss Ursula eyed the straggle-feathered bird warily. "Strange that is precisely what he should lose," she said. "But does forgetfulness alone absolve him from the crimes of his erstwhile existence? Listen to the wisdom of Destiny, maggot child. You hold in your embrace a viper. He might not be dangerous now, but beware him. If his mind ever recalls his true identity and nature, then he will undoubtedly turn against you. Only one master does that creature serve."

"Quoth wouldn't hurt me," Neil objected.

The raven chirped in agreement. "He is mine friend who succoreth me!" he chattered, shying away from the woman's suspicious glance.

A knowing smile appeared upon Miss Ursula's stern features. "How very intriguing," she said. "Memory was always peppering his conversation with ridiculous proverbs and sayings. Remember, maggot child, I warned you. Not all the chambers of this creature's mind are closed. Do not put your faith in him. The essence of his real disposition is betrayal and malice."

"I'll choose whoever I like to be my friend," the boy told her impatiently. "You can't order me around anymore. I've already done what you wanted. It's up to that Dorkins girl now."

Miss Ursula grew serious again and took a shallow breath.

"Yet Edith is departed," she said. "Perhaps your path is entwined in the tapestry still."

With a rustle of her taffeta gown, the old woman

stalked forward and looked as though she was about to speak when, abruptly, she halted and held up her hand for silence.

"Go, child, answer the door."

Neil frowned. "Why?" he protested. "There's no one there."

Even as he uttered the words, there came a faint tinkling noise from the main entrance.

"Let him in," Miss Ursula commanded. "There may yet be time. The day might still be saved."

Grudgingly, Neil brushed past her and descended to the hallway, still clutching Quoth in his arms.

* * *

Standing on the steps outside, Aidan removed his top hat and quickly ran his fingers through his hair.

Straightening the red bandanna and primping the lapels of his frock coat, he wondered if he ought to press the small brass button a second time, but then he heard the sound of footsteps, and he held his breath expectantly.

Slowly the heavy wooden entrance swung open, and he found himself looking into the face of an eleven-year-old boy holding a fretful one-eyed raven.

Not prepared for this unexpected door warden, Aidan cleared his throat and respectfully touched his forelock.

"I am here," he said, "as requested."

With one hand still on the door, Neil stared at the short, oddly dressed man and recognized him as one of the people who placed flowers about the drinking fountain.

"Requested?" he mumbled. "You'd better come in, then."

Pulling the door fully open, he stepped aside, and the stranger crept forward apprehensively, his eyes bulging with awe and reverence.

Into the somber, dusty entrance hall of the Wyrd Museum, the place of his annual pilgrimage, Aidan stepped, and his throat dried to think of the astounding honor bestowed upon him.

"Be quick and close the door, maggot," came a terse female voice. "There are drafts enough within these walls."

Neil obeyed, and edging a little farther inside, Aidan sought to find the owner of that haughty voice.

Poised with infinite dignity and frosty composure upon the middlemost step was the figure he had venerated for the whole of his life, and he choked back a humble, yet jubilant cry before dropping to his knees and bowing his head.

"Mighty Urdr!" he breathed worshipfully.

Arrayed in her black evening gown, the jet beads glinting in the morning light, her head tilted slightly as she considered him, Miss Ursula Webster remained upon the stairs like a regal spider awaiting a fly.

"I expected you sooner," she finally said.

Too afraid to raise his gaze from the floor, Aidan swallowed the lump in his throat and nervously fingered the brim of his hat. "I came as soon as I received the summons," he apologized, "but the tires of my van are not as devoted as I. One of them chose to burst while I was still only halfway here."

"Save your excuses," she rapped. "The harm is

already done—and do stand up, man. I refuse to address the top of your head in this fashion. Such archaic manners, together with the times that bred them, are long crumbled into the dust."

Aidan did as he was bid, and Miss Ursula gracefully descended the stairs.

In the boy's arms, Quoth peeped out at the old woman and twitched uncomfortably.

"Ware that dam," he cawed under his breath. "He that sups with her requireth a long spoon."

"Harm?" Aidan muttered when Miss Ursula was standing before him. "What harm do you speak of?"

"The girl I was to send with you," she said, "the one we have hoped and waited for all these years, has disappeared—and Veronica has gone with her."

Aidan's face clouded over. He understood the grave implications of this, and his dark brows knotted together. "They have been taken? But how? What power can enter the sacred shrine of the Fates?"

"I did not say such," she snapped. "No, they have been lured away from here."

"Lured? But how? Who?"

"Only one voice other than mine would Veronica attend to. Listen to me, Aidan. In you the blood of Askar runs true. Tremble then when I tell to you that the age-old enemy of the Spinners of the Wood has returned. It is His hand that lies behind this."

"The Gallows God?" he breathed, shooting a cautious glance at the raven in the boy's arms. "Then that answers much."

The old woman clasped her hands before her and pressed her thin lips together. "Yes," she affirmed.

"Veronica and Edith do not know of the dangers they are heading into. A dread is upon me, Aidan. Yes, I who wove the fabric of destiny and ordained all that has been—I am mortally afraid."

"What must I do?" he asked.

Miss Ursula took his hands in her own and squeezed them imploringly.

"Stop them!" she begged. "Bring them back. He who has enticed them away desires only their destruction. I would go myself, but I may not pass over the boundaries of my small realm. Do this for me, Aidan, descendent of the city beneath the Ash."

The man's emerald eyes sparkled with a fierce fire, and he nodded somberly.

"Where will I find them?" he asked simply.

Taking a step toward the entrance, Miss Ursula stared out at the brightening day and sighed. "Where else?" she said. "He will deceive them into bringing that magical device into his own blood-soaked hands. Although she has taken the measuring rod with her and without it I cannot see further than my eyes allow, Veronica and Edith have most certainly gone to Glastonbury."

Aidan backed away. "Then I must set off at once!" he cried.

"Wait!" she commanded, and to Neil's surprise he found that the old woman was now staring at him.

"In the past, boy, I have treated you harshly," she began. "If you are able, forgive me."

Neil shifted uneasily and wondered what she wanted from him.

"If you wish your thread to be sundered from the

web," she said, "then speak now. Yet, if you desire to remain a part of the weave then journey with Aidan. Go with him to Glastonbury."

"Me?" Neil spluttered in disbelief.

Miss Ursula nodded, and he could tell she was in deadly earnest.

"You understand us better than I dare to admit," she said. "But, most of all, you know Edith."

Neil opened and closed his mouth, but no sound came out. He wanted to refuse, yet he realized that this sinister old woman would not have asked him if it was not of the greatest importance.

"W . . . What about Dad?" he stammered.

"I will make your father understand," answered Miss Ursula. "You can trust Aidan. What do you say, boy? I do not order you, not this time. Yet if Veronica and Edith are not returned to us, then the end of all things creeps a little closer."

This forbidding thought made the hairs on the back of Neil's neck rise, but it was not that which finally made up his mind. Remembering the melancholy that had engulfed him when he believed his adventures were over, and realizing that this was his chance to be a part of something exciting again, he found himself saying, "I'll go, but Quoth comes with me."

Miss Ursula narrowed her eyes as she contemplated this condition, then assented. "Well decided. You are indeed bound up with the business of the Fates, for a little while longer at least. It will be a time of trial for your newfound companion also. Before it is over we shall see if Quoth is capable of keeping faith with you. Yet if Memory returns, then it will be an extra peril for you to contend with. Now, there is no more time to waste. Go immediately."

Without even a chance to say good-bye, Neil was ushered to the door. Miss Ursula turned to Aidan one last time and said, "Find them. Do not fail me."

Hastening down the three steps outside, the strange little man raised his top hat and flourished it theatrically as he pointed his toe and bowed.

In Neil's arms the raven nudged the boy and murmured, "Fools and little dogs are ladies' playfellows. As she hath no love for me, I hereby say unto ye thy trust in her shouldst be thin as a rasher of wind."

"Don't worry," Neil assured him, glancing cautiously at Miss Ursula. "I know just how treacherous she can be."

Reaching his van, Aidan cried, "Fear not! They are as good as found."

With that the little man clambered inside. Taking one last look at Miss Ursula and wondering what lay ahead, Neil climbed into the passenger seat with Quoth upon his lap.

Alone on the step, the eldest of the Webster sisters watched in stony silence as the engine started and the blue van pulled away.

"But I do fear, Aidan," she murmured. "I fear very much indeed."

Lifting her hand in farewell, she waited until the vehicle was out of sight before turning to gaze at the sculpted bronze figure at her left.

"And you, Veronica," she whispered, staring up into the unseeing, verdigris-stained eyes, "there truly was no other way. I really am so very, very sorry."

CHAPTER 14

MISSING THE DAWN

It was the sound of birdsong that finally roused Lauren Humphries from slumber. Although she had attempted to stay awake for the rest of the night, her eyelids had eventually slid down and her head nodded to her chest well before the dawn came.

Now, like a drowsy hedgehog, she unfurled from the increasingly uncomfortable curled-up position and stared drowsily around her room, wincing when her neck clicked stiffly.

Then she remembered all that had happened, and ignoring the complaints of her cramped muscles, she hurried to the door.

"Sheila!" she cried, storming onto the landing and charging into her parents' bedroom.

"Dad! Dad!"

Suddenly, Lauren stumbled to a standstill, and the girl stared at the bed in disbelief.

Unwilling to open his eyes just yet, her father

stirred grumpily, scratching his receding hairline and groping for the alarm clock. The figure at his side, however, continued to sleep soundly.

With the coverlet pulled up to her chin, her skin a bloodless shade of gray and sparkling with perspiration, Lauren's stepmother lay there as large as life.

Doubting her own senses, the girl moved closer, while Guy pried open one eye and slowly let the digital numbers of the clock impress themselves upon his mind.

"That can't say ten past six," he grumbled, flopping back onto the pillows. "What's the big idea?"

Lauren touched Sheila's cheek. The flesh was hot and clammy.

"I don't have to be up till seven-thirty," her father continued. "Too early for breakfast in bed, Lorrie."

When his daughter didn't answer, Guy blearily forced his eyes open.

"Don't wake her up as well," he said crossly. "She doesn't get a decent night's sleep as it is without you looming over her."

Lauren looked up from the unconscious woman at his side. "Dad," she said quietly. "There's something wrong. Look at her."

Still groggy, Guy wearily pulled himself up and leaned across his partner's pale form.

"She's burning up," he exclaimed, finally surfacing from his doze. "Sheila! Sheila!"

Worriedly he shook her, and with her eyes still firmly closed, the woman muttered under her breath.

"Hlökk . . . Hlökk."

"What was that?" Guy asked, his face frowning with concern. "Sheila, wake up!"

Lauren shuddered as a chill gripped her, and she stared at the object hanging innocently from the bedpost.

Suspended on its thread, its glass eyes oddly bright and gleaming, the crow doll appeared exactly the same as when Sheila had first taken it from its wrappings, but Lauren disliked it more than ever. She studied the letters embroidered on the calico apron with suspicion.

"Wait," she murmured to herself. "It wasn't there. Last night—it wasn't there."

Guy glanced up at her, but the question on his lips was lost when Sheila's eyelids fluttered open and he saw that her pupils were dark and dilated.

Grimacing at the light that streamed through the open window, the woman quickly turned away.

"Honey?" Guy began. "What's the matter? Shall I call the doctor?"

Sheila shook her head. "No," she grunted. "I'll be fine. Just so tired . . . very tired."

"Sheila . . ." Lauren asked, "do you remember anything about last night? Did you go out for a walk or anything?"

Her stepmother attempted to laugh but found the effort too much. "Really, Lorrie . . ." she uttered faintly, "the things you say. I died as soon as my head touched the pillow, but to be honest . . . I feel as though I spent the entire night running a marathon. I can hardly keep . . . keep my eyes open."

"You lie there, then," Guy said calmly. "Don't you

worry about anything. You get your rest. It'll be all right."

Slipping from the bed he closed the window, failing to notice the claw marks gouged into the sill, then led his daughter to the landing.

"Looks like she's got this bug that's going around," he said in his usual efficient manner. "Thank goodness there are no guests in at the moment. Look, Lorrie, I know it's a lot to ask, but I've got an important meeting today that's going to drag on for ages. It's a two-hour drive and . . ."

The girl sighed and folded her arms in resignation. "All right," she agreed before the favor was even asked. "I'll skip class and stay with her."

"That's my girl," Guy said, gently nudging Lauren's shoulder with his fist. "I'll call the doctor before I go and make sure he comes out to check on her. Probably won't last more than a few days, anyway."

Returning to her room, Lauren sat on the edge of the bed and tried to make sense of what she had heard and seen the previous night. No matter how she strove to explain it, however, there was simply no rational answer.

Looking at her plump reflection in the bedside mirror, she dragged a brush through her masses of red hair and longed to believe that the experience was all an invention of her weary imagination.

What had made that dreadful shrieking noise, and why hadn't it awakened her father? Laying the brush down, she stared at her freckled face and watched her forehead crinkle as she scowled.

Sheila was certainly not suffering from any ordinary illness, and remembering the large feather she had found, Lauren could not help but think of the crow doll hanging above the woman's head.

"I don't get it," she said aloud, pouting at the face in the mirror as though it ought to know the answers. "What's going on?"

* * *

In the next room, the girl's stepmother lay exhausted under the bedcovers. From the bathroom she could hear the squirting shower water and Guy's voice raised in some tuneless, half-remembered song.

Sheila smiled wanly. No trace of the night's trauma remained to plague her waking thoughts, but when she closed her eyes and drifted on the threshold of sleep, chaotic flashes leaped into her fatigue-filled mind.

She felt herself traveling high above the ground, riding on the wind, while all around her large shadowy shapes called in harsh, cruel voices. Sometimes the sounds changed into terrified screams, and then, flickering fleetly in and out of her weariness, she could see a great burst of flame blasting and blossoming in the dark like a beautiful burning marigold.

Yet throughout all this, one feature remained a constant. Whether she was soaring into the night or swooping low over a wood, there were always feathers. Black, suffocating feathers that scored and irritated her flesh, choking and catching in her throat as she gagged and bawled in that hideous, grating voice.

"Hlökk!" the woman whimpered, and with a jolt, she came to once more. Heaving a sigh of relief, Sheila found herself still in the bedroom.

From the kitchen downstairs the deliciously mingled scent of frying bacon and percolating coffee was rising, and its pervading aroma floated up into the bedrooms.

Usually Sheila adored this time of the morning and loved the mouthwatering smells of breakfast, but today the odors made her wretch and balk. She threw the bedclothes from her to stagger to the bathroom.

Yet as she hastened to the door, the woman stared back at the bed and covered her mouth in dismay.

About the imprint her body had made in the rumpled sheet was a filthy collection of twigs and straw. When she looked down at her feet, she discovered that they were covered in grime and dried mud.

"What's happening to me?" she whispered desperately.

CHAPTER 15

DROWNING IN LEGENDS

"You ever been to Glastonbury?"

Neil shook his head. "Isn't Glastonbury where they have the music festival and everyone slops around in mud?"

"That's a very minor part of its charm," Aidan said. "It's like saying 'England is where fish and chips come from.' It might well be true, but a very lame and unenlightened summary of a place all the same."

Neil smiled. After nearly five hours on the road, he had grown used to Aidan's pattern of speaking and anticipated the imminent lecture with interest.

Up on the boy's shoulder, the place where he felt most comfortable, Quoth watched the landscape race by and glared at the cars that passed them.

Occasionally he would join in the conversation, but his contributions were never really relevant, and so he contented himself with pretending that he was actually flying down the highway on his own. Now and again the raven would try to spread his wings to heighten this pretense, but he could never keep it up for long and would resort to nursing his damaged limb morosely.

After a faltering start, Neil was soon chatting about anything and everything, for Aidan had quickly put him at his ease, and the boy almost forgot that they were embarking upon a potentially dangerous journey.

Aidan's talk was mesmerizing, and Neil listened in fascination as the curious-looking man told him of the time before the World Tree was destroyed and many of the tales of Askar.

"So what happened when the tree was poisoned?" Neil asked.

Aidan's face became set and grave. "It is said that there dawned a morning that was the darkest my ancestors had ever known. The sky grew black, as a cloud of pestilence blew across the city.

"Then the foul ogres of the north marched upon the World Tree and they hacked and chopped at it.

"A wild, insane panic seized the people, and they ran like scared sheep as the Ash quivered and trembled. Only the bravest stood their ground: those of the royal house, the city guard, and the Captain who had gained godlike powers and wisdom by hanging upon Yggdrasill for nine nights—Woden."

"Woden?" Neil broke in. "You mean Odinn?"

Aidan's eyes glittered. "He must have been a letter carrier's nightmare, the number of names he had: Odinn, the Gallows God, Father of the Slain, Grimnir, Wodenaz, Sky Father, Leader of the Wild Hunt."

Upon Neil's shoulder, Quoth drew his bald head

into his neck and listened to all that was said.

"But no one now has ever heard of the battle between the people of Askar and the lords of the ice and dark. With Woden at their head, they rode out of the city, though the stink of death was about them, and bravely charged to vie with the enemy."

Quoth closed his eye and sank against Neil's neck as a vision of a storm-lashed day abruptly flooded into his thoughts.

He was surrounded by an army of mail-clad warriors on horseback, and their thunderous shouts of challenge echoed inside his poorly repaired mind. Above and behind him, countless green banners bearing the badge of Askar were torn by a black wind that came blasting from the north, and those whom the diseased mists touched swooned and fell, stricken from their mounts.

Like a tremendous cliff face, the titanic girth of the World Tree reared high on the army's right flank, yet in his fragmented memory, Quoth's attention was focused solely on a figure before him.

Riding a great ebony-colored steed, sitting tall and fearless in the saddle, with a bright sword drawn in his gauntleted hand, a silver helm upon his head, and a sable cloak flapping about his shoulders, was the Captain of the City Guard—Woden.

Unexpectedly the glorious pageant faded from Quoth's thoughts, and although he tried to recall more of the desperate scene, all he could make out was the shape of another raven swooping past him to alight upon the Captain's shoulders. Then the vision was gone, and Aidan's voice broke into the bird's mind.

Quoth shook himself uneasily.

"Most of the Askar folk were butchered that day," the man told Neil. "It was a hideous, bloody massacre—humans are no match for the Frost Giants. It lasted only until the Queen was killed, and then the rest of the city's host were finally routed."

Quoth shivered, for the image of an auburn-haired woman flared momentarily in his thoughts.

Clothed all in blue, with a circlet of gold about her brow and riding a dappled mare, the fleeting vision screamed suddenly, and her ghastly shrieks reverberated within the bird's skull.

A jagged spear of ice had been savagely thrust through the woman's throat, and the cream-colored mane of her horse was spattered with royal blood as she tumbled from the saddle.

Crashing to the ground, her body was immediately engulfed in a dark, freezing shadow, and the raven whined fretfully as a horrendous, rime-covered apparition started to form inside his mind.

"Sshh!" Neil told him. "Go on, Aidan."

Quoth winced, not wishing to recall anything further of that terrible day, and he recklessly banged his head against the window to jolt those unwanted memories back into hiding.

"When she saw her mother die," Aidan continued, "the eldest princess called to her two sisters and rode with them into a vast, unexplored forest."

"The Websters?" Neil breathed.

Aidan nodded. "Yes, but back then they were known by different names: Urdr, Skuld, and Verdandi.

"At the outskirts of the forest, they were met by a

magnificent white stag, who guided them through the woods until, at last, they came to a wide clearing. There, about a clear, shimmering pool, the sisters beheld for the first time the surviving root of Yggdrasill.

"In that momentous hour, the stag and his brothers, who were standing around the sacred pool, fell to their knees and bowed their heads to the princesses. Urdr saw that upon the banks was the loom that had been made from the fallen bough.

"Then the earth shook.

"In the great distance Yggdrasill toppled and went crashing to the ground. No earthquake, no tempest, no flood or erupting volcano has since matched the violence of that time.

"As Nirinel quivered and trembled, the sisters heard the legion of ice lords come roaring over the plain in pursuit of them. Woden tried to beat them back but they hurled him aside, and louder their fierce, unholy roaring bellowed until the three sisters knew that they would be killed and the final root destroyed— heralding a new eternity of darkness for the world."

* * *

Aidan fell silent as he maneuvered the van into the streets of Wells. Then, in a voice filled with respect and reverence, he said, "But, of course, that didn't happen, or you and I wouldn't be here now. Because in that dreadful moment Urdr did what she had been born to do. To the loom she went, and with the trumpeting yells of the enemy raging at the fringes of the forest, she strung it.

"At once a protective mist rose around the clearing and shielded them from the ice lords' fury. But as soon as the first weft was created, the fate of the world was written and the Nornir came into being. The princesses became the mistresses of destiny, yet to it they were irrevocably bound and there was no escaping."

"So they've been stuck there ever since," Neil said, suddenly feeling sorry for the three old women.

"The museum is built upon the site of the original clearing," Aidan explained, "and they have never left its protecting walls—not until now. That is why Urdr fears for her sister."

"So what happened to the Frost Giants?"

"They returned to the frozen wastes and the shadows beneath the cruel mountains. What else could they do? Until Nirinel dies they cannot reclaim the everlasting dark, and so they wait."

"Then Veronica and Edie going off has nothing to do with them?"

Aidan shook his head. "No, nothing they could do would entice Verdandi from the sanctuary of the museum."

Neil let out a deep breath. A somber mood had descended upon the driver, and the boy attempted to lighten it once more.

"So if it's not the mud-caked hippies," he began cheerfully, "then what makes Glastonbury so special and marvelous?"

Aidan grinned. "Ah," he said. "You'll see, soon as you get a look at it. Not far now. This is Wells, and you'll have your first view of the Tor in a minute. A ravishing place it is, a haunting, beautiful land."

"Beauty draweth more than oxen," Quoth cawed, reaching up to push the tip of his beak into the narrow gap at the top of the window, where a delightful draft was blowing.

Aidan glanced at the bird and scratched his sideburns. "A stranger passenger I've never had," he declared. "But Urdr must know what she's doing, letting it come with us."

"There's nothing wrong with Quoth," Neil said defensively. "Don't start messing with him."

Through the picturesque city of Wells the van drove, and Neil looked out at the huddled jumble of old buildings that reared up on either side of the narrow roads. Behind the high slate rooftops he spied the stately towers of the cathedral jabbing into the gray sky, and they reminded him of the spires and spikes that rose from the gables of the Wyrd Museum.

"Yes," Aidan said, "it's a roly-poly, buttery landscape around here. But for all its sedate, picture-postcard prettiness, Somerset holds the most inspiring spot you'll ever see outside of dreams."

Then, leaving Wells behind, the van took a country road that was flanked on both sides by open fields. Trees and hedges dashed by, and as the boy stared out across the great flat fields, he suddenly felt Quoth's claws pinch his shoulder tightly. He sucked the air through his teeth in irritation.

"Hey!" he told the raven. "Let go."

But Quoth was not looking at him. The bird was leaning forward, murmuring softly to himself, his eye peering through the windshield.

Neil followed the raven's gaze and forgot at once the mild pain in his shoulder, for in that instant he caught sight of Glastonbury.

*   *   *

In the distance, rising like an island from a sea of slate-clad rooftops, rearing majestically up into the sky, its grassy shoulders kissed by the wintry midday sun—was the Tor.

With the tower of Saint Michael standing alone and mysterious on the summit, the great breast-shaped hill was an extraordinary, enigmatic spectacle. Neil had never seen anything quite like it before. It was as if he was viewing some ancient, mythical land.

Above the clustering houses, its massive grandeur dominated this unreal, magical world, and a marveling grin spread across the boy's face. Now he knew. Seeing it overshadow the small town and climb heavenward, he understood everything he had ever heard about this place. A slumbering power resided in that graceful green mountain, and a tremendous desire to reach it suddenly burned in his heart. He wanted to charge up the slopes and run around the tower, shouting at the top of his voice.

"Above Queen or Captain," Quoth muttered quietly, "such folly is love. Intimately doth I recall the curve of knoll and mound. Every shelf and hillock of yon lofty wold doth this poltroon know."

"You recognize this place?" Neil asked.

Quoth shifted his weight from foot to foot and ruffled his feathers uncomfortably. "Yea," he answered, squinting up at the Tor, "the aspect of this terrain tickleth the dust of mine moldered wits."

"Not surprising that you remember it," Aidan said, easing his foot upon the brake and pulling to the side of the road. "The Captain's ravens were often here. It was to this spot they brought the princess Verdandi many times, according to the legends that have been passed down the generations of my family. Yet after he had lashed himself to the World Tree, Woden never met her there again. He was beyond her reach, you see—not mortal anymore."

The van came to a halt, and Aidan rested his chin on the steering wheel as he stared at the distant hill.

"Heavy with myths is the air about Glastonbury," he said in a far-off, spellbound voice. "Fair to drowning in them it is, the blessed isle of apples."

"Isle?" Neil asked. "It's not an island."

Aidan smiled. "Not anymore," he muttered. "But once, many thousands of years ago, it was. Somerset means Summer Land. In the winter the sea would flood in, and the Tor, together with Chalice Hill next to it and Wearyall Hill across the valley, would become a true island. Then, in the hot months, the water would retreat again and leave a treacherous marshy bog all around here."

"The Summer Land," Neil echoed. "But Chalice Hill . . . why is it called that?"

The man breathed deeply and fingered his bandanna. "Oh, just one of the more recent traditions hereabouts," he replied. "Don't they teach you anything in schools these days?"

"Not about this place. Why should they?"

"Haven't you ever sung the hymn/*And did those feet in ancient time/Walk upon England's mountains green?*"

"Course I have," Neil said. "What's that got to do with it?"

Aidan half closed his eyes. "Listen to the words next time," he whispered, "that's what they're there for. *And was the Holy Lamb of God/On England's pleasant pastures seen?* This is where that happened. Did no one ever tell you that Jesus Christ came to these shores?"

"Don't be crazy."

"A good thing I never attended school then," Aidan tutted, "or I'd be as uninformed as you."

"That can't be true."

"What? That I was never sat down and educated? There's much more to learning than books and chalkboards."

"No, that stuff about Jesus. You don't seriously believe it!"

The man looked at Neil, and the boy was astonished to see that his swarthy face was completely serious. "A fine rule in life," he said with an edge of impatience in his voice and a glimmer of emerald kindling in his eyes, "and one that you would do well to learn, is to not contradict one who knows better than yourself. Closed minds learn nothing, Neil Chapman. Remember that and you might one day be happy with what is around you."

"I'm sorry," Neil found himself saying. "You just didn't strike me as being particularly religious. Not the happy God Squad type anyway. I didn't mean to offend you."

Aidan stared at him a moment longer then started

the van once more. "I wasn't talking of religion," he said. "Merely relating that about two thousand years ago a boy, probably about the same age as yourself, visited this land with his great uncle, who was a wealthy merchant. Tin was an important trading commodity, you know, and the Cornish mines are not that far down the coast—not compared with the great distance between here and the Holy Land.

"It would have been quite natural for Joseph of Arimathea to set out upon one of these trips. You don't get rich by staying at home, and why shouldn't he let his nephew come along to see something of the world? A much happier voyage, that first one with the young Christ, I imagine, than the one that finally brought Joseph here some time later."

"What happened on that one?" Neil asked.

Aidan's dark brows twitched as he answered. "It was Joseph who took Jesus's body down from the cross," he said, "and his was the tomb that Christ was supposed to lie in afterward. A most courageous man that merchant must have been. Associating so openly with such a troublemaking kinsman would have cost him dearly. Eventually he left his homeland and came back to Britain, but he did not come empty-handed. That's why Chalice Hill is so called. Somewhere around here The Grail resides—Joseph brought it with him."

"The cup used at the Last Supper?" Neil breathed, unable to conceal the skepticism in his voice.

Aidan shrugged and looked at the outlying houses they were now passing. "Well, maybe not a cup as such," he said. "Standing at the foot of the cross, he was supposed to have collected the blood and the sweat of Christ in two vessels. Cruets they're called, and they've nothing to do with oil and vinegar before you start asking."

"I wasn't going to."

"Well, anyway, The Grail myth leads us straight into the tales of King Arthur, which are also linked with Glastonbury, and I haven't even mentioned the Holy Thorn yet. I told you the air is thick with legends around here."

"Like unto bees which doth swarm about the honey pot," Quoth put in.

"Well said." Aidan chuckled.

Turning off the Wells Road, the van made its way down a long sloping street in which the windows of the ordinary, everyday newsdealers and grocery stores were interspersed with more intriguing displays of crystals, strange ceramic figurines, colorful esoteric posters, and vegetarian menus.

"Might as well take the scenic route through the town since we won't be staying long," Aidan remarked. "Keep your eyes peeled for Verdandi and the young girl, although I'm certain they'll be heading straight for the Tor when they arrive, if they aren't here already."

As the van passed by the entrance to a courtyard that basked in the title The Glastonbury Experience, Aidan twisted around to see if he recognized anyone in there. But it was too cold to sit outside the café that day, and only a handful of young people with studs in their noses and a short-haired terrier tethered by a piece of string were gathered in front of the New Age shops.

Steering the vehicle left onto Magdalene Street, the man sucked his teeth and pointed behind the buildings.

"The town grew up around the ruins of the sixth-century abbey over there," he told Neil. "Very important it was in its day—quite a dandy little metropolis, until Henry the Eighth had his way.

"The first Christian church to be constructed aboveground was built here, you know, and it was here that the monks dug up Arthur and Guinevere—if you believe in them, that is."

When they came to a gap between the buildings, Neil could see the impressive remains of the ancient abbey rising out of a wide expanse of meticulously tended lawn. Even in this advanced state of decay the weathered, honey-hued stones were splendid and beautiful to see. A crumbling moss-crowned husk of its former glory, the abbey stood with silent composure, the empty Romanesque windows and arches politely permitting visitors to view and tread its august, roofless interior.

"Don't you believe in King Arthur?" the boy asked, turning aside from the decorous ruins.

Aidan wrinkled his hooked nose. "Not the fairy-tale version," he said. "But behind everything there is a kernel of truth. Those romances are a collection and corruption of much earlier tales. One of my favorite parts though was always the bit where the dying Arthur is taken from the mortal shores by three royal maidens."

"The Websters again?"

"Can't get away from the Spinners of the Wood." Aidan chortled. "Their influence is everywhere. Avalon is where tradition says Arthur was brought and lies sleeping—until England needs him again."

"But you just said he was dug up."

"Oh, that was the Abbot's twelfth-century version of a tourist attraction," Aidan scoffed. "Like putting a big sign saying 'sale now on' in a store window. It was just a con to bring in the pilgrims. No, if there is someone who sleeps under this blessed soil, I'm pretty certain it won't be any Celtic chieftain."

Crouched on the boy's shoulder, Quoth had grown unusually quiet. He no longer quested the breach in the window with his beak, and when the draft did blow upon him and stir his scruffy feathers, he cringed and buried his face beneath his wing. His delicate senses had detected something terrible out there, and his little heart began to patter in his breast.

Veering left again the van headed up Bere Lane. They had skirted around the center of the town, and now the Tor reared up before them once more.

"We'll park in front of the Chalice Well Gardens," Aidan said. "It's not far from there."

"Chalice Well," Neil murmured. "This is all so bizarre."

"Two springs does this town boast. The red spring and the white. Perhaps that's where the story of Joseph's cruets comes from. Do you know that even in the worst droughts they have never failed?"

"When Miss Ursula spoke of a magical device that Woden wanted Veronica to find for him," Neil said slowly, "do you think she meant this Grail, chalice—whatever it is?"

Aidan shook his head. "No," he said with absolute certainty. "What possible use could that be to them? If it is hidden hereabouts, I doubt that it possesses any power the Nornir might desire. Their sovereignty over mankind reaches farther back than any religion. I can't see how The Grail could help them ward off Verdandi's Captain, can you?"

Turning onto Chilkwell Street, they pulled into a gravel-covered area before a high stone wall, and with a wry smile, Aidan said, "This is where the fun begins. Welcome to Avalon."

Opening the door, Aidan stepped from the van and waited while Neil clambered out of the passenger seat, but the raven refused to come with him and hopped stubbornly onto the handbrake.

"Come on," Neil urged. "We're here now."

Quoth nervously bobbed his head up and down and shied away from the open door.

"Nay," he cried with a dread-laden squawk. "A miasma of blood doth taint the sweet air. Canst thou not perceive the violent deeds committed in these environs, Master Neil? Mine innards are as weak as blue milk. I doth bewail and afright to feel such vileness around us. This morn 'twas gore and gizzard which did feed the dew-dripped sod. The reek of death, most cruel and heinous, fair choketh this unhappy chicklet. Let us begone afore this evil o'ershadows our path."

Neil looked at the bird in surprise. Quoth was genuinely frightened, and he reached in to comfort him.

"I can't smell anything," he said. "Come on, it's probably just your scrambled brains playing tricks. I'd have thought you'd appreciate being let out of the van after all these hours."

Quoth goggled up at him and shook his head, but

Neil was anxious to find Miss Veronica and Edie and wouldn't stand for any more nonsense.

Placing his hand at the raven's feet he told Quoth to climb onto his fingers, and so, fearfully, the bird obeyed.

Neil brought him out of the van, and Quoth waddled up the boy's arm to perch upon his shoulder again while peering warily about them.

"What's the matter with your little companion?" Aidan asked, seeing the bird's agitation.

Neil closed the passenger door. "Thinks there's something wrong about this place," he replied. "Although it might have more to do with having to leave the warmth of the van."

Placing the crumpled top hat on his head, Aidan eyed the bird curiously.

"Gall and wormwood art more toothsome to me than the fetor of this odoriferous stinkpot," Quoth cawed, glaring at the swarthy-faced man with an obdurate frown and a firm clack of his beak.

Aidan scratched his chin and gazed around them. "I think perhaps your pet might not be as addled as we would both like to believe," he informed Neil. "Let's waste no more time—to the Tor."

Crunching over the gravel, they walked back to the road, but before they could proceed any farther, there came the sound of running footsteps behind them.

"Aidan!" a voice cried. "Aidan, thank heavens it's you."

The gypsy and Neil turned to see, hurrying from the entrance to the Chalice Well Gardens, a middle-aged man with a pot belly, dressed in dark blue overalls and carrying a hoe.

"Did you hear?" the man called. "Isn't it awful?"

Aidan's dark brows lifted high into his forehead as the man came puffing up to them.

"George?" he muttered. "What? . . ."

"It was on the radio this morning," the man gasped, leaning upon the hoe and clutching his stomach to stop it from wobbling. "Then Nancy called. Everyone's been stopping in to talk about it. There's precious little peace in the garden today, I can tell you. How did it happen? Do you know? The report was very vague. I still can't believe it."

Aidan put his hand upon the man's shoulder and stared questioningly into his mournful eyes.

"George!" he said forcefully. "Calm down. I've been away and only got back this minute. What are you babbling about?"

The man drew a sharp breath and sucked his bottom lip forlornly.

"Then you don't know," he whispered. "Oh, I wish I didn't have to be the one to tell you."

"Tell me what, George?" Aidan insisted, becoming stern.

"Tales of blood!" Quoth suddenly interjected, and the man in the ill-fitting overalls gaped at the bird in astonishment. "Grisly doings, I'll be bound. Murder! Treason! Fe, fi, fo, fum!"

"George!" Aidan commanded.

The man turned his attention from the raven and in a solemn, dejected voice said, "It's Rhonda and the others. . . ."

Aidan stiffened. "What about them?"

"Last night, their bus . . . it said on the radio it blew up. . . . Oh, God, it's so dreadful."

Neil glanced at Aidan's face. The swarthy features had frozen. He said no words, but Neil could tell by the fierce emerald blaze that burned in his eyes that the boiling emotion threatened to overwhelm him.

"They used to love coming to the gardens," George said feebly. "Dot and Patrick were here only yesterday filling their bottles with water from the spring. Liked it better than the white one they did. Said they could feel it doing them good . . ."

The green fires dancing in Aidan's eyes daunted the man into silence, and he sorrowfully hung his head.

"Accursed be the pasture that feasts on blood," Quoth chimed in, "and bitterer still the slaughter-grown harvest of offal-fed fruit."

Aidan turned slowly and stared at the bird with a glance seething with such reproach that Quoth gave a plaintive quack and shielded his face with his wings.

"I must go to them," the gypsy said. "I have to know what happened."

Tearing back across the gravel he yanked open the van door and threw his hat inside.

"Wait!" Neil shouted. "You can't go. What about Veronica and Edie?"

Aidan's features twisted as the turmoil raged within him, until finally he said, "I won't be long. This is all part of it, don't you see, Neil? I have a horrible feeling I know what's happened to my friends. I have to find out for sure."

"But what about me?"

"We can't both go. You'll have to remain behind.

Go up the Tor. If Verdandi and the girl are there, bring them down here and wait until I return. An hour at the most, that's all I'll be. I promise."

Neil ran forward, but his guide was already climbing into the van.

"Why can't you tell me what's going on?" the boy protested. "Aidan, what if something happens? Aidan, listen to me! Wait a minute!"

With a roar the engine started and the van reversed back into the road.

"I won't be long!" Aidan yelled through the closed windows. "Don't worry, lad, don't worry!"

Neil ran after him. "I can't believe you're doing this!" he bawled angrily. But the driver never heard him, for the tires screeched over the blacktop and the van sped off, leaving Neil standing in the middle of the road, alone and confused.

Watching the exhaust fumes disappear around a bend, the boy worriedly turned to the raven upon his shoulder. They were stranded in an unfamiliar place, with no one to help or advise them, and it seemed that Quoth's foreboding portent had been confirmed. Something malevolent was at work here, and Neil felt a twinge of fear grip his stomach.

"That's it then," he muttered. "We've been dumped. What do we do now?"

Quoth squinted up at the clear, pale blue sky, and adopting an ominous, warning tone, he said, "Little under four hours doth remain of Phoebus's rays. If thou dost fail in the task set before thee, then beware of the darkness when it falleth. This night we shalt all be steeped in a mire of blood."

CHAPTER 16

TWO LOST SOULS

Following Aidan's counsel, Neil took the Wellhouse Lane approach to the Tor. This route began as a narrow track fenced in on either side by a thick growth of trees and bushes. It finished abruptly at a metal gateway, beyond which the great hill swept impressively upward.

It was not until Neil was halfway up this momentously steep slope that the boy's anger began to diminish. The climb was not difficult, for a stepped pathway had been cut into the inclining turf, but his leg muscles ached all the same.

From this direction, however, a trick of perspective lent the tower of Saint Michael the illusion that it was retreating behind the mountainous hill, sliding steadily down the bank opposite to the one that Neil was doggedly toiling up.

Pausing to gaze at the odd, solitary structure, that tall stone finger that claimed the pagan site in the name of the Archangel, the boy assured himself that it could not be much farther. Yet, just when he thought he had neared the summit, he discovered that he had only reached a shoulderlike formation and that there was still some distance to go along the Tor's deceptively long spine.

Exhausted for the moment, he took the opportunity to look around him and turned to gaze down upon the town of Glastonbury.

Neil was high above it now, and from that uncanny vantage point, it felt as if he was standing on a circle of grass that had been cut adrift from the anchoring earth and was floating up to the clouds.

Sitting patiently by the boy's ear, Quoth delighted in the lofty airs that streamed through his mangy feathers, and he flexed his primaries experimentally, longing to be able to soar over the treetops. But his right wing was still too weak, and he tucked it glumly by his side, jealously watching the other birds casually traversing the sky.

"Thou must learn to endure thy affliction," he grumbled softly. "Envy may shooteth at others but doth ever wound herself."

"It doesn't look real," the boy said, contemplating the small houses below. "Like a toy landscape for a model railroad."

In the middle distance, the collection of buildings and streets branched out to form a spur of brick and slate, neatly lassoing a humpbacked mound slightly smaller than the one he was currently standing on.

"That must be Wearyall Hill," Neil muttered. "Aidan would know why it's called that. Do you think he really will come back? Miss Ursula said that I could trust him."

Quoth rocked back and forth. "Trust him, verily," he chattered darkly, "yet look to thyself."

Neil resumed the climb, and the tower grew larger with every step, until finally he was standing before its gaping arch.

Exposed to the ravaging gales that on wild, wintry days whistled and ripped through the two doorless entrances at its base, this striking monument to resilience was a comforting beacon for every latter-day pilgrim who came to town in search of enlightenment.

Craning his neck to look up at the crenellated upper story, Neil paced around the four solid gray walls before turning his back to the tower and gazing at the shrinking countryside.

"Well, there's no one else here but you and me," he said to Quoth. "If Edie and Veronica did arrive before us, it looks like we missed them. Either that or they haven't made it yet."

The raven proffered no reply, for he was shooting suspicious, darting glances into the tower's shadowy interior.

"We'll just have to wait," the boy remarked, buttoning his blazer and wishing he'd had the foresight to bring a coat with him from home.

"There's no rain due—not this day nor the next," came a sudden, unexpected voice.

Neil jumped in surprise and whirled around, wondering how anyone could have scaled the Tor so quickly without him noticing.

"You be a real dafthead standing out there in the

wind though!" the voice added. "No scarf, nor hat neither."

Neil stared into the archway and noticed a shabbily dressed old man sitting on a stone bench, half-hidden in the shadows.

"Get a nasty head cold you will," the man commented, his wrinkle-framed eyes peering curiously at the boy and narrowing when regarding the bird perched on his shoulder. "But there's other reasons, better 'uns. Only loonies stand about in the open like what you do. Tommy wouldn't do that—he knows as to keep out of sight."

Neil moved a little closer but remained outside.

"Arr," Tommy continued, rising from the stone seat and shambling forward. "Gets you in under cover, afore *they* spots you, lad. Listen to Tommy. He knows, he saw 'em. Oh, yes, he saw 'em all right and wishes he hadn't."

"Who did you see?" the boy asked. "Was it an old lady and a young girl? Were they here?"

With a shake of his head, the trampish figure pulled off his grimy cap and pointed purposefully at Quoth.

"Never been so scared in his life has poor Tommy," he gibbered, staring at the bird and shivering. "Almost had him they did, sure to come back an' all. Makes him homeless again that does, for Tommy won't never dare sleep down in that place again, not for a hundredweight of cabbages he won't."

Neil folded his arms, and Quoth muttered softly in his ear, "Methinks thou couldst truss up the wits of yon muggins in a wren's egg."

"Feathers black with beaks and claws deadly sharp!

Tommy clapped his peepers on 'em, but he were lucky. He was watched over, so them nasties never spied him a-hidin' there."

The boy gave him a humoring nod. The old man's face rumpled into a sorry display of misery, and he twisted the cap in his large hands and uttered a forlorn whimper.

"Soon as he could, soon as the day came, Tommy ran from that barn," he wailed, "but he forgot somethin', didn't he? He left it behind. Not so clever as he thinks, sometimes he ain't, but only natural under them circumstances. He had to leg it real quick. But, oh, how could he have forgot his precious belongings—lost without 'em he is. When the night comes he won't have no protection this time. Tommy doesn't want them horrors to get him."

Burying his ruddy face in the greasy lining of his cap, the old man gave a morose sniff, then his eyes lit up and he rammed the hat back upon his brilliantined hair.

"You'll go with Tommy and see he's safe, won't you, lad?" he declared suddenly, with a wide smile that revealed his few remaining teeth. "He won't be so afeared with a bit of company, and it won't get dark for a while longer. Tommy's got to fetch his bits and pieces, see."

Neil shook his head. "I'm sorry," he began, wondering why he always had to contend with the local lunatics. "I've got to wait here."

Tommy stepped from the archway, glanced warily at the clear sky, and grunted. "That's all well and good, but we won't be long. Just nip down and collect Tommy's gear."

"I'm not going anywhere," Neil insisted.

Pausing, the old man lifted the peak of his cap and studied the boy carefully. "Funny, the company you do keep," he said, indicating the raven. "A right scruffy-looking specimen that is. Been in a real skirmish that 'un. Nearly got plucked for Christmas, did he?"

Quoth cleared his throat indignantly and let out a low, insulted caw.

"Still," the tramp rattled on, "you always did have mighty rum pals. Tommy liked the look of that teddy bear of yours best, though."

Neil stared at him in complete amazement. How could he possibly know about Ted?

Tommy chuckled. "Oh, yes," he announced. "Hasn't always lived here, hasn't Tommy. Used to live in London he did."

"In the war?"

The old man rubbed his stubbly chin in concentration. "Now which war would that be?" he mused.

"The second."

"Arr!" Tommy agreed, snapping his fingers. "That'd be it. He was out of the hospital by then and lodgin' in one of them dingy houses right alongside it. He saw you then, boy, oh, yes."

"What did you see?"

"Enough to know you're a lad who'll help him get his belongings back."

With that he turned and headed for a second track that lay behind the tower and zigzagged down the Tor.

"Tommy!" Neil called. "Wait."

Uncertain of what to do, the boy gazed back at the

road, but there was still no sign of Edie, Veronica, or Aidan.

"For all his years the clot is fleet of foot," the raven observed, watching the old man disappear below the rim of the hill.

"Okay," Neil decided. "I'll have to go after him. He *must* be linked to this. If only you could fly, then you could stay here and come find me when Aidan or the others arrive."

Quoth hung his head in shame and trilled a pathetic cheep.

"Oh, never mind," Neil told him, breaking into a run.

* * *

Down the far side of the immense hill they went, with Neil plying the old man with questions. But all Tommy cared about was the retrieval of his beloved possessions.

"'Tain't far," he said when they left the Tor path and entered one of the surrounding fields. "Tommy used to like it there, snugger than anywhere else he'd found for a long while. Been there a tidy few years now—a sore pity he has to leave it."

Plodding alongside him, the boy listened to his concerned mutterings as they crossed the barren fields, until Tommy abruptly halted and caught hold of Neil's arm to prevent him going any farther.

"This is it," he exclaimed, jabbing a thumb over the hedge toward a dilapidated and disused barn. "Tommy's homestead."

"Well, let's go and get your stuff," Neil prompted.

"Not so hasty," the tramp answered, doubtfully scrutinizing the derelict building. "Might not be safe. Though it's still early, they could've come back."

The boy looked at him intently. "Who is this 'they' you keep talking about?" he asked. "Why won't you say? Is it social workers or something? Are they trying to put you in a home?"

Tommy snorted and wiped his nose on the sleeve of his disheveled overcoat. "Why doesn't you ask that there bird of yours?" he murmured. "See if it can't smell anything bad over there."

"Why would I ask my raven?" the boy replied cautiously.

The old man stomped his ill-fitting boots into the plowed soil, and his florid jowls quivered when he shook his head in frustration.

"Drat it, boy!" he hissed. "Tommy done heard that feather duster speak to you before. If there's anyone who can sniff these demons out, it'll be the likes of him!"

Quoth blinked and looked at the tramp questioningly.

"All right, then." Tommy addressed the bird bluntly. "Does you sense anything nasty in the air? Be there somethin' harmful in that there barn?"

The raven looked over at the neglected structure. It was a forsaken outbuilding of some small farm that had long ago been swallowed by a larger concern, and the surplus barn had been left to stand idle and crumble into the soil.

Its corrugated roof was rusted and pitted with

holes, and halfway up the nearest wall, the shutters to the hayloft were hanging from their hinges. Standing in an overgrown yard at the edge of the field, it was a sad yet endearing sight—a remnant of farming history that would one day succumb to the gusting winds and collapse in upon itself.

Quoth paced up and down Neil's shoulder as he ducked and jerked his head, leering at the building and lifting his beak into the breeze to sniff and analyze the cold air.

"It would help if he knew what he was supposed to be looking for," Neil put in.

"He'll know it if it's there," Tommy assured him.

Presently the bird drew himself up, and spreading his good wing, he declared, "Nay, though the reek of violence doth make my quills tingle hereabouts, I fail to find aught of special mark touching yonder hovel. 'Tis as empty and wanting as mine noddle."

The tramp smacked his lips and rubbed his hands together. "That's good enough for Tommy," he proclaimed, happily pushing through the hedge.

Neil followed him across the weed-tangled yard, and the old man led him around the side of the barn to where a rotting wooden door stood wide open.

Tommy scampered into the gloomy interior, and with a brief glance at Quoth, Neil crept after.

A pleasant, sweet-smelling dusk filled the ruined barn, punctuated by spears of light that stabbed down from pinholes in the rusted roof above. With the aid of their glittering beams, the boy gazed around him.

The outbuilding was crammed with dismantled fragments of useless farm machinery and various pieces of discarded furniture. Old tractor engines stood alongside three-legged or seatless chairs, and plowshares rested against the splintered remains of a Welsh dresser. A jumbled assortment of corroded traps sat on a moldering leather trunk, and leaning on an upright piano that was sadly bereft of keys was a collection of broken rakes, shovels, and pitchforks.

It was a hoard of junk. If there was ever an opposite to a miser's treasure, then this was surely it.

"Here we are. Here we are," Tommy chatted to himself, negotiating his way between the heaps of lumber and crossing to the corner where a mound of bald tires was partially covered by a tarpaulin.

"This is where Tommy done hid himself last night," he told Neil. "Ducked under there real quick he did, as soon as he heard them a-circling overhead. But 'twas only cuz he had his collection with him that he was spared."

Stooping to fish out his cherished mementos, the old man cast a timid glance up toward the hayloft.

"Good nose on him, that bird of yourn," he called out. "Now, where's Tommy's pretty beauties?"

Lifting the tarpaulin, the tramp reached into one of the tires and brought out an old satchel. Tommy hugged it to himself then trotted over to Neil and cleared a space on the rickety dresser before emptying the contents of the bag for the boy to see.

"There!" the old man said with undisguised pride. "Them's Tommy's treasures. Have a gander, boy."

Neil obeyed and saw that the tramp's valuable collection was nothing more than a mass of religious trinkets: postcards, small plastic figures, key fobs,

scraps of gift wrapping, a torn advent calendar—
anything, in fact, that depicted an angel.

Quoth clicked his beak in mild scorn, but Tommy
didn't notice and grinned so broadly as he lovingly
sorted through the dog-eared icons that Neil was
reminded of the broken piano nearby.

"Angels have always kept Tommy safe from hurt an'
harm," the old man murmured, picking up a blue
plastic cake decoration molded in the form of a
cherub and turning it reverently in his clumsy fingers.

"That's how he made it through the Great War.
Came down to rescue him from the Kaiser's soldiers
they did."

Neil leaned forward. "You mean the Second World
War," he corrected. "And I don't think there were any
angels around then—a demon or two perhaps, but no
angels."

The old man's pale blue eyes gleamed at Neil and
he sucked his gums thoughtfully. "No," he said at
length. "'Twas the Great War. Tommy was at Mons,
you see. In the great retreat, through the clouds of
gunsmoke, he saw 'em, the heavenly host—and that's
where Tommy fell. In the miry mud's where the
medics found him, and they shipped him off home."

"But that can't be . . ." Neil mumbled, ignoring the
ludicrous story of the angels for the moment and
puzzling over the more practical problem. "If you were
fighting then, you'd be nearly a hundred."

"Arr," the tramp sighed. "Tommy's had a good
run, that's true enough, exceptin' for a touch of the
sciatica now and again. But after the battle, when he
woke up in the infirmary, he couldn't remember a

thing—not a sausage. So bright and glorious were the shining ones as they came charging out of heaven that it made him forget. That's all he could remember. If Tommy did have a family or friends to go back to, or a sweetheart a-waiting, then he never knew, and so he was kicked out of the army."

Lapsing into regretful silence, the old man wiped a tear from his eye and began to gather up his collection again.

"Verily canst this addled goose fathom thy loss," Quoth commiserated with a self-pitying sniff. "Melancholia ever sets in when I dwell upon the blank pages which doth lie behind me. To be ignorant of whom thou art and whence thou came—'tis a dry meat to chew and a bitter draft to sup."

"Then you and Tommy is both lost souls," the old man commented. "But as he always says, may angels and ministers of grace defend us."

Idly listening to the pair of them, Neil wondered why he had wasted his time following the old man to this dingy place.

"Never did like that there spiky mansion," the tramp piped up with a bewildering switch of subject as he slung the bag over his shoulder. "Forever gettin' lost in room after room Tommy was."

It took a moment for Neil to realize what he was talking about. "Do you mean the Wyrd Museum?" he ventured. "Are you saying you've been inside it?"

"That place weren't no museum!" Tommy stated emphatically. "Infirmary he told you it was. That's where he went after he clapped eyes on the angels a-flyin' over the battlefield. Spent a long while there did Tommy, getting his strength back and such. Didn't care for it one bit neither."

An uneasy prickling sensation tingled down Neil's spine as he realized what the man meant. Tommy had been a patient at the Wyrd Infirmary, but the boy remembered that between the wars the place had been a lunatic asylum.

Immediately, Neil began to feel uncomfortable. What if the tramp had escaped from the institution? He was certainly crazy, that was abundantly clear, but what if he was dangerous? Although he seemed harmless enough, his genial humor might swing into a violent one without any warning.

Biting his lip, Neil edged away and moved toward the door, but Tommy had already shuffled in that direction and blocked his escape.

"Tommy don't never want to move from around here," he muttered. "London was a bad place. He reckons this is the best place for keeping a lookout now. Lots of holy things here, boy, bound to attract celestial bein's to them sooner or later—like mice to grain or foxes to chickens. They'll come, you'll see."

From the yard outside could be heard the ugly sound of crows calling, and the tramp instantly shrank fearfully behind the door.

"Keep quiet now!" he hushed. "Them's might be ordin'ry birds, and then again they might not."

"I've got to get back to the Tor," Neil insisted.

Tommy turned to stare at him, and the boy was startled to see a ferocious scowl contorting the tramp's face.

"You'll not go nowhere till Tommy tells you!" he

growled, reaching for a pitchfork and guarding the entrance with it.

Neil glanced at Quoth. "He's completely nuts," the boy hissed out of the corner of his mouth.

The bird squinted at the tramp belligerently then looked around them, and with a faint cackle, he slyly nodded toward the hayloft and its broken shutters.

The boy understood, and when the old man turned his attention back to the yard, spying on the crows through a crack in the door, Neil crept toward the wooden ladder that led to the barn's upper level.

Silently, with Quoth keeping a watchful eye on Tommy, Neil climbed the aged rungs, praying that they would support his weight. Yet, as soon as the boy reached the straw-covered platform above, the bird gave a frightened shriek and toppled head over claw from his shoulder.

With a flurry of hay dust, Quoth landed on the loft's floorboards, gasping and squealing in dismay.

"What is it?" Neil cried, crouching beside the floundering bird and lifting him in his hands.

"Nay!" Quoth croaked, struggling to be free and leaping back onto the straw. "A terror is upon me, Master Neil, a dread so mighty I doth fear mine flesh wilt shrivel."

Down by the entrance, Tommy stared up at the hayloft, and glowering, he strode toward the ladder with the pitchfork gripped tightly in his fists.

"Fie! Fie!" the raven shrieked, running around in a circle, thrusting his beak into the straw and shaking his head in despair. "I'll betide this place. Fiends cruel and murderous hath been here. Upon this very board they did stand—I perceive each of their foul scents. Ten at least were their number. How it freezes the blood of this ailing lambkin to be sensible of their presence."

Neil could only look on as the bird scurried along, troweling his beak through the piles of dirty straw and clasping his wings behind him in dejection and anguish.

"What sort of fiends?" the boy asked. "What are you talking about?"

With his face powdered gold with hay dust, Quoth stole up to him and in a woeful, hollow voice cried, "Alas, alack! Large and terrible these nightmares doth loom in mine mind, yet from its locked chambers I cannot grasp neither their history nor title. All this fledgling knoweth is that thou must shun these creatures. They are bringers of death."

Shaken by Quoth's words, Neil rose and walked over to the opening where the shutters hung from their hinges and gazed out at the Tor in the distance. Already the daylight was growing dim, and the boy reproached himself for ever leaving the vicinity of the tower.

Lowering his eyes, he stared down at the ground and wondered if he could jump without hurting himself when, suddenly, a warning cry from Quoth made him spin sharply around.

"No, you don't, boy!" Tommy snapped, seizing hold of Neil's arms and dragging him from the edge.

"Get off!" Neil yelled, battling to free himself, while Quoth lunged for the tramp's feet and pecked at his ankles.

"Back off, you crazy bird!" the old man called, pulling Neil farther into the loft. "Tommy won't hurt him. Tommy would never hurt his pals."

Letting Neil go, he jigged and danced across the floorboards as Quoth continued to nip him.

"Ouch! Ow!" the tramp yelped. "Tommy didn't mean to scare. He were worried about them crows, that's all. Ouch!"

"Quoth!" Neil commanded. "Leave him alone."

Obediently the raven bounded back to him, and Tommy eyed the boy with gratitude.

"Punch holes in oak fences your chum could." He smiled ruefully.

"Why did you drag me away like that?"

Tommy's face was a picture of puppylike innocence, and already Neil was beginning to doubt his suspicions about him being dangerous.

"You was too close to the brink," the tramp breathed. "You might have fell."

"All you had to do was tell me."

The old man wiped his nose and stared dismally at the floor. "Tommy was scared of them crows," he whispered. "He don't think too good when he's frighted. All his braveness ran out in the Great War. He's not had an ounce since. He's mighty sorry if'n he spooked you. It were them dratted flappy crows."

"Well, they've flown off now," Neil said, feeling foolish for ever doubting Tommy's good nature. He might be odd, but looking at his guileless, lined face, Neil saw there wasn't a shred of harm in him.

"This is where they were," Tommy blurted, blithely forgetting the boy's suspicions and dropping to his knees to forage and grub among the straw with his bare hands.

"Awful noisy an' all, with their nasty voices and foul way of talking. Tommy heard them scrabbling about—and look!"

The old man brushed away the loose straw, blew the dust from the floorboards, then gazed triumphantly up at Neil.

"There," he breathed. "See how sharp them claws must be."

Neil stared down and murmured in surprise. Scored and sliced deep into the wood were the marks of three barbed talons.

"What on earth could have? . . ." the boy began, but at that moment Quoth came scuttling over the floor, yammering with excitement.

"Master Neil! Master Neil!" he cried. "Observe that which I too hath found!"

Neil and Tommy turned as the raven scampered back to the corner, where he hopped around the things he had discovered.

There, poking from the hay, were two huge black feathers.

Neil reached out to take them, but Quoth beat his hand back with his wings.

"Hold!" he squawked. "Touch not that evil filth."

"The little fellow's right," Tommy agreed. "Better to pick up hot coals than mess with those."

Neil looked up at the old man in confusion. "What's going on around here?" he mumbled.

"This is where they've made their gatherin' place," the tramp uttered fearfully.

"But who? What are these creatures?"

"The same as what killed that young couple in the car a week back," Tommy answered darkly, gripping his satchel and assuming a haunted, anguished expression, "and what did the same to them nice folk in the bright bus late last night. Heard 'em croaking about it Tommy did. Heard 'em lickin' their claws and cleanin' their beaks."

Removing his cap in respect for those who had perished, Tommy held the precious satchel close to his chest, then he turned his startling blue eyes upon Neil.

"We must leave here," he said urgently. "Right away—or sooner. See how the light fails outside. This is nowhere to be after dark. They're certain sure to be back tonight!"

Calling for angels to help and guard them, the tramp hurried back to the ladder, telling Neil to follow.

"Been here too long!" he cried anxiously. "You must meet your pals by Saint Michael's tower. Get a move on, lad! Stir your stumps!"

Lifting Quoth up to his shoulder, the boy clambered down behind him. The tramp picked up the pitchfork he had left at the bottom of the ladder only to throw it down again.

"Won't do no good 'gainst them," he whispered. "Only angels can save us from them, boy, only angels."

Neil hurried after him. But, even as they set off toward the Tor, the afternoon was fading and it was already too late.

CHAPTER 17

SKÖGUL

In the center of Glastonbury, just outside the town hall, a small Badgerline bus came to a halt, and among the people who alighted, a young girl stuck out her lower lip and waited impatiently.

"Thank you so much." Miss Veronica's frail tones drifted from the open doors as she enthused her compliments to the driver. "I did enjoy myself. You've been most kind, and it was so pleasant conversing with your delightful friends back there. I do hope fortune favors you, Mr. Badger. I shall be sure to tell my sister next time I see her."

"Veronica!" Edie called. "We ain't got all day."

The elderly woman waved to each of the other passengers and gingerly stepped from the vehicle, leaning heavily upon her cane.

It had been a long, tiring journey. They had spent most of the night finding their way to Paddington Station, and when they arrived, they had discovered that they would have to wait until morning for the first train.

When it pulled out of the station, however, they were not aboard, nor were they on the one that followed, because Miss Veronica had somehow managed to lock herself in the ladies' bathroom, and more than an hour was wasted endeavoring to get her out.

The train they ultimately boarded was very crowded, and the pair of them formed a curious spectacle wandering up and down the cars searching for two seats together.

Eventually they settled themselves close to the dining car. Miss Veronica caused a great commotion when she asked for jam and pancakes, and she tapped her stick petulantly upon the counter after the steward informed her that the nearest they could offer her was a jelly doughnut.

As there was no station at Glastonbury, they were forced to change at Bristol and travel the remaining distance by bus. Standing at the wrong stop, they squandered another hour, but they had finally made it, and Miss Veronica waved a grimy handkerchief after the bus as it rumbled away.

"Look at those charming folk gazing back at us," she sighed. "How enchanting it was to pass the time with them, and how captivated they were by my company."

"They ain't gazin'." Edie laughed. "They're gawkin', and that's cuz you told 'em you hadn't been back here for thousands of years. Thought you were out of your mind they did."

But the old woman didn't seem to hear and looked adoringly at the buildings around them.

"My, my, how it has altered," she cooed. "Yet still I can feel the thrum of the ancient power that flows through the ground here. Can you not sense it, Edith?"

The child nodded. From the moment she had set foot upon the sidewalk, an electric thrill had buzzed inside her head, and the silver tinsel in her pixie hat sparkled fiercely.

"Over this very spot my barge carried me in my youth," Miss Veronica murmured, dreamily closing her painted eyes. "And in the marsh time, only he and I knew the secret way to our special place. Joyous days, Edith, joyous days."

Taking the girl's hand in her bony fingers, she hobbled up the street. The wizened old woman with a white-powdered face and garish vermilion lipstick smeared all around her mouth carefully picked her way alongside the grubby little urchin, who was dressed in clothes that would not be fit for a rag sale. Yet in Glastonbury, no one batted an eyelid.

Then, turning the corner, Miss Veronica let out a delighted squeal that swiftly evolved into a peal of twittering laughter.

"There it is!" she cried, madly thrashing her cane in the air and jabbing it toward the end of the lane. "Ynnis Witrin. Oh, we were so happy there, Edith, me and the Captain. How wonderful to see that it has changed so little in spite of everything around it. I can hardly believe that I am to see him again after all this time, after all that has happened."

Edie Dorkins said nothing as she stared at the Tor. During her short life she had never been to the countryside, and the unfamiliar sights and smells excited her. Yet as she gazed upon that beautiful green mountain, a coldness crept into her heart, and she held her breath, fearing that something dreadful was about to befall them.

* * *

Hunched over the handlebars of her bicycle, Lauren Humphries pedaled furiously down Bere Lane. She hardly glanced at the figures of Edie and Miss Veronica when she flew past them, for the red-haired girl was troubled and determined to find an answer to the riddles that agitated her.

She had remained in the bed and breakfast until shortly after lunch, when her stepmother had come down the stairs holding her head and groaning for an aspirin. Sitting in the kitchen, mustering her dwindling strength, Sheila had decided that she had lain in bed for far too long, and although she was still unwell, she had stubbornly driven off to the store to stock up in case any last-minute guests arrived.

Lauren knew she shouldn't have allowed her stepmother to leave, but trying to talk Sheila out of anything was difficult at the best of times, and the woman dismissed the girl's concern outright.

Listening to the car pull out of the driveway, Lauren was suddenly relieved to be alone in the house, and gripped by a sudden rash impulse, she ran to find her father's toolbox.

Shortly afterward she hastened to the rear of the building and emerged carrying a long ladder, which she dragged around to the front and propped up against the chalky blue wall.

Then, stuffing her pocket with a handful of three-inch nails, the girl tucked a hammer into her belt and carefully climbed the ladder until she was level with the window of her parents' bedroom.

Quickly she closed the wooden shutters, and in twenty minutes she had nailed them firmly closed.

"There!" she panted, inspecting her handiwork. "That'll keep it out—or her in."

With one problem still to solve, she returned the ladder and rode off on her bicycle toward the town.

Into Magdalene Street she sped, her flame-colored, curly hair flowing behind her. But when she rounded the corner of the main street, she took her feet off the pedals and dismounted.

Lauren wheeled her bicycle through the entrance of The Glastonbury Experience and leaned it against the statue of a Celtic goddess that stood in the courtyard beyond.

The pungent, almost sickly fragrance of burning incense laced the air, imbuing the atmosphere with a surreal, decadently exotic quality. The girl nervously nibbled her fingernails, feeling almost stupid for having taken Sheila's no-doubt mundane illness so seriously.

The collection of New Age shops encompassing the pleasant enclosure exhibited their enigmatic wares. Signs advertising "crystal healing" and "color reading" hung in some of the windows, while others displayed the work of local artists who specialized in depicting the Tor wreathed by rainbows or rising from a sea of ethereal mist. Tie-dyed scarves fluttered just within the doorways, and the sweet tinkling of wind chimes played an endlessly random, tuneless jangle.

One shop in particular held Lauren's attention. In the windows of the small craft emporium called Moonshine squatted row upon row of grotesque, big-bellied ceramic earth mothers, and after a moment's doubtful hesitation, the girl entered.

The lilting music of panpipes mingled with birdsong filled the shop's interior—just one of the many relaxation tapes available to the vacationing, harmony-hungry city dweller. But this kind of earnest, slickly packaged serenity always grated on Lauren's nerves, and she strove to ignore it. This was where Sheila had purchased the sinister crow doll.

Glancing quickly around, the girl saw that she was not the only customer in the shop.

A middle-aged American couple was examining an unattractive ceramic bowl, which had been fired in a glaze that was the dingiest shade of mud conceivable, and they were bickering in low whispers about whether to buy it or not.

"Jo-Beth would just hate it!" the woman mouthed to her husband. "I tell you, Murray, you get that monster for our daughter and I'll break it over your head."

Lauren suppressed a smile, and pretending to admire a lumpy vase, she looked instead at the owner of the shop, who was sitting behind the cash register.

In her early forties, Dulcima Pettigrew had lived in Glastonbury for five years and had run Moonshine for the past three.

Normally an attractive, bubbly woman, that afternoon she looked irritable and tired. Around her eyes were dark circles, which she attempted to conceal by wearing a pair of sunglasses.

Lauren studied her keenly. The striking bleached-blonde hair that usually tumbled down her shoulders was hidden beneath a black headscarf, and today was the first time Lauren had seen her without ludicrously long earrings dangling from her pierced lobes.

In accord with this new, puritan image, the girl noticed, Miss Pettigrew's wrists were also unusually bare, for they routinely clinked and rattled with over a dozen bracelets.

Sneaking another glance at Dulcima's tired face, however, Lauren wondered if the woman's current aversion for ornament might not simply be because she was too exhausted to bother decking herself out. She appeared to be as drained as Lauren's stepmother.

Why Miss Pettigrew had felt compelled to open the shop when she was so ill was another matter, but before the girl could give it much thought, her gaze shifted to an object that was hanging behind the woman's head.

Wearing a hat of black straw and a dark brown–checked dress was a crow doll.

Only the color of the material and the dried plants sticking out of the apron pocket distinguished this creepy little effigy from the one Sheila had brought home, and Lauren moved forward to examine it.

"Oh, now, Murray—if that isn't the very thing for Jo-Beth!" the American woman abruptly cried, pointing to the doll with her pearly pink nails. "It's so cute and quaint. She's just gotta have it!"

Barging past her husband, she tapped the counter and waved at the object eagerly.

"I'll take that please, Miss," she told Dulcima. "I've never seen anything like it before. Such sweet twiggy fingers—oh, I just love it. Are they made locally? Could I get one with my daughter's name stitched on it?"

Miss Pettigrew regarded the woman through her sunglasses, and in a polite but firm voice, she said, "I'm sorry, it isn't for sale."

"Not for sale?" the customer moaned. "Oh, Murray, she says I can't have it."

Her husband stepped forward and reached into the pocket of his plaid sports jacket for a bulging wallet.

"How much do you want for the doll?" his rich, rumbling voice drawled. "I know you Britishers like to haggle."

Dulcima lowered her glasses. "It isn't for sale," she repeated, a little more forcefully this time.

The American narrowed his eyes and put his wallet away. "Come on, honey," he said, taking hold of his wife's arm and leading her to the door. "We're leavin'."

"Did you see her eyes?" his wife declared. "Is she on drugs?"

"Who cares. This whole backward country's full o' crazies. Let's go on down to Bath like I wanted to do in the first place."

With a slam of the door the couple departed, leaving Lauren alone with Miss Pettigrew and feeling rather uncomfortable.

"Do you need any help there?" Dulcima asked.

Lauren shook her head. "Only browsing, thanks . . . but about those Americans . . ."

"What about them?"

"I'm just curious. You sold my stepmother one of those crow things yesterday. Why wouldn't you let them have that one?"

A ghostly smile appeared on the woman's face. "Because the dolls are very special," she replied. "Don't you think so?"

"Not really," Lauren confessed.

"Take a closer look."

The girl edged nearer and peered at the cloth figure hanging on the wall.

"I like to know that they're going to a good home," Dulcima said. "Somewhere nice and local. That's why I let your stepmother have one."

"You talk about them as if they're children."

"Perhaps it is we who are the children," Dulcima said mysteriously. "Sometimes we're the ones who need guidance."

She reached up, took the doll from the hook, and offered it to Lauren.

"Why don't you have it?" she said. "It's the last one; there were only twelve. No need to pay me. I know you'll look after it."

Trying to hide the revulsion she felt, Lauren gazed at the cloth crow creature. If anything, it was more horrible than Sheila's. Those tiny black-bead eyes seemed to be watching her, and she wondered how the American woman could have possibly been enamored of it.

Lauren couldn't explain why she disliked it so much, but all her instincts told her that the effigy was malignant, and she didn't want to have anything to do with it. She even went so far as to put her hands behind her back in case they accidentally brushed against the fabric.

"Who made them?" she brought herself to ask. "Was it you?"

The woman laughed faintly. "Me? I'm not . . . gifted enough. No, I merely sell them. Someone far cleverer than I is responsible. The first time I saw them I was captivated and simply had to claim one for myself."

"What does the writing on the apron mean? This one's different from my stepmother's. Hers says 'HLÖKK,' but the stitches here read 'GÖLL.'"

"'Shrieker' and 'Screamer,'" Dulcima informed her, drawing out the vowels—relishing the sound of the words. "And the one that owns me is 'SKÖGUL,' which means 'Raging.'"

"Owns you?" Lauren murmured.

The smile disappeared from Miss Pettigrew's face as she realized she had said too much. "Do you want the crow doll or don't you?" she demanded curtly.

"No, thanks," the girl replied.

"Then you're making a very big mistake."

Lauren backed away. The woman's tone was hostile and threatening.

For a moment Dulcima glared at her, then she relaxed and shrugged.

"You'll never see their like again," she resumed in a more normal manner. "Well, there are plenty of other people around here who might be tempted. Now, was there anything else you wanted?"

The girl answered that there was not, and she made for the door.

Dulcima watched her leave then, giving the crow doll a loving pat, returned it to the hook.

"Perhaps she wasn't suitable after all," the woman whispered into the fabric.

*　*　*

In the courtyard outside, Lauren sat at one of the café tables, struggling to figure out what was happening.

For over half an hour she stayed there, watching the tourists mill in and out of the shops until, eventually, a woman she recognized as being local wandered into Moonshine. After several minutes she came out with a parcel wrapped in dark blue paper printed with silver stars and circles.

Lauren guessed at once what the package contained, and her suspicions were confirmed when Miss Pettigrew closed the shop a short while later and strode purposefully out into the street.

"At last!" she heard the woman cry with a laugh. "We are complete!"

CHAPTER 18

CHARRED EMBERS

Like the webbed strands of a great, luminous spider, a network of fluorescent yellow tape crisscrossed the country road, fencing off the grass shoulder and threading into the nearby wood.

A line of police cars, their lights idly flashing and radios crackling, lined the edge of the trees. Somber-faced officers paced about the cordon, exchanging grim looks. One young policeman stood away from his colleagues. All the color had drained from his face, and he took deep breaths of the acrid, burned air to try and conquer the nausea that had seized him.

"You all right now, Col?" a corpulent sergeant called.

The man waved back but remained where he was and stared blankly at the darkening sky. If he ever saw another sight like the one that had just turned his stomach he would resign from the force. How the forensic guys managed, he couldn't begin to imagine.

At last the queasy fluttering in his guts subsided,

and although his face was still ashen gray, he mopped his forehead, preparing to rejoin the others.

Wandering back, his legs still a little shaky, he saw a small blue van skid to a halt in the middle of the road. An oddly dressed man, who was obviously a gypsy, came leaping out to charge toward the tape barriers.

"Hey!" the policeman yelled, his voice combining with the shouts of his colleagues. "You can't come through here!"

Aidan slithered beneath the cordon, and at once five burly officers came running to stop him.

"Let me pass!" he demanded when strong hands grasped his shoulders.

"This is a sealed area, sir," the overweight sergeant snapped, roughly bundling him back toward the tapes. "The scene of a very serious incident, and we don't want any ghoulish souvenir hunters. Now get lost before I charge you with something."

As he was frog-marched through the cordon, Aidan's temper exploded, and in one smart movement he ducked and slipped out of his much-patched coat to round furiously upon his captors.

"Be still!" Aidan commanded, and such was the tremendous authority that rang in his voice, the officers froze and stared at him in stupefied amazement.

"Now," he continued, taking his coat from the sergeant. "Let's have no more nonsense and be a bit more civilized, shall we?"

The policemen swayed unsteadily as though stirring from sleep.

"You can't come through here," the sergeant reiterated, albeit with less confidence this time.

Aidan glared at him. If there was one quality he couldn't stand it was bullheaded stupidity. It would be so easy to daunt them with a few of the simple tricks he knew, but in spite of his anxiety to discover what had happened to his friends, he knew he would learn more if he followed their tedious procedures.

"Who's in charge here?" he demanded.

The sergeant wanted to tell the funny little man that police matters were none of his business, yet when he looked at those emerald flames he found himself saying, "Chief Inspector Hargreaves, sir."

Aidan's grave expression brightened considerably. "Charlie Hargreaves?" he cried. "There's a bit of luck. Be a good fellow and fetch him, would you?"

"I don't think so, sir," the officer refused, avoiding those weird glittering eyes. "Like I said, this is an extremely serious incident."

"I know that!" Aidan snapped, dragging his fingers through his long hair in frustrated outrage. Mastering himself, he leaned forward and spoke to the plump officer in a low, conspiratorial whisper.

"Listen," he growled. "If you continue to obstruct me, I for one really will lose my temper, and I don't think your superior would appreciate this shameful treatment of one of his oldest friends."

The sergeant swallowed audibly. "You really know the Chief Inspector?"

"He and I used to steal apples together when we were boys. Terror of the orchards we were."

A skeptical sneer formed on the sergeant's face, but the gypsy was so assured that his doubts rapidly trickled away.

"Colin!" he called out to the young officer. "Go tell the Chief Inspector there's a Mr. . . ."

"Aidan."

"A Mr. Aidan to see him."

The gray-faced policeman hesitated before following the yellow tapes into the trees.

"Don't worry, lad," the sergeant told him. "It'll all be bagged up by now."

The young officer nodded feebly and hurried into the wood.

"Bagged up?" Aidan muttered, staggered by the man's crass insensitivity. "Would you care to explain that deplorably callous comment? What exactly did you mean?"

"Can't say, sir," came the unhelpful reply.

Aidan considered him anew and, in a cold, cryptic voice, earnestly intoned, "You want to watch those night shifts. Too fond of fast food, aren't you? And then a few beers with the boys.

"I'm a good reader of people, my fine, fat sergeant. Faces are the maps of our lives, did you know that? Well, by my reading of your ugly, pugnacious mug, you've got two years before your first heart attack, and six months after that—it's the biggie."

The policeman opened his mouth but said nothing and could only gaze at him in consternation.

"Aidan!" a deep voice cut through the uneasy atmosphere. "Thank goodness."

Hastening through the trees came Chief Inspector Hargreaves—a tall, solidly built man with dark hair turning gray at the temples. His caved-in-looking face was framed by a neatly clipped brindled beard.

"Let him by, Sergeant!" he barked gruffly.

Aidan gave the rotund officer an infuriating wink as he slid past, but before joining the chief inspector, the gypsy paused.

"Never too late to change," he said more gently than before. "A little less beer, a lot more exercise, and a huge helping of good manners will get you another forty years. Think about it."

The sergeant wagged his head and stared after the curious man in wonder.

"Teasing my officers?" the chief inspector murmured when Aidan approached.

The gypsy put up his hands in mock surrender. "I admit I lost my temper," he said. "But they really are a pretty dumb bunch."

"They're good people doing a difficult job. Not surprising if they're a bit rough around the edges today—it's not been a particularly happy one. At least the reporters have packed up and gone now."

The men regarded one another. The one now putting his brown frock coat back on was the shorter of the two, but the man in the uniform looked up to him all the same.

"It's good to see you, Leader," he whispered, throwing his officers a cursory glance as he led Aidan aside. "You have no idea how relieved I am now that you're here," he confided. "This is beyond me. It's got us all completely baffled."

"So, Charlie," Aidan said quietly, "tell me what happened."

Hargreaves conducted him along the edge of the road to an area where the grass was flattened. An assortment of objects lay unattended and curiously out of place on the grass.

"This is how they left it. We haven't a clue how the vehicle was moved. No tire marks, nothing."

Aidan gazed with profound sadness on the campsite of his friends. This was where he had visited *Eden's Bus* only the previous evening. There was the box the dogs slept in, and there, lying on its side, was a large water container.

"Did you find anything?" he asked.

The chief inspector moved a little farther across the grass. "There was some blood over here," he stated. "We don't know whose yet. Leader, they . . . they're all dead, you know."

"I guessed that they would be. Now, take me to it."

Through the trees Hargreaves led him, and as they pressed deeper into the wood, the unpleasant smell of burned timber mounted steadily.

"It was a mighty big blaze," the chief inspector commented. "Could spot it for miles—but you'll see just how big for yourself when we get there."

Tramping over the leaf mulch, Aidan noted numerous policemen scattered about the woods searching through the thickets with long sticks.

"Not all of them were in the bus when it exploded," Hargreaves uttered, choosing his words delicately. "One of them . . . well, we still haven't found all of him yet."

Aidan squeezed his eyes shut as the information cut through him, then, with renewed determination, he forged on.

Now the trees they passed were coated with a film

of soot. A little farther in they became charred and withered. Then, as they progressed onto ground that was still smoldering, the chief inspector turned stiffly.

"This is it," he said. "It's not pretty."

Moving aside, he let Aidan view the horrendous scene ahead, and the little man staggered forward.

It was like stepping into a vision of Hell.

The world was suddenly stripped of every color, and only a stark coal-black wasteland remained. All that was left of a wide area of dense woodland was a stunted forest of cindered stumps that chinked and chimed as they cooled, pouring countless strings of bitter smoke heavenward.

A thick carpet of ash smothered the incinerated soil, and Aidan's feet sank deeply into the downy layers of carbon as he gazed on the wreckage that lay in the center of this blasted devastation.

There, ruptured into three large, twisted fragments of buckled and mangled metal, were the shattered remains of the cheerfully painted bus his friends had once lived in.

Unrecognizable in its cremation, the vehicle's fractured frame sprawled across the fired landscape like the crashed ruins of an airline disaster.

Blistered and burned in the inferno, the once-vibrant colors had given way to a blackened shell whose windows had melted, and patches of bubbled glass dotted the surrounding embers.

In and around the vehicle's tortured skeleton, forensic teams wearing white paper coveralls were meticulously sifting the debris and hunting through the scorched remnants, overlooking nothing.

"Rhonda, Luke, Owen, Dot, Patrick," Aidan grieved. "An evil way to die."

The chief inspector came and stood beside him. "The bodies have been taken to the pathology lab," he said grimly. "Can't be many worse ways to go than burning to death."

"That's assuming they survived the fall."

Hargreaves stared at him. "Fall? If you could shed any light on how this accident could possibly have happened, I'd be most grateful. How does a bus get inside a wood, without leaving any kind of trail, then blow up like this? It just doesn't make any sense."

"There you go assuming again," Aidan told him. "This was no accident. Something is stirring, Charlie, something great and terrible."

Crossing the desert of ash, the tails of his coat flapping behind him, Aidan went to take a closer look at the roasted wreck, to the astonishment of the forensic scientists in their sterile coverings.

Hargreaves hurried behind him, gesturing to the others that the odd little man had his permission to be present.

Like a dog searching for a scent, Aidan roved amid the destruction, halting occasionally to squint at a battered scrap of bodywork as he tried to figure out which part of the bus it had originally come from.

Watching this eccentric interloper weave in and out of what should have been their exclusive domain, the scientists became gradually more irritated until they finally put down their instruments and complained to the chief inspector, who attempted to placate them.

"Charlie!" Aidan shouted abruptly. "Over here."

Hargreaves hastened over to where the gypsy was kneeling before a distorted sheet of perforated metal and crouched beside him.

"This is a section of the roof," Aidan remarked. "But what do you make of these ragged holes?"

"Looks almost deliberate," the chief inspector breathed. "Too regular to be a result of the explosion. As if something ripped clean through it on purpose."

"That's exactly what happened. The bus was seized by the roof and hoisted off the ground—must've been pretty high, too—then it was dropped here."

Hargreaves rose. "That's impossible," he hissed. "Apart from a huge crane, what could have done that?"

Aidan ran his fingers over the jagged rents and, in a quiet, despairing voice, murmured, "*Valkyrja.*"

A deathly expression stole over the chief inspector's face, and he choked back an exclamation of horror.

"Valkyries . . ." he gasped. "But that's preposterous!"

Lost in turbulent thought, Aidan slowly drummed his fingers upon the punctured metal before stretching to stand beside his old friend.

"Don't disappoint me, Charlie," he said in a hushed, mournful tone. "Where's your learning? You're descended from Askar folk same as me. You go to the museum ever year like I do to adorn the fountain and to look for a sign. You know there are all sorts of possibilities in this world."

"Even so, Valkyries in this day and age? They were supposed to have been destroyed in the early time."

Aidan held him with his powerful eyes. "The tales say that only the human hosts were vanquished," he reminded him. "The unclean spirits were never captured. Somehow the twelve servants of Woden have returned. Those malevolent creatures He created to overthrow the Nornir are back among us."

There was silence as both men considered this terrifying prospect.

"The Fates are in hideous danger," Aidan said eventually, rousing himself from his doom-filled thoughts. "I have to get back to Glastonbury—I've been away too long already. Verdandi has left the museum; she is heading for the Tor. If those nightmares find her . . ."

The chief inspector agreed, but scanning the devastation around them and looking at his officers, he wondered what he should tell them.

"Charlie," Aidan snarled, knowing what his friend was thinking. "It doesn't matter anymore. The end is coming, don't you understand? If the Valkyrie are loose, there's nothing any of us can do! They're not human. Those vile abhorrences are beyond us, and the best you can do is to quell the panic for as long as you can. Say what happened here was a freak accident. Don't let the public know—not yet."

Hargreaves nodded solemnly. "I won't," he promised. "Now you go, Leader. The Nornir need you. Don't fail them."

Taking hold of the policeman's hand, Aidan shook it desperately, then he whisked around and sped over the cinders to plunge into the trees beyond.

"The destiny of the Fates themselves is in your keeping now," the chief inspector whispered hoarsely. "From the darkness that awaits us, I pray we will all be spared."

CHAPTER 19

VERDANDI

Reaching Wellhouse Lane, where the outlets for the two springs came washing down the road to gurgle into the sewer grates, Miss Veronica leaned on her walking cane and drew a hand over her eyes, smudging the lashes painted along the lids.

"Oh, dear," she panted. "What a long road that was. Celandine could have danced its entire length— I wish I had her stamina. It's so very tiring being away from the museum, so very, very tiring."

At the old woman's side, Edie Dorkins was watching the rust-colored water of the red spring mingle with the clear of the white.

Laughing, she jumped from the sidewalk and capered to the center of the sloping lane, where she kicked and splashed in the shallow channel, stomping to the other side, where she spun around on the tips of her toes.

"This the way up the hill?" she asked, pointing to the track that lay behind her.

Miss Veronica peered at the tree-lined path and carefully picked her way through the swashing spring water, drenching the dirty white satin of her gold-embroidered slippers.

"It does appear to be the only route," she agreed. "Edith, dear, hold my hand. I do believe I'm trembling wth nerves."

The girl took the shriveled, shaking hand and wondered how long it would take the old woman's feeble legs to stagger up the Tor. Together they walked across a cattle grid and stepped onto the narrow path.

Twilight had come early to the trackway, hemmed in on both sides by tangled briar and tall hawthorn trees. Through this shadowy murk, Edie and Miss Veronica doggedly plodded as the path curved around and upward, but already the strain of even this simple climb was beginning to take its toll upon Miss Veronica.

Presently the bordering trees and hedges came to an abrupt stop at a metal gateway, and the inspiring spectacle of the Tor was unveiled before them.

At once Edie ran to the railed barrier and poked her head between the bars. From here on, the ground rose more sharply than before, and she could hear the breath wheezing in Miss Veronica's throat.

Ignoring the imposing view for the moment, she studied the old woman and pouted truculently.

With one hand upon her cane and the other pressed against her breast, the youngest of the Websters looked as though she might collapse. Under her overcoat, her frail form was shivering with exhaustion, and her haggard face was pinched with fatigue.

"You park yourself down for a bit," Edie told her, patting one of the two upright stones that formed an unconventional, graveyard-like stile at one end of the gate. "There ain't no way you can get up there without a breather."

Miss Veronica shook her head and gazed at the child with a curious gleam in her milky eyes.

"No," she said, gasping for breath. "There can be no delay. Soon the sun will be setting."

"But you won't make it!" Edie sternly told her, folding her arms and jutting out her chin.

A secretive smile flickered over Miss Veronica's white-powdered face. "Oh, Edith," she uttered with amusement, "did you really think I could ever allow my Captain to see me as I am now—a hunchbacked, decrepit old hag? No, my dear, I am not as mad as all that. I know that it is Verdandi he wishes to meet, not this raddled, liver-spotted, painted cadaver."

The child didn't understand what the old woman meant, but Miss Veronica leaned against the gate, and taking the walking cane in both bony hands, she lifted the pearl handle to her crabbed, vermilion-smeared lips.

"Awaken," she crooned softly. "Verdandi summons you, O rod of life and doom. Though you are far from the seat of your power, listen to my command and do my bidding."

Holding it out in front of her she waited. Then, as Edie watched, faint filaments of glimmering light began to rise within the wood's grain, just as they had done in the Websters' poky apartment in the museum.

Up around the stick the light spiraled. It pulsed and sparked with a livid glow that dispelled the gathering shadows and poured a verdant brilliance upon the old woman's infirm figure.

"Here me now," Miss Veronica's cracked voice ordered, "you who were made from sacred timber torn from the mighty Ash. With your aid I did tally and measure the span of all who dwelt outside the circling mists, and I know too well the extent of your strength. Grant this, then: bestow upon Verdandi one final service. Count back through the score of my years—give me back a day. Let me be as he remembers, for a little while."

The cane crackled in her hands, and the glare blazed upon her withered features as she closed her bag-ringed eyes. Above her, the knotted branches of the hawthorns flashed in and out of the settling dark, and the wondrous radiance flooded over the pathway, bejeweling the stones and dappling the weeds with a lustrous splendor.

Bathed in the dazzling beams, Miss Veronica bowed her head. "Thank you," she murmured.

Edie held her breath in anticipation as the flickering rays danced in her wide eyes, but Miss Veronica was now ready to continue.

Squeezing her brittle bones through the gate, she set foot upon the open, grassy slopes of the Tor. The magical light began to waver and dwindle, until only occasional flecks of cold green flame lapped about her walking cane.

"Hurry child," she said anxiously. "See how the night gathers in the distance. I must not be late."

Edie scampered after her.

The late-afternoon sky had darkened, and the summit of the great hill was already shrouded in shade as they started to climb, yet from the moment she caught up with Miss Veronica, Edie was aware that something remarkable was taking place.

Wherever the old woman's slippered feet trod, the scrubby winter grass writhed and flourished, becoming rich and luxuriant, and the lush footmarks shone as though basking in the light of a bright summer morning.

Wheeling around to gawk at this glorious shimmering trail, Edie squealed in delight, for the thick grass was spreading to form a wide, sunlit path that stretched ever outward, flowing in all directions until it reached the railed gateway and the hedges beyond.

Suddenly the naked trees burst into bud, and the new leaves gleamed in the unnatural sunshine, even though the sky above was just as dark as before.

Gamboling across the sweet-smelling grass, Edie gulped great lungfuls of the now warm, deliciously perfumed air.

"Don't dawdle," Miss Veronica called to her. "Stay by me, or time will rumble over you and you will be lost."

Feeling the invisible sun of a fair June day that had ended long ago upon her upturned face, Edie stared at her companion, amazed.

With every step she took, the old woman was changing. Her strides were becoming increasingly vigorous, and even as Edie watched, her bent spine clicked and groaned until it was straight and strong.

Like melting ice, the ages were dissolving from Miss Veronica. The chalky powder crumbled from her face, and the crudely daubed lipstick faded as her mottled, scraggy flesh was drawn tightly over her cheekbones.

Beneath the fine eyebrows, which only a moment before had been charcoal arcs drawn too high upon her forehead, Miss Veronica's eyes sparkled a beautiful cornflower blue, and her long jet-black hair flowed behind her lithe figure like a river of shadow.

Gone was the weary, shambling crone who had wasted with the innumerable centuries, and in her place walked a lovely, statuesque woman in the first flush of youth.

Halting for an instant, she removed her drab, cumbersome overcoat and cast it to the ground, as the dirty silk robe that Miss Veronica always wore now rippled and shone like a searing white flame.

As a goddess she appeared, so pure and enchanting was her beauty. Her countenance was one that mortals would worship and die for, gladly perishing for the smallest smile from her lovely lips.

Verdandi, of the royal house of Askar, was the fairest creature ever to have blessed the earth with her presence, and no longer in need of a prop to support her, she carried the walking cane lightly while extending her other elegant hand tenderly toward the dumbfounded child.

"Do not fear, Edith," her fluting voice said. "Verdandi is returned as she was in the spring of her days, before the frost of age blighted her. Behold, it is a day filled with hope and wonder."

As she spoke, Verdandi raised the rod and the

lowering sky peeled away. From the remote horizon, across the glowing landscape, the gathering shades of evening were torn aside and scattered to uncover a brilliant canopy of sapphire blue.

A perfect summer day unfurled about them, and without uttering another word, the lovely young woman clasped Edie's small hand and marched up the Tor.

Edie cast her eyes around them. The town of Glastonbury had completely vanished. Not a house, not a road, not a lamppost, not even a garden remained, and only a vast stretch of uninhabited marshland extended toward the encompassing hills.

In shedding the years from Miss Veronica, the measuring rod of the Nornir had taken them both back to a time in her youth, and Edie's face was split by a huge, exhilarated grin.

Higher they ascended the terraces that banded the Tor much more prominently in this ancient age, and Edie noted that even the solitary tower had disappeared. Yet the crest of the Tor was not deserted, for a single tall figure was standing up there waiting for them.

"Do you see?" Verdandi exclaimed, catching her breath. "He is there—my Captain."

Silhouetted against the brilliant azure sky was the outline of a man, a great sable cloak billowing about his shoulders, and circling above his helm-crowned head flew a large black raven.

Verdandi's pace quickened as they approached, and Edie studied the Captain with great interest.

Drawing closer, she could see that he was dressed

for battle. Beneath the black cloak he wore a corselet of burnished mail that winked and scintillated in the sunlight when he raised his hand in greeting.

Within a gem-encrusted scabbard, a long sword hung at his side, and on his feet were great spurred boots, but Edie could see no sign of a horse anywhere.

He, like Verdandi, was young. Long flaxen hair curled past his shoulders, and a forked beard covered his chin. In the shade of his silver helm a pair of dark eyes glittered. It was a proud, rugged face in which the lust for victory in combat could easily be read.

Yet there was also an air of unease about him that Edie could not understand. He seemed restless and uncomfortable. After everything Miss Veronica and the others had said about him, the child had expected someone bold and heroic who would throw back his head with a fierce, terrible laugh or hurl his sword into the air in greeting, then catch it again in his teeth. To her surprise, Edie found that the Gallows God was something of a disappointment.

"Woden!" Verdandi cried, releasing Edie's hand to run the remaining short distance and throw her slender arms about him.

Edie pulled a wry, disgusted face while the couple embraced, then she looked up at the familiar black bird lazily flapping its sleek wings, remembering that she had some nips and scratches to repay.

"Too many years have divided us!" Verdandi said, resting her head upon the Captain's armored chest. "Why did you not return sooner?"

The man looked down upon the dark tresses of her

hair, which streamed like fine smoke in the breeze, but he appeared troubled and did not reach out to hold her.

Even through his armor, Verdandi could feel him tense, and she drew away in confusion.

"What is wrong?" she murmured, glancing at her hands to ensure they were still young and beautiful.

"I . . . I can't," Woden stammered.

At once the raven fluttered down to land upon his cloaked shoulder and bowed his head to the striking woman.

"Hail, Princess," he rasped. "My Master knew thou wouldst not break thy vow. Behold, my Lord, is she not as fair as ever?"

The Captain could only stare at her with a dazed expression upon his noble face, and Verdandi's fine brows twitched with uncertainty.

"Do you still blame me for Urdr's actions?" she entreated. "When Thought came to me, I was led to believe . . ."

"Verily!" the raven interrupted with a coarse squawk. "Thou must forgive my Master's tangled tongue, Princess. He is smitten by thy loveliness. That is all."

"Is this true, Woden?" she asked. "Have you remembered at last the promises we made upon this very hill?"

The man opened his mouth to answer, and Thought shook his wings, scraping his feathers across the Captain's neck as a gentle but intimidating reminder.

"I could never forget them," Woden uttered.

"How I have cursed Urdr for making me ride with

her to Nirinel," she said, her voice racked with regret. "I would have stayed by your side in the battle, you know that. We ought to have died together on that field of slaughter, yet even that was denied me. If you had not listened to my sister, we could have both found peace long ago."

"I . . . I am sorry."

"When I found and cut your tortured body from the Ash, I knew I had lost you. What happened afterward was not of my doing. From that moment you were the rightful one—it is you who should have been the Master of Destiny. The war was never of my making."

Swiveling his beady eyes at the Captain, Thought coughed hastily. "Why dwell upon such days of woe?" he crowed. "'Tis the present thou must give heed to."

The woman smiled in agreement. "As ever your messenger displays his wisdom," she said. "Let us bury what is behind us."

"I would like that," Woden told her.

"Let it be as though the intervening ages never were. Titles and rank meant nothing here. In this special place we are just two ordinary people, and the customs and edicts of the court are far, far away."

Having sat down upon the grass, Edie groaned as Verdandi embraced him once more, but her silvery blue eyes were more interested in the antics of the raven. Thought appeared to be continually prompting the Captain, either with a muttered whisper from the corner of his beak or by a surreptitious dig with his claws.

To Edie's shrewd scrutiny it didn't seem as though

Woden relished Verdandi's attentions one tiny bit. If anything, he looked anxious and afraid.

"Something is the matter," Verdandi said, as she too observed Thought's continual goading.

Woden glanced at the raven and let out a guilt-ridden sigh.

"I cannot do this," he declared, unable to meet her gaze and staring shamefully at the ground. "Listen, I must tell you the truth . . ."

"The truth!" Thought hastily interjected. "Wouldst thou burden this maiden's heart with such grave tidings?"

Verdandi stared at the Captain anxiously. "What news does Thought speak of?" she asked in a wavering voice. "Tell me, my love."

"Princess," the bird cawed, "permit me to speak for my Master. Thou knowest full well the tally of the ages that have passed since last thee met. Bitter it may have been for the three sisters, yet for Him the trial of enduring was too great."

"Woden!" she cried. "Your messenger's words frighten me!"

The Captain shook his head in dejection.

"My Master did not want to speak of it!" Thought blustered. "To glimpse you once more was all He craved afore the end, yet too well doth thou know Him. Witness how swiftly the deceit was uncovered."

"End?" Verdandi repeated. "Now you talk in riddles."

"Nay," the raven muttered. "An end is indeed nigh for thy Captain and my Lord. Know this, Princess, the Gallows God is soon to die."

The woman stepped back, aghast, and stared at the man in disbelief.

Chewing a blade of grass as she sat cross-legged on the ground, Edie was certain that Thought was not telling the complete truth. She didn't trust him at all and doubted everything that came out of his ugly black beak.

"The carrion bird lies," Verdandi breathed. "You are hale, Woden. The power within you, the same spark that burns in both of us, cannot be extinguished. For such as we there can be no death."

"Assuredly to thine eyes my Master appears strong and as permanent as the stones," Thought said with a great show of sadness. "But 'tis only an artful guise, a phantom reminder of what was. I am certain thou canst comprehend such a connivance, Lady. Yet 'neath this vision dodders an old and ailing sack of bones. Of the enduring life bestowed upon him by Yggdrasill, little remains."

"Is it true?" she whispered.

Woden frowned as though struggling to answer, and Thought's eyes glinted warningly at him.

"It is," the man finally said.

Verdandi clutched his hands and pressed them to her cheek. "Then we can never be together," she wept. "This will be our very last meeting."

"Perhaps," the raven said archly, "and yet perhaps not. There might yet be a chance."

The woman looked at him bewildered. "What chance?"

Thought moved from side to side, and a cunning gleam shone in his eyes as he answered.

"One slender hope doth my Master and His loyal servant foster. He can indeed be saved, yet by one rare and precious thing and that alone."

"Tell me."

The bird jerked his head and pointed across the marsh-filled valley with his beak.

"I speak of that which was brought thither from over the sundering waters and lies now upon the breast of a hermit, long dead below yonder ground.

"From a desert land he came. In former times he was a merchant, yet when he settled here, a missionary had he become and one great device did he have in his keeping. A golden prize imbued with such power it couldst lift the shadow that doth threaten thy Captain. If thou canst fetch the gilded treasure of Joseph, then naught wouldst e'er come 'twixt the pair of thee."

Verdandi spun around to scan the flat swamp at the foot of the Tor, and Edie was disturbed to see a frightening resolve ingrained on her face.

"Where is this grave?" the woman asked. "I would plunder a thousand tombs to save him."

A low cackling grated in Thought's throat. "Only thou canst find it. Only one who has drunk of blessed water may open the earth and take this hallowed, costly device from the hermit's interment."

The woman turned back to her Captain and kissed him tenderly.

"Verdandi shall fetch this thing for you, my love," she promised. "Rest here and save your strength. Soon we will be united forever."

"Wait," Woden blurted.

At that, Thought gave an agitated cry and dragged his claws through the midnight fur of the sable cloak.

"Master," he warned, "do not detain my lady. The grains of thy life are near run out. Forget not the glorious outcome once this most trifling of deeds is accomplished. Think long on that and consider well thy next words."

Woden heard the unmistakable edge in the raven's voice and knew what was meant.

Turning to Verdandi, he smiled weakly. "Go, then. Do as Thought suggests, bring it to me."

Lifting her cane, Verdandi faced the wide, reed-crowded marsh, and in a desperate, forceful voice she cried, "Reveal to me, Verdandi of the royal house of Askar, show unto her the resting place of he who came from over the seas."

Edie rose to her feet, glancing suspiciously at Woden and the raven, then gazed out at the sprawling, overgrown bogs and brackish pools in which the sunlight glittered and danced.

"Yield your secret," Verdandi asserted. "The might of Doom and Destiny commands it."

As soon as the words were out of her mouth, a tremendous silence descended across the valley. The warm air became still and charged with expectation.

In the midst of the treacherous tracts of mud, where islands of firmer terrain encroached into the dun realm of pond and ditch, Edie saw, the ground was beginning to move.

Slowly at first, the earth bulged and heaved, causing every plant to tremble and quiver, until suddenly a piece of the land fell away. Down into a gaping hole it dropped, and from the darkness below there shot a brilliant silver-green flame.

Into the sky the dazzling beacon soared, and the raven shrieked with triumph.

"The entrance!" he screeched. "Behold, it is uncovered! Go, my lady, save my Master. Bring to Him that which wilt heal His hurt."

With a last look at her Captain, Verdandi began to hurry down the Tor.

"Wait!" Edie yelled, scrambling after her. "You ain't leavin' me behind!"

Down the steep slopes they hastened, with Edie skidding and sliding over the grass, trying her best to keep up with Verdandi, who ran as swift as a deer fleeing from the hunt.

Snagging even more holes in her woolen stockings as she bounced and tumbled in Verdandi's wake, the child followed her into the shade of the apple trees that fringed the lower terraces of the majestic hill. It was a mad, haring race, dashing through the blossom-covered, leaf-dappled orchard, then out to where the safe ground gave way to sinking mud. Edie was glad to see that here the woman stopped, and she managed to catch up with her, only to puff and blow in the struggle to draw her breath.

"Take care, Edith," Verdandi warned, not waiting for the child to recover and tentatively planting her foot upon a patch of bog-beset weeds. "The marsh is perilous if you do not know the secret paths. Copy my steps."

Gulping the air down, Edie tucked the hair that had worked itself loose and flew in her eyes back under her pixie hat and did as the woman instructed.

Over the squelching, miry ground they went, as fast as the meandering routes allowed. But driven by the urgency of her task, Verdandi often forgot that the child was not able to leap across wide ditches as she could, and she was forced to return to direct her through less difficult ways.

Edie didn't like the marsh. Although she enjoyed trudging in the sticky black mud, she hated the clouds of gnats and mosquitoes that flew up to buzz about her face and zoom into her mouth and eyes. When the pinnacle of enchanted flame was almost reached and could be seen rearing above the tall grasses ahead, the girl was very much relieved. Halting, she blew her nose upon her sleeve as a gnat chose that moment to go exploring up her nostril.

"The entrance will not remain open for long," Verdandi said, her diaphanous robe now splashed with silt and her slippers caked in clay. "We must find this golden device as soon as we can."

At last the labyrinthine paths and spongy causeways came to an end, and the woman crossed over a quagmire-filled trench to a large island of solid ground.

"We are here," she cried when the child bounded over to join her. "Now, let us find the grave of this missionary."

Through the tall, obstructing reeds they crashed, stumbling into the clearing where the silver-green flame towered over them in a pillar of crackling, blazing light.

Shielding her eyes, Edie edged closer, intrigued to

discover that it radiated no heat. But just as she was about to put her hand experimentally into the heart of the leaping column, it gave a ferocious roar and boiled upward in a momentous fireball that exploded high above the marsh and dissipated to the farthest reaches of the clear blue sky.

"Quickly," Verdandi declared, staring at the deep fissure in the ground from which the beacon had blazed, "the way is open."

Edie rubbed her eyes, for the harsh glare had imprinted bright streaks upon her vision. But peering over the edge of the yawning hole, she could see that beneath the soil, a roughly fashioned staircase had been cut into the underlying rock and plunged steeply down into a tunnel of absolute darkness.

Casting a worried glance back to the Tor, Verdandi ran to the topmost step, and not wasting another moment, she began to descend.

Edie scampered after her, pausing only briefly as she left the warm sunshine behind to wonder about the raven's strange behavior and the peculiar, subdued mood of the tall warrior-captain.

But in front of her, Verdandi's white-clad figure was already vanishing into the shadowy gloom, and so the girl put her doubts aside, and the stone walls of the narrow passage rose above her head as she followed.

Into the earth they pressed, the daylight rapidly fading to a spectral dusk that was barely enough to illuminate the steps beneath their feet. Edie had to fumble against the rocky wall for balance as she cautiously proceeded.

Deeper the tunnel delved, the still air becoming

musty and suffocating. Then the girl heard Verdandi sigh with relief.

"The steps are ended," echoed the woman's voice, "but here another passage begins. I cannot tell how far it stretches."

Eager to join her, Edie lost her footing, and the child slid down the remaining stairs, landing at Verdandi's muddy feet with a bump.

"Edith!" the woman cried, stooping to help her. "Are you injured?"

Edie snorted, despising the fuss, and picked herself up. "Only a few more bruises. Take more'n that to . . ."

Her high, fearless voice was suddenly lost as the surrounding rock trembled and a loud rumbling resounded throughout the tunnel. Down the stairs cascaded a torrent of soil and stones, and Verdandi hauled the child to one side as the avalanche thundered into the passage.

"No!" the woman cried. "Not yet."

The pale, shadowy light failed completely as, up above, the two sides of the fissure moved together and the passage was engulfed in darkness.

Her back pressed against the quivering rock, Edie heard Verdandi shriek in the consuming night, but when she reached out to hold her the strong, forceful voice dwindled and cracked and the hands she clutched withered in her grasp.

"What is it?" the girl cried. "What's happened?"

Invisible in the strangling blackness, the woman sobbed then answered in a dry, weary voice, "We're sealed in and time has rushed by above. Oh, Edith, I am old once more—I am Veronica."

Unable to see her, Edie ran her fingers over the weeping woman's form and found that it was shrunken and bowed, the face corrugated with age.

"We got to get out," she said.

"Not yet," Miss Veronica told her, tapping her cane along the wall and shambling forward. "I must save the Captain. Please, help me find the hermit's grave, Edith. Veronica needs you."

And so, into the tunnel that lay at the foot of the now buried staircase the two of them blindly blundered, and the darkness claimed them.

* * *

Above the ground, in Glastonbury, the ages blurred and the centuries careered by as the marshes faded and the stones of the magnificent abbey rose, only to crumble into a familiar ruin as time drew ever closer to the present.

The Tor alone remained steadfast in the madness that whirled about it, and the figure of Woden stared at the astounding spectacle in wonder.

Then, as the shadows of evening closed over the great hill once more and the tower of Saint Michael loomed behind him, Verdandi's Captain turned to the raven upon his shoulder and the false, deluding image that had arrayed him melted into the gloom.

Silently the sable cloak shredded in the breeze, and the silver helm, sword, and chain mail evaporated, becoming skeins of pale mist that were snatched into the night. Like a disturbed reflection in rippling water, the warrior's face shimmered, the long flaxen hair turned dark and unkempt, and the forked beard was straggly again.

Staggered by the visions he had just experienced, the Reverend Peter Galloway shook his head and drew a hand over his face.

"Incredible," he finally managed to utter. "Amazing!"

Thought looked at him sternly. "Thy foolish tongue near spoiled our Lord's intricate design," he cawed with scorn. "Thou didst play thy part most poorly."

Peter turned and stared down into the valley, where streetlights now shone and vehicles barged along the Shepton Mallet road.

"I'm sorry," he apologized. "But I still don't understand why we had to lie. Who were that young woman and the strange little girl? Why won't you explain properly?"

The raven cackled. "Thou art here to fulfill our Lord's wishes, not query or gainsay them. Verdandi hath been chosen to bring this glorious prize unto us. That is all thou needeth to know."

"But the deceit can't be right. Already I've stolen a car, and now I've been part of a cruel fraud. You made her think the person she loved was dying! Surely this isn't how it should be?"

A sly smirk appeared on Thought's ugly face.

"What matters a score of falsehoods if the goal is won?" he muttered. "Think only of His suffering. If thou doth wish to aid Him further, then hearts must be broken and tongues must betray. Better to fix thy mind solely upon the outcome of this most noble of quests. He shalt be returned, the world will believe in Him again. The proof we seek must be found."

"You're saying that the end justifies the means," the vicar said wretchedly. "I can't accept that."

"'Tis folly to believe otherwise."

Peter's eyes closed, and he tried to unravel the confusion in his soul.

"But that pretty young woman," he continued. "If she is the only one who can get us the holy treasure, then why couldn't we simply tell her the truth?"

The raven's hunched shoulders shuddered as though he was laughing silently. Then, fixing the vicar with his beady stare, he croaked, "Verdandi and the whelp art in no danger. Turn thy thoughts and concern to thine own future. This night all thy prayers shalt be granted. Prepare thyself for new marvels."

Peter wasn't sure that he could, but he steeled himself for whatever trials and tests still lay ahead for him and nodded slowly.

"Then let us begone," Thought crowed, beating his wings and rising into the air. "The time of the gathering is upon us. Dost thou not sense it? The Twelve are waking!"

CHAPTER 20

THE CRIMSON WEFT

"Be safer to go back to Tor Hill by way of the road," Tommy said when he, Neil, and Quoth left the derelict barn. "Them fields is too wide an' open with nothin' to hide us if'n we need it."

Keeping the looming, shadowy bulk of the Tor upon their right, the tramp led them around the dark expanse of plowed earth, tottering warily along.

"Safe for now," he mumbled to himself, patting his satchel. "Just 'nuff time for Tommy to get to the tower."

"That's not where you're thinking of sleeping tonight, is it?" the boy asked. "You'll freeze."

Raising a large, red-knuckled hand, Tommy pointed across the murky gulf to where the yellow streetlights stretched from the main part of town to climb the lower rise of Wearyall Hill.

"Either that or Tommy sleeps next to the Holy Thorn," he said. "Them nasties dursn't touch him there, but that'd be even worse cold, what with no walls nor no stone bench fer Tommy to lie on."

"You don't think you'd be better off in a shelter or somewhere?"

The tramp pulled a disgruntled expression and aired his tongue as if he had tasted something unpleasant. "Not on no one's Nelly," he mumbled. "Tried to get Tommy put away lots of times they did, but he won't have it. 'Sides, them places ain't no use in keeping the bird women out."

"Bird women?"

Tommy's pale eyes turned on Neil, and the tramp put a finger to his lips. "Hush now," he urged. "Not so loud. It's dangerous to tempt fate. You should know that, boy."

The country lane they had taken now joined the main road, and the dazzling headlights of the oncoming traffic made Quoth shake his head and keep his one eye half-closed.

"We'll just get on along Coursing Batch," Tommy told them, "then us can go up the Wellhouse Lane way."

The old man hurried along. Soon he would be climbing the Tor to claim the sanctuary of Saint Michael's tower, and with his collection of angels to protect him, he was sure to come through the night unscathed.

Beaming his toothless smile, he suddenly noticed a single light traveling shakily down the road, and he immediately recognized the plump figure that sat behind it.

"How do!" he shouted. "You hurry on home, girlie!"

Her eyes fixed upon the rear lights of the car in front, Lauren Humphries looked up sharply at the sound of the tramp's voice.

Since leaving The Glastonbury Experience, the girl had not known what she would do when she returned home, but now a wild idea came to her and she swiftly applied the brakes of her bicycle.

"Tommy!" she cried, putting one foot on the sidewalk. "You were right. There is something weird going on here."

Caught in the beam of her bicycle lamp, the tramp halted when he saw the distress written on the girl's face.

"Now then," he muttered gently, "what's got you so worked up?"

It was then that Lauren noticed Neil, and remembering how the local boys had bullied the old man the other day, she looked at him suspiciously—although she was astonished and even a little afraid to see a large, one-eyed raven perched upon his shoulder.

"Don't you be spooked by this 'ere lad now," the tramp reassured her. "He be Tommy's newest pal."

Neil nodded politely at the girl, but he was anxious to continue to the Tor, and the narrow sidewalk made it impossible to squeeze past Tommy's large frame.

Quoth, however, was willing to be more communicative and gave a hearty chirp while viewing the girl and her wheeled contraption with much curiosity.

"Hail and well met!" he chattered. "O fine, dumpy damsel! Fie, 'tis surely false when 'tis said that a pretty pig doth make an ugly old sow. Thou hast a most comely face."

Lauren stared at the bird in shock, and Neil hastily wrapped his fingers over Quoth's jabbering, offensive beak.

"Sorry about that," he quickly interjected. "He's not right in the head."

"Perhaps you should teach him a better repertoire," the girl suggested coldly before turning back to Tommy.

"Don't you mind that overgrowed, baldy sparrow," the tramp told her. "He's good as gold, really."

"Forget the bird!" Lauren said in a frantic rush of words. "I have to talk to someone about what's happening before I explode. At first I thought it was just my imagination. But I know now that it's real and horrible, and my stepmother's caught up in it."

Lifting the peak of his cap, Tommy sucked his gums, and his white, whiskery brows formed a deep frown.

"Always hoity-toity, that 'un," he muttered. "But she don't deserve none of what's in store. Real sorry, Tommy is, but there's nothin' no one can do if'n she's been got. There ain't no use you goin' back home neither. Safer to stick your head in the mouth of a lion whose belly's rumbling. You best come with us."

Lauren shook her head. "It's not too late!" she protested. "I know what's causing it all—it's the crow dolls! I don't understand how, but they're responsible! You've got to help me, Tommy."

"Help you do what?" he spluttered. "Tommy don't know squat about dollies, nor want to neither. He's got to get up that hill double quick."

"But Dad won't be back yet, and there's no one

else who'll believe me!" Lauren pleaded. "If we can just get home before my stepmother goes to bed, then I can throw the foul thing onto the fire and she'll be all right. Please come with me, Tommy. I don't want to go on my own."

The old man gazed at her forlornly. The girl was shivering with emotion and fear, so, casting a sorrowful look at the dark shape of the Tor, he assented.

"Tommy'll go with you," he agreed. "But if'n we're too late, then he ain't stoppin', even if he does have his angels to guard him."

"Thank you!" Lauren cried.

Brushing her gratitude shyly aside, the tramp turned to Neil. "Tommy can't come with you now, lad," he said. "But you know the way from here. Just keep on down this road and cut into Wellhouse Lane."

Neil was secretly relieved that the tramp was heading off with the girl. He was desperate to meet up with Aidan again. So far he had failed to do anything Miss Ursula had requested, and the consequences of not finding Edie or Miss Veronica didn't bear thinking about.

Sitting close to his ear, however, Quoth had grown still and silent. Lauren's words concerning the crow dolls had triggered some vague memory deep in his decayed brain, and a horrendous sense of foreboding flooded over him.

"Hold!" he squawked suddenly. "Avast! Belay! Desist! Master Neil, Master Neil!"

The boy grimaced as the raven's shrieking spiked through his eardrum.

"What is it?" he demanded impatiently.

"Go with these goodly folk!" Quoth instructed. "The plight of yon portly maid doth concern us most highly."

"But what about the others?"

The raven's eye glinted and in a harsh, woeful voice he replied, "Put thy trust in mine counsel. A specter of the past is rising, and mine heart forewarns that we art all in peril. Dark pictures churneth in this addled pate, and dread, riddling words of ill omen doth speak unto me from mine former life."

Hearing Quoth's earnest, fearful speech, Neil glanced at Tommy and Lauren then said simply, "We're coming with you."

*   *   *

A short while later they were all walking up the driveway to the Humphrieses' bed and breakfast. Sheila's car was parked at the side of the house, and a wedge of cheering yellow light streamed across its hood from the kitchen window.

"Well, she's home," Lauren commented, leaning her bicycle against the wall.

"Tommy can see that," the tramp whispered, breathing upon the vehicle's rear window before rubbing it with his elbow.

Lauren laced her fingers together nervously as she moved toward the kitchen door. "Perhaps you ought to stay out here while I check what's going on," she suggested. "If she hasn't gone to bed then I could run upstairs and swipe the creepy thing without her knowing."

"I thought you wanted us to come in with you?" Neil objected.

"I do, but you don't know what she's like. She can be a real pain sometimes, and I don't want to upset her unless I have to."

The tramp nodded sagely. "Arr," he agreed. "Don't like Tommy's sort, that daft woman don't. Every time he done sees her, she crosses the road to get out of Tommy's way. Ha! Tommy sometimes follows her just for fun!"

"She sounds awful," Neil muttered.

"You don't have to live with her," the girl replied.

Standing on the step, Lauren pushed open the door and cautiously peeped into the kitchen.

"Hello?" she called. "You in here?"

Waiting by the car, Neil and Tommy heard no response, and Quoth craned his neck forward to catch the scents that flowed from the brightly lit room.

"Zoodikers!" he croaked under his breath. "This place doth possess an evil air."

The kitchen was empty, but on the table where Sheila had left them were five large shopping bags still full of groceries. With mounting unease, the girl saw that not even the frozen food had been unpacked and put away.

Unnerved, she quickly ran to the living room, but with the exception of the kitchen, the rest of the ground floor was in darkness.

Returning to the back door, she called the others inside and glanced uncertainly up the stairs.

"She must have gone to bed already," she said. "I'll go see if she's asleep."

"Don't you do anythin' crazy now," Tommy cautioned. "You put your ear to the door first and see if it's snoring or screeching you can hear."

Neil stared at him, but Lauren obviously knew what he meant.

"I'd already thought of that," she told him.

Switching on the landing light, Lauren ascended the stairs.

In the kitchen, Tommy pulled the hat from his head and wrung it in his hands. Quoth shuddered upon Neil's shoulder and roved his eye around the room, murmuring apprehensively to himself.

When she reached the landing, Lauren crouched on the carpet and breathed a sigh of relief, for a gentle, rosy glow was shining beneath the door. If the bedside lamp was turned on, that could only be a hopeful sign—her stepmother might still be awake.

With her heart in her mouth, the girl crept closer. Then, brushing her flame-colored hair out of the way, she placed her hands on the door frame and pressed her exposed ear against the stripped pine.

For what seemed like ages she waited, straining for the slightest sound, until at last, she heard Sheila's weary voice groan miserably.

Lauren glanced down the stairs at the others and gave a cautiously optimistic sign, then pointed to the door handle to tell them she was going in.

Lifting his satchel, the tramp held it up toward her encouragingly and muttered, "Tommy's lovely angels are watching over you, lass."

"Sheila," Lauren whispered, tapping lightly on the wood, "are you all right?"

Gingerly she turned the handle and pushed the door open.

Down in the kitchen, all of Quoth's ragged feathers stood on end, and the raven pulled a pained, horrified expression.

"'Tis here," he choked, urgently tugging on the collar of Neil's shirt to get his attention. "The stink of death this chicklet didst fear in the hovel. That dread is on me once more! Those terrors I didst sense amidst the straw, one of their number hath been here, verily—'tis here now!"

Neil and the tramp stared at him then looked sharply up the stairs.

"Wait, girlie!" Tommy hissed. "Come you back down!"

But it was too late. Lauren had already entered the bedroom.

* * *

Lying on top of the covers and still fully dressed, the girl's stepmother stirred feebly when Lauren approached.

Going to the grocery store had been too much for the woman. On her return she had almost collapsed in the kitchen and had only managed to struggle upstairs by a supreme effort of her failing will. She felt as though her life was ebbing away, seeping from her limbs to leave only a barren, vacant void to be influenced and controlled.

Even with the warm pink glow of the lamp falling on her features, Sheila's skin appeared ashen and clammy. Her eyelids fluttered, and her dilated pupils slid across to gaze up at the anxious girl.

"L . . . Lorrie . . ." she whimpered. "I . . . feel . . ."

Lauren laid a hand upon the woman's sweat-streaming forehead. It was hot and fevered.

"You'll be all right, Sheila," she said, trying to sound calm. "Everything'll be fine. Just concentrate on getting well."

Her stepmother's eyes rolled upward, leaving a hideous sliver of white showing, and the girl looked away to glare at the object that she knew she had to destroy.

Hanging from the bedpost above Sheila's head, the effigy of the crow woman appeared just as Lauren had last seen it—a primitive cloth figure with beads for eyes and twigs for feet and fingers.

As the crow doll dangled there inert and dormant, it seemed ridiculous to believe it wielded power over her stepmother, but after talking to Miss Pettigrew in the craft shop, Lauren knew that her instinctive dislike of the sinister image was justified.

Warily the girl glanced at the ailing figure upon the bed. Sheila had fallen back into a swoon and was rambling incoherently in a hoarse whisper. So, taking this chance and curbing her natural revulsion, Lauren reached out to steal the vile thing.

As soon as the girl's fingers closed about the fabric of the small checked dress, Sheila's eyes snapped open.

"Stop!" she yelled in a high-pitched, frantic shriek. "What are you doing?"

"I'm taking the doll away," came the swift reply. "Can't you see? That's what's making you ill!"

Sheila's large, dark eyes stared at her in horror. "No!" she cried. "Lorrie—don't! You mustn't! Give it back. Give it to me!"

Lauren shook her head and edged toward the door as the woman let out a piteous, mewling cry.

"I have to have it!" she wailed. "I will have it!"

Without warning, Sheila flung herself from the bed and lunged at her stepdaughter, knocking her off balance.

Lashing out with more strength than the girl could have imagined possible, Sheila snatched the crow doll from her grasp and leaped back across the room to dive under the bed, where she gripped the effigy fiercely and glared out like a cornered wild animal.

"Sheila!" Lauren gasped in dismay. "What are you doing?"

"Get out!" the woman sobbed from beneath the bed. "Leave me. Leave us."

"I can't."

Sheila's labored, fitful breathing was her only answer, and so, not knowing what else to do, Lauren opened the door.

"I'll be back in a moment with help," she said.

"Hlökk," came a despairing hiss. "The crimson weft must be woven."

Hearing those words, Lauren hurried out onto the landing, closed the door after her, and ran down the stairs to where Tommy and Neil were waiting.

"It's no use!" she told them. "I tried to take it, but she went berserk and snatched it back."

"She'm still your stepmother then?" the tramp ventured.

Lauren nodded vigorously. "Yes, but I don't know for how much longer. You have to help me take the doll from her before it's too late."

"Halt, I say unto thee!" Quoth cried abruptly.

The girl looked around. The raven was no longer standing upon Neil's shoulder, for the boy had put him down on the table at his own request, and he had been nosing around in the shopping bags.

"Get that filthy thing off there!" she demanded.

Neil ignored her. "What is it?" he asked the straggly bird.

Quoth paced forward to the table's edge, his beak covered in the telltale crumbs of the loaf he had been nibbling, but his face was grave, and when he had finished chewing, he looked long and hard at the girl.

"Pray tell," he began solemnly, "didst the dame have aught to say?"

Lauren frowned at the creature in disbelief. "It's really talking!" she exclaimed. "Not like a parrot at all. How on earth—?"

"Well, answer him then," Neil told her.

"There was something," the girl said. "When I left her she was babbling but not making any sort of sense. Something about a crimson weave."

Quoth swallowed fearfully, and his wedged tail drooped as his beak opened to emit a forlorn whine.

"A crimson weft," he corrected with dread.

"How did you know that?"

Leaning upon the table, Neil peered at the raven quizzically.

"You're remembering something, aren't you?" he marveled. "Tell us, please."

Quoth turned to him, his one eye nearly bulging from his head.

"Go not up yonder deadly stair," he rasped, mortified. "She who waits above is beyond all help and hope. The chambers of this wretch's mind are locked no longer and canst recall the nature of the evil that wakes in this land. Alas for Quoth, would that he could not!"

"You know what these bird women are?" Tommy asked.

The raven hung his head as he sorted through the disordered jumble of released memories now crowding his thoughts.

"In the distant days when this hapless booby didst serve another," he began softly, "after the Ash had fallen and the ogres of frost were abashed and didst retreat away, Quoth's Lord had dominion over all things. Yet over destiny His power was as naught, for the three sisters hadst yoked that burden unto themselves. So His resenting festered, and He became wrath with them."

"Look," Lauren butted in, "we have to get that doll away from my stepmother!"

Tommy put his hand upon her shoulder as she moved toward the stairs. "No, girlie," he said gently. "Hear the little fella out."

"A god He was," Quoth continued darkly, "yet subject to the Spinners in the Wood, same as any base beast or lowly worm. Thus, in his envy and rage, He misused His wisdom to perform a heinous deed and so didst sink into madness and folly.

"From the dread night the first master of Quoth

did invoke spirits of death and despair, and unto them He sacrificed maidens, in which they made their earthly abodes."

"Oh, no," Lauren gasped.

"Twelve such terrors there were, fiends of savagery and carnage, and into them He poured His might and strength. To mock the Fates they didst choose those who went to die in battle, and all feared and reviled their hated name."

Quoth paused and looked at each of the three people in turn.

"Valkyrie," he cawed hollowly.

Tommy fidgeted with the buckles of his satchel and glanced nervously at the windows, where the darkness seemed to press and push against the glass.

"And these things are here now?" Neil asked.

The raven bowed. "To overthrow the Nornir they were created long ages since. A loom of their own devising didst they fashion in their vileness. Spears were its frame and entrails of the slaughtered did form the warp, weighted below by hacked, hewed heads. An arrow was the shuttle, carrying a weft of crimson, and from this devilish web a river of gore didst flow.

"Against the circling mists they rampaged, yet the enchantment of the Fates could not be breached and the host of Woden wast scattered or slain. Now 'twouldst seem the Twelve are rising once more. He hath summoned them a second time. The ending battle draweth near, Master Neil."

Lauren pulled away from the tramp's restraining hand. "I've got to stop it!" she cried. "I can't let that thing take her over again."

"Too late!" Quoth rapped sharply. "Thy mother hath already been claimed by a fell spirit. When the Twelve unite there canst be no road back."

"But the last doll was only sold today!" the girl insisted. "There's still a chance."

Suddenly, from her parents' bedroom, there came a horrific, terrified scream, and Lauren bolted to the steps in despair.

"It's got her!" she yelled. "We've got to save her!"

Upon the table Quoth shook his wings in fright and leaped up and down, squawking, "Hold hard! 'Tis too late. Stop the dumpy one!"

Both Neil and Tommy charged after the girl to drag her back to the kitchen, while, from the second floor, Sheila's bloodcurdling howls were joined by frenzied bangs and crashes as the furniture was hurled aside.

"Let me go!" Lauren bawled, battling to tear herself free. "It's attacking her!"

"Ain't nothin' we can do," Tommy warbled, cowed by the awful shrieks and clatterings above.

Scampering from one side of the table to the other, Quoth squealed in fear, but his bleating voice was drowned by the woman's resounding screams.

"The midnight spirit possesseth her," he jabbered. "Thou art the only human maid here now, and on the morrow she wilt be enslaved for years unending, with no respite. When the Twelve art together the charm is complete."

"No!" Lauren wept, her flailing arms sagging as she ceased her struggles and sank to her knees.

"The Valkyrie draweth its violent breath only to slay and berserk," the bird added. "If it doth not fly from here, it shall scent us out and hunt our blood."

Everyone turned to the stairway. Sheila's voice was changing. The agonized howls were now raucous screeches—grating, gutteral, and totally inhuman.

"That's it!" the old man whispered in recognition. "That's the racket Tommy heard last night. That's what was in his barn. Oh, Lord, send us angels. Save us!"

Neil shivered and his skin crawled. The creature's voice was hideous. He slowly backed away from the stairs, cursing himself for ever yearning to be involved with the Websters' business again.

At that moment there came the noise of splintering glass, followed by a deranged, riotous battering that vibrated and hammered throughout the entire house.

"What's it doing?" Neil muttered. "Why doesn't it just fly out the window?"

Still kneeling on the floor, Lauren gasped in alarm. "Oh, no," she said, rising shakily and gripping Tommy's sleeve. "The shutters. I nailed them closed. That monster's trapped up there!"

"No, it ain't," the tramp whispered, his voice trembling. "There be another way out."

Neil stared up at the bedroom door. "Lock it!" he cried.

"There's no key!" Lauren answered. "Wait, listen. The noise, it's stopping."

Upstairs the insane pounding clamor ceased, but the tense silence that followed was almost worse.

"What's happening?" Neil murmured, turning to look at Quoth.

"Death approacheth," the raven cawed.

Behind the bedroom door a muffled scrabbling began, and the people in the kitchen looked at one another in dismay as they realized the creature was clawing at the handle.

"Fie!" Quoth barked. "Flee! Retreat! Escape! The Valkyrie is upon us!"

All at once the clumsy raking noises came to an end, then everyone heard the ominous squeak of hinges as the door slowly opened.

Tommy stumbled backward, blundering into the counter, while Lauren held her breath and waited, too afraid to move. By the table Neil glanced around for something to use as a weapon, and chittering like a captured rabbit, the raven scurried inside a shopping bag to hide himself among the bread and cookies.

Upon the landing an immense dark shape appeared.

As it threw back its ghastly head, a high, prolonged, piercing screech blasted from the nightmare's gullet.

Downstairs, everyone clapped their hands to their ears as the horrendously shrill note ripped through their nerves. Then, with a tremendous, shattering roar, the windows split and cracked. Glasses shattered on the shelves, bottles smashed, jelly jars fractured, and up in their sockets, the lightbulbs exploded.

Darkness engulfed the bed and breakfast. Neil heard Tommy sobbing wretchedly, and Lauren cried out, while in the plastic shopping bag Quoth was quailing.

And the Valkyrie descended.

CHAPTER 21

HLÖKK

Down the stairs it came, an apparition of feather, claw, and beak.

Paralyzed with fear, the three figures swamped in the gloom could only gape at the evil spectacle, hearing its great barbed quills scrape against the walls, bite through the patterned paper, and scratch into the plaster beneath.

Large and cruel were the hooked talons that stole down the creaking steps, snagging and ripping rents in the carpet. From powerful splayed toes covered in scaled, leathery skin they stabbed, great curved blades capable of tearing metal and crunching through bone.

Its massive wings furled in order to squeeze its hulking bulk down the narrow stairs, the Valkyrie was a malignant vision of despair and hopelessness.

As the creature towered above the people huddled in the kitchen, its two round jet black eyes penetrated the shadows and fixed upon the petrified forms.

Her heart beating wildly, Lauren could not wrench her stricken gaze from the deformed abhorrence as it stalked ever closer. Tears streamed down her cheeks as the rancorous, repulsive travesty of a face emerged from the deeper murk that eclipsed the landing.

Framed by a mane of spiked, ragged feathers, like the black petals of some sickly, poisonous flower, the mordant, misshapen head was a nauseating fusion of human features combined with those of a monstrous raven.

Gray, scab-ridden flesh crusted the grotesque, pitiless countenance, which was dominated by a vicious, spearing beak that slowly opened and closed, as though savoring the fear that flowed up to greet it.

Crowned by a knotted profusion of quill and bristling hair tangled with twigs and thorns, the abomination reached the lower steps, and a bass, discordant rattle, like the warning hiss of a cobra before it strikes, issued from the venomous gullet.

Pressed against the counter, Tommy threw his hands before his face and slid to the floor, cringing behind his satchel and gibbering for divine protection.

"Gabriel, Uriel, Michael, help us. Oh, sweet heaven, protect Tommy and his pals. Only angels can save 'em now."

But all he heard in answer was a repugnant, chilling shriek as the horrible monstrosity eyed its victims greedily.

Quoth's bald head reared from the shopping bag, his one eye goggling in terror at the foulness that loomed beyond the table. Sickened and scared, he saw the repellent, loathsome face move with deliberate slowness from the tramp on the floor, over to the girl, and finally to Neil.

"Hlökk!" the raven squealed. "Shrieker is here! We art already slain!"

Backed against the table, Neil stared at the savage, blood-craving horror, frozen with fear. Not since he had first witnessed Belial rise above the bomb site had he known such dread, but then the Wyrd Museum had been close by with the blessed water of its drinking fountain to help. This time he was trapped in a building in the middle of nowhere, with an enemy equal in ferocity and motivated only to slaughter and destroy.

The evil-brimming eyes flickered momentarily as they settled on him, and a low, menacing gargle began to sound in the dark, dry throat.

"Master Neil!" Quoth cried, tumbling out of the bag. "Beware! Beware!"

The bird's warning came too late, for in that instant the Valkyrie screeched, and the kitchen became wrapped in an even greater veil of shadow as the huge wings suddenly unfurled. With shrill, murderous shrieks gurgling from the ravening beak, the creature lunged straight for Neil's throat.

Before the boy could dodge aside, the fiend was upon him.

Sharp, clattering quills thrashed and beat upon his face, and cruel claws came ripping through the shadows to seize him by the arm and waist, smashing him violently to the ground.

Neil yelled in terror, but Hlökk pinned him down, sending the table and chairs flying across the room with a careless smack of its powerful wings. It pressed a curved talon over Neil's windpipe to crush and choke until the boy's voice became a strangled, retching gasp.

Against the cabinets the table crashed, its legs scraping a frightful note across the quarry tiles, and from its surface were flung the shopping bags and one wailing raven.

Shaking its vile head, the Valkyrie crowed in triumph. Then, with sadistic malice, it lowered its razoring beak to rip the life out of its wriggling prey.

As the distorted, harrowing face descended, Neil snapped his eyes shut and waited for the blow. Suddenly his attacker let out a furious screech, and he stared up to see Lauren gripping the great, hideous head in her hands, battling to drag it back.

The lethal beak snapped ferociously as the creature tried to twist itself free from the girl's desperate grasp.

Lauren cried out in pain and panic. The feathers were like razors; they sliced deep into her hands, and she knew she could not hold on much longer. Bucking and writhing before her, the apparition yammered and shrieked, bellowing a terrible outraged screech. But as the monster shifted and tried to throw her off, its deadly claw lifted from Neil's throat, and the boy squirmed out from under it.

Now Lauren was in peril. The Valkyrie tore its head away, and the girl was left clutching a handful of bared feathers.

Incensed, the unclean specter reeled about, stretching its wings out wide as it glared at her.

Bubbles of frothing spittle dripped from the enormous beak as the horror pounced. Lauren fled before its ravaging fury, and Hlökk thundered in pursuit.

The girl tried to run to the door, but her enemy was swift, and the way was barred by a fence of quill and feather.

In the darkness, Neil heard Lauren's piteous screams, and though his neck was bruised and the air wheezed in his throat, he snatched up one of the dining chairs. Lifting it above his head, he charged toward the horrendous mass of towering shadow.

Snarling, he brought it crashing down upon Hlökk's briar-crested skull, and the Valkyrie let out a deafening roar.

Still cowering against the counter, Tommy peeped out from behind his satchel only to see the terrible bird woman rear up, its bristling, thorn-tangled hair scratching on the ceiling.

In the gloom he could see Neil, still with the chair in his hands, preparing for another strike, but with a flash of the monstrous claws the seat was plucked from the boy's grasp and hurled out of the window.

The creature's shrieks were unbearable now, and Tommy felt as though his brain would burst.

Rigid with terror, all he could do was watch as the foul black shape knocked Lauren to the ground then lashed out at Neil.

Across the floor a much smaller patch of darkness scampered and hopped, wailing and yowling as it ran toward its master.

"The Valkyrie cannot be defeated!" Quoth squealed. "When host and doll art joined, all efforts art in vain. Alack and woe! Fie and damnation!"

With hideous, brutal force, a massive wing threw

Neil across the room, and he landed awkwardly on the floor, his skull striking one of the cabinets.

Dazed, he raised his head to see the monster lumber toward him, dragging a struggling Lauren behind it.

"The controlling doll!" Quoth howled, desperately flapping his wings but unable to take to the air. "'Tis thine only hope. If I wert thrice and thirty times as big . . ."

With a contemptuous flick of its vicious talons, Hlökk sent the irritating raven careering over the floor to sprawl tail upward in a puddle of jam and broken glass.

Groggily, Neil glanced up at the devilish, corpse-like face that now floated above him, but this time he was too stunned to challenge or contest it.

The suffocating blackness that lay beneath its wings came crushing over his face, smothering and choking as the terrible claws closed about his side and went ripping through his shirt.

Neil winced when the talon pierced his skin and a trickle of blood oozed out, but his fight was over now. The Valkyrie had both him and Lauren, and that was the end of them.

In another moment a dreadful scream resounded in the kitchen.

*   *   *

Picking himself out of the jam, Quoth wheeled around and saw a flurry of feathers thrashing in the darkness.

Still shrieking its nerve-shredding screech, Hlökk fell backward. Its grotesque head cracked against the quarry tiles, and in a frenzied chaos of flailing wings, its clawed feet tore everything in their raking path.

His head still resting against the cabinet, Neil blearily opened his eyes to see the toppled black shape seized by violent, convulsing spasms that racked its entire vile being. Uncontrollably the monster twitched and jerked, the shadowy awning of its wings battering the air as it tried unsuccessfully to right itself.

Neil groaned as the pain in his head started to play tricks on him, but then, becoming more alert, he propped himself up and leaned forward.

Hlökk was shrinking.

The giant, repulsive shape of the Valkyrie was dwindling. The great span of its mighty wings was already diminished, and the claws that scraped along the tiles were retreating back into the scaly flesh of the splayed toes.

Amazed and relieved, Neil suddenly heard Lauren's elated voice cry, "Tommy, you did it! You saved us!"

Standing just out of the yammering, withering creature's reach, the old tramp blinked at the sight before him and nodded dumbly. In his large hands he held the crow doll he had torn from the monster's neck, and he stared down at the now lifeless cloth effigy in disgust.

Pattering over the tiles, leaving sticky, strawberry footprints in his wake, Quoth hurried over to Neil.

"Art thou injured?" he asked.

"I think I'll live," Neil replied, grimacing when he

ran his fingers over the bloody but shallow wound in his side.

"Tommy's collection was what saved the day," the tramp muttered, patting his bag thankfully. "It's them what gave his braveness back. But he'll not touch this filth no more. Get gone, you dirty nasty!"

Unable to bear holding the crow doll any longer, he cast the cloth image across the kitchen, where it spun over the floor and was lost beneath one of the splintered cabinets.

Lauren gazed down at the melting darkness that had been the Valkyrie. Already it was human again, and she knelt beside the now motionless figure of her stepmother to see if she was alive.

Dressed in the torn, ragged fragments of her clothing, Sheila lay unconscious on the floor, and nothing the girl could do would wake her.

"I need light," she said. "There are matches and a few candles in the drawer over there. Could somebody get one?"

Clutching his side, Neil moved to the drawer and rummaged in the shadows until he found what he sought.

But in the heavy darkness beneath the broken cabinet where Tommy had thrown the crow doll, a faint glimmer of red light was already sparking to life once more.

On the sinister creation's calico apron, the thread that formed the embroidered letters of the evil spirit's name began to shine brightly as the indwelling, malignant force roused itself and the glass beads glittered with hatred.

With a slow, jerking movement, the doll turned its head to view its victims, and flipping itself over, it began to worm its way out of the dusty space.

Fumbling with the matches, Neil lit one of the candles and set it on one of the few remaining saucers, but before he could give it to Lauren, he heard Quoth's dismayed voice squawk out in alarm.

"Gadsbud!" the raven yelped.

From under the cabinet the crow doll had dragged and heaved itself, and even as they all turned to stare, it tottered to its twiggy feet and purposefully advanced toward them.

"Defend us, defend us!" the tramp wailed. "Tommy's braveness is gone again. He has to get himself to the tower. He has to go!"

Incapable of facing any more horror, the old man lurched for the door and scuttled outside.

"Tommy!" Lauren called after him. But it was no use. Clinging to his precious satchel, the tramp hastened over the gravel and was gone.

Watching the small crow doll approach from the shadows, with the fiery letters emblazoned across its apron, Quoth scratched the ground as an impetuous and brash desire raged within him. The bird bullishly lowered his head, only too pleased to have a foe more suited to his own size.

"Woebegotten spirit of evil design!" he growled, flexing his primaries and jutting out the lower part of his beak. "Prepareth thou to be unstuffed!"

Whooping at the top of his croaky voice, Quoth recklessly barged forward to butt the eerie mannequin in its soft stomach then stamp upon its foolish straw hat and unpick the raddling thread that held it together.

When the crow doll saw the raven charging toward it, the creature dodged nimbly aside and spun sharply around to catch Quoth on the back of the head with its stick fingers.

Quoth cried out in astonishment, for the blow was more forceful than he had anticipated. The effigy was possessed of a terrible strength that sent the hapless bird sailing, beak over claw, through the air, to land in a sorry, disheveled heap.

"The fool's bolt is soonest shot," he groaned, mourning for his bruised dignity.

Rotating upon its spindly feet, the doll whirled about to proceed on its way, back toward the unconscious woman it had claimed as its host.

Into the flickering circle of candlelight the animated cloth mannequin waddled, and to Lauren's distress, she saw that the twigs were already shooting from the checkered sleeves, snaking out to wrap about her stepmother's neck and knot within her hair.

"No, you don't!" Lauren yelled, diving across to snatch up the infernal creature just as it leaped at Sheila's head.

"This time you're definitely going into the fire!" the girl declared, gripping the wriggling object tightly in her hands. "Bring me that candle."

Neil came forward, but as he did so, the candle glow fell upon Sheila's face, and the boy beheld the woman for the first time.

"Quick!" Lauren snapped, and she turned her head to see what was keeping him. The boy was staring at

Sheila, utterly thunderstruck, although Lauren could not begin to guess why.

All Neil's senses withdrew from his surroundings, and the saucer shook in his wavering hand as he peered long and hard at the woman's pale, weary features.

"Mom," he whispered.

There on the floor, Lauren's stepmother, the human host of Shrieker, who only minutes before had tried to butcher them all, was Neil's own mother, Sheila Chapman.

Since she had abandoned her family over four months earlier, this was the first time the boy had seen her, and a raw, empty numbness consumed him. What should he feel? His mother had left them to live with a man she had met at evening classes. He recalled that day with surreal clarity. She had coldly lined him and Josh up to inform them that she was going, and that dreadful moment had, up to that point, been the worst of his young life.

Between then and now he had wished many times that she had taken him with her, but not any longer. He was now happy to have remained with his father.

Yet there she was, lying at the boy's feet, and Neil did not know what to do.

He could only gape in confusion, and his stupefied delay was all that Hlökk required.

Its stunted arms flapping and waving, the doll in Lauren's grasp gazed up at the curling mass of carrot-colored hair that trailed down the girl's shoulders, and the fabric of its face creased and puckered into a parody of a smile.

Having exposed the back of her head to the repository of Hlökk's unhallowed spirit, Lauren had placed herself in the same danger as her stepmother, for she was just as vulnerable a target as Sheila.

"What's the matter?" she asked Neil. "I have to burn this—"

Into her hair the twigs suddenly went winding, spiking into her scalp and stretching about her neck.

Not expecting the sudden onslaught, the girl was totally unprepared, and she screamed in panic as the growing branches lashed around her skull and the first black plume came rupturing from her forehead.

"No!" she screeched. "No!"

At once Neil snapped out of his bewilderment, but it was too late.

As soon as the crow doll had leaped onto Lauren's neck and tangled itself in her hair, the girl's flesh had turned gray and a festering crust of scabs and ulcers had crackled across her face.

Locked in torment, she doubled up with agony as her arms snapped and splintered, stretching and rearing back to form the skeletal frame of a huge pair of wings.

Throwing the candle down, Neil darted over and plunged his hands into the girl's hair where the crow doll had rooted itself, but nothing he could do would pry it loose.

"I can't do it!" he cried. "The thing won't budge! It just won't budge!"

Lauren's shrieks altered as her jaw split and cracked, the now papery skin flaking back as the first points of a lethally sharp beak pushed and speared forth.

"It's no good!" the boy sobbed, his wrists surrounded by a rising collar of quills and feathers. "The doll's welded to you! God knows what Tommy did before, but I can't do it!"

A harsh gurgling note crept into Lauren's voice as she howled, and Neil backed away in despair. There was nothing he could do. Lauren was changing into the Valkyrie before his eyes.

"Master Neil!" Quoth suddenly cried, reeling toward him. "Thou must flee whilst ye may. Go now, afore the portly maid is utterly consumed!"

"We can't just leave her!"

Quoth yanked at the boy's shoelaces. "She is gone!" he squealed. "An instant more and she shalt be feasting upon thee!"

Lauren was now completely unrecognizable. Her eyes had swollen, and the beak had grown to its full size. Enormous feathers were tapering from her dwindling fingers, and in a chilling rasping voice she croaked, "Hlökk . . ."

"Master Neil!" Quoth begged.

But the boy was looking in anguish upon the body of his mother, and grasping her by the arms, he tried to drag her toward the door.

"What madness is it thou doest?" Quoth yelped. "Leave this one, leave her!"

"You don't understand," Neil shouted. "I'm not going anywhere without her—she's my mother!"

The raven blinked in astonishment then spun around to see that Lauren's transformation was nearly complete. Already the great dark eyes were fixed upon them.

Chirping in fear, Quoth bounded up onto Sheila's

unconscious body and hopped onto her lolling head to stare urgently up into his master's face.

"Go now, afore 'tis too late!" he squawked. "Hlökk will not harm this one. The scent of the Valkyrie is still strong upon her. 'Tis thou it shalt rend and devour. Fly! Fly!"

Neil stared at the raven then glanced across to the feathered nightmare.

A shrill, strident shriek issued from the creature's gullet as it reared up to its full, menacing height and shook its massive wings.

"I hope you're right!" Neil muttered, letting go of Sheila and plucking up the raven.

"Make haste!" Quoth yowled.

With the wailing bird in his arms, the boy bolted for the door and flung himself through it. Then, slamming it behind, he pelted out into the darkness.

Along the driveway he ran, as fast as he had ever run. Within the kitchen, the Valkyrie screeched in fury, and Neil glanced over his shoulder to see a dark, horrendous silhouette thrown across the gravel as the door splintered and buckled before the monster's might.

"Aaiiieee!" Quoth squalled.

Neil wrenched his eyes away from the terror behind, but too late he saw a black shape step out in front. Before he knew what was happening, two strong hands had caught him by the shoulders.

"Let me go!" the boy yelled. "Let me go!"

The raven in his arms helplessly beat his wings against Neil's captor, then whimpered as the kitchen door was suddenly shattered from its hinges. Onto the gravel the Valkyrie came hunting.

CHAPTER 22

THE TOMB OF THE HERMIT

Deep in the earth, far below the streets and sewers of Glastonbury, Edie Dorkins and Miss Veronica Webster stumbled through the black passages, blindly tripping over unseen stones and grazing their shins against outcrops of the invisible, encasing rock.

With no method of measuring the passing hours, it seemed as though they had been sealed down there for ages, yet neither of them was dispirited.

Although she was old and haggard once more, Miss Veronica kept her thoughts fixed upon her beloved Captain.

Holding the old woman's hand, listening to the walking cane tapping out the way before them, Edie Dorkins was actually enjoying the experience. She adored the enveloping dark. If it had not been for Miss Veronica, she would have liked to have gone scurrying into the perpetual shade to wallow for an eternity in that resplendent, embracing night.

In silence they wandered, following the tunnel's curving walls, until, gradually, they became aware of a lessening in the profound blackness ahead.

In the distance a faint, pallid radiance began to glimmer, and when she raised her hand, Edie could just make out its outline against the waxing glow.

"Our goal is near," Miss Veronica said.

As they advanced down the passageway, by degrees the light welled up, bathing the surrounding rock in a cold, silvery gleam.

Into this pale aura went Edie and the old woman, discovering that it emanated from the far end of the tunnel, where a low archway was cut into the stone.

Eagerly, Miss Veronica's halting pace quickened, and Edie leaped away to be the first one to reach this intriguing portal.

The arch was an opening to a much larger space, and standing on the threshold, with the soft, silvery light playing across her young features, Edie peered within.

Beyond the low entrance was a great round chamber whose one encircling wall curved inward to form a geometrically perfect dome.

Yet the vaulted space was devoid of any decoration or device. Apart from the rushes that were strewn upon the floor, it contained only one, albeit unusual, object.

Situated in the center of the chamber, and looking distinctly odd in this peculiar environment, was a large wattle hut.

Built of woven strips of reed and willow, with a pitched thatch roof, this primitive structure housed the source of the bleak glimmering effulgence, almost as if a detached luminous nugget of the lustrous moon had been placed within.

Through the gaps between the interlaced branches, countless argent rays fanned out to form a dandelion-shaped path of light, whose radiating beams dappled the cavern with a ravishing, dancing pattern.

Beguiled by the shimmering display, Edie stole inside, stepping through wavering beams that painted her clothes with pearlescent patches of gentle brilliance. Tilting her head back, she held out her arms and spun wildly around until she ran out of breath and fell dizzily against the wall.

Pausing in the archway, Miss Veronica gazed on the scene and gripped the handle of her cane as her legs buckled beneath her. A power equal to that of the Nornir was manifest in that chamber, and the unexpected force of it took her breath away.

"Edith," she called, "assist me. I am weaker than ever."

At once the child ran over to her, and steeling herself, Miss Veronica entered.

"What is this place?" Edie asked.

"A tomb, dear," the old woman answered feebly. "Now, stay by me, child. I have need of your strength. Here, I am no longer sustained by Nirinel and must not remain. What we seek lies in there. Let us take the device and go quickly."

Over to the wattled hut the old woman limped with the girl, staggering purposefully around its blank wicker sides and halting when they came to an ancient tapestry draped across one of the four walls.

Edie looked at the hanging's faded fabric. It was crudely woven and the images it depicted were simply executed, yet she could still tell what they were intended to represent. In the middle of the time-stained cloth, upon a field embroidered with stylized droplets alternately picked out in red and white thread, were two thorny boughs that formed a rudimentary cross. On either side of this was a vessel fashioned in silver wire.

Miss Veronica studied the motifs carefully. "The arms of he who lies within," she reflected. "Draw it aside, Edith, dear. I'm afraid we must disturb the poor man's peace."

Edie stepped forward to pull the curtain, but when her fingers touched the cloth, the fibers disintegrated into powder and the entire tapestry went crashing to the floor, sending up a billowing, musty cloud of dust and dry decay.

At once the hidden light burst through the suddenly exposed doorway, turning the swirling particles into a brightly churning tempest of glittering rain. Edie stepped back, covering her mouth and nose so as not to breathe it in.

Yet Veronica could not wait, and seeing her stride through the entrance, the child rapidly followed, only to gaze in wonder upon the origin of the beautiful glare.

"Lor!" she marveled.

Within the hut, upon a long, low plinth of granite and flanking a large lead box, were two sealed vessels made of the purest silver.

Like supernatural lanterns, ceaselessly shining and glimmering in the subterranean darkness, they stood on the stone table. Beating from their untarnished, brilliant metal, the heavenly radiance steadily poured.

Steeped in the glittering glow, Miss Veronica eyed the fabulous treasures and nodded as though listening to a voice only she could hear. At her side, Edie Dorkins was too enthralled by the captivating spectacle to notice, and with the light blazing in her eyes and flaring in the tinsel strands of her pixie hat, she reached out to touch the vessel nearest to her.

"No, Edith," Miss Veronica said sharply. "They are not what we have come for. Listen to your senses. Can you not understand what these hallowed cruets contain?"

Edie's forehead creased as she strove to look beyond the splendor, then she raised her eyebrows as she said, "Life! This one has life and magic in it!"

"I suppose it does, in a way," Miss Veronica considered. "But what it really holds is blood."

The child chuckled with relish.

"Yet from the veins of no mortal did that precious fluid drip," Miss Veronica added. "It is the blood of a divinity, and the other vessel houses sweat that was bitterly wrung."

"I want to see," the child insisted.

"Do not break them open," the old woman said. "One day another shall come to this place. Do not cheat him of his destiny. Ursula would be so displeased and cross."

"Well, what have *we* come for?" Edie grumbled.

Miss Veronica shuffled alongside the granite plinth and placed her bony hand upon one end of the large lead box.

"What we seek lies in here," she said. "Within this coffin."

"That's a coffin?" the girl breathed. "Is there a skeleton inside?"

Miss Veronica looked at her in mild astonishment. "Oh, Edith, dear," she apologized. "I didn't stop to think you might be afraid."

"I ain't scared of no old bones," the child retaliated, already prying the lid off with ghoulish glee. "I want to see what's in there!"

Quickly her small, nimble fingers worked the soft lead flanges of the cover free, and with Miss Veronica's help, she pulled it clear and sent it thudding to the floor.

At once Edie sprang forward to peer inside, but the sight she saw was not what she had been expecting, and the child staggered back in astonishment.

Within the open coffin lay an elderly man dressed in simple hermit's robes. An expression of perfect peace and contentment was upon his old face. The lids of his eyes were lightly closed, and the skin of his brow was smooth and free from the furrowing cares of the world. About his head, as though it had continued to grow throughout the centuries, a mane of dark gray hair filled the surrounding casket, twining with the whiskers of a long white beard that spread over his chest and stretched down to his waist.

Edie had seen many of the various faces of death from her time in the war, but this one was new to her. It was as if the man was merely sleeping, and she prodded him suspiciously.

Miss Veronica knew what she was thinking and put

her doubts at ease. "He is dead, Edith," she said, "and he has lain here for what you would consider to be a terribly long time."

"But why haven't the worms been at him?" the girl asked in disappointment.

The old woman sighed. "Who can say?" she murmured. "Yet here lies the uncle of the one whose blood and sweat is contained within the cruets. Perhaps it is their influence that has kept the corruption at bay, or else it is the power of that which we have come to take from him. I do not know."

"He looks like a king," Edie remarked, "even though he ain't wearin' no crown."

Leaning upon the edge of the coffin, Miss Veronica studied the noble face wistfully.

"I remember," she began in a quiet, thoughtful tone, "when this man's nephew was born. Ursula said that a great cry rang out from the sacred groves and along the eastern shores, proclaiming the death of the ancient gods.

"She was rather irritated, I recall, but none of that actually happened until much later, and not all of the old deities were completely forgotten. Some of them survive still, in neglected pockets and turgid backwaters of the world. How much longer they can continue only Ursula can tell, but this at least I can do now. The time has come to heal one who is fading. The weak must be made strong, Edith. That is why we are here, and I must violate the serenity of this grave."

Reaching into the coffin, the old woman combed her fingers through the luxuriant white whiskers that flowed from the dead man's chin, searching among the thick swathes of tangled beard for what she needed to save and restore the life of her Captain.

Parting a space through the dense, haylike layers, Miss Veronica revealed a pair of hands folded over the hermit's chest and saw, placed reverently above them, ensnared and snarled by the soft branching growth, a circular golden object.

"There it is," she whispered. "The healing treasure. Forgive me this act of robbery, my dearest sir. There is another whose need is more desperate than your own."

With infinite gentleness, she closed her fingers about the precious yellow metal and lifted it from the dead man's breast.

A sound like a heavy escaping breath filled the wattle hut, and even as Miss Veronica withdrew the trinket from the lead casket, the body of Joseph of Arimathea sagged and shriveled beneath his hermit's robes. The peace faded from his noble face as it rapidly withered and decomposed, exposed and conquered at last by the ravages of the bygone millennia. Into black dust the ancient preserved flesh crumbled, leaving only a grinning skull surrounded by a sea of flowing hair, until that too rotted and sank into the mounting mold.

Soon nothing was left inside the coffin but a heap of powderous decay, and Miss Veronica shook her head sadly.

Edie Dorkins tore her eyes away and stared at the treasure now held in the old woman's hands.

Encrusted with gold and polished gems, the device was a curious shape. In appearance it was like a large bracelet, hammered and curved from one single piece of tapering metal that was worked into a shallow spiral. Even in the glare of the cruets, she could see that it gave off a pale light of its own.

Miss Veronica examined its richly adorned surface but winced and shuddered as though the very touch of the gold pained her.

Edie eyed the gleaming treasure curiously. "Can't see how that'll help," she said flatly.

"Nor can I," the old woman whispered, "but there is a power within it all the same. It prickles and stings, like holding a garland made of nettles. It is all I can do to keep from dropping it."

"That's the same thing what Ursula wanted me to fetch, ain't it? She said it were dangerous."

Miss Veronica began to limp toward the doorway. "I really couldn't vouch for anything she might have said," she told the girl. "Ursula is always so close and secretive. She rarely bothers to explain anything to me or Celandine."

"Don't you miss them?"

The old woman faltered then pretended she had not heard and went out into the dome once more. "Hurry, Edith. We must take this valuable device to Woden. He will know the secrets of its healing power. It is time we made our way back to the surface."

Edie lingered in the hut for a moment more. It seemed a shame to leave the two cruets behind. She was sure they might be useful, and besides, they looked so pretty. Perhaps if she took only one it wouldn't do any harm.

"Hurry, Edith," the old woman called.

Standing beside the granite plinth, the child looked longingly at the shining silver vessels, and darting a wary glance at the doorway, she suddenly reached over to take one.

As soon as she touched the cold, brilliant metal, a tremendous roar shook the domed chamber like some terrible, calamitous alarm.

Edie let go and sprang backward immediately, but it was too late. The ominous splitting sound of fracturing rock thundered about the cavern. The walls of the hut started to quiver as a great crack splintered down the center of the low granite plinth.

"Edith!" Miss Veronica cried, lurching back to the doorway. "What have you done?"

The child whirled around. Now the floor was subsiding, and the hideous crack grew wider as it buckled, becoming a deep rift that ruptured the entire length of the chamber, dividing it in two. Shaken by fierce, jolting forces, the lead coffin jerked and tilted as one half of the broken stone table dropped abruptly, and the silver cruets toppled over to go rolling onto the quaking ground.

Edie stared about her in horror then fled toward the doorway, leaping across the ever-growing fissure to be at Miss Veronica's side.

"Hurry!" the old woman shouted. "The tomb is collapsing!"

Abruptly the hut's ancient wattle walls shattered with the violence of the shifting ground. Like a million strands of finely spun glass, the brittle reeds and osiers exploded behind them, and with a mighty avalanche of dust and straw, the thatched roof came crashing down.

Grasping hold of the young girl's hand, Miss

Veronica tried to lead her from the chaos and destruction that engulfed them. But she was too old and weary, and when the next tremor seized and rocked the chamber, she was thrown to the floor, dragging Edie with her.

Then, with an almighty, tumultuous rending of stone, huge chunks of the fractured ground tipped and tumbled, falling down into a black abyss that yawned open below.

Deafened by a horrendous clamor as the area where the hut had stood finally gave way, Edie raised her head in time to see the fragments of the plinth and the lead coffin slip down into the chasm. Then, like two fiery white comets, the vessels containing the blood and sweat of Christ plummeted after.

As their glimmering radiance plunged into the gulf, the domed chamber was lost in a darkness that only the bracelet in Miss Veronica's tightly clenched hand alleviated.

In the ghastly golden glow the old woman searched for the arch that led to the tunnel and pointed to it wretchedly.

"We must reach it!" she cried. "It is our only! . . ."

At that moment the floor surrounding the gaping fissure broke free from the curving walls, and with a sickening, jarring crunch, the remaining rock heaved and pitched into the waiting void.

Shrieking, Edie Dorkins clawed and clung to the jagged fragment of ground beneath her as it slithered downward, while Miss Veronica was flung helplessly into the empty darkness and the circlet they had come so far to find was sent spinning out of her grasp.

CHAPTER 23

THE GATHERING

"Fates preserve us!" cried Aidan, letting go of Neil's shoulders when he saw the horror of the Valkyrie burst from the kitchen. The twisted abomination that was Hlökk threw back its deformed head and let out a ghastly shriek.

Aidan shuddered. With its large black eyes glinting, consumed with malice and lusting for slaughter, the nightmare came pounding toward them.

"Aaaiiiyeee!" Quoth yammered. "We art caught! We art killed!"

"Not yet we're not!" Aidan yelled, setting off down the path, hauling Neil after him. "Get into the van. It's just down by the road!"

The Valkyrie's horrendous screeches skirled into the night as they fled out of the Humphrieses' driveway. Across the path the creature's murderous talons clattered, raking up a hail of gravel with its long pursuing strides.

Feverishly, Aidan yanked open the van door, and Neil tore around to the passenger side to clamber within.

"Hlökk is nigh upon us!" Quoth whined, cowering under the boy's arm as the grotesque shape stampeded from the gates, its vicious beak thrusting the air, eager for blood.

Hurriedly, Aidan turned the key in the ignition, but just when the engine roared into life, the monster caught them.

Framed in the windshield, the malignant, quill-maned face appeared. A low, gloating cackle issued from the yawning throat as the beast eyed the van's succulent contents.

Aidan's fingers closed tightly about the steering wheel as he gazed upon that evil countenance, knowing that a similar sight had heralded the final moments of his friends who had been killed in the bus. His own face grew hard as his fear turned to hatred.

"What are you waiting for?" Neil cried.

Spreading its wings, Hlökk shook its feathers and crowed exultingly, raising one of its savage claws to bring it smacking down on the hood, jolting the van violently.

A vile, piercing squeal sliced through Neil's ears as the creature dragged its talons across the metal. Then the loathsome beak lolled open, and the Valkyrie lunged forward to smash its way through the windshield.

"Not this time!" Aidan shouted, and in that instant, he slammed his foot on the accelerator and the van leaped forward.

Startled, the monster was flung off balance, crushing

the hood and cracking the windshield when its horrible weight came thundering down. Then it somersaulted high over the roof as the vehicle roared away.

Hlökk's hulking shape crashed onto the road behind with a flailing mass of feathers, and its furious, dismayed screeches split the night as it struggled to right itself.

"Hurroosh!" Quoth cheered, bounding onto the backseat of the van to watch the floundering shape recede in the distance. "Forsooth, 'twas grandly done. Like a reed cut down by the sickle she did fall! Behold how the grooly fiend doth squirm and . . ."

The raven's voice dwindled to a hoarse whimper, and his jubilation was curtailed, for the Valkyrie was already rising from the ground and spreading immense wings.

"Woe betide us," Quoth uttered dismally, sliding down the seat to scamper back onto Neil's lap. "It hath taken to the air. The Valkyrie flies!"

Trees and hedges rocketed by as the van hurtled along the lonely road toward Glastonbury, but with every passing second the ravaging Valkyrie closed in.

"What about the Tor?" Neil cried. "Tommy said it'd be safe up there in the tower. He said they couldn't touch us there."

"Is that where he was going when I saw him run from that house?" Aidan asked. "Well, I'm afraid the tower's out of the question for us. We'd be dead before we even got halfway up the hill. There's no way of fighting those things. We have to find someplace else, somewhere those devils dare not go."

"The church?"

Aidan shook his head. "That wouldn't keep them out. Sacred ancient sites are what we need now."

At that moment the roof buckled and warped as a curved talon came ripping inside. The van lurched across the road, the tires skidding over the blacktop as the vehicle was dragged aside.

Quoth squealed shrilly and Aidan hunched over the steering wheel, trying to wrench it to the left, as up above them the apparition raged in fury.

With a rasp of metal the claw slipped free. The van bolted away, careering madly toward the town, zigzagging from side to side, attempting to avoid the swooping horror that dived upon it again and again, battering the ruptured roof.

"Hold on!" Aidan yelled, turning the van sharply around to career down Bere Lane.

"The weavers of the crimson weft are wont to chase unto the direst end!" Quoth squawked, the fierce motion of the vehicle hurling him off his feet. "Never doth their prey escape them."

"Tell that bird of yours to keep quiet!" Aidan shouted.

Another savage blow struck the roof, and a second rent was torn in the metal as this time the cruel beak stabbed downward.

Into the van the nightmare's iron-like bill spiked and ripped, and Neil dodged aside to avoid it impaling his shoulder.

Slaughterous shrieks blasted within the vehicle, and Quoth gibbered in terror when more of the roof was peeled away and the creature thrust its grievous head still farther inside.

The houses bordering the street were quickly ablaze with light as the inhabitants ran to the windows to find out what was happening. But as soon as they saw the small blue van race by, tormented by the horrific black shape that clawed and screeched upon its roof, many hurriedly closed their curtains and locked their doors.

Nearing the end of the long lane, Aidan suddenly sent the van into a sickening spin, whirling out of control across the road until the wheels hurtled onto the sidewalk and Hlökk's unclean shape was thrown into the shrubs of a tidy front garden.

Snarling, Aidan revved the engine, and the vehicle shot away, but this time the terrifying creature did not follow. Leaping onto the low garden wall, it jerked its disfigured head back to focus on a spot beyond the Tor, as though hearing a distant call. With a powerful sweep of its great wings it soared into the night and vanished into the darkness above.

"I thought you said they never gave up," Neil gasped to Quoth.

The raven clacked his tongue in warning. "It hath gone to fetch aid," he said. "To the gathering Shrieker doth fly. Then others shalt come, Screamer and Raging, Biter and Tearer. Like unto a mouse set before a dozen cats shalt we be."

"Then we've got to get help before they find us," Neil cried.

Aidan said nothing. A grave resolve was carved upon his swarthy face, and leaving Bere Lane, he drove the van away from the center of Glastonbury and up a rising narrow street called Hill Head.

"Where are we going?" the boy demanded. "The police station?"

"Boys in blue won't be no use to us, lad," the man replied tersely. "No point getting even more folk butchered."

Neil stared out of the window at the cottages that raced by, and he saw the lights of the town fall behind them.

"This is Wearyall Hill," he suddenly realized. "What's up here?"

"Something to keep you safe!" Aidan rapped back. "Could be the only thing that can, aside from Saint Michael's tower."

Abruptly the buildings that flanked the road ended, and where the cramped way bent around to girdle the lower slopes of the long, low hill, Aidan stopped the van and got out.

"Hurry!" he shouted, sprinting to a muddy track at the corner of the road where a wooden stile led to the desolate darkness of the humpbacked hill beyond.

Neil and Quoth followed him in confusion.

"You're crazy!" the boy cried, gazing at the empty expanse that stretched before them. "If more of those things come, we'll be done for out there."

"I said you'll be safe," the man repeated sternly. "Get yourself up there as fast as you can and stop only when you reach the Holy Thorn."

"The what?"

Aidan ground his teeth. "Joseph of Arimathea," he explained impatiently. "He came ashore here and rested on this hill, hence the name. When he planted his staff in the ground, it took root and flowered. A scion of that tree is up there on the hillside. Just keep running straight and you can't miss it; it's fenced in by a railing. As soon as you reach it, hold on and don't let go for anything."

"But . . . what are you going to do?"

Aidan stared back across the valley to where he could just make out the black silhouette of the Tor.

"They'll all be swarming this way in a minute," he said firmly. "Urdr sent me to find Verdandi and the girl, but I failed her. There's only one thing I can do to redeem myself now. She told you to trust me. Well, I'll not break that faith. This is where we part company, Neil."

The boy grabbed the man's arm. "You're not leaving me again."

"I'm getting back in the van," Aidan told him, his mind made up. "Your raven was right. Those creatures never abandon their prey when they give chase. They are the Wild Hunt, Woden's raven women. They'll hound my little motor until they catch it. If I leave now I just might be able to lead them off and give you time enough to reach the Thorn.

"Perhaps you'll even find Verdandi—that's who they're really after. The Gallows God has lured her here to destroy her, don't you see? After that he'll dispatch his Valkyries to London to attack the museum. If I can buy even five minutes more for the Nornir, then that's what I have to do. As a descendant of Askar, it's my duty."

Dismayed by what he was hearing, Quoth scurried over the mud to tug at the man's trouser leg. "Thine flesh shalt be their feasting!" he declared fretfully. "Thy death is assured if thou chooseth this path."

"Listen to him!" Neil cried. "You don't stand a chance!"

The gypsy's emerald eyes glinted in the darkness as he pulled his arm free of the boy's grasp and hurried back to the van.

"I know," he said solemnly. "So don't let it be for nothing. What are you waiting for? Get running—go now! Find the Thorn, and may the hand of Fate guard you!"

"Wait!" Neil cried, but Aidan had already slammed the door behind him and the engine turned over.

Hastily the boy ran to the van and banged his fists on the window.

"Don't do this!" he pleaded. "Aidan! Aidan!"

The man held up his hand in farewell then swerved the vehicle around and drove it back down the hill.

"Stop!" Neil shouted. But it was no use. The lights of the van quickly waned in the distance then disappeared altogether as it reached the main road.

Standing in the middle of the lonely narrow road, Neil could not believe what the man had done.

"Good luck," was all he could bring himself to say.

"Master Neil!" came a squealing squawk. "Thou must do as he bid thee. Find this Thorn!"

The boy looked across to the stile, where Quoth was wriggling between the bars. Then, with a final glance down the sloping lane, Neil climbed over the rail and rushed into the darkness ahead.

* * *

Deep shadows filled Tommy's derelict barn, but now a different figure stole into the gloom, and the beam of a large flashlight shone over the neglected interior.

A furtive rustling sounded from somewhere nearby. The Reverend Peter Galloway jumped in alarm as he cautiously crept into the secluded, dilapidated building.

"What was that?" he cried. "Who's there?"

Behind him there came a fluttering of wings, and Thought, the raven, flew over his head to alight upon the remains of an old tractor.

"Quell thy craven heart," the bird told him. "Dost thou fear the foraging of rodents?"

"Mice?"

Thought sniffed and chuckled dryly. "Rats," he corrected. "Now the hour of the gathering is at hand. Let us betake ourselves to yonder loft and await our guests."

The vicar shone his light over to where the ladder rose to the upper level, and Thought flitted in and out of the beam as he leaped from his perch and flew upward.

"Pox and plague!" the raven exclaimed when he landed on the straw-covered floorboards. "Others hath been here this very day. Two at least."

By the time the Reverend Galloway had ascended the ladder, the bird was busily hunting through the scattered hay, snouting and questing his beak from one corner to another in perplexity.

"What is it?" Peter asked. "Could it have been that young woman and the child?"

Thought glared at him and ruffled his feathers.

"Not they," he denied. "Yet I am uneasy. A third presence I doth detect. A scent familiar—yet not so. I like it not at all."

The vicar sat on an old bale of straw. "Is there danger here?" he asked, worried by the bird's uncharacteristic concern.

Thought prowled over the floorboards for a further inspection, then stamped his clawed feet. "For my Lord's sake, I pray not," he croaked. "Yet this riddling trail discomforts me. Who would dare meddle in our affairs? I shalt not brook such presumption."

"About that woman," Peter persisted, unnerved by that last, callous comment. "Isn't it time she returned with the Chalice? She and the girl have been gone for hours now."

Thought cocked his ugly head to one side, and his beady eyes gleamed in the beam of the flashlight—almost mockingly, it seemed to Peter.

"Faith, fellow servant," the bird assured him. "Soon they wilt return and this . . . this golden prize shalt prove our Master's existence beyond doubting."

The vicar give a weak smile. "I know," he said. "I'm just finding it difficult to take it all in. From this night on the world will be a different place. The good news will be pronounced in every country, and when He is ready to speak, there will be no more wars, no sickness, no pain."

"The world will indeed be changed," Thought admitted. "Yet prepare thyself for the wonders thou shalt behold this night. Afore the dawn thy faith wilt be tested. Flinch not from what awaits thee, and obey my bidding."

Peter nodded. "I am rather nervous, though," he confessed. "But whatever lies ahead, I shall not shrink from the most holy office I am charged with."

The raven concealed a guileful smirk and strutted over to the wide opening where the shutters hung from their hinges.

"Yet not alone shalt thou perform thy duties," he said cryptically. "*They* approacheth. The servants of my Master wilt soon be here."

"Who are these others we're waiting for?" Peter asked. "And why do we have to meet them in this forsaken place? I just don't understand all this secrecy. Surely we should be proclaiming this from the rooftops!"

Thought gazed up into the midnight sky before answering.

"Until the time appointed, the way of stealth is the only course open to us. He hath said unto thee to prepareth the way, and this have we done and shalt continue to do."

"But these others," the vicar pressed.

The bird cackled faintly. "If 'twill mollify thee, know then that their number is twelve," he said, reveling in the effect his words had upon the man.

Peter gasped. "Twelve . . ."

"A most sacred host are they," Thought continued. Then, with a more chilling edge creeping into his cracked voice, he added, "Yet their aspect wilt fright and afflict thee. Staunch now the humors of thy terror and snuff out thy lanthorn. My Lord's messengers wilt be unlovely in thine earthbound eyes, but fear them not and stand to greet them."

The vicar thought he understood and remembered what he had told the children at Neil's school.

"I know," he answered gravely. "They're not likely to appear as shining white figures with wings and haloes. I must expect to be mortally afraid, just as the shepherds were."

The raven leered up at him before turning back to the opening. "Thou art wise to dread them," he muttered. "Yet this only I doth admit: they art indeed possessed of wings."

Trembling, Peter fidgeted with the whiskers of his straggly beard as an anticipating silence fell. A few minutes later he stiffened and sat bolt upright as a faint yammering came from outside, and Thought glided over to the man's shoulder.

"They are here!" he cried. "The Twelve art gathered at last. Harken to their delightful voices."

The Reverend Galloway thought that the growing clamor was the most evil noise he had ever heard, but he steeled himself and prepared to be overcome by the sight of this angelic host.

Outside the barn, the strident shrieks of the Valkyries mounted as they surrounded and swooped about the ramshackle building. The night was filled with their ghastly screams, and when vast patches of black shadow began to rush across the entrance to the hayloft, the vicar felt a surge of ice-cold fear travel down his spine. He forced himself to stand his ground and keep his eyes open.

The screeches were unbearable now. The rush of mighty wings shook the corrugated roof, and a fine rain of rust drifted down to settle on Peter's unkempt hair.

Suddenly, screaming at the top of its foul, rancorous voice, the first of the nightmares plunged in through the opening, and the vicar threw his hands in front of his face at the repellent sight. Although it was dark within the barn, he could see enough of the creature's vile silhouette to despair, and his skin crawled when the atrocity shook its feathers and its grotesque, inhuman eyes glittered malevolently at him.

"Sweet mercy!" Peter quailed, recoiling from the horrendous spectacle.

The Valkyrie snapped its beak menacingly. A bloodthirsty screak vibrated the barn as the quilled abhorrence displayed its fury, incensed that the meeting place had been invaded.

At the same moment, a second and a third nightmare came crashing inside, and their baleful eyes roved in their scabious sockets to fix upon the petrified vicar.

As more of the deformed scourges burst into the loft, Peter flattened himself against the wall.

"They are sent by the Lord," he kept telling himself. "I am in no danger."

But for all his theological ponderings, the vicar had never dreamed of such inexorable hideousness as was displayed now before him, and he felt both faint and sick.

Yet upon his shoulder, Thought waited until the last of the horrors had entered before making any kind of move. He could feel the Reverend shivering beneath him. The terrified motion jiggled through the raven's body, but he made no effort to comfort or appease the man and looked instead with pride upon the hellish congregation.

Here then were the local women transformed by

the crow dolls that Woden had compelled Dulcie Pettigrew to distribute. Thought laughed under his breath to see the most feared slaves of his Master gathered together again.

Eleven ghastly feather-fringed heads now bobbed and twitched within the cramped loft space, the black ruffs and twig-tangled hair scraping the crumbling roof and clattering against the rotting rafters. A fetid stench came from their hot, rancid bodies, and their malicious gazes were trained solely on the man cowering in the farthest corner.

Every bitter beak croaked and screeched with slaughterous intent. The lethal talons splintered through the sagging floorboards as they pushed and jostled one another, tensing and preparing to pounce upon the defenseless, paltry human who had dared to intrude.

Peter's heart thumped and pounded against his ribs when he heard the creatures' revolting, gutteral speech as they yelled for his destruction.

"Hot blood! Ssweet man flessh. Tear it, rend, and sstrike! Gorge on sspleen, crunch the bone, ssnap the sspine! Ssuck out brain, chew grisstle, devour, and drain. Death! Death! Death!"

The din within the barn was tremendous, and with one lurching movement, the Valkyries rushed forward to rip out the man's throat and slake their thirst with his blood.

At once, Thought left Peter's shoulder and flew before their repulsive faces, emitting a high, shrill squawk that knifed through the inflamed yammering. To the Reverend Galloway's amazement, the monsters halted and turned their awful countenances toward the circling raven.

"Be still!" the bird cried as a hush fell. "I, Thought, command it."

The creatures croaked and hissed in response, and the raven dived in among them, his wings brushing against the sides of their unclean heads. They snorted the air suspiciously before rattling their quills and honking like gruesome, gargantuan geese in recognition.

"All know me," Thought declared. "Did I not lead you into battle on that final day when we were routed by the mists?"

Croaking sounds of agreement rippled through the assembled mob. The raven weaved in and out of the hulking, misproportioned bodies, swaying them with his words and calling them back into his service.

"Biter!" he crowed. "Thou didst bear the standard. Raging and Screamer, Torment and Ruin, the cloth of war didst thee uphold. Hate, the arrow of doom wast thine. To contend with the enemy of our Lord we rampaged over the plain, only to be confounded at the last by the witchery and devilment of those within the wood. Now the wheel is turned, the hour is here once more, and this time we shalt not fail. The mists are departed, and they shalt pay most dearly."

The Valkyries caterwauled their pleasure, and Thought whirled around them one final time before returning to Peter's shoulder.

"This mortal is high in our Master's regard," he told them. "No injury nor hurt wilt I permit thee to inflict upon his person."

A low, disgruntled hiss issued from the nightmarish

audience as their eyes glowered disdainfully at the man whose tender flesh was denied to them.

"'Tis the Lord's bidding!" Thought reiterated forcefully. "Thou must all yield to my . . ."

The bird broke off as he suddenly realized how many Valkyries were present.

"One of thy number is absent!" he cried, screeching furiously. "Where is Shrieker? Was this day not appointed for the final moot? All were to be ready. Where is the last of thy company?"

The apparitions twisted and turned, wondering what could have become of her, but just then the noise of beating wings came rushing about the barn, and into the hayloft Hlökk flew.

Furling its wings, the unholy creature that had consumed Lauren Humphries stood upon the ledge, threw back its head, and gave a calamitous scream.

At the far end of the loft, the Reverend Galloway winced at the sound and prayed for deliverance from this unceasing parade of terror.

"*We are betrayed, my ssissterss!*" Hlökk thundered in a fearsome, gargling voice. "*The dessign of our Masster iss in hazard. A traitor iss aiding the Nornir. With my own eyess I ssaw him.*"

The others snarled and snapped, raking their talons through the floor when they heard this. Then Thought called for silence, and Hlökk's hostile glance burned upon him.

"*Why are you here?*" the monster demanded.

The raven blinked in astonishment at the insolent question. "I am the emissary of thy creator!" he declaimed. "'Tis not thy place to challenge me! I am

Thought, he who is deep in His counsel, who knoweth all the reaches of His subtle mind."

"*What truth iss there in your wordss?*" the creature demanded, lowering its foul head and stealing forward. "*When your own kinssman asssisstss our enemy!*"

Thought scowled in confusion. "Kinsman?" he squawked.

"*Yess!*" Hlökk growled. "*Your own brother!*"

The raven jerked his flat head left and right as at last he understood the strangely familiar scent that had perplexed him earlier.

"Memory!" he screeched. "My brother lives?"

"*He doess and hass renounced our Masster!*"

"Thou liest, Shrieker!"

"*Even now he ridess with two who sstink of Nirinel. They are here to defeat uss. Thiss very night I wass asssailed and wrenched from my hosst. A power wass with them I could not undersstand.*"

The other creatures spat and clacked in dismay, but Thought narrowed his eyes and hunched his shoulders.

"Memory must be found!" he declared. "If he hath indeed turned traitor then we cannot allow him to thwart us. Hark, O devoted servants, the hour long awaited fast approacheth. Verdandi hath been enticed from the shrine's protection, and unto us she shalt deliver the device our Lord doth seek."

A macabre, croaking chorus rang about the loft as the Valkyries screamed their approval, and Thought stretched his wings dramatically.

"My brother must be taken! Go search him out. Shrieker, lead us to these vainglorious fools. They must be slain!"

The barn shuddered as the monsters shook their feathers and thundered from the opening to soar into the dark night.

"What's happening?" the Reverend Galloway asked when the raven flew back to him. "I don't understand this."

Thought sneered at him, but knew he had to keep up the pretense a little while longer.

"A Judas hath been discovered," he snapped. "We must find him afore the prize is brought to us. Our Lord must not be betrayed. Now, make thyself ready."

Peter shivered. "What for?"

"The war twixt good and ill hath begun anew," Thought told him with a devious grin. "Thou must come with us."

"Me?" the vicar blurted. "Out . . . up there?"

The raven cackled. "Thy presence is needed," he said with a laugh. "Into the heavens thou shalt be drawn. Come, ride with these angels."

To Peter's dismay, the bird ordered him over to the opening, where he stared fearfully up at the horde of black shapes now swarming above the barn.

"Biter!" Thought cried. "I have a burden for thee."

There came a fierce rush of feathers, and a putrid stench blasted into the vicar's face as one of the circling Valkyries plunged toward him.

"Hold up thy hands!" the raven instructed.

Peter obeyed and felt mighty talons seize his arms, the hooked claws snapping like vices around them, squeezing and clutching so tightly that he yelled in pain.

But his voice was lost in the surrounding uproar.

He felt his arms almost wrenched from their sockets as the winged horror above snatched him into the air and his feet were plucked off the floorboards.

With sickening speed the vicar was hoisted into the sky to join the others, and Thought fluttered before him, crowing his instructions to the waiting, slaughter-starved nightmares.

"Dear Lord!" Peter howled, closing his eyes, unable to gaze down at the empty gulf beneath him and unwilling to look upon the terrifying spectacle of the dark host that bayed and screamed on every side.

Like a black storm the assembled Valkyries hurtled through the sky, and with the Reverend Galloway dangling helplessly from their claws, they went screeching into the tortured night.

CHAPTER 24

WITHIN THE FROZEN POOL

A blast of freezing air sliced into Edie's lungs as she struggled to make sense of what had happened.

Down into the pit she had fallen, clinging to her splintered section of rocky floor, until the bottom of the great dark chasm was finally reached. With the dreadful, jolting violence of the impact, the child was thrown clear.

Shattered pieces of rubble still rained down from above, and Edie could hear them rattling onto the ground. Fortunately she had been flung out of their path, and for the moment she was content merely to listen to the clattering percussion of pebbles and debris.

The girl's eyes were squeezed tightly shut and she felt bruised and sore all over, yet it was not until an icy numbness began to bite into her limbs, especially her legs and hands, that she started to feel afraid. What if the terrible fall had broken her back? What if she was to die slowly in this forsaken abyss? No one would ever find her. She would become just another fossil in the unexplored roots of the world.

Edie cackled to think of it. Perhaps she too would one day be placed in a museum as a dried and shriveled exhibit.

Opening her eyes, she sat up to find herself in a large drift of feathery frost that had cushioned her fall. Scooping a handful up to her lips, she licked it and stared around her.

The cavern that had lain beneath the hermit's tomb was immense. All around, rising like a forest of shimmering crystal columns, were momentous pillars and towers of ice. Up from the hoary, rime-covered ground they thrust, rearing high into the blackness above. From that same dark ceiling, the tips of mighty icicles came spearing, hanging threateningly over the child's head.

It was like being in the palace of winter. In the distance Edie could see galleries and cloisters formed entirely from ice, and gingerly stepping from the frost drift, she moved toward the center of the huge glittering space to where the remains of Joseph's grave lay in fractured ruins.

Lying on their sides, dented but not broken, the silver cruets still blazed their glorious light, and it was this that illuminated the gargantuan space. Twinkling over every frost-bristled surface the hallowed vessels steadily shone, turning the monstrous glacial trees into distorting mirrors and warped prisms that threw back the beautiful, lustrous gleam a thousand times.

Normally, Edie would have been enraptured by the

vivid display, but now only one thought burned within her.

"Veronica?" she called. "Where are you?"

Sticking out from beneath one of the larger chunks of rock was a mangled mass of flattened lead—all that was left of the coffin. The child could not help but think that somewhere, under all those tons of broken stone, the old woman lay similarly crushed.

"Squashed into jam," she said sadly. "Poor Veronica."

Suddenly an eager, delighted voice drifted to her from out of the darkness that lay beyond the reach of the magical lanterns.

"I hope it's strawberry!" it cried. "Save some for me!"

There, stumbling into the light, was Miss Veronica.

The old woman looked only slightly the worse for wear after her hideous descent. Her already pale and powdered complexion was thick with dust, and splinters of gravel were caught in her dyed tresses. The silken robe was ripped and tattered, and she had lost one of her satin slippers, but Miss Veronica had managed to keep hold of her walking cane. Waddling forward, her stalklike, knobbled legs bleeding with cuts and grazes, she had a great, glad smile on her face, and she held out a trembling hand toward Edie.

"Are there pancakes also?" the old woman called. "How scrumptious! I do feel peckish."

Edie ran across the rubble to hug her as Miss Veronica peered hungrily about the glittering cavern.

"Oh, but I can't see any," she muttered sulkily. "I hope you haven't eaten it all, Edith, dear."

The girl shook her head impatiently. "There ain't

no jam," she said. "But why ain't you killed after droppin' all that way?"

"The same reason you aren't, dear," came the amused reply. "We are the Fates. Well, two of them anyway. I remember Ursula saying how there was very little that could actually do us serious harm. We have drunk of the blessed waters, and the threads of our lives were never part of the tapestry, you see. We are outside of the web, even though we are enslaved to it."

Clasping a hand to her bosom, she stared up past the lofty heights of the glimmering pillars to where the darkness reigned and sighed wistfully.

"I did enjoy that little fall," she confessed. "Do you think we might do it again? Celandine and I could have amused ourselves by leaping off the museum's roof when we got bored. She would have enjoyed that so. I wonder what she's doing now? Still practicing the steps to one of her dances, I expect. What a pity there are no pancakes after all. I was dearly looking forward to them."

Edie stared at her. The old woman seemed to have forgotten why they were here and the seriousness of their predicament. It was as if she had regressed into the idiotic ramblings of her former self, before the old memories and resentments toward Miss Ursula had surfaced in her fuddled mind.

"Veronica!" the girl snapped. "What about Woden? What about the bracelet? Don't go all stupid on me again!"

The old woman pressed her arthritic fingers to her temples.

"The Captain!" she exclaimed, becoming lucid

once more. "The healing treasure—it fell from my hand. Help me find it, Edith! We must take it to him!"

Separating, they each chose a section of the cavern in which to search, knowing that as long as the golden circlet was not buried under the slabs of granite it would be fairly easy to find.

As she passed between the enormous ice pillars, Edie let her sharp eyes scan the way ahead, hunting for both the treasure's pale yellow glow and a possible way out of this great wintry chamber.

Yet there was no escape. There were no hidden exits and no steps to take them back to the destroyed tomb chamber above. Edie and Miss Veronica were trapped.

Reaching the slippery far wall, where the soft beams of the silver vessels mingled with dim shadows, Edie began to follow it around as best she could.

After several minutes of having to squeeze between the translucent stalagmites and constantly losing her footing on the treacherous frozen floor, the child suddenly saw a pale radiance ahead, where fewer of the titanic pinnacles jutted into the dark.

Hurriedly, Edie slipped toward it, leaving the chill, glasslike forest behind her. She ducked beneath a draped formation of iridescent ice and slid to a wide area of white frost, ringed about by boulders of polished black rock.

In the center of this strange circle, half buried in the snowy carpet, lay the golden ornament they had removed from Joseph's grave.

Keeping her eyes fixed upon the wavering buttery gleam that flowed from the precious enchanted metal,

Edie clambered over the bordering stones and quickly ran across to retrieve it.

Kneeling on the freezing ground, the girl lifted the bracelet, and a cloud of vapor issued from her lips as she gasped and let it fall once more.

The metal was horrible to touch. It tingled and stabbed her skin, and she pulled her hands up into the sleeves of her coat before attempting to pick it up again.

"That can't be why Ursula was so scared of it," she pondered aloud, inspecting the brightly glinting jewels. "P'raps it's a magic wish-giver."

Balancing the circlet upon her head like a tiara, Edie closed her eyes and commanded, "Take me and Veronica out of this hole and plop us back outside."

Nothing happened. The girl looked about her in glum disappointment, then, when her gaze fell upon the place where the treasure had lain, she squealed in surprise and the bracelet fell from her pixie hat as she toppled backward.

"Blimey!" she yelled. "Veronica! Over 'ere!"

From the far side of the cavern the old woman's answering voice called back, but Edie was already scrabbling at the frost beneath her, sweeping it wildly aside and peering down excitedly.

Clearing a wide space around her, pushing the snow to the edge of the boulder-ringed area, she held the golden bangle close to the floor and breathed a great, steaming plume of amazement.

The polished black stones that surrounded her were the edge of a great pool, and she was crouching upon its frozen surface. Down into the shadowy, ice-locked depths shone the pale glow of the treasure, and the child bit her lip as she gazed upon the incredible sight it revealed.

A pair of large round eyes were staring up at her from the solid murk below, and the girl burnished the ice with her sleeve in order to see more clearly.

The eyes were mirrored globes, and the light of the bracelet curved and glittered around them, so that they burned like lamps filled with a cold, wintry flame.

Endeavoring to see more, Edie squashed her nose against the frozen water and tried to pierce the dim dark.

Yet the creature was too far down for the gentle golden rays to penetrate. Beneath those baleful eyes that appeared to be staring straight back at her, the unearthly face disappeared into the gloom, and all the girl could make out was a wide forehead crowned by a mass of hair that resembled tangled river weeds.

Edie had never seen or imagined anything like it.

"Oh, well done, Edith, dear," came Miss Veronica's voice as the old woman approached the frozen pool. "Now let us find a way out so we may take the healing device up to the Captain. We've been gone such a woefully long—"

Carefully climbing over the ring of boulders, Miss Veronica crept to the young girl's side, where her jaw dropped open in bewildered astonishment.

"Gracious me!" she cried. "I don't believe it! It's impossible!"

Edie tore her face from the ice, peeling a layer of skin from her nose in the process.

"Do you know what it is?" she asked eagerly.

The old woman stared down at the unblinking bulging eyes and backed away to sit down with an ungraceful bump upon one of the bordering stones.

"I do indeed," she whispered. "Though I thought never to see its like again."

Edie slithered over to her.

"Tell me!" she insisted.

Miss Veronica tried to calm herself but could not prevent a thrilled grin from breaking across her withered face.

"It's an undine, Edith!" she declared. "You have found an undine. And a male one at that!"

The girl grinned back at her then folded her arms. "What's one of them?"

"Undines are water spirits, dear. I thought they had disappeared from the world ages since. I cannot quite believe that I'm seeing one now, I truly can't."

Rubbing her eyes in case they were deceiving her, the old woman took another look and clapped her hands together with childlike glee.

"In the beginning of things," she told Edie, "before the lands were raised, undines roamed in the great oceans. They are the font of all sacred wells and springs, and long ago, such a glorious being dwelt in the pool beneath Nirinel."

Edie turned back to gaze upon the frozen creature sealed within the ice. "You had one of them under the museum?" She whistled. "What happened to it? Why ain't it there now?"

"It left us," Miss Veronica replied. "The creature was lured away. That is why when the well was drained, the blessed water was never replenished. If only Ursula and Celandine were here now, I should love to see the looks on their faces. They will never believe my word alone, or yours either—if we ever go back, that is."

"Is it dead?" the child asked.

The old woman sucked in her cheeks. "Oh, no, dear," she said. "When a water spirit perishes, it returns back to the element from which it is made, becoming a mighty wave or a squalling tempest. No, there's nothing the matter with that fellow as far as I can tell, except that he's imprisoned in the ice, of course. This really is stupendous."

But Edie was no longer listening. Her head was buzzing within the pixie hat. Now she knew why she had insisted on accompanying Miss Veronica to Glastonbury. Scampering back to the center of the pool, the girl threw herself down and started to scratch and scrape the surface ice with her fingernails.

"Edith!" Miss Veronica called. "What are you doing?"

"I want to let it out!" she cried.

The old woman's hands fluttered nervously before her mouth. "Oh, I'm not sure what Ursula would say."

"Stuff Ursula!" Edie shouted. "I got me an idea. Will you help me or not?"

Miss Veronica's high painted eyebrows crinkled upon her forehead as she muttered to herself. "Stuff Ursula!" she repeated. "Yes, why not. Why should I care what she thinks anyway?"

Gripping hold of her walking cane, she eased herself from the boulder and rose while clearing her throat.

"Stand aside, Edith," she instructed.

The girl obeyed and watched as Miss Veronica held out the cane and tapped it once upon the ice.

A flicker of green flame traveled down the black rod, shooting out over the frozen water, and the old woman waited expectantly.

The livid light of the emerald fire burned briefly over the surface of the pool until a loud crack resounded throughout the cavern, then the glow vanished as the ice split and shivered.

Up through the deep crevices the thawing waters bubbled, and Edie leaned across the boulders to see a fine film of skin slowly close over the large mirrored globes of the undine's eyes.

"It's working!" she gurgled. "Look! He's movin'!"

As the splintered chunks of ice melted and dwindled, the creature within the pool began to stir.

At first only the eyelids blinked. Then, as the dark hair began to swirl and wave in the warming waters, the head shifted, and choking back a cry, Edie saw at last the undine's face.

It was like looking at an ogre of the unlit deep. The undine's countenance was a frightening creation of scale and muscle. Between the great staring eyes two slits served as nostrils, and below them a wide, lipless, fishlike mouth opened to draw its first liquid breath in countless years.

Edie could see no neck to speak of; the scaly chin simply joined onto the creature's chest. The undine's shoulders were huge knots of shining, sinewy flesh fringed with webbed spines, and above them she saw a row of gills twitch and flare.

With the inky cloud of the water spirit's hair churning

thickly about its face, the creature's eyes swiveled within their froglike sockets, glaring up at the rippling world above until they finally came to rest upon the two figures standing beyond the rim of its domain.

Edie beamed and waved joyously, but Miss Veronica drew close to her and tried to lead the child away from the edge.

"Careful, Edith," she warned. "Folk are never at their best when they have just awoken. There's no knowing what sort of mood he might be in. Besides, not every member of his race was benevolent. They were apt to be untame and capricious. The undines were extremely powerful. They were here long before the land, long before Yggdrasill, long before us."

"You mean he might be bad?" the girl asked.

The old woman nodded fearfully. "The lords of the ice began as water spirits," she said. "Oh, dear, what have I done?"

But it was too late to repent of her actions now, for at that moment the pool boiled and seethed as, from the cold darkness, the undine rose.

Over the polished black stones the icy water crashed, drenching the figures of Edie and Miss Veronica as they stared helplessly at the ancient power that came bursting to the surface.

Into the upper air the undine erupted, throwing back its huge head to open the wide, razor-toothed mouth and roar in a voice like the pounding of the sea on the shore and the full fury of the raging storm.

As the bitterly cold waves smashed and battered over her, the girl could only splutter and gape up at the terrifying spectacle that reared from the pool like a dark vision dredged from a mariner's nightmare.

Shaken by the bellowing blare of the creature's sonorous clamor, the massive icicles that filled the cavern began to resonate and chime, while the immense glacial columns vibrated and tinkled as fragments shattered and fell away.

Edie jumped when one huge block of ice came tumbling down and exploded with a tremendous crash, then the clangorous din fell silent and she saw that the undine was glowering at them.

Deep ridges formed on the glistening skin of the creature's wide forehead as it considered them, and Edie felt a pitiless, indomitable force beat down upon her.

At her side, Miss Veronica caught her breath as she too felt the potency of the undine's overwhelming power.

Like a mounting, destroying wave, the monstrous figure towered over them, a drizzle of rain teeming from the long hanks of dark green hair that hung heavily over the pulsating gills, splashing into the pool and against their upturned faces as they anxiously waited.

"Your pardon, Lord!" Miss Veronica suddenly piped up, her frail voice sounding rather comical before that lowering countenance. "Long has it been since I was privileged to encounter one of your noble, exalted race. I am Veronica, a Spinner of the Wood, attendant of the last remaining root, and this is Edith, whom my sisters and I have taken to be our daughter."

Resting her hand upon the child's shoulder for balance, the old woman executed a clumsy curtsey then dabbed the dribbling water from her face.

Edie noticed that the furrows in the undine's brow had vanished and the tension in the wintry chamber was easing gradually.

"Eldest of all things are you," Miss Veronica continued in her praise. "Only the rolling waters and the flame that burns at the world's heart are older. You were ancient when the Ash first took root, and I honor you with great reverence."

Bowing her head, the old woman nudged Edie to do the same, but the child ignored her, for the undine let out a long, rumbling sigh and began to sink back into the pool.

Down into the dark water the gigantic bulk descended, until only the great head remained above the surface and the mass of hair snaked about the submerged shoulders like billowing fronds of pond weed.

Then, as the pale lids languidly slid over the sparkling mirrors of its eyes, the undine spoke.

A sound like trickling streams and rushing, rapid rivers came to Edie's ears from the lipless, gaping mouth, and to her delight, she found that she could understand what the babbling, splashing voice was saying.

"Grateful am I to you," the undine said, "measurer of petty destinies. The cold, binding shackles are undone at last, and the time of my captivity is over."

"Who did this cruel and wicked thing?" Miss Veronica asked.

A deep, rolling growl echoed from the creature's throat. "My brothers," came the dissonant reply.

"They forged for themselves chill flesh in which they left the waters, seeking dominion over the new continents. Yet I would not join them; enamored of the oceans as I was, the land held no fascination. My rebellion angered them, and so they tethered me with the biting chains of their new raiment. Here have I remained through the endless lonely years."

The eyelids closed, and the corners of the great mouth drooped despondently.

"So alone," the undine lamented. "Forsaken and forgotten in the chill, bleak darkness, without hope of light or companionship."

Miss Veronica tutted consolingly. "At least I had my sisters," she admitted. "However annoying they were, I was never alone."

"May the blessings of the deep be upon you," the creature said gently, in a voice like the rush of the foaming surf. "Now I am eager to return to the boundless blue seas. The grots and caves of this land I shall be most glad to leave. Farewell."

The old woman bowed a second time, and the water spirit slid farther into the pool.

"Hey, Fishface!" Edie suddenly shouted. "Don't you go yet!"

Only the large bulbous eyes were now above the surface of the water, and they turned upon her curiously.

"Edith!" Miss Veronica trilled in a fluster. "How dare you speak to him like that!"

"Why shouldn't I?" the girl answered defiantly, assuming a belligerent stance as she placed one foot on the boulders and jabbed a finger at the creature.

"I think you're downright mean and ungrateful!" she accused. "Leavin' us 'ere like this, after we went to the trouble of lettin' you go. Ain't you ashamed?"

Miss Veronica threw up her hands, scandalized. "You impudent child!" she gasped. "Button your lip at once."

"Won't!" the girl cried grumpily. "He's not only selfish but crazy as well. Ain't no point goin' back to the sea. There's none of his sort left—you said so yourself."

The undine raised his massive head from the pool, but this time his face was clouded with anger.

"What say you?" he thundered.

Edie placed her hands on her hips. "You're the last one," she said obstinately. "When you leave 'ere, you'll be on your lonesome all over again, with only sardines and kippers to talk to."

The cavern trembled as the water spirit snarled, and the pool churned as his wrath mounted. A dark shadow fell on Edie Dorkins, but the child simply laughed and snapped her fingers rudely.

"Blast and blow all you want," she told him with an unimpressed sniff and a curt toss of her head. "I don't care no more. All I wanted was to be friends. If you'd have come back to the museum with us, you could have stayed in our well and I could've chatted to you every day and kept you company. Would'a been good, I reckon. You wouldn't be lonely, and the well'd be full again. But you go off, go swim in your ocean. Leave us stranded 'ere where we found you."

The very air quivered as her insulting talk angered the ogre of the deep. Then, without warning, and as

Miss Veronica buried her face in her hands, the wide mouth opened and the creature chuckled softly.

It was a beautiful, melodic sound, like the gushing of rapid water over pebbles, and Edie grinned to hear it.

"I see you are a keeper of a different kind of sacred spring," he said. "The spirits of the waters are wise beyond your understanding, yet in you I see the hope of the world."

"Then you'll come live in our well?" she pressed.

The undine threw back his head and laughed more loudly this time, and the joyful noise rebounded throughout the vast cavern.

"Persistence should be your name," he told her. "But I will not trade one cramped jail for another. The wide waters are calling, and I must travel them."

"Oh, what a pity," Miss Veronica said. "It would have been quite like the old days. I know Celandine would be thrilled, and even Ursula would have to admit she was pleased. She couldn't be angry with me for running away then, could she? It would be as if nothing had ever changed."

The undine held them both in his keen, considering gaze. "Perhaps the time has indeed come for change," he said with unexpected sharpness, as his mood swung yet again. "Why should the well beneath the final root be replenished? The time of the Nornir is gone. Their ancient strength should not be restored to them."

"What are you saying?" the old woman cried.

"To all things there is an end," came the sinister reply. "Is that time not come for the attendants of Nirinel? Let the final root die."

"But if that happens—" Miss Veronica began to protest.

Again the creature laughed, but this time the sound was unpleasant and scornful.

"What care I?" he rumbled. "If I am the last of my race, then let the brethren who imprisoned me rule over a new darkness. Why prolong it further? The final, eternal night will come."

With that his immense head submerged beneath the surface of the pool, and his voice was lost in the bubbling waters.

"Get back 'ere!" Edie bawled, leaning over the edge and shaking her fist. "I hope you get torpedoed and end up fried and battered!"

Down into the dismal dark the undine descended, his vast bulk melting into the fathomless depths. But Edie continued to shout and rage until she saw two points of light flash and glimmer at her from far below, and she knew the creature was laughing at her.

Disgusted, she spun around and brandished the golden circlet with a ferocious determination upon her young face.

"Time we got out of 'ere," she cried, stomping over to the draped ice formation and ducking beneath it. "Got to be some way out. Let's find it and take this up to your Captain."

Miss Veronica agreed, but glancing worriedly back at the pool, she let out a frightened wail, and the child whirled around.

"Edith," the old woman yowled. "Look."

Hurrying back to her side, Edie saw that the water within the boundering black boulders was bubbling wildly and beginning to spill over the stones.

Across the frozen ground it flowed, flooding past their feet and seeping out into the cavern to swash against the farthest walls and fill the night-black crannies.

Like a spouting fountain the pool continued to swell, gushing its contents over the cavern floor, and the level quickly began to rise.

Miss Veronica gripped her cane in despair. "We shall never leave this place," she whimpered. "The undine's heart must have been hardened by the cold. He is no better than his brothers, the Frost Giants."

The water was up to Edie's ankles now, and she began to paddle back toward the center of the cavern, where the silver cruets were still blazing brightly.

"Sooner we get out the better then," she said. "Don't worry, Veronica. 'S only a bit of water, nothin' to be scared of. If we can fall all the way from up there with just some cuts an' bruises, we'll be all right."

The old woman swallowed fearfully as she stared down at the rising flood. "You don't understand," she muttered. "The power of the undine is behind this deluge. It is his will that flows about us."

"So?"

"He and his kind are mightier than the Nornir," she despaired. "Edith, can you not see? Do you not understand why they were our most bitter enemies? They and their works are capable of destroying us."

The water was up to the girl's knees now, and she gazed at Miss Veronica anxiously.

"So that's why he was laughing," she murmured. "What happens if we can't find a way out?"

"Then we're certain to drown," the old woman

said. "Oh, Edith! There is no way out—there isn't!"

"Has to be!" Edie yelled, wading through the fast-flowing water. "We have to find it!"

With growing panic, she floundered through the galleries of ice toward the cavern wall. But the glittering halls and corridors had become sluicing rivers, smashing through the fragile frozen screens in their path. Strong currents eddied and whirled around the high colonnades and dragged at the child's small frame as she pushed and trawled her way past.

Suddenly the steady brilliance of the silver cruets was thrown into turmoil as the waters lifted them up. The hallowed vessels were borne upon the tenacious tide, bobbing their way through the vast chamber, their blazing light shooting wildly around.

Shadows dipped and swamped as the magical lanterns rode the rising, churning waves, their splendor spinning giddily over the shimmering surfaces of rock and ice.

With the erratic glare flashing on her distressed face, Miss Veronica labored through the foaming channels after Edie and called to her desperately.

"It's no use, Edith!" she wept. "We'll never make it!"

Yet the child's anger would not let her rest, and when she reached the enclosing wall she frantically searched for a handhold or cleft, anything that might lead to a way out. With bitter determination she battled on, her arm thrust through the spiral hoop of the bracelet, exploring the stone by its pale radiance.

The water continued to swell and rise. By the time it had surged up to the girl's neck, she had still not found any means of escape. As the dragging, towing currents grew stronger, she finally abandoned all hope.

Sobbing, Miss Veronica blundered toward her. The water had reached the girl's chin, and Edie had to stand on tiptoe to breathe.

With tears streaming down her face, the old woman threw her arms around Edie and tried to lift her above the raging torrent. The child spluttered and clung on to her, jumping up and down to gulp the cold air, but Miss Veronica's limbs were too frail and weak even to lift her off the floor, and she sniveled desolately.

"Forgive me, Edith," she wept. "It was my vanity that brought you to this. Oh, I'm so sorry."

Edie shivered, thrashing madly with her arms as she tried to float above the surging waves. But it was no use. The undertow was too great, and despite her frenzied splashes, it hauled her down.

The girl's ears filled with freezing water as it closed above her head, and she choked as it flooded her mouth and nose.

With the silver cruets reeling a deranged wheel of light across the cavern, Miss Veronica did everything she could to drag the child back to the surface. Summoning all her puny strength, she tugged on Edie's sleeves, and the girl came up gasping and retching.

But the old woman could do no more. The fierce currents snatched the child from her grasp, and with a howling, terrified scream, Edie Dorkins was dragged down into the dark, seething waters.

"No!" Miss Veronica shrieked. "No!"

And then she too was lost.

CHAPTER 25

BATTLE OF THE THORN

Wretched and afraid, Neil Chapman scrambled over the stubbly grass of Wearyall Hill, his feet slipping in the unseen mud. The great bare mound that faced the Tor across the valley was shrouded in darkness. It rose like the back of an enormous whale from the surrounding sea of streetlights that glimmered in the remote encircling distance.

Barely able to see the rearing outline of the hill, Neil lumbered blindly upward, slithering onto his hands and knees when the ground abruptly rose even more steeply.

Before him, bounding and scampering, with his one eye ogling the way ahead, Quoth urged him on, squealing the directions.

"Keep true to this path!" the raven instructed. "We art upon a slender ridge. If thou dost stray but a little ye shalt tumble down."

"Any sign of the Thorn yet?" the boy cried. "There

doesn't seem to be anything growing up here!"

Quoth spied into the darkness ahead. "Not far!" he warbled. "Not far!"

Neil picked himself up, but before he could resume the stumbling climb, a faint yammering sound floated to him upon the night breeze. Turning, he looked across the twinkling valley below to where the Tor blotted out the horizon like a huge black cloud.

Quoth's goading encouragement choked in the raven's throat as he too heard the chilling noise. Although he could not see them yet, he knew that the Valkyries were racketing through the sky.

"Hlökk hath fetched her sisters," he muttered dismally.

Neil strained his eyes and thought he could see specks blacker than the enveloping night veer over the Tor and Chalice Hill and swing out across the flatlands toward Wells.

"They're chasing Aidan," he breathed.

Quoth sniffed and hung his bald head. "Though the darkness rideth o'er him, his goodly name shalt keep its luster everlasting."

In silence they waited, wondering what was happening beyond the screening hills.

* * *

Leaving Glastonbury behind, Aidan had headed for Wells in order to lead anything that followed him as far away from Neil as possible.

The van sped along the deserted country road, and the cold air rushed in through the clawed roof, battering against the gypsy's grim face and tugging at his long, dark hair.

The fleeting blur of trees and hedges raced by as the vehicle roared down the winding way, but Aidan's thoughts were elsewhere. Ruefully he remembered how he had told Miss Ursula Webster not to worry, that he would bring Veronica and Edie back to her. Yet ever since he had arrived in Glastonbury everything had gone wrong. What if the raven women had already captured Verdandi and the girl? What hope could there be for them now?

"Please, let there still be a chance," he muttered under his breath.

As if in answer, he suddenly heard the rising clamor of repulsive, skirling voices, and Aidan's face contorted with anguish and desolation.

"So soon," he whispered. "I thought there'd be a little more time. . . ."

He pressed his foot down, and the van careered recklessly over the road, the beams of the headlights streaking into two flaming smudges of light. The air that poured into the jagged rents was whipped into a pummeling gale that sang in his ears. Yet it could not drown out the tremendous baying and screeching that echoed about the sky, and Aidan knew that the end would not be long in coming.

Down the twisting lanes the vehicle shot, skidding around sharp bends, the brambles scraping against its sides in its mad, bouncing dash. But soon the air above was thickly alive with a frenzied thrashing of feathers. Over the meandering lane the host of the Valkyries soared, their hideous, abhorrent faces glaring at the small blue van bolting below them.

At the forefront of the hellish horde, with oaths of death and bloodshed screaming from its cruel beak, Hlökk began spiraling down, plunging through the air, leading the others in the attack.

Glancing up through the torn roof, Aidan saw the Valkyries descending, and before he knew it, the van was swamped by a mass of flailing black plumes and clattering feathers.

Desperately, Aidan battled to keep the vehicle on the road as savage claws buffeted and hammered into it. Down ripped the ravaging beaks, shredding what remained of the roof like tattered fragments of paper. Then up onto the grassy banks and back again the nightmares hurled the battered, beleaguered van, and their harrowing screams of derision rose to a malevolent crescendo.

At the height of the screaming, four curved talons ruptured the side windows, hooking around the frames, and two pairs of mighty wings began to lash the air.

Trapped in the driver's seat, Aidan felt the van judder and lurch, and the rear wheels whined in complaint as they were lifted off the road.

Up from the ground Raging and Screamer hoisted the vehicle, hauling it above the hedgerows, then higher than the trees.

As the van swung perilously from side to side, Aidan let go of the steering wheel and threw himself back against the seat. There was nothing he could do now. All further struggle was futile.

Staring up through the torn ceiling, he saw the

loathsome forms of the two Valkyries eagerly flap their filthy wings. Beyond their odious shapes he glimpsed something more horrifying: the figure of a terrified man dangling from the claws of another monster.

His arms aching and his face numb with cold and shock, the Reverend Galloway could hardly believe what was happening. At the top of his voice he called to Thought to put a stop to this ghastly ordeal. The raven ignored him, and the vicar was left hanging like a limp rabbit in an eagle's claws.

Unable to reconcile the horrible reality of the actions of the Valkyries with the tenets of his faith, he now doubted everything the raven had said.

Twisting his head around, Peter gazed on the suspended van, dazzled momentarily by the headlight beams slicing through the night as the vehicle tipped and rocked. He then looked at the driver within. For the briefest instant the men exchanged glances, each sharing their fears, each pitying the other.

Aidan narrowed his eyes, but he was not permitted to wonder about the identity of the unfortunate soul or why the Valkyries had captured him, for at that moment there was a flutter of smaller feathers. Diving between the creatures above, a sleek raven with sharp, cunning eyes perched on the edge of the roof and leered feverishly inside.

"What trickery is this?" Thought cried when he discovered that the van contained only Aidan. "Where is my brother? Where is Memory?"

A look of defiant recognition crossed Aidan's face. "You must be Thought," he shouted above the rushing wind. "I wondered if we'd meet."

The raven spat at him. "Bandy no words with me, thou progeny of peasants. By the slenderest thread dost thy paltry life hang. Naught would give my Master's servants greater glee than to let thee fall."

The gypsy laughed bleakly. "You were pickled in the museum too long," he tutted with a fearless shake of his head. "Otherwise you'd know that threats never work on someone you're going to kill anyway. I'd say it was time to give up your stripes and retire, old boy. You're not the bird I've heard you were."

"Thine ill-mannered tongue shalt be ripped from the root!" Thought hissed in outrage.

"What is the pension for the likes of you?" Aidan jeered. "Three worms a day, is it? Or do you get millet and a cuttlefish thrown in as well? If you're really lucky you might get a dinky little mirror to keep you company."

Incensed, the raven threw back his head to bark out the order for the Valkyries to send the van hurtling to the ground. But at the last instant he wavered, and his beady eyes darted back to gloat over the audacious gypsy in the callous hope of seeing him squirm.

Yet Aidan was no longer looking up at him. The man was staring out of the shattered passenger window. Thought followed his glance to see the lights of Glastonbury sparkling in the distance and the dark mound of Wearyall Hill rising just beyond.

"Ho!" he squawked, puffing out his chest. "Thine own eyes betray thee."

Aidan turned away quickly, but the raven could see the anxiety he was so desperately striving to conceal.

"What of thy arrogance now?" the bird cackled.

"Art thou sapped of thine taunts to be so silent?"

Furious with himself, Aidan growled and without warning leaped up from his seat to grab the insidious, malicious raven and wring his neck.

But Thought was too quick. With one sweep of his wings he was out of the gypsy's reach, and his mocking laughter floated down to him.

"Now thou shalt drink at the bitter cup of thine own providing!" the bird's harsh voice scorned. "Raging, Screamer, bear thy charge a little farther. We return to Ynnis Witrin!"

The atrocities above shrieked their obedience, and the van whirled about as the horde of raven women flew back toward Glastonbury.

Gazing out of the windshield, Aidan saw the small shape of Wearyall Hill grow ever larger as they stormed through the heavens. He hoped that Neil had managed to reach the Thorn in time.

* * *

"Danger approacheth," Quoth whimpered, starting to back away up the slope. "The Valkyries are returning. To the Thorn, Master Neil, whilst there still be time!"

Holding his wings out wide, the bird scuttled up the hill in panic. With the screeching rising steadily in the distance, Neil Chapman tore after.

Louder grew the braying shrieks as the boy ran the final stretch to the Glastonbury Thorn.

Situated just short of the summit, the tree was a tortured-looking specimen that had been sculpted by the wind and was surrounded now by hooped railings.

The Thorn leaned rakishly to the left, its dense knot of tangled branches resembling a cloud of spikes and needles. As he stared at it, Neil wondered if Aidan's story had been only a joke. How could that puny tree possibly be any defense against the power of Woden's conjured monsters?

The screeches were nearly deafening now. He knew that the Valkyries were closing fast, yet the boy dared not turn around in case the fearful sight of them rooted him to the spot.

"Almost there!" Quoth called, his eye flicking from Neil to the evil rushing toward them. "Quickly, quickly!"

Neil sprinted the remaining distance, but just as he neared the Thorn, two circles of light flashed across the hillside. Hearing the noise of an engine overhead, he had the wild idea that the air force had been called to contend with the winged enemies. He spun around gladly to catch a glimpse of the arriving helicopter, only to reel back in horror.

The glare and noise were coming from Aidan's van, and Neil spluttered in fright to see it swinging high above.

"Master Neil!" Quoth squealed. "The Thorn—reach for it."

But the boy could not tear his eyes from the horrendous spectacle, and the draft of many wings beat down upon his upturned, stricken face.

Ducking under the railing, the raven wailed when he saw that Neil had halted, and he came blustering back to tug at his shoelaces.

Three of the grotesque nightmares plummeted out

of the sky, wings tucked behind them and talons outstretched, ready to snatch the boy from the ground and shower the soil with his blood. Transfixed, Neil could see their malignant eyes fixed upon him. Their demoniacal yells blared in his ears, but still his legs would not move, and the Valkyries opened their murderous beaks to snap through his bones.

At the boy's feet, Quoth tried in vain to rouse him. Then, as the great quilled specters came ripping over the grass in a deadly, swooping dive, the raven pushed his head forward and bit Neil sharply on the ankle.

Neil yowled, and at last his paralyzed terror left him. He staggered toward the Thorn, only to slam into the railings that surrounded it.

With an almighty scream, the raven women shot after him, their feathers battering and raking over his back as their talons reached to slit his flesh. Neil screwed up his face as the first claw slashed his blazer, but before it scythed into his skin, he thrust his arms between the rails, threw them around the tree's gnarled trunk, and hung on for dear life.

On the grass behind him Quoth was flung backward as a brilliant light suddenly burst over the hilltop, and the despoiling, triumphant shrieks of the Valkyries were at once transformed into shrill screams of agony.

Rolling down the sloping ground, Quoth came to a sprawling stop. With his head tucked awkwardly under one leg, he gazed up at the wondrous sight in amazement.

The knotted branches of the Thorn were erupting with fiery blossom. Every petal crackled and shone like the sun reflected upon rippling water, until the whole tree was bathed in one enveloping, blinding flame that drenched the hillside with a holy rose-colored light.

Beneath the blazing boughs, Neil felt the hairs on the back of his neck prickle and rise. But despite the intensity of the flaring, lambent fires, he felt no heat. Staring upward he saw that the branches were neither burned nor scorched.

Above the radiant Thorn, whirling in dismay and alarm, the three Valkyries brayed their angry frustration. The fabulous light pained their unclean eyes, and if they strayed too close to the flame their primary feathers smoked. They squawked in outrage at this unlooked-for threat to their ferocious and brutal authority.

High over the hill, the other creatures clamored to see their sisters so confounded, but Thought flew among them to assuage their rising panic.

"Fear not!" he crowed. "Such useless chicanery poseth no obstacle."

Glaring down at the shining Thorn, the sour-faced raven suddenly spotted a black dot tottering over the grass. He recognized it at once.

"The time of judgment is nigh!" he hissed, thundering down.

* * *

"Cleave to the tree, Master Neil!" Quoth hollered, bowling forward, overjoyed to see the Valkyries held at bay. "Thou canst come to no harm in its blessed shelter."

Scuttling forward to join the boy in the Thorn's

protection, the bird stopped abruptly and whisked wildly around.

"Brother mine!" called a terse, strident voice. "Where goest thou?"

In a flurry of feathers, Thought landed lightly on the grass, and Quoth's one eye goggled at him as a turmoil of emotions flooded through every fiber of his being.

Woden's lieutenant eyed him shrewdly. It was plain that the power that had restored his brother to life had been lacking and the regeneration was not complete. If he could only reach those damaged areas of his brain, if he could only deliver him back into the service of the Gallows God.

"Memory!" Thought cawed in an insidious, truckling voice. "I did think ne'er to look upon thy visage again. It pleaseth me greatly to find thee now."

Quoth's beak fell open as his brother's wheedling words stirred the vague images of his past, and he recalled the terrible craving for war and carnage his former self had reveled in.

"No greater love exists than that of brother for brother," Thought asserted, putting forth his power. "Divided we are naught, yet together none may assail us. Join me, Memory, be what thou wert. A most excellent crusade awaits our commanding, and great renown shalt be ours."

Swaying unsteadily, Quoth floundered in the resurging memories. Images that had been transient glimpses now reared almost tangibly around him.

In the last hour of his former existence, the forces of Woden were charging over the plain toward the enchanted wood, where the three usurping females had made their abode, dispensing their destinies and mocking the might of his Lord.

The sound of battle raged all about as those faithful to the royal house of Askar clashed with the legions of their erstwhile Captain. The turbulent noises of death were like glad music to the dumbfounded raven. Flying low over the enemy's green banners and weaving in and out of their upraised spears, the twelve terrible servants came storming after, and the Valkyries strung their hideous, gore-dripping loom with the entrails of their butchered victims.

It was a magnificent, victorious day. While his Master's army was trampling over the bodies of its foes, Memory shot clear of the fray to go speeding toward the wood, laughing raucously at the top of his brash, haughty voice, singing the praises of the Gallows God and deriding the hated Nornir.

Trumpets and drums proclaimed this the finest moment of his life as he rushed recklessly through the outlying trees to be the first to mock the three sisters and herald the end of their dominion over fate and fortune. Yet even as the jubilant, conceited song of victory sprang from his gullet, the mist rose about him and into darkness and oblivion he tumbled.

Quoth teetered upon his scrawny legs, the shock of his unleashed pernicious personality jolting through him. Thought snickered to himself to see it.

"Let us be as we were in the early time," Woden's raven invited. "Join me, brother, and we shalt feast on victory ever after."

Clinging to the Holy Thorn, Neil Chapman

watched anxiously as his tattered companion wavered. The boy recalled Miss Ursula's warning concerning the treachery of the bird should its memory ever be restored.

"Quoth!" he shouted. "Don't listen to him!"

Steeped in the splendor of the tree's flames, the one-eyed raven glanced back at the boy. Then, returning his hooded gaze to his brother, in a defiant, sublime voice, he announced, "'Tis better to nibble a morsel of sweet pudding than gorge upon the stale and wormy pie. Hatchlings we may have been, yet no more. The bond betwixt us is sundered. Memory didst perish in the mists long ages since. Now I doth dance to a different tune, for I am Quoth, and zooks-hurrah for that!"

Neil could have hugged him, but Thought's face contorted with rage and his eyes burned with rancor and bitterness. Squawking in fury, he leaped into the air and let loose a piercing shriek to the Valkyries high above them.

"Behold then the dire consequence of this thy imbecile choice!" he ranted. "Look on what thou hast done."

Neil and Quoth glanced up to where Raging and Screamer wheeled in circles above the hill. Suspended from their talons Aidan's van swung precariously, but hearing their leader's signaling cry, the monstrous creatures responded with a foul, jubilant screech and slackened their grip.

To the boy's horror, he saw the vehicle fall from their grasp and come toppling out of the sky.

"No!" he yelled. "Aidan!"

CHAPTER 26

DEJECTED AND DOWNCAST

Quoth trembled and hurriedly buried his face in his feathers as the van tumbled down. Somersaulting in the darkness, the headlights spun a demented whirl of light as they rocketed toward the hilltop.

With a splintering crunch of metal, the vehicle thundered into the ground, smashing onto the hill a sickeningly short distance away from the Holy Thorn.

"Aidan!" the boy bawled.

Impacted on its side, the shattered wreckage rocked momentarily before tipping over and crashing onto its roof. With a grating clank of buckled metal, the driver's door popped from its hinges to go slithering down the hillside, and like a rag doll, the gypsy's broken body was thrown out onto the grass.

Neil stared at him in despair. The man was covered in blood, and he was so badly crushed and smashed that the boy wrenched his eyes away to press his face against the weathered tree trunk. But he could not escape the revulsion that boiled and tore inside him, and he cursed Woden's raven with all his might.

"You murdered him!" he bawled.

Thought gave a chilling chortle as he flew around the tree. "A fitting punishment," he cried, "and one which thou shalt surely share. Didst thou truly think this burning briar couldst hinder my Master? Nay, 'tis a sanctuary no longer. Easily canst thou be torn from thy petty shield."

"You just try it!" Neil dared. "I'd love to see you burst into flames!"

But the raven mocked him and gave a loud chittering cry.

At once Biter descended, with the Reverend Galloway dangling in its clutches, and seeing the man who had danced at his school assembly come swooping out of the night, Neil thought he had finally lost his mind.

*　*　*

Peter had witnessed everything. When the Thorn had erupted with divine flame, his heart had leaped as he took it for a sign that all would be well. But when he realized that it was repelling the winged atrocities he had believed were angels, he was once again consumed with an anguish that turned into abject despair as the van was sent hurtling down. In his distress he prayed for the man who had been inside.

The ground raced up to meet his trailing feet, and when Biter released his aching arms, the vicar was thrown roughly onto the grass.

Staggering, he stared woefully at the wreckage where the gypsy's motionless body lay then stumbled away from it.

"What have you done?" he wailed when Thought came fluttering toward him. "This is evil! You've lied to me from start to finish!"

"Silence!" the raven scolded. "Yonder rogue didst betray our Lord. His seditious crimes wouldst have prevented His return."

Peter shook his head. "That's no reason to kill," he sobbed. "I want no part of this!"

"Fainthearted worm!" Thought shrieked. "From thy path there is no returning. My Lord hath need of thee yet awhiles."

"I can do no more than I have," the vicar refused. "I only wish I had not done that much."

The raven flew before his face, his voice ringing with compelling command. "Obey me!" he demanded. "Obey the Master! Dost thou wish for countless others to perish?"

"You know I don't."

"Then undertake this simplest of tasks."

Peter nodded wearily. "What must I do?" he asked.

Thought swept back to the Thorn. "Remove this whelp!" he ordered. "Tear him free!"

"Don't do it!" Neil shouted. "Don't help them."

The Reverend Galloway turned back to the raven. "He's just a child!" he protested. "Suffer the little children!"

"Shrink from this one act and thou art denying thy faith," Thought screamed back at him. "Thus far, through trial and ordeal, thou hast come, and He is best pleased in thee. Do not balk at this, the bitter end. Shall it be said of thee that thou wast found wanting at the last?"

Peter pressed his fingers to his temples. He didn't understand anything anymore. He was tired and shaken, and the raven's raucous urging was subverting his own force of will.

"Very well," he found himself saying.

"You keep away from me!" Neil warned when the vicar approached.

"I'm not going to hurt you," Peter promised. "Why don't you just let go?"

"You're crazy listening to that lying bundle of filth!" the boy cried. "He'll kill us all!"

"Master Neil doth speak the truth!" Quoth pleaded. "Avaunt and leave him be. Thou art deceived and duped!"

But the vicar strode up to the hooped rails and put his hands through them to take hold of the boy's arms. Then he started to pull them from the tree.

Furious, Neil lashed out and kicked him. The man grimaced under the raining blows, but eventually he dragged him away. At once the Holy Thorn flickered; the fiercely blazing blossom withered, and darkness returned to Wearyall Hill.

"Beware!" Quoth yelped as the horrendous black shapes of the Valkyries came swooping down.

There was nothing Neil could do to save himself. A searing pain pinched his shoulders as Hlökk's vicious talons grabbed him, and the boy was torn from the hillside and carried aloft into the night.

"Master Neil!" the one-eyed raven whined.

The Reverend Galloway watched Neil's wildly wriggling figure soar heavenward, and he turned an ashen face to Thought.

"What'll it do with him?" he asked.

Woden's lieutenant sniggered wickedly and cocked his head over to the van's wreckage. "The cur shalt pay for the trouble he hath caused, as do all who rise against the Lord," he muttered hollowly.

"You'd kill a child? How can this be the will of God?"

Thought smirked at him. "Thee and thy conscience shalt not wrestle much longer—the time is almost upon us. But first, one more score remaineth to settle."

Spreading his wings, he glided down to where Quoth hopped dejectedly on the grass, whimpering Neil's name and staring disconsolately up at the sky.

"Fawning mouthpiece of the despised Nornir!" Thought spat. "Thou hast been spared till the last. If Memory, mine brother, be truly dead, so too art thee, traitor!"

Sprinting forward, he rammed his flat head into Quoth's chest, and the startled bird blundered helplessly onto his back.

"Die then!" the malevolent raven cried, lunging down to claw three bloody rents across the side of Quoth's face. Neil's companion squealed in pain as he struggled to right himself.

Lashing out with his feet, Quoth kicked his opponent under the beak, and Thought was thrown off balance.

Seizing his chance, Quoth sprang up, but Woden's lieutenant was strong and his wings were powerful. Snapping and biting, he charged at the bald bird, plucking a cloud of mangy feathers from Quoth's scraggy neck as they grappled and vied with each other, scuffling and rolling over the grass.

Yet Thought had the mastery, and soon Quoth was pinned down with a fierce claw squeezed about his throat. Woden's raven sneered his contempt as he casually scored his talons through his brother's flesh.

"Thy trifling attempt to foil my Lord's design hath failed," he crowed. "The palsied hags shalt be destroyed, and the Gallows God wilt take his rightful place as the Master of Destiny."

Bruised and bleeding, Quoth bleated forlornly, unable to struggle any longer.

"The breath from thine body shalt I wring," Thought said sadistically. "Against the stones thy skull wilt be dashed, and thy carcass become a haunt of wasps and maggots."

His beak gaping open as he gasped and choked, Quoth felt the life ebb away from him, and his flailing wings flopped limply at his side.

Throwing back his ugly head, Thought gave an odious, gloating chuckle and prepared to snap his brother's spine.

Suddenly a feverish yammering resounded above the hilltop, and the raven glared upward as the Valkyries began shrieking more excitedly than ever.

"'Tis time!" he cried. "The Twelve hath seen it!"

Giving Quoth's inert, battered body a scornful kick, Thought flew to Peter's shoulder and shouted in his ear.

"Hark! We must fly. The final moment is come!"

"Do I have to go with you?" the vicar complained. The raven pointed up to where the Valkyries were circling and cackled darkly. "Behold the boy thou didst pluck from the Thorn," he said. "Perform this last act, and I swear unto ye his life shalt be spared."

"You promise?"

Thought's eyes glittered at him. "Assuredly I do. Yet think on the marvels that lie ahead. The golden prize hath been found."

And so, for the last time, Peter agreed and lifted his arms in the air. Once again they were seized by Biter, and he was swept up into the darkness above.

Alone on the hilltop, Thought gazed at the destruction around him, and his black, merciless heart was gratified. Then, anxious to oversee the last stage of his Master's intricate plan, he stretched his wings and rose into the sky.

Across the tormented heavens the ghastly host raged away from Wearyall Hill, following the course of the road that led to Chalice Hill, and their horrendous voices dwindled in the distance.

*   *   *

With his open beak squashed in the mud, Quoth groaned miserably and waited until he had gathered enough strength to push himself over before attempting to move.

Wincing from the agony of his wounds, he somehow managed to squirm onto his side. Then, looking about him, he was horrified to discover that he was lying right next to Aidan's body and was gazing straight at his upturned face.

The gypsy's eyes, glazed with pain, were staring

fixedly up at the night, and Quoth shuddered woefully.

"Master Neil," he lamented. "To what ignoble end hath we all come? Wouldst that I could die at thine side."

"Neil . . ." a weak voice whispered.

The raven blinked in astonishment and sat up in spite of his raw cuts and throbbing bruises.

The voice was Aidan's. The man was still alive.

Lurching to his feet and dragging his damaged wing behind him, Quoth hobbled closer to the dying human and looked forlornly upon his blood-soaked face.

"Alas," he wept. "Lackaday, our hopes art in ruin and thy valor wast for naught."

Aidan's lips quivered as he strove to speak, but death was stealing over him, and in a hoarse whisper he said, "The tramp . . . Neil . . . find him . . . find Tommy . . ."

And with those words, the leader of the descendants of Askar died.

Quoth sniveled into his feathers and solemnly laid his head against the man's bloody brow.

"So passeth a noble knight," he mourned. "And hereafter the day shalt be a shade more dark than before."

A tear trickled from the raven's downcast eye and ran the length of his beak to splash onto the ground. Then Quoth's bald head crinkled with a frown, and the bird looked at Aidan in wonder as he realized the importance of his dying words. One single, slender chance still remained, and only he could prevent the awaiting doom from descending.

Staring out across the valley, Quoth watched the Valkyries swarm above the town. The Tor, where he knew Tommy would be hiding, appeared an awfully long way off, and he would never reach it in time even if he ran without stopping. Yet as he gauged the great distance, a new resolve hardened in his breast, and the bird's hope swelled.

"Master Neil," he murmured, "thy ragged raven shalt save thee, else die in the attempt."

Pattering across the grass to where the broad, sloping hillside stretched down before him, Quoth opened his useless wings and gave the ground a determined scratch with his claws.

"Upon my shoulders dost doom now lie," he told himself, summoning his strength and flexing his feathers. "Craven and timid thou art, Quoth, yet cringing shalt avail thee naught at this, the last hour."

Hopping from foot to foot he gave an experimental flap of his wings then began beating them more forcefully as he set off, running down the hill.

"Thou canst do this," he squawked. "'Tis no great matter. The lowly sparrow and base gnat doth accomplish the feat every day."

Over the ground he charged, leaping into the air, feverishly thrashing his feathers, but no matter how hard he tried, he never rose more than a few inches.

"Do not abandon hope!" he yelled. "Think of thy master!"

But in Quoth's mad, frantic rush, his foot caught on a stone, and wailing fearfully, he tripped and fell headlong into the wind. Squeezing his eye shut he waited for the crash as he tumbled beak over claw, and his hopeful spirits were utterly crushed.

Yet the expected crunch into soil and sod did not

occur. When the raven tentatively opened his eye, to his overwhelming joy he found he was sailing high above the ground, riding the night air and gliding over the hill. He was flying.

There was no time for the fledgling to enjoy the new experience. Fanning out his wings still farther, he flew over the roofs of Hill Head, and taking a circuitous route across the fields to avoid the horde of raven women, he made for the Tor.

Cold was the gale that streamed through the meager feathers about Quoth's head as he shot like a bullet toward the lofty summit of the majestic mountain and circled once around the tower of Saint Michael before diving into one of the two archways at its base.

Within the solitary building, Tommy sat upon the hard ground, his collection of religious icons spread meticulously about him in a carefully arranged circle. Surrounded by the angelic cards and cherubic figurines, with the flames of three candles flickering over the enclosing stones, he chewed his toothless gums and covered his face with his cap as the noise of the Valkyries echoed about the vaulted sky outside.

Suddenly, into his sanctuary, a manic bundle of quacking feathers came bursting, and the tramp cried out in alarm as Quoth tumbled to an ungainly, skidding halt before him.

"Fie! Fie!" the raven shrieked, even before he had picked himself up from the sorry heap he had landed in. "Thou art needed, old man!"

Tommy stared at the demented bird and huddled into a frightened ball. "You get out of Tommy's refuge!" he shouted. "Leave him alone."

"The future doth teeter upon a knife edge!" Quoth cried, scampering over to him. "The Twelve hath made Master Neil captive. He shalt be killed less thou aid him! I can do naught alone. I beseech thee, old one."

The tramp shivered and averted his eyes from the imploring raven. "Tommy can't!" he gibbered. "Them bird women are out there. They'll get him if he steps out of his hidey-hole."

"Then a curse upon thee!" Quoth snorted, his temper raging. "Sit here and wait for the end, yet when my master is thrown from the heights, know that his blood is upon thy hands, and none of this foolish litter shalt comfort thee then!"

Barging about the tramp, the raven kicked the figurines and scattered the scraps of card and paper he so desperately treasured, then flicked his tail up in disgust.

"No!" Tommy warbled, groveling to retrieve them and repair the circle.

Quoth glowered at him then turned to leave. "Puny use shalt I prove to be," he declared. "Yet I must do what I can. Unto thee doth I bequeath any white feathers I didst possess—to add to the great store of thine own. Aidan was wrong about thee!"

With that he bolted from the tower and shakily took to the air once more.

Sitting in his lonely sanctuary, Tommy wiped his dribbling nose and sobbed piteously.

"Mercy on us," he burbled, shamed by the bird's great courage. "Send angels to save them. Oh, listen to them devils out there. Won't someone do something? Help us, the everlasting darkness is here!"

CHAPTER 27

THE PROPERTY OF LONGINUS

Suspended from Hlökk's powerful claws, with the monstrous crowd of Valkyries swooping around him, their reviled clangorous voices crowing and screeching in triumph, Neil Chapman ceased his struggles and gazed desolately down.

The world seemed horribly far below. Beneath his dangling legs a sickening gulf dropped and fell away to where the lights of Glastonbury appeared as tiny jewels.

Hlökk's hideous croaking voice sounded above him as the creature called across the sky to its sisters, "*Verdandi iss near. The reek of her chokess and sstifless!*"

Diving in among them, Thought twirled in the air and laughed proudly. "This is the moment for which our Master hath waited these long empty years," he exulted. "Behold, down yonder—the witch ascendeth, bringing with her the instrument of her own destruction."

Flying high above Chalice Hill, the raven women

turned their baleful glances down to Wellhouse Lane, where the two springs gushed and gurgled into the grids. Stretching their murderous beaks wide, they honked with hellish glee.

The surface of the road was trembling. Even from his lofty, perilous vantage point, Neil could see the lane buckling and bulging with the pressure of some tremendous force that pushed and stretched it from below.

Creaking, the blacktop heaved as the soil beneath it thrust and churned. The metal grates by the pavement clanked and rattled, until suddenly the spreading cracks burst apart and up from the ruptured road exploded a hail of dirt and rubble.

Clods of earth and grinding stones were scattered over the lane as the fissure widened. Out of the depths of this newly formed chasm there came an almighty roaring. Then into the night spouted a torrent of water.

High the massive fountain towered, its foaming maelstrom of cascading spray snatched by the breeze to go drizzling over the town. The roads were turned into rivers as the wild, unstoppable deluge came racing out of Wellhouse Lane to flood across Chilkwell Street and course down the length of Bere Lane.

Like an icy volcano, spewing freezing water into the air, the crevasse continued to rage and grow until, all at once, the surging column dwindled, its might spent. With a final squirting rush it ceased, but the brimming chasm continued to bubble and quake as, up from the deep reaches of the earth, the controlling might of the last undine propelled two figures into the chill night air.

From the frothing fathoms Miss Veronica and Edie came, and when their heads broke through the surface of the water, they gasped and gagged, gulping for air.

Edie quickly scrabbled for the side, but the undine's power gently lifted them both clear as the ground swelled, carrying their buoyant forms out of the fissure and depositing them safely on the road.

So was the debt he owed them for his release repaid. Edie and Miss Veronica lay upon the lane, panting and puffing like stranded fish while the waters retreated back into the gulf and the red and white springs resumed their idle gurgling.

Soaked to the skin, Edie coughed and spluttered and squelchily rose, a puddle forming about her sodden, dripping figure.

"See, Veronica," she began, shaking herself like a dog. "He weren't bad after all . . ."

Only then did she hear the wild, baying calls in the sky. She lifted her eyes to see the dark-winged nightmares slowly descend.

"Strewth!" she squealed, splashing over to where the old woman was attempting to stand. "What's them things?"

Miss Veronica gripped her cane and peered upward. "*Valkyrja*," she gasped, shivering at the sight of them. "My Captain's most terrible servants. They are horrible, Edith. Why has he summoned them here, I wonder? I hope we have not come too late!"

"Can they hurt us?" the girl asked.

The old woman looked anxious. "The creatures

fear the Spinners of the Wood," she answered. "We despatched them long ago, and they won't have forgotten that in a hurry. But Woden wouldn't let them harm us."

Taking the glimmering golden circlet from around the child's arm, Miss Veronica flourished it for all to see and hurried toward the narrow trackway that led to the Tor.

"There cannot be much time left," she told the girl. "We must reach the Captain quickly."

Edie followed her up the sloping path, stumbling often, for her eyes were trained upon the skirling raven women above.

Miss Veronica, however, attempted to put the distressing creatures from her mind, for she was anticipating the moment when her Woden would be made well by the magical device she had taken from Joseph's grave. Hastening between the bordering trees and hedges, she arrived at the gate that opened out onto the Tor and lifted her walking cane as she had done before.

"Awaken," she called. "Verdandi summons you, O rod of life and—"

The old woman broke off abruptly as, through the overhanging branches, Thought came darting.

"Fairest princess!" the raven cried, coveting the bracelet she held as he alighted upon the gravestone-like stile. "A thousand thanks and more! No reward is too great for thine intrepid deeds. Thou hast returned not an instant too soon. The grains of His life are near run out. Come, thou must heal Him."

"Wait," Miss Veronica begged. "He must not see

me like this. I must be young and beautiful again. It is Verdandi he wants, not this dried-up old hag."

Thought pranced up and down in agitation. "No time, no time!" he cawed desperately. "What use thy former beauty if it shineth only upon death?"

"Is he really that close?" she breathed. "Then hurry, fly. Take this thing to him! Don't wait for me."

The old woman held the circlet out to the raven, but the action took Thought by complete surprise, and he seemed almost afraid to touch it. Squawking in alarm, the flustered bird nearly toppled from the perch as he dodged to avoid coming into contact with that precious glowing metal.

"Nay, Nay!" he cried, leaping into the air, where it was safer. "My Master shalt be carried hither."

"Is that why the *Valkyrja* are here?" Miss Veronica demanded.

Thought bowed, feigning respect. "Thou hast no need to fear the Twelve," he told her. "They art my Master's bearers. If 'twould appease thy dread, only the one who conveyeth His ailing form shalt descend."

"No, no, I'm sure there's no need for that. They are his servants, after all."

"As thou sayest. Now I shalt lead them hither so thou may surrender thy most marvelous prize unto His own hands."

Edie watched the bird as he soared upward to call down the Valkyries, and the girl pouted. She didn't trust that creature and suspected that everything his treacly, toadying voice said was one fat, continuous lie.

But Miss Veronica was too anxious to save her Captain to notice any of this. She passed through the stile to stand in the open ground beyond as the raven cried out to the Valkyries.

* * *

High over the Tor, Hlökk croaked jealously as the eleven other nightmares started to descend, and with malicious spite, it squeezed Neil's shoulders even tighter until the boy yelped.

With Biter at their head, the apparitions rushed down to the lower slopes of the great green mountain. In the leader's talons, while they were still far above the ground, the Reverend Peter Galloway quivered as he felt the shadowy webs of illusion form about him once again. Shimmering strands of deceit appeared from the ether to wind tightly around the vicar's body, weaving the same image of the young Askarian Captain that he had worn that afternoon.

From his shoulders the sable cloak streamed in the wind, and a silver helm materialized about his brow as the mail armor glittered like stars in the darkness.

The fantasy was completed long before Miss Veronica or Edie Dorkins could possibly see the transformation take place. Thought flew up to remind the man what he must do.

"The prize is thine for the taking," the raven told him. "Yet remember thy part; act it well and the boy shalt be spared."

"I understand," the blond phantasm of Woden assented. "Whatever you ask."

Down on the Tor, Miss Veronica Webster could hardly contain her mounting excitement as the great dark shapes grew nearer. With a momentous buffeting gale as huge wings churned the air, the Valkyries landed and the false vision of Woden was deposited with the utmost reverence upon the ground.

As Biter fell back, the other raven women bowed low to the deluding image, humbly laying their horrific heads upon the grass in mute obeisance.

Edie stared at their grotesque unnatural shapes with amazement then looked long at their sharp hooked claws. It was not difficult to imagine the carnage they were capable of, and she wrinkled her nose at the rancid odor that drifted from their repulsive quilled bodies.

At her side, Miss Veronica focused her attention upon her beloved Captain, and she hobbled over to him with the bracelet in her hands.

"Woden!" she cried. "Oh, I'm so glad there is still time."

The tall warrior spluttered as Peter remembered he was supposed to be dying and gave the old woman a weak smile.

"I knew you would not fail me," he murmured with a convincing weary gasp. "You have saved me, Verdandi. Give the thing to me, and we will be together forever."

Miss Veronica blushed coyly. "I'm not as you remember," she apologized. "Time has not been kind to me, Woden. I am old and ugly. What future can there be for us?"

Looking through the illusion's eyes, the vicar

viewed the ancient shriveled face. Her garish makeup had been washed away in the flood, and she looked like any other old lady. Her back was bowed and crippled, the flesh exposed by the flimsy gown was mottled and sagged, and the hands were swollen and arthritic. And yet, perhaps by the aid of some unexpected power the deceiving image afforded him, he could also see beyond the wizened exterior and glimpse a fraction of Miss Veronica's indomitable spirit.

Undying and eternal was the flame that burned in her heart, and her nobility was pure and supreme. Trapped in her frail shell, this remarkable woman had risked everything to save the life of the man she had adored in the days of her youth and whose memory she had never stopped loving.

"To my eyes you will always be beautiful," Peter found himself saying, and the sincerity in his voice was unmistakable.

Miss Veronica smiled and offered the bejeweled circlet up to him.

The bangle's pale buttery gleam flowed out over the slopes, and the Valkyries hissed in dismay when they saw it. Everyone present could sense the power that beat from that curious device, and the raven women shuffled backward, taking flight into the trees to escape its cold, biting glow.

As he looked down upon the treasure, a blank confusion stole over the false Captain's face. But before he could speak, Thought urged him to take it.

"Thy life is saved," the raven crowed, continuing the pretense for a moment more, his beady eyes shining with greed and exultation as Peter raised his hands to accept the glittering device.

"Halt!" shrieked a sudden interrupting voice as Quoth came tumbling into their midst. "Desist! Belay! Old crone, thou art misled!"

Miss Veronica blinked in astonishment as Neil's raven landed with an unceremonious bump on the ground and scurried over to her, flapping his wings in alarm.

"Memory!" the old woman exclaimed. "What are you saying? I must restore your Master to health."

"No, Veronica!" Edie joined in sharply. "Listen to him."

"This imposter is not the Gallows God!" Quoth decried. "'Tis but a trick to lure and deceive! Even Woden feareth the might of the bauble thou doth hold in thy hand. He is far from this place."

The old woman stared at the image of the warrior before her, then gazed down at the bracelet. At once Edie snatched it from her and stuffed it under her coat.

"The scruffy bird's right," Edie agreed vehemently. "That ain't your Captain. We been had."

Perched in the trees, the Valkyries snarled, and their beaks clacked as they ruffled their feathers.

"Grumble all thou wilt!" Quoth shouted back at them. "Against the Nornir thou art powerless. Cruel and mighty the Gallows God made thee, yet thy strength is no match for they."

"Is it not?" Thought raged, zooming over Quoth's head and scratching the bald scalp with his claws. "We shalt soon see."

Alighting on Peter's shoulder, the evil raven leered

down at Edie and in a foul, menacing voice said, "Surrender the device into our keeping."

"Won't!" she rapped back. "An' if you try to grab it, I'll pull your wishbone!"

A revolting cackle issued from the bird's throat.

"'Ware him," Quoth cautioned.

Thought's dark eyes blazed with cruelty and loathing as he contemplated the girl. Then the raven gave a loud cry.

Staring upward, Edie and Miss Veronica exclaimed in dismay as the dim outline of Hlökk spiraled slowly down and in its clutches they saw Neil Chapman.

"The caretaker's boy!" Miss Veronica gasped.

"If thou dost not obey me," Woden's lieutenant threatened, "the young dog shalt plunge to his death. Deliver unto us that most precious object."

Edie looked at Miss Veronica, and the old woman nodded. "We must," she told her simply.

"Here," the girl said sullenly, as she pushed the bracelet into Peter's hands. "But it won't do you any good."

At her feet, Quoth was relieved that his master had been spared. He could see Hlökk swooping down to drop him among them. But Thought was hooting with foul glee, and the sound was hideous to hear.

"Fools!" Woden's lieutenant crowed. "Didst thou not guess the true nature of yon golden trinket? Didst the shape strike no chord?"

Edie didn't like that conceited, confident laugh, and she pressed closer to Miss Veronica.

The old woman, however, was looking at the man she had been tricked into believing was Woden, for the illusion was fading. Tears brimmed in her wrinkle-ringed eyes as she finally beheld him for who he truly was.

"Ursula was right," she whispered bitterly. "I am a fool and always have been. He did love me once, long ago, I'm sure. But a greater love fanned the flames of his heart—his ambition. It was the craving for power and position that usurped me in his affections. He sought Ursula out and begged her knowledge, and she is blameless. I see that now. Here at the end I see it."

Upon the vicar's shoulder, Thought twisted his face with malice and derision. "Now thy reign hath concluded!" he spat. "The instrument of thine own destruction ye hath brought from the deeps of the earth. Henceforth the Nornir are no longer Mistresses of Destiny. They are vanquished at last!"

"Go lay an egg!" Edie rallied. "There's nothin' the likes of you can do to us."

A sly, knowing light flickered in Thought's eyes as he regarded her. "Is there not?" he cawed.

Confused by everything he had heard, Peter glanced up briefly to see Hlökk cast Neil onto the ground. He watched the loyal Quoth go scampering over to him. Then he returned his studious gaze to the glittering object in his hands.

"I don't understand," he muttered. "This is no chalice. It's just a piece of jewelry. It proves nothing!"

Hearing him, Woden's raven tutted in a mock injured tone, enjoying the last part of his Master's intricate plan.

"Not true," he denied. "Thou didst desire testimony to The Passion of thy Lord and Savior, and these misguided dolts hath provided it for thee."

"What are you saying?" the vicar cried. "It's only a lump of bent gold! Is that what all this has been about? Some stupid treasure hunt?"

Thought grinned sadistically. "Look again," he goaded. "No proof could be more concrete, in that thou wert not deceived."

As Neil stumbled toward them, keeping a cautious eye on the large and sinister shapes waiting in the trees, the Reverend Galloway turned the circlet over in his fingers. Suddenly his stomach lurched as he finally recognized the twisted shape.

"No!" he breathed.

Thought chuckled callously, savoring the poor man's horror. "Unbend the bangle," he prompted. "Return thine evidence unto its former guise."

A cold sweat pricked out over Peter's forehead, and his hands trembled when he began to uncurl the coiled, tapering piece of gold.

As the yellow metal warped and unfurled, hairline cracks broke through it and the gemstones burst from their settings to go rolling into the grass. But no one paused to find them, for all eyes were upon that glimmering, buckling ornament.

From the original base metal to which the gold and jewels had been applied, the rich encrusted gilding flaked and shattered. When Peter had finished, he stared at its true, tarnished shape, and a desolate cry of revulsion issued from his lips.

There in his hands was a plain, if distorted, spearhead.

The object's baneful form imprinted itself on the

vicar's collapsing mind, and the raven on his shoulder screeched with evil laughter.

"Only now dost thou comprehend the full measure of thy folly!" Thought scorned. "Behold, the spearblade that Longinus, the centurion, formerly didst own.

"Witless dolt, thy faith wouldst not suffice thee, and thou wert ripe for the choosing. In thy impatience thou didst crave to show unto the world proof that the Christ did live.

"Look then to thine hands. What better witness than the very dart that robbed him of his life?"

Peter's eyes filled with a fevered madness, for he was in no doubt that the object in his hands was the weapon that had pierced the side of the man from Nazareth as he suffered upon the cross.

From the tarnished metal a rust-colored powder stained his fingers, and he let out a strangled shriek of torment when he realized that the substance was dried blood.

Falling to his knees, the Reverend Galloway finally went tumbling into the madness that Woden and the raven had planned and prepared for him, and the broken man sobbed uncontrollably as his mind was reduced to ruins.

Rising above him, Thought squealed with infinite malevolence.

"Now thou knowest!" he snapped at Edie and Miss Veronica. "I hath in mine power the most potent instrument of destruction there hast ever been, and the one most fitting to wield it. Behold thine own destruction!"

Chapter 28

Blood on the Tor

"No will of thine own dost thou possess," Thought hooted at the shivering figure upon the ground. "Hear me now and arise, O slave."

Still clutching the spearblade, Peter Galloway rose mechanically. No expression was upon his face, and in his eyes no light shone. The man's shattered reason was now totally subject to the whims of the raven, and the disgusting bird returned to his shoulder.

Thought's beady glare flicked from Neil, to Quoth, then Edie, and finally came to rest upon Miss Veronica.

"Old witch," Thought croaked venomously. "Too long hast thou cheated death. Go now into that cold embrace, and tell the reaper thy sisters shalt soon be following."

Cackling, the raven opened his wings and in a forceful, commanding voice cried, "Raise now the blade. Plunge it deep into the harridan's breast! Let the font of her heart's blood spill o'er the soil of her trysting place."

Peter gripped the spear fiercely as he lifted his arm and stepped forward, but Neil and Edie pushed between him and Miss Veronica.

"Stop this!" the boy yelled. "Listen to me. You can't do it."

With a brutal sweep of his fist, Peter sent Neil flying. Edie leaped up to bite the hand that held the blasphemous blade, only to be knocked violently aside.

Thought laughed to see their futile efforts, and in the trees behind, the watching Valkyries uttered abhorrent chants of death.

"Naught thou canst do wilt stop my vassal from executing the task set for him!" the raven vaunted. "He doth hear only my voice and knoweth only my will."

The way was clear now. Only Quoth fluttered through the air quacking impotently, and defenseless, Miss Veronica staggered back toward the gate as Peter strode after her.

"Kind sir," she said. "Come to your senses. I have done no harm to you. I know you will not strike me down."

Thought sniggered, relishing every instant.

Gripping her cane, the old woman shambled down the grassy slope until she bumped into the railings and any further escape was made impossible.

Pinned against the gateway, Miss Veronica looked into the man's face, searching for a spark of humanity. But Thought's unbounded malice consumed Peter totally, and there was nothing she could do.

"Kill her!" the raven screeched, rising to his full height, his eyes blazing with hatred. "Impale the withered hag!"

Tossing back her head, Miss Veronica threw up her arms to fend off the terrible blow as the spear came stabbing down.

Into the night the old woman's despairing cries ripped, cleaving through the deep shadows. But the blade never reached her, and Thought shrieked with rage when he saw a grubby, red-knuckled hand gripping Peter's arm.

Whirling a cartwheel in the air, Quoth gave a shout of joy as a timid, friendly voice spoke from the shadows.

"Why don't you just put that nasty spiker down, son? You got no call to go murd'rin decent folk."

Edie ran over to Miss Veronica. The old woman hugged her desperately, while Neil stared across at the shabby-looking figure who had stepped from the darkness.

"Tommy!" he cried, laughing in spite of the savage hisses that sounded in the trees above them as the raven women shook their quills in readiness.

"Kill the oaf!" Thought yelled while Peter wavered, his arm still locked in the tramp's large grasp.

"You listen to Tommy now," the old man told Peter. "No use hidin' in that head of yourn and turnin' into a daftie. Tommy knows—he tried it."

To Thought's fury, his newly created slave gradually turned his head to stare at the ridiculous toothless tramp. Tommy's pale eyes shone softly in the light that glimmered from the spear.

"Come back, son," Tommy coaxed gently. "You can't dance with the devil on your back."

Flying from the vicar's shoulder, Thought beat his wings in Peter's face and screamed at him.

"Hear me!" he demanded. "Thou must tear thyself from this vagabond and slice the hide of Verdandi. My Master shalt not be thwarted. Thou must obey!"

But whatever Peter Galloway had seen in the tramp's face was enough, and his mind was already clearing.

"Gut her!" Thought shrieked, putting forth all the power that Woden had bestowed upon him. "Split her! Gore! Slit! Stab! I want her dead!"

At that, the battle for Peter's soul was finally won. Yanking his arm loose and glancing at Miss Veronica, the vicar threw back his hand, and the spear went hurtling through the air.

Shrill were the screams that resounded across the lower slopes of Glastonbury Tor.

Straight through the evil raven's heart the blade of Longinus went plunging, and the bird's diabolic screeches were turned into yowls of surprise.

With the blade caught in his ribs, Thought was flung back as the spear crunched clean into solid stone, and the raven was impaled against the stile. With a final jerk of his ugly head as it lolled limply onto the tarnished metal, Woden's deceitful, pitiless lieutenant expired, and a cloud of sawdust flew from his gullet.

At once the spells that had rejuvenated the bird were broken. The feathers fell out of his skin as it perished and decayed, crackling like parchment and crumbling to powder. Into the skull the gleaming black eyes shriveled, and the jaw clattered to the ground when the bare bones turned to chalk. Soon only the spear remained embedded in the stone.

Fluttering down to land on the nearby rail, Quoth gazed at the sorry pile of dust scattered over the ground and shook his head sadly.

"Farewell, brother," he mourned.

But his voice was overwhelmed by a sudden outcry from the unholy monsters perched up in the trees. Screaming in outrage, the Valkyries came ravaging down, their talons outstretched.

Like a raging tempest of quill and claw, the twelve raven women flew from their perches. With Thought gone, nothing could check them. They screeched at the top of their infernal voices, baying for slaughter as their beaks savagely snapped and clashed.

Frantically, Peter Galloway reached for the spear and wrenched it free of the stile.

"Stay here!" he cried to the others as he rushed to meet the oncoming nightmares.

"Wait!" Miss Veronica called to him. "Stay by Edith and myself. The *Valkyrja* fear us."

But the vicar did not hear her and ran forward, shouting fearlessly.

"Come on, then!" he cried, brandishing the blade above his head. "Who wants to taste this next?"

Charging into the enemy's midst, he leaped underneath the first of the crazed, harrying furies as its raking talons reached wildly for him. Peter brought the gleaming spear slicing down to cut and hack through the vicious hooks. Black blood gushed from the scaly toes as the curved claws were shorn away.

Above him the Valkyrie shrieked in pain, and Peter laughed grimly, thrusting the blade up into the mass of razor-sharp feathers. A hideous scream discharged from the murderous beak. With a flurry of black quills, the misshapen brute toppled from the air, and the vicar swerved aside as it came crashing down.

Onto the ground the fiend smashed. From its twig-crowned head a prickling black mist steamed into the night. The creature quivered and screeched in its death throes, and every trembling feather melted into smoke.

All that remained lying upon the grass was the unconscious body of a woman, and tangled in her hair were the slashed tatters of a crow doll.

"One down!" Peter yelled triumphantly, but more of Woden's unhallowed conjurations came shrieking in wrathful vengeance, rending their claws through the vicar's clothes and scoring bloody gashes across his face.

In the chaos of flaying quills and plunging beaks, the gleaming spear ripped and stabbed, but there were too many of the hellish horde for Peter to contend with, and the lethal, yammering storm seethed slaughterously about him.

Edie wanted to run to help him, but five more distorted terrors had fixed their unclean sights on Neil and Tommy and came whooping in to snatch them away from her and Miss Veronica's presence.

"Get back, you 'orrors!" Tommy wailed, abruptly seizing Miss Veronica's cane and thrashing it in the malformed, feather-framed faces as the ferocious claws gripped his coat and started to drag and pull at him.

Defying the abject terror that consumed him, the tramp brought the stick cracking down against the corpse flesh of the grotesque heads. He clattered it roughly from side to side, jabbing it into the great dark eyes, incensing the winged abominations all the more.

Flesh-freezing screams rang over the slopes of Glastonbury Tor, and the tramp was clawed and bitten, but still he battled, striking and prodding, clouting and beating.

Edie ran to his aid, and the Valkyries shied away from the fey, spritelike child, caterwauling in disarray, for the forces of doom sparkled in her pixie hat and they dared not attack her.

Despairing, Neil wondered what he should do, but he had no weapon to fight with. He stared helplessly at Tommy's valiant figure, with Edie capering around him, before turning to the dark, frenzied cloud that roared and assailed the Reverend Galloway.

Peter was totally obscured by the screeching monsters, their battering wings and scything talons engulfing him completely. Yet in the midst of that furious mass of hate and malice, the spear sliced arcs of light and the grass smoldered where the poisonous Valkyrie blood dripped and splashed.

From the clamoring mob there came a curdling yowl, and another of the feathered ogres crashed to the ground, shortly followed by a third. Their bodies blistered and scorched, withering down to the human frames beneath, and the ragged remnants of the controlling dolls were whisked away by the wind.

But Peter's strength was failing. The numbers were too great, and their evil might finally overcame him. Neil and Miss Veronica watched in dread as, torn and bleeding, the vicar gradually succumbed to the destroying, shrieking creatures.

His attacking blows were beginning to miss their mark, and the spear floundered in his grasp, overshooting the plumed targets and swiping through empty air.

Stumbling, he toppled unsteadily on his feet, and at once a bitterly sharp beak snapped at his neck and tore out a hunk of flesh.

Peter howled and clasped his hand to the wound. Lashing out feverishly, he ripped the blade through a flailing wing, but the creature leaped up and hit out fiercely with its claws. The barbed talons hooked into the vicar's wrist. His arm was flung back over his head, throwing him to the ground, and the blade went spinning from his grasp.

With triumphant yells of carnage and bloodshed gargling over their slavering tongues, the apparitions pounced upon his fallen body, and their dark wings wrapped about them.

High over the heads of Neil and the others, the enchanted blade catapulted, ratcheting through the overhanging branches before plummeting down and embedding itself in the soft mud of the narrow trackway behind them.

Horrified at the sickening spectacle of the tormenting Valkyries, Neil bolted through the stile to retrieve the spearhead, and Quoth flew after him.

Hearing the vicar's howl of pain, Edie whirled

around and gasped to see the hideous raven women clawing at his body.

Hollering, she barged across the grassy slope, her arms outstretched. The foul creatures hissed their displeasure but fell back all the same.

Edie knelt by Peter's battered figure, but she was too late. He was already dead.

Wheeling overhead, Hlökk viewed the scene below, and a hideous, profane plan formed in the monster's corrupt mind.

* * *

Flying in pursuit of his master, Quoth urged the boy to hurry.

"Haste! Haste!" the raven gaggled. "Nine terrors yet remain!"

Glimmering in the darkness, the spear's upturned blade pulsed and shone, and Neil dashed down the path to fetch it. But before he had run three steps, there came an urgent clattering of huge primary feathers and the misshapen form of Hlökk swooped through the trees.

With its malignant travesty of a face contorted into a vision of despair, the terrifying servant of Woden dived toward the helpess boy, shrieking and bellowing, and Quoth was cast aside as it thundered down.

Racing toward the pale, shimmering light, Neil could feel the creature's hot, putrid breath blast upon his neck, and suddenly Shrieker's massive wings were beating and thrashing all around him.

With a barbarous snarl, the Valkyrie jerked its head

to one side, then brought it swinging around, and its powerful beak smashed against Neil's skull.

There was a horrible crack, and with a cry, the boy collapsed senseless onto the path.

"Master Neil!" Quoth yelped from the hedge where he had crashlanded. "Avaunt from him, thou base scavenger of carrion! I shalt put out thine great gogglers if thee touch him!"

Hlökk's ghastly face regarded the insignificant bird for a moment, then a chilling, rasping cackle rattled in the specter's throat.

"*Your brother iss dead,*" it croaked, "*but we sstill sserve the Gallowss God. He made uss, he called uss, we will obey him.*"

Quoth quickly clambered from the brambles to carry out his threat as best he could, but with a tremendous sweep of its wings, Hlökk left Neil unmolested and returned to its sisters.

Frantically the raven bounded over the path. "Master Neil!" he cried. "Shrieker is gone. Quick, awaken! The peril is not yet over. Methinks a new evil is afoot."

But to Quoth's dismay, the boy did not move. The raven glanced fearfully back to the gateway and watched two of the Valkyries taunting Tommy, driving him farther along the hillside, away from the stile, where Miss Veronica stood alone and anxious.

Edie Dorkins looked up from the Reverend Galloway to see Hlökk circle overhead, croaking its instructions, and to her astonishment, the other raven women reared up in answer and came lumbering toward her.

The girl narrowed her eyes and rose to stand her ground. She could see that the creatures were afraid of her, but still they came, and a twinge of doubt surfaced in the child's thoughts.

Thrashing their enormous wings, the Valkyries stalked forward. Edie raised her arms in challenge and took a prowling step nearer.

The braying din from the horrors' beaks grew louder, but this time they refused to be cowed, and Edie glanced back at Miss Veronica nervously.

"Here, child!" the old woman called. "Hurry!"

Edie fled back to her, and the feathered nightmares charged after.

* * *

In the pathway, Quoth saw all of this and perceived that Hlökk was executing some loathsome dark design. Torn with anguish, the raven wanted to stay at his master's side to watch over him, but he was also greatly distressed to see the others so beset with evil, and he understood that the spearhead was their only way of fighting those horrendous apparitions.

Scuttling down the track, he approached the glimmering blade and fluttered around it, attempting to pluck it from the thick mud it had fallen into. Yet the weapon was too large and unwieldy for the bird to lift. It had embedded itself firmly in the soft ground so that the blade pointed upward, and the sharp edges cut his feet when he tried to grasp them.

"It budgeth not!" Quoth wailed. "What am I to do? All is woe—alas, alack!"

Glancing from his master over to where the Valkyries were assailing Edie and Miss Veronica, the raven flapped his wings to go and help them. Suddenly he heard Tommy's dismal cries and didn't know who to fly to first.

Distraught with indecision and panic, the raven finally chose the girl and the old woman, for Woden's servants were concentrating their ghastly energies upon them and Miss Veronica was crying out in fright.

Soaring over the path, Quoth rushed to join them and do whatever small service he could, but before he reached the gateway, Aidan's dying words came to him once more.

"'Tis madness!" the raven spluttered, as at last he realized what the gypsy had been trying to say. "Loon ravings, no more! And yet, what other hope have I?"

Darting through the trees, he flew over the open ground of the lower slopes, leaving Edie and Miss Veronica to confront the infernal foes on their own. He veered across to where the tramp was beset by Biter and Screamer, the walking cane still flailing in his hands.

Up to that point the raven women had been toying with the old man, afflicting and tormenting him, relishing the terror ingrained upon his florid, craggy face. But the sadistic sport was over now. Hlökk needed them elsewhere, and they set about the tramp in deadly earnest.

Feverishly, Tommy thrashed the stick at them, shouting for all he was worth, desperately calling upon aid that never came.

Suddenly, Quoth came sweeping through into the frenetic fray and landed on the tramp's shoulder.

Tommy was so frightened by the horror of Biter and Screamer as they clawed and pecked at him that he didn't even notice.

"Old one!" Quoth was forced to squawk in his ear. "Harken to me!"

Tommy jumped, startled by the bird's unexpected voice, and turned his head, distracted.

Immediately Biter pounced, snatching the cane from the old man's hand and hurling it across the hillside. Screamer's talons flashed out and tore through Tommy's forearm, shredding the sleeve of his coat and gouging a savage wound in his skin.

The tramp wept with the agony and stumbled back as they attacked him, but upon his shoulder Quoth steadfastly remained and yelled at him.

"Save thyself!" the raven cried. "Save us all! Thou hast the power!"

Sobbing in terror, Tommy waved his hands before his haggard face and staggered under the Valkyrie's horrendous battering.

"With his dying gasp Aidan named thee!" Quoth continued, ducking and dodging the slashing claws that reached for the tramp's throat. "Think! Why wouldst he do such? Why couldst thou remove the crow doll when no other could? What is thy hidden secret? Why hast thou forgotten?"

Tommy blundered on, his face cut by the vicious quills that churned about him.

"Tommy doesn't know!" he wailed. "Save him, someone—Gabriel, Uriel. Send him angels! Oh, dear God, hear him!"

As Quoth clung grimly to Tommy, the raven's eye

grew wide with excitement and he hooted with joy.

"Zooks-hurrah!" he shrieked. "I have it! Thy tale of war, of the battle where thou didst see the shining ones—'tis all true! Canst thou not see, canst thou not recall?"

"No!" the tramp screamed as Biter tore three jagged rents along his back, and he fled up the hill in the vain hope of reaching the tower.

"Tommy's angels!" he howled. "He must have them!"

Screeching bloodily, the Valkyries snapped at his hands and plunged down to bite his legs, and the tramp could run no farther.

"Thou wast not a foot soldier!" Quoth cried, scrabbling to remain by the tramp's ear as he was overwhelmed by the destroying raven women. "Thou art no mortal. Thou art thyself a shining one, stranded in human flesh! Tommy, *thou* art the angel! Dost thou not see?"

His face streaming with blood, the tramp stared at the raven dumbfounded, but it was too late. Screamer and Biter slammed into him, and Tommy fell to the ground; squealing, Quoth was dragged with him.

Buried beneath the baying, trampling Valkyries as they pecked and feasted on Tommy's flesh, the old man's shrieks were quickly lost, and Quoth was swamped in the unholy pair's foul shadow.

* * *

Away from the terrible scene of slaughter, Edie Dorkins and Miss Veronica flinched from the gathered monstrosities that screeched and squalled before them, and they edged through the stile.

"What's happenin'?" Edie cried as a frenzied blur of sharp quills whisked the air before her.

"They're driving us back," Miss Veronica answered. "Herding us down the Tor like sheep."

"But why?"

The old woman shook her head. The Valkyries propelled them along the path, hemming them against the hedge with their furious beating, controlling every footstep of Woden's hated enemies.

"I don't like this!" Miss Veronica whimpered. "Some vile purpose lies behind it. Look at their horrible faces. They're afraid to be so close to us, but something's mastering their fear. They're excited, all of them. Listen to their blaring voices. Something's going to happen. Oh, Edith, I'm frightened."

Driven farther down the muddy trail, Edie held on to the old woman's hand and stared along the path to see where the raven women were directing them.

Close by she could see Neil Chapman lying unconscious in the mud, and a little way ahead . . .

"Veronica!" Edie cried. "We've got to stop this! Don't let 'em take us down there! I know what they're doin!"

Desperately the girl tried to push her way clear of the goading feathers, but the Valkyries screamed at her and seven sets of brutal claws lashed out to bar her way and thrust her back onto the desired route.

"It's no use," Miss Veronica told her. "We must go where they want us to."

"But we can't!" Edie yelled. "Look!"

The old woman stared down the track and sharply drew her breath when she saw what awaited them.

"By the great Ash!" she exclaimed.

Seeing their horrified expressions, Woden's hulking winged servants crowed and yammered eagerly and proceeded to jab and poke with their sharp beaks, pushing their victims more swiftly down the path.

"*Death to the Nornir!*" Hlökk chanted, and the other malignant creatures joined in, croaking and rasping as their grisly goal drew near.

Past the spot where Neil Chapman lay, Edie and the old woman were marched, and their forbidding destination shimmered in the shadows.

With its tip pointing to the sky, the spearhead they had gone through so much to find shone coldly, and the captives were driven unerringly toward it.

The Valkyries were beside themselves with excited, rapturous zeal. Woden would be pleased with them. Even without Thought's cunning to lead them, they had discovered a way to kill the reviled enemy, and Hlökk crowed with rejoicing glee.

"*Kill! Kill! Kill!*" the nightmare shrieked.

Like an enveloping cloud of darkness and despair, the atrocities whipped one another into a greater frenzy than ever before, and their claws smashed into the prisoners, knocking them off balance.

"Veronica!" Edie cried when the old woman staggered under a vicious, battering blow.

Miss Veronica tried to steady herself, but the Valkyries pushed her again, and she lurched precariously over the upraised spear.

"No!" Edie bawled, rushing forward to save her from falling.

The old woman regained her balance at the last moment, but the spectral horrors around them were furious. Hlökk tore its way through, lowered its plumed head, and with a ferocious, trumpeting shriek rammed the girl in the chest.

Screaming, Edie was thrown backward and fell sprawling toward the waiting, glistening blade.

A horrendous chorus erupted from the assembled Valkyries as Nornir flesh was punctured and sacred blood went seeping into the mud. But their jubilant cackles were swiftly curtailed, for at that moment the entire Tor shook. They turned their repulsive, gloating heads to gaze fearfully up the pathway as a deep, rumbling quake vibrated through the ground and an almighty bellowing roar boomed out across the earth.

Up on the grassy slopes, where Biter and Screamer caroused in the tramp's stringy flesh, the two raven women were suddenly catapulted into the air, and a tremendous rush of searing flame boiled heavenward.

Into the darkness the brilliant pinnacle of light went shooting, and from the ground a vast, billowing cloud blossomed and swelled. It burgeoned up into the night, rearing above the great green hill and flaring with dazzling color as fierce jags of lightning burst from its heart.

A ravishing, blazing splendor like the noonday sun blasted out across the whole of Glastonbury, and the surrounding countryside was flooded with blinding radiance.

Higher the gargantuan cloud expanded, and within

its fulminous vapor a colossal, cataclysmic vision rapidly took shape.

Inside the mushrooming mist three stupendous serpentine silhouettes snaked and coiled, and from the haze, one of the golden horn-crowned heads exploded.

High over the tower of Saint Michael the staggering revelation reared. The Tor was dwarfed by its soaring dimensions as a pair of hook-clawed wings unfurled with a sound like rolling thunder.

Like slivers of the sun the fiery eyes burned in that mammoth, dragonlike head. The burnished scales scintillated and flashed, and from the gaping lips torrents of destroying flame cascaded over the plowed fields, scorching the soil and kindling the hedges.

So was the angel that had descended to the mortal world in 1915 finally released from the trammeling flesh of the corporeal form it had assumed and in which it had been locked ever since.

Over Glastonbury the shining celestial being was revealed in all its apocalyptic glory, and the mortals shuddered at the violence of its reawakening.

Writhing from the crackling cloud, the three gigantic heads twisted upon winding, arching necks. A mighty gold-armored tail wrapped itself around the summit of the Tor as the angel's searing eyes glowered down.

Flung clear of the divine flame, Screamer and Biter were stricken with terror, thrashing their tattered wings to flee the awful sight that towered above them. But from the celestial being there was no escape. Out of one set of fiery jaws there hailed a tempest of flame, and the two Valkyries were utterly swallowed in a mesh of light.

From the sky the human hosts dropped, and the controlling dolls squealed shrilly as they were devoured by the hallowed fires.

On the path below, the remaining raven women burst toward the trees, fiercely beating their dark wings and rocketing out over the town, dismayed and defeated by this unforeseen catastrophe.

Terrible though they were, Woden's grotesque servants were no match for this one marooned member of the heavenly host.

Tearing through the bewildering, lustrous night, shooting past its screeching sisters and leaving them behind, Hlökk heard the ominous rumbling roar reverberate from the Tor, and the sky was filled with flame as the Valkyries withered and were consumed.

But Hlökk rampaged ever faster, hurtling out across Wearyall Hill and over the flatlands beyond. Shrieker would not be consigned to ashes. Its malevolent spirit would never return to the dark recesses of the infinite void.

Throwing back its monstrous head, Hlökk, last of the Valkyries, crowed joyously, but that screech was its final one. Down streamed a jet of flame, and the creature's malignance was wholly obliterated.

Wreathed in the scorching, devouring heat, Hlökk fell like a stone. Down to the bare fields it plummeted, the agonized screams echoing over the land as its spite-filled, seditious spirit was sent back to the farthest reaches of the abyss.

With a shattering crunch, the hideous shape

crashed onto the ground, then melted. The plump figure of Lauren Humphries lay insensible across the furrows, with shredded ribbons of burned and smoldering cloth fluttering in her carrot-colored hair.

The Twelve were conquered at last. Above the Tor the wondrous vision of the angel lifted its heads to unleash a tremendous bellowing roar. Silhouetted before its golden magnificence, a tiny black speck dared the dripping flames and spiraled upward to sing and squawk in gladness.

Unafraid of the lethal resplendence that blazed all around him, a one-eyed, scraggy-looking raven quacked a song of victory and basked in delicious splendor as he dived in and out of the glimmering gigantic cloud.

"Merrie meetings!" Quoth crowed. "'Tis better to be happy than wise! Zooks-hurrah! Zooks-hurroosh!"

Warbling in delight, he fanned out his feathers and twirled deliriously. Then he saw it, the scene upon the ground far below—and the raven's celebrations ended.

* * *

Neil Chapman groaned and sucked the air through his teeth as the dull pain in his head throbbed and pounded. Groggily he opened his eyes, but he quickly closed them again as the blazing light from the angel on the Tor blinded him.

Lying in the mud, he waited until he was ready, and shielding his eyes, he gazed up at the momentous being rearing above the hillside.

Then the boy wrenched his attention away, for a desolate, soul-rending sob came to his ears. He looked down the path to where Edie Dorkins was crouched upon the ground.

Great tears were tumbling from the child's almond eyes as she knelt in the soft earth, and her entire body shook with her weeping.

"Edie?" Neil murmured, a dreadful fear coming over him. "What's wrong?"

The girl did not answer, and as the boy drew near he understood why. Miss Veronica Webster's frail figure lay motionless on the path. Edie had lifted the wizened head onto her lap and was sobbing uncontrollably over her, stroking the old woman's long dyed tresses with her small, trembling fingers.

"She . . . she pushed me . . ." the child wept bleakly. "When . . . when those things threw me down, she . . . she pushed me out of the way."

Neil gazed down at Miss Veronica and closed his eyes at the sight of the spearblade that was sticking up through the flimsy white robe, now stained with her royal blood.

"She . . . she slipped," Edie cried. "Slipped and fell on it. Oh, help me, I can't lift her off it. Please, we might save her."

Gravely, Neil slid his hands under the old woman's shoulders and gently raised her from the ground as Edie pulled the spear from Miss Veronica's back.

"There now," the child sniffed, dragging the pixie hat from her head and dabbing it on the wound in the vain hope it would staunch the blood and heal her.

"You'll be well," she said huskily. "You're a

Webster. You'll mend and get better. I know you will. Please, Veronica, you have to."

As Edie bent over the old woman, Quoth flitted down to join them, and the raven hung his head in sorrow.

A faint, expiring breath floated from Miss Veronica's wrinkled lips, and the webbed eyes fluttered open.

"Edith," she uttered in a barely audible whisper. "The spear has done its work."

"No," the girl denied. "I won't let you go!"

The fingers of the old woman's hand twitched feebly, and Edie clasped them in her own.

"Tell her," Miss Veronica breathed with difficulty. "Tell Ursula. I'm sorry—I forgive her. Poor Celandine, who will watch her dance now?"

"We both will!" the child insisted.

The pale eyelids slid shut. "No more," the hoarse, vanishing voice whispered. "No jam and pancakes."

"Don't go!" Edie wept.

But the wizened woman eased into death and with her final breath murmured, "I love all my family, the youngest not leas . . ."

"Veronica!" the girl bawled, squeezing her hand and brushing the hair away from the aged face. "Veronica!"

Thus the youngest and once most beautiful of the three Fates of the ancient world perished. Edie Dorkins pressed her face next to that of Miss Veronica and whined piteously.

Wiping his eyes, Neil staggered away as a fierce rush of wind tore about the lower slopes and the shining vision upon the Tor was enveloped in a searing flash of light.

Greater the gale grew, ripping through the trees, and the ground shuddered. Then, as suddenly as it had appeared, the angel was gone and darkness reclaimed the night.

Stumbling down the path, Neil Chapman heard the blare of sirens as fire engines and police cars finally arrived in the street below. Feeling utterly lost and alone, the boy gazed back at the young girl grieving over Miss Veronica's body, and he knew that an ending that should never have occurred had come to pass.

Nothing would ever be the same again. The structured order of things beyond his understanding was broken, and he looked up at the solitary tower of Saint Michael. But the Tor was lost in profound shadow, and as Neil lowered his eyes, a feathered head gently rested against his cheek.

Deep beneath the ancient, brooding building, within the Chamber of Nirinel, the lone figure of Miss Ursula Webster stood still and silent.

Her gaunt features were turned toward the mighty withered root that arched above her. She waited for the moment that she knew must come, an expression of dread and suffering etched upon her face.

Then it happened.

A hideous pain ripped through her breast at precisely the same moment that the spearblade stabbed into Miss Veronica far away in Glastonbury.

Crying out, Miss Ursula fell to the ground, gasping and weeping as she experienced her sister's dying moments.

Above her the last root of Yggdrasill trembled ominously, and a deep, resonant groan reverberated throughout the chamber.

"It's done," the old woman howled. "The Cessation has begun!"

Slumped upon the earthen floor, Miss Ursula Webster sobbed uncontrollably, and the torchlight dimmed about her, plunging the cavern into a deep, despairing darkness.

Outside, in the hollow night, Miss Celandine's hysterical screams rang from the small apartment until a tremendous splitting of stone and metal abruptly drowned out her dismal wails.

The grand Victorian entrance to the Wyrd Museum was shuddering. One of the bronze figures that flanked the oaken door suddenly toppled from its plinth and went crashing to the ground, where it shattered and exploded.

A deathly calm descended as Miss Celandine's insane screeching gradually faded, and into the alleyway a dark gray mist swiftly flowed.

Through the curling fog a hooded figure came, the profound shadows beneath its cowl fixed intently on the broken fragments of sculpture. A faint sigh hissed from his unseen lips.

"Verdandi is no more," the sepulchral voice whispered. "The Witches of the Loom are divided at last. Soon Skuld and the mighty Urdr herself will fall victim. Such is the will of Woden."

Turning, the sinister figure stepped back through the spectral mist and melted into the consuming gloom.